THE LEGACY
of EDEN

THE LEGACY of EDEN

NELLE DAVY

Recycling programs for this product may not exist in your area.

ISBN-13: 978-0-7783-2955-8

THE LEGACY OF EDEN

For questions and comments about the quality of this book please contact us at Customer_eCare@Harlequin.ca.

www.Harlequin.com

Printed in U.S.A.

First Printing: February 2012
10 9 8 7 6 5 4 3 2 1

For Jack

PROLOGUE

I WAS CALLING FOR HER.

I pointed the flashlight into the darkness, puncturing the purple haze of the evening with circles of white. The air was full of the smell of azaleas and the sound of crickets, and I began to think of how much I would miss my home. For a moment, I was truly scared of leaving the farm, and I was stricken with both the fear of the unknown, and my desire for it. I gave up a shudder.

And then I heard it.

The sharp snap of twigs being twisted into the earth. I swung around and moved off the path, down to the rose garden. I heard them before I saw them. His voice was low, half in a whisper, but in the stillness of the night, it carried.

"Say it," he urged, and then more forcefully repeated, "Say it!"

And then another noise. At first, I didn't even know it was her. It was a sound I had never heard from her before.

I have relived that night so many times. Once, I had dared to believe that I was different from my family, that I was the one who did not fit. But as my grandmother Lavinia, the catalyst for my family's mottled history, once said, "Blood will out."

Perhaps you would have made a different choice that night. If so, your heart would not be heavy with such deep regret. But knowing who I am, who my family was, how could anyone have expected anything else?

MEREDITH

The Path to Remembrance

1

TO UNDERSTAND WHAT IT MEANT TO BE A Hathaway you'd first have to see our farm, Aurelia.

If my family's name is familiar to you, it may be that you have either already seen it, or at least know something of its reputation. In its day our farm was notorious for being one of the most prosperous estates in our county in Iowa. An infamy only surpassed in time by that of the family who owned it.

I have spent the past seventeen years trying to forget it, forget my family and forget my past. For seventeen years I was given a reprieve, but after that length of time, you stop looking over your shoulder and you forget how precarious your peace is. You take it for granted; you learn to bury your guilt and then you convince yourself that it will never find you.

And then he died.

My cousin Caledon Hathaway Jr. left this earth in late October at the age of forty-five. The cause of death was cirrhosis of the liver. As seemed to be the curse of all Hathaway men after my grandfather, he would die young and alone and how he was found I do not know: he lived with no one and by then Aurelia had ceased to be a business and had become merely a vast space of withering land. Though a notice was placed in the local newspaper, his death was mourned by no one and his funeral attended only by the priest and an appointed lawyer from the firm who handled our family's assets. His body rested in the ground, at last unable to hurt or harm anyone else, and that should have been the end of it.

But then eight months later, at ten to three on a Thursday afternoon, I received a letter. I settled into my armchair next to the window, my hands still stained with streaks of clay from the morning's work in my studio. Ever since I left art school I have dedicated myself to sculpture, though it has only been in the past five years that I have made a decent enough living from it in order to do it full-time. Before that I was like any artist-cum-waitress, come every and any menial job you could find. I don't earn much but I get by and as I fingered through the array of bills and fliers, the stains of my morning's endeavors trailed across the envelopes until I came across a stark white one, different from the others in its weight and the crispness of its paper. It bore the mark of an eminent law firm whose name seemed familiar to me, but I thought nothing of it and slit open the mouth of the letter with my finger. Why wouldn't I? I had forgotten so much—or at least I had pretended to.

By the time I had finished reading it, the damage had been done. I looked up from the typescript to find my apartment an alien place. Sunlight was streaming through the windows and reflecting off of the counter surfaces and wood floors.

I could feel a prickle of sweat on the back of my neck and my mouth tasted hot and sweet with what I realized was panic.

I rushed to the bathroom and was violently sick.

Pushing myself upright I brought my hands to my face and then ran my fingers through my hair, clawing the strands back from my forehead. I caught sight of my phone and even though my stomach was filled with dread, I had to know, I had to know if they have been told. The letter said that they had tried to contact other members of the family. Who else, who else? I closed and reopened my eyes but it was no use. As soon as I began the thought, they swam across my vision, the living and the dead, diluting the reality of my kitchen with memories I had striven to bury for nearly two decades: my grandmother in her caramel-colored gardening gloves pruning her roses; my father throwing water over his head to cool himself off so that his great mop of blond hair slicked back, grazing the top of his shirt; Claudia in a white two-piece with her red sunglasses; my uncle Ethan shaking a cigarette out onto his palm from a pack of Lucky Strikes. I leapt away from the counter and ran into the studio. I darted around my sculptures to my desk and rooted through the drawers until I found the battered Moleskin address book and flicked through the pages until I found her number.

Where would she be now, I thought as I dialed her number? Is she even home? I knew she had gone part-time at the clinic since she had the girls, but I don't know her shift schedule. But my thoughts were abruptly cut off as she picked up on the fourth ring.

"Hello," she said, slightly breathless.

I opened my mouth to speak.

"Hello?" she said again.

There was a pause. I pictured her hanging up.

"Hel—"

"Hello?"

"Hello?"

Our voices overlapped. She withdrew. In the interim I somehow managed to ask, "Ava?"

She was shocked. I heard a sharp intake of breath. I said her name again.

"Meredith," she said finally and then sighed with impatience. I wound the telephone cord around my finger at that and squeezed.

"Can you talk?" I asked

"Yes."

"I thought you might have been at the clinic. I wasn't sure if you were in."

"I just finished a shift."

"Are the girls around?"

"I'm alone, it's okay."

I closed my eyes and swallowed.

"Good, I—I need to talk to you. It's—"

"Is this about Cal Jr.?" she asked abruptly.

My eyes flew open. I felt winded. My voice, when it came out, was harsh, animal.

"How?"

"The family lawyers called me."

"When?"

"A few days ago."

"Why?"

"Same reason I suppose that they contacted you."

"They did not call me," I said, looking down at the letter, which was crumpled in the fist of my hand. "They wrote instead."

"I told them straight out I didn't care. Not about him dying, not about the farm or how he had driven it so far into the ground it was halfway to hell. They talked about my 'responsibility.' I told them I had done above and beyond more than my duty by that place."

I bit my lip so hard I thought I tasted blood.

"I suppose I was a bit harsh," she said reflectively, "but I got the feeling that they would just keep calling if they thought they could get anywhere. I guess that must have been why they tracked you down." She paused. "Have you heard from Claudia? Do you know if they contacted her, too?"

I thought about our eldest sister, probably dismissing shop assistants with a bored wave of her hand in some mall in Palm Beach.

"No, but she has a different name now. She's married."

"Did not stop them from getting to me. Or to you, or don't you go by our mother's name anymore?"

I swallowed hard at the reproach. "No, it's still Pincetti."

She snorted. "And there was once a time when Hathaways were crawling out of our ears, now none to be found. I suppose I was the first person you rang when you got the letter, was I? I am so touched. I wonder why that would be?"

I closed my eyes, blocking out the orchestra of sounds from the taxis and crowds on the road below and the various cacophony of voices that rose in a fog from the streets. I forced my mind to blank, to hold my breath in my chest, to keep everything still.

"So you knew then?" I somehow managed. For a moment I thought she had gone, as there was only silence and then, "Yes."

I digested this. "I see," I said and I did, with painful clarity. This was a mistake.

"I told them I didn't want anything to do with it," she volunteered. "They could do what they wanted." She gave a small laugh. "They even asked me about funeral arrangements. I told them the only way I would help would be if I could make sure he was really dead."

I winced. I hate this side to her, especially because I am part of the reason why it is there.

"It's all gone you know? The farm…" she began. "In the end it was riddled with debt. They're going to sell it, did you know that?" She stopped and when she began again, her voice broke. "It was all for nothing and she'll never know it."

There was a pause.

"What will you tell them?" she asked eventually.

"Huh?"

"What will you do?" Her voice was careful, deliberate, and I realized with a small shiver that I was being tested and that she had no expectations that I would pass.

"I suppose I will have to call them."

There was a silence. There was nothing for a moment; just a blank and then when she next spoke her voice had degenerated into a repressed scream of fury.

"Why?!"

This time I spoke without thinking, so that what I said not only surprised me because of my daring, but also because it was true.

"I guess I'm just not ready to walk away yet."

Even to my mind they were an interesting choice of words. They hung there in the silence between us. I waited for her to speak and I could tell even in the pause how much she wanted to attack me, to use my words as a noose and hoist me up, legs kicking, desperately searching for ground.

"I have to go. I need to pick up the girls," she said.

All of a sudden I was exhausted. It would never end, I thought. There was still too much damage left to inflict. I had long since ceased to engage in this trading of blows. I had marked her once and that was enough. Nearly two decades later it was still pink and raw, but she was not yet finished.

"I'll call you back," she offered.

"Okay," I said and we hung up. Even as we did so I knew she wouldn't call back. As if we were still children, she spoke again in code, a code she meant for me to decipher:

You did not do as I expected. You failed me—again.

Aurelia. I don't know what it looks like now. It has been years since I last saw it from the back of a car window, but I don't fool myself for an instant that even if the place was rotted out and the fields of once bright corn are now nothing but broken earth, that I wouldn't still feel the same pull to it, a need to do the unspeakable for it.

That is one of the reasons why I have never gone back.

Why does it have this effect on me? Because of this: regardless of my mother and her lineage, I am a Hathaway. Even though I have taken her maiden name (and no one except my college alumni association asking for money, or Claudia in postcards, refers to me as anything else) it does not matter. I may live in New York, have changed my hair color, name and friends, but tug at the right thread and all this carefully constructed artifice will fall away.

Blood will out.

In its heyday, my family's farm was impressive: it stretched three thousand acres when the average farm was about four to five hundred. But more than its size, our farm was infamous because it was unusual. Unlike any farm in our county, or indeed any farm that I have ever heard of, my grandmother took it in hand and developed it into something more than just a business, but a thing of real beauty. She did the unthinkable, and even more astonishingly, it worked.

Farms are meant to concentrate solely on that which will

maintain them: crops, livestock, tools. They are a place of work and where I come from, the farms that were considered the most impressive were those that embodied this: well-tended fields, a full harvest, up-to-date machinery. This was the attitude of our fellow farmers and their own farms reflected this. If there had been such a thing as Farm Lore, this would be it.

But my grandmother wanted more. She didn't see why she shouldn't and somehow, to the puzzlement and then mockery of their neighbors, she succeeded in convincing my grandfather, the son of a seasoned farmer who had been raised on all the principles I have just described, to ignore what he had been taught and bend to her will.

The result was months of gossip, whispers in the grocery store, lingering stares and tight smiles when they were passed on the street. The farmers themselves made fun of my grandfather behind his back; lamented his impending ruin to each other and begged him to his face to curtail his wife's madness. You must understand, our town was a community, and that meant that everyone had a small stake in everyone else's business.

"It'll end in tears," they said, and secretly hoped.

In little over a year, my grandmother decided that her initial vision was completed enough to her satisfaction and she threw a party. My grandfather, Cal Sr., was relieved—he saw it as a peace offering. She let him believe that.

How can it be so easy for her? I thought, as I sat in my studio, my conversation with Ava repeating in a continuous loop through my head. She who, unlike me, spent years forcing herself to remember when I was struggling to forget. The light was beginning to die outside, eager lamps from the streets sharpening against the encroaching dark. I sat in the corner of my room, surrounded by the half-formed clay models, whose shadows threw deformed specters on the walls behind them. I could tell as we spoke that unlike me she did not see an arched sign hung between two columns of oak with the farm's name written on it in curlicue black lettering or the gravel paths that wound through sculptured green lawns on which were planted pockets of flowers. It was a path that swung down to a sloping mound on top of which stood a house so impressive that seventy years ago, when it was first revealed to our neighbors, it caught the eyes of every guest carrying their various dishes of dessert and dressed salad and forced them to stop.

The old house where my grandfather had been raised, the one that had been just like their own, had been torn down. In its place, built in a mock colonial style, was a tall square building. What struck them first when they gazed up at it was the color: it was white. Even before they entered it they knew on sight that it was a place of polished woods with the smell of tall flowers in clear vases.

No, my sister did not see this and I knew she would not have cared to do so even if she had.

She did not see the rose garden with American Beauties puncturing the trellis walkway or the grove with the fountain of the stone god blowing water from his trumpet. Her memory had pulled down the shutters onto all the things my grandmother had fought so hard to accumulate and on which she had lavished such loving attention. I could hear in her voice, how little she cared now, how much she almost rejoiced in its demise. What had once been a thing of beauty abundant with fields upon fields of corn, which in the summer took on such hues of yellow mixed with orange that you could be fooled into thinking you were viewing the world through a haze of amber, was now an empty husk, reflecting only the various corruptions and losses of its last and most destructive owner.

She did not always think so. If you had seen the farm in its golden age, you would have called it a halcyon and known in your heart that to live there was to be happy. Secretly everyone thought so. My grandmother knew it and relished it. I could not fully understand why at the time. Her reaction to people's envy and admiration was almost victorious. Only later did I come to realize how she had longed to be at the receiving end of such jealousy, that she had geared her life toward that moment. It had for so long been the other way around.

Can you understand? Can you discern even from these fragmented recollections the hold that place could have? Why those who lived there would do anything to protect it regardless of the consequences? It was stronger than the bonds of community, this love, stronger in the end than that of family. It affected all of us. Not the same, never the same, but it always left its mark and you knew then who you truly were and why you bore your name.

On the rare occasions my sister and I have talked since resuming contact a few years ago, our conversations have tiptoed around her bitterness—her, I should say, justified anger. Out of fear or diplomacy we have steered clear of anything that might have forced us down a path on which we would have to confront what is between us. I have done this dance mainly on my own. There were times when I think she would have gladly allowed things to degenerate into the spectacle of recrimination and blame that I so desperately hoped to avoid, but she never pushed it. When the time came, and I think we always knew it would, she would have nothing to fear. She was the betrayed, not the betrayer.

And now, here we finally are, because the one time when

she expected me to revert to type and walk away I wouldn't. The irony was not lost on me as I put the phone back on its rest. I know what she thinks—that I'm being deliberately contrary, hurtful, cruel. The rational part of me knows I have no right to blame her for thinking this—haven't I proved myself to be all these things already? But I am still furious with her, because I so want to be able to do what she is asking and leave the farm to its fate with no regrets, and I can't. Then I could show that what happened—what I did—was a mistake, it wasn't me. I can change. I have changed.

I was calling for her. It was I who had offered to find her.

Oh, God, if I had never…if I had never opened that letter today, if she hadn't told the lawyers she had wanted nothing to do with them, if Cal Jr. had never inherited the farm, if I'd done the things I'd believed I was capable of, if I hadn't been capable of the things I'd done, if…if…if…somewhere out there, all the potential versions of my life floated on parallel planes. In one I never went out that night, in another more likely alternative, she does not put down the phone. Instead she stays on the line. We talk for a long, long time.

She listens.

She forgives me.

Do you believe in ghosts?

I didn't until I started living with them.

Two days have passed since the letter arrived. I walk past my mother sitting in my armchair mending my pinafore, or my father at the fridge humming to himself as he scans my feeble purchases of organic whole foods. The walls between my memories and reality are disintegrating and everything from my past that I have tried to push back, now rushes forward to escape.

Once while on the way to the bathroom, I passed my

cousin Jude, who I have not seen since I was ten. He cracked a hand on the back of my legs. "Toothpicks," he chortled; I gave him the finger.

Part of me is terrified. I wonder if I am losing my mind. But I find their intrusions oddly comforting. It is like turning up at a reunion I have been dreading only to remember all the things we had in common, all the memories that made us laugh, and I am reminded of a time when it was easy to be yourself.

At one point when I was flicking through the channels and stumbled on a soap opera my grandmother used to love, I hesitated. Even though I knew it was crap, and I have never watched it, I left it on for her, imagining she was behind me, waiting to hear her slip past and the soft creak of the wicker chair as she settled down to watch it. Just before it broke for commercial I said aloud, "This is madness."

Swift in reply, she answered, "Only if you expected a different outcome."

It was at this point that I decided to call the lawyers.

"Good afternoon, Dermott and Harrison, how may I help you?"

"Yes, this is Meredith…" I hesitate. What name do I use? And then with a sense of weariness I think, what's the point in trying to pretend. "…Hathaway. May I speak with Roger Whitaker, please?"

"Will he know what it's regarding?" the receptionist asked.

For a second I was struck dumb. "Yes."

I was sitting down this time. I took a deep breath and leaned back into the headrest as I was put on hold. After a few seconds the line was picked up and a male voice answered the phone.

"Miss Hathaway, so good to hear from you."

"Is it?" I asked.

"Of course. I assume you've had time to think over what we detailed in the letter?"

"What part? The part where you told me my cousin was dead or the other bit where the farm's going to be sold off and auctioned to the highest bidder to settle against his debts?"

"I know this is difficult to take in—" *no, I've been waiting for this for seventeen years* "—but we think perhaps it would be best if we spoke face-to-face about this. One of our senior partners was a friend of your grandfather's. He knows how important the farm was to your family."

"Was it?"

"Excuse me?"

"Was it important to us— I mean how many of us had you tried to contact before you found me? How many times did you get hung up on or ignored? Probably got cursed out a few times, too, huh?"

The voice was deliberately gentle at this point. "We were aware that there had been a significant rift between several family members. We know this is a delicate situation and for the sake of your family's past connection with this firm we wanted to make the process as smooth as possible...."

I saw that I was in for the lengthy legal homily.

"You can't."

"I don't think that—"

"You can't ever make it better. You can't make it nice and easy or simple, so do yourself a favor and don't try."

There was a pause. "There was talk here that perhaps it might be more effective if you or a family member could sign over the responsibility of handling the dissolution of the farm and its assets to us. Of course this could prove to be difficult, considering that there is no direct claimant to the farm and others could contest the process if they should hear and—"

"No one will."

"Well, uh, even so there is the matter of personal items, artifacts. We weren't sure if someone would want to come down and sort these out from what should be sold with the farm and what would be kept."

I saw my childhood home, the one a mile down from the main house with its yellow brick. Suddenly I was in our blue living room with the window seat behind the white curtains I used to hide under while I perched there waiting for Dad to come home.

"Of course."

"When can you come down then?"

"What?"

"When would you like to come to the farm and do this? The sooner the better, to be frank. I don't know if you are working, or if it would be a problem for you to take time off—"

"I work for myself. I'm an artist—a sculptor actually."

"Excellent, then when shall we set up an appointment?"

I opened my mouth, suddenly utterly bereft. I raised my eyes from the floor and shuddered. They had lined themselves up all around me in a crescent of solemn, knowing faces.

"I don't know."

Our farm was on the outskirts of a town surrounded by the farms of our neighbors: people whose children we played with, whose families we married into, whose tables we ate at. Together our farms formed a circle of produce and plenty that enveloped our small town, a hundred and seventy years old with its red-and-white-brick buildings and thin gray roads. Simple people, simple goals, old-fashioned values: this is where our farm is still to be found. I had not seen it in nearly two decades, but as I looked at the crowd of faces glaring at me from the other side of the room, I realized with a thin sliver of horror I had no choice, I would be going back. And I shuddered so violently, I had to clamp a hand over my mouth to stop myself from crying out.

"We'll leave you to think about it. But please—" his voice retracted back into smooth professionalism "—don't take too long."

It took me three hours to find it. There was a lot of swearing, I tore a button off of my shirt and scratched my arm, but eventually I sat cross-legged on the carpet and smoothed the crackled plastic of the front before I opened the album.

Ava had packed it in my suitcase the night before I left for college, the night I found her in the rose garden. I had opened my trunk in my new dorm to find it slotted between my jeans and cut-off shorts. I couldn't bear to look at it for a long time. I had left it in the bottom of the trunk and when I had to repack for Mom's funeral, I had tipped it out on the floor, daring only to look at it from the corner of my eye. I am a firm believer in what the eye doesn't see, can't be real. That was why, much to my mother's deep disappointment, I became a lapsed Catholic.

But this time I flipped back the covers and stared. I drank it in. The photos had grown dull with age. The colors, which were once vibrant blues and reds, were now tinged with brown and mustard tones. I slipped my fingers across the pages, watching the people in them age, cut their hair and grow it out again. From over my shoulder, my father leaned down and stared at himself as a young man on his wedding day. The light behind my parents was a gray halo surrounding the cream steps of the New York City courthouse. They had married in November, just before Thanksgiving, and you could see behind the tight smiles, as they stood outside in their flimsy suits and shirts, how cold they were.

"Phew, wasn't your momma a dish?" he said.

And she was. She wore her hair in the same way she would continue to for the rest of her life: center part, long and down her back. A perpetual Ali McGraw. Decades after this photo was taken, she would be widowed, her children would be scattered and broken, her home rotted out from beneath her. In her last moments, did she think of this? I don't know. I wasn't with her, only Ava was there.

She was not alone if she had to face her past and all its demons. And neither am I. I could feel them all pressing against me: the smell of my father's breath...chewed tobacco and Coors beer somewhere to my left.

I took my time with the album, even though inside I started to scream. My hands trembled but I continued to turn the pages. Each new memory sliced its way out of me, taking form and shape with all the others. I didn't mind the pain—it was just a prelude to the agony that has been biding its time for the right moment and now it was almost here. With one phone call it was as if all those years of running away were wiped out in an instant. My life is a house built on sand. That should have made me sad but it only made me tired. I turned another page. We looked so normal. In many ways we were, except all the important ones.

I flicked the page and saw my aunt Julia, whom I never got the chance to meet. Her hair was still red, before she started to dye it blond. From what I've heard from the strands of people's covert conversations, Claudia was a lot like her.

And then I looked up from the album and saw him standing there, the cigarette smoke separating and spiraling above his face. He was named after my grandfather, who was lucky enough never to realize what his namesake would grow into.

"Are you in hell, Cal?" I asked him.

He laughed at this. "Aren't you?"

"What do you remember?" I asked, suddenly urgent.

"Same as you," he said with a sly grin. "Only better."

"Don't listen to him, honey," my father said, lifting his chin in disdain.

Cal Jr. shot him a look of pure hate. "How would you know? You weren't even there!"

I stood up and walked out of the room. *This is it,* I thought to myself, *I've snapped.* I'm finally broken.

"You're not fucking real," I suddenly shouted.

"Dear God, girl, still so uncouth," my grandmother said, stepping out from the kitchen, her tongue flicking the words out like a whip. "I always told your mother she should have used the strap on you girls more often, but she was too soft a touch."

I turned around to face her, my fists clenching and un-clenching by my side. "You—if you hadn't—"

She turned away from me, disdainful, bored. If this were all in my head, what did that say about me?

"Enough excuses, Meredith."

I was shaking so hard, my voice tripped over itself.

"You were a monster, you know that? A complete mon-ster."

"Made not born," she said and looked at me knowingly.

"Oh, no—" I shook my head "—I am *nothing* like you."

"No, Merey—" and she smiled "—you exceeded all of our expectations."

I took a step toward her—toward where I thought she was.

"I'm going back to the farm. To sell it, to take what's left of your stuff and hock it at the nearest flea market."

"Oh, Meredith." She sighed. "You'll have to do better than that. Have you learned nothing? In terms of revenge we both know you can do so much more."

I shook my head and rubbed the heels of my hands into my eyes until the light grew red.

"You're not here," I said again, but even so I could feel the light pressure of her hand on my wrist.

"Neither are you," she whispered.

I opened my eyes and lifted my head. There: the fields on fields of cereals and golden-eared corn from my memory, from my dreams. They lay before me, an ocean of land, the colors all seeping out in a filter of gray.

Exasperated, I finally asked her the question I knew she had been longing for. "Why are you even here?"

"Darling." She chortled, suddenly filled with unexpected warmth. The silk of her green dress grazed past my arm as she came to stand beside me. "We never left."

LAVINIA

The Good Soil

2

I GREW UP SURROUNDED BY STORIES. EVERYONE had a story about someone or something: it was our town's way of reinforcing its claim on its inhabitants. And they have talked to me and around me all my life, so that my memory is not just mine alone, but goes back far beyond my birth.

In the half gray of a reminiscent twilight they stand there, waiting for me to allow them to be remembered. I can see them begin to open their mouths and flood me with their explanations, their whys and wherefores. They want forgiveness just as much as I do and they long for it now more than ever.

But who should start? Who needs it more? And then she disengages herself from them, her form hardening from mere silhouette to actual shape. In a swathe of green she steps forward, out of time and dreams—a ghost who has walked the earth of my memory so many times, the ground is worn underfoot.

★ ★ ★

What's hard is not starting at the beginning but trying to decide where the beginning is.

If my grandmother had to choose, for her the beginning of our story would be in May of 1946. We would find ourselves at a church fair with its fairly standard gathering of paper plates, white balloons tied to the end of red checked tables and the food is potluck.

Father Michael Banville stands before a bowl of salad and dressing, chatting amiably with Mrs. Howther about the state of her geraniums. To the left of him stands a small knot of farmers' wives chewing over the latest town news between mouthfuls of sweet potato pie, and farther on from them, dressed in a loose flower shift, her auburn hair bobbed to curl against her shoulders, stands a tall woman putting the finishing touches to her layer cake. She had brought the icing in a tube that had been wrapped in wet tissue and kept in her handbag throughout the service in the small white church.

Every time someone passes and catches her eye she makes the same apologies about some problem with her oven the night before and how she had to run down to her uncle's home to finish off the cake before the service, so she has had no chance to do the icing until now. People have nodded at these comments, even offered a smattering of sympathy, but mostly they have moved away wondering why on earth she would have persisted with something that circumstance was so set against. Why not bring a salad instead, or something simple? But no, they guessed correctly, she had to prove something. That was Anne-Marie Parks all over, they all thought.

The potluck was a rowdier affair than usual. Enclosed by a series of collapsible tables with honey-colored deck chairs, the gathering on the small knot of green at the church entrance added a season of color to the otherwise mundane scenery of white building and sky. It was the first one held in the town since the end of the war. Soldiers still dressed in their GI uniforms bore the weight of the grateful wives holding on to them, as they attempted to play with babies who did not know them. People mingled, smiled, and there was even a gramophone propped up on a stack of magazines on a chair. Everyone chatted as they ate and swayed along to the music, all of which Anne-Marie Parks ignored as she continued to ice her cake.

Across from her, standing next to a dish of chicken legs, her husband, Dr. Lou Parks, a tall man with long hands, stood balancing a plate of coleslaw and ham as he tried to pretend that he could not see what his wife was doing. His companion, Joe Lakes, a local farmer, did the same and therefore most of the talking. He chatted about his produce, his animals, his work, anything to keep the talk away from the subject of wives and home. It was this kindness that made him bring up a subject of gossip he would never usually raise, but as he saw Anne-Marie use the flat of a spatula to swipe away a piece of icing that did not suit her, he grasped at the last piece of news he could find that might keep them going until the silly woman had finished.

"You know they say Walter's boy is coming home?"

"Hmm?" At this, Lou Parks raised his face from his plate and fixed his graying eyebrows into half moons of surprise.

"Don't know for sure though, of course. But there's been a lot of talk. Walter's been laid up a while and Leo's been manning things alone on the place for so long now, but they say Walter's been getting worse."

Lou Parks kept his features stiff as he watched Joe scan his face for confirmation.

"How'd he hear?" he said at last.

"Telegram. Old Florence said how Leo sent a message by the wireless a few weeks back. She won't say what it was or nothing and there weren't no name as such, but she said the reply come back all the same and though she didn't know what it was exactly, Leo opened it then and there in the office—he couldn't wait. She couldn't think what else could be so urgent."

"That's not much evidence to suggest it was about his brother," Lou persisted as he swallowed another forkful of ham.

"No, no…true, but Mac at the hardware store said how their sister Piper had come down to get some more linen and stuff. Good kind, too. And when he'd asked her about it she'd sniffed and said they may be expecting visitors."

"Could be just that," said Lou.

"Nah, everybody knows Walter don't know nobody outta town. Whole family what's alive and they talk to is right here—all except his boy."

Lou was chewing thoughtfully when he caught a glimpse of his wife slicing away a piece of cake for the minister. The layer cake was all white now, with small red rosebuds lining the corners and forming a heart of sugar flowers in the center. He saw the minister pick up the fat piece in his fingers and his head nodded in silent agreement with whatever he was thinking as he devoured it.

"Very nice, Mrs. Parks," he said as he strode away licking his thumb thoughtfully. "Very nice."

A shadow of something passed over Anne-Marie's face. What, he could not tell, and then she picked up her icing and the tissue and pulled off her apron before leaving the cake. She did not take a slice for herself, or for her husband.

"I haven't seen that man in a long, long time," said Joe wistfully. Lou stared after Anne-Marie as she wove her way

through the crowds, which parted for her, though not one
person looked at her or interrupted their speech to address
her. Lou's jaw slowed to a stop. Quickly he turned back to
his companion.

"So how's your knee, Joe? I noticed you seem steadier than
you were last week."

"Mmm-hmm" said Joe, looking over his shoulder.

"Another piece of ham, Joe?" asked Lou, setting his fork
down and reaching to cut a slice.

"Hmm? Oh, yes, thank you."

"No trouble," said Lou, heaping the plate high and then
Joe pulled up a chair and began to sit down. Relieved, Lou
settled himself beside him and took in another mouthful of
coleslaw as they silently and methodically began to eat.

Later that night, as he waited in bed while she finished
up in their bathroom, Lou thought back to the church fair.
He thought of the cake and the delicate rosebuds, of the
look on his wife's face as she had stared at the minister who,
blissfully ignorant, had greedily relished the slice she had
cut him with only the barest of acknowledgment. She had
lost herself for the rest of the afternoon, until finally she had
slipped an arm around his waist just as he was thinking he
would like to leave. They had passed the table with the cake
as they walked to their car and he had noted that it was still
as she had left it with only one slice taken away.

He wanted to tell her his thoughts: to say them and wait
for her response so that maybe then he would fully understand the meaning behind what he had seen, but as ever
when she stepped into the room, her body pale beneath the
white cotton nightdress and her hair crowding her shoulders in waves tinged with red, he opened his mouth and
the words seemed to fail him. Instead of voicing all these

thoughts he said, "You know there's talk that Cal Hathaway may be coming home."

"Who?" his wife asked.

"Walter's boy."

"Oh. Why does that matter?"

He turned to face the ceiling. "No reason, I guess." He shifted so that his back faced her when she slipped in beside him. "Just nice for Walter to have his family back."

"What did you say his name was?" she asked.

"Abraham technically, 'cept almost everyone calls him Cal."

"Why's that?"

"It's his middle name."

"Like me," she said quietly.

"I like Anne-Marie," her husband said, an unexpected tenderness suddenly tugging at him. He waited for her to say something else, but she didn't and so he untensed himself and settled down to sleep.

Outside, crickets chirped before the milk of a half moon and Anne-Marie Parks heard them well until the early hours of the morning when she finally fell asleep. She did not think about what her husband had told her; there was no immediate reason why it should be relevant to her. She did not know that she would later marry the man whose name she had so casually forgotten as she lay hugging her pillow, waiting for sleep to come. Nor everything else that would come to her: things she stayed awake aching for, night after night, until she woke beside her husband, hating the rise and fall of his back because that, and not what she had dreamt of, was her reality. She was so unaware of what lay in store, of what she was capable, or who she really was.

This was all when she was still just Anne-Marie Parks, the

local doctor's wife; seven months, four days and ten hours away from becoming Lavinia Hathaway.

When Abraham Caledon Hathaway finally returned home, it was to find his father dying. The man who had once wrestled him down and cast his belt on his back at sixteen after he had stolen the family truck and gone drinking, had withered to a husk and now lay in blue-striped pajamas on white linen sheets.

Cal had stood in the doorway of his childhood home contemplating how close his father looked to death. He was not horrified by this. He had met death already over a year ago. His wife had been decapitated in a car accident while he was out at work as a salesman. A truck with a load of metal ladders had slammed on its brakes at a red light, but the ladders had not been properly tethered to the back. At the force of the stop, one of them had dislodged and shot straight through the windshield of his wife's car and smashed into the base of her head at the neck. Their three-year-old daughter, Julia, had been in the passenger seat next to her at the time, although miraculously she was unhurt. Cal had picked her up at the hospital after he had identified his wife. Her skin and cherry-patterned dress were still covered in her mother's blood. He stared into the calm brown eyes of his child and had known then and there what death really was, and also, that at the tender age of three, she now knew it, too.

That was why he let her come upstairs with him to see his father when they first arrived at the house, even though his sister, Piper, had protested.

"It ain't right," she had called after them both from the bottom of the stairway.

"What isn't?" their brother Leo had asked, coming in to take the lunch she had laid out for him on the kitchen table.

Piper turned. "He's taking Julia up to see Pa."

Her brother had humphed as he tore into a cold beef sandwich with mustard. "So they've arrived, have they? Anyway what do you care? It's his kid."

"Would you let yours come up?"

"I don't have none so I wouldn't know. Anyway, I'm thinking that'd be more along the lines of their mother's call. She don't have no mother."

Piper jutted out her chin in irritation. "Still ain't right."

"He say how long he staying for?"

Piper watched her brother as he stared at her over his plate.

"I didn't have time to ask. He just dropped his bags and went straight up."

"No sense beating 'round the bush, I guess. He's only here for one reason and we all know it."

When Cal came back downstairs, he paused at the bottom step at the sight of his younger brother. Piper ignored them both and, bending down low, she faced the silent unflinching gaze of her niece.

"Do you want some lunch Ju-bug?"

Julia looked up at her father, who stared at her in silent agreement.

"She'll ask for it when she's hungry," he said.

He looked at his sister. She was still as she ever was: thin, wiry, her hard jaw and her overly inquisitive eyes searing everything with their gaze. He looked at his brother sitting at the table, staring at him thoughtfully as he ate. Already he could feel the enmity wash over him. Suddenly he was incredibly tired, and he longed for the silent confines of his small apartment back in Oregon.

He nodded in greeting.

"Long time," he said. Leo raised his eyebrows; Piper looked at the floor.

"Could say that," Leo replied.

"I heard you got married," Cal said.

"Yeah. Just before the war."

"You fight?" Cal asked, suddenly curious.

Leo used the last of his sandwich to mop up the mustard sauce on the plate.

"Yeah." He looked up and stared at his brother. "I did my time."

Cal looked away, as if lost in thought, before he cleared his throat.

"Did you see any action, Cal?" his brother asked softly.

Cal met his brother's unflinching gaze.

"I saw plenty."

"Pa's glad to have you back," offered Piper, the light notes of her voice grating against the air in the kitchen.

"Pa barely knows his own name," Cal snapped. Piper looked away out onto the porch and sniffed.

Julia frowned and began to swing against the grip of her father. Cal looked down at his daughter as if he had forgotten she was there.

"Julia, this is your uncle Leo," he said, raising a finger. "Remember the pictures I showed you?"

Julia looked at her uncle and then shook her head.

"Well, it don't matter," said Cal. "He was much younger in them than he is now."

"Hi there, girl," said Leo and gave her a halfhearted wave. He turned back to his plate. "You both gonna be here long?" he asked sharply, without looking up.

Cal gave him a level gaze and then shrugged.

"Don't think so. Got to get back to work, for one thing."

"Didn't you tell them the circumstances?" asked Piper, shocked.

"Of course I did. They said I could take as much time as I

needed but, uh, I just don't think I'll be needing that much time."

Piper's eyes slid away from her brother to the floor. Leo paused and then pushed back his chair before wiping his mouth on the back of his hand.

"Well then," he said, "well then. No need to make no fuss."

"My thoughts exactly," said Cal.

Of course that wasn't how it turned out.

It began when Piper came down from their father's bedroom a few days later and started making a list at the kitchen table of things to get in town. Not from the local store, but up in the city from the place their mother had always used when she needed something special. Then she went out to see Leo. When she found him hoisting hay bales in the barn, she told him to keep the seventh free.

"What for?" he'd asked between grunts of exertion.

"Pa's planning something," she'd said.

"Pa can't wipe his own ass. You're planning something for him."

"And?"

"And what is it for?"

"For the family."

Leo had grunted again but he did not speak.

Then three days later, as she went to pick up some meat for dinner, Anne-Marie Parks saw Piper Hathaway order up two sides of beef, three hams, four chickens and a hog.

"You hibernating?" asked Dan Keenan from behind the counter. "If so you're early, it ain't even fall yet."

"Luck favors the prepared," said Piper as she counted out the money.

Later that week over mashed potatoes with sausages and

onions, Lou Parks told his wife about the invitation they had received.

"Walter's having a party up in the house," he said.

"Where?" asked Anne-Marie.

"Aurelia, their farm. We're invited."

"Oh," said Anne. "Why?"

"To celebrate Cal coming home."

"That's nice," she said halfheartedly.

"Leo won't think so," her husband muttered in reply, before turning back to read his paper. And so, because he was preoccupied, she didn't bother to question him, and as usual they finished the remainder of their dinner in silence.

Two weeks later and my grandmother stepped foot on Aurelia for the first time. The place as it was then would be unrecognizable to me: no sign in curlicue lettering, no pockets of flowers, no white house. I have seen pictures of what it used to be like. Instead of the daisies and hyacinths, the entrance to the farm was simply a sandy drive that wove its way along the crab grass. The house on the mound was not white and tall, but gray and flat with dark shutters and a roof that peeked over the front in a slanted fringe. In the distance the grass swept on and on, periodically knotted with thatches of prairie grass until eventually it found the fields of corn and the stream. It was large and expansive and Anne-Marie's first thought when she saw all of this was that it was ugly.

Did she see everything then that it could be? Did she re-envision the sight before her and see in her mind the potential that could arise from beneath her guiding hand? It would not have surprised us if she had. In fact in some ways it is what we would have expected from her, because in the end the way she knew exactly how to mold the farm

to suit her tastes and bring out the beauty in it was almost
prophetic. She was so intuitive that we all assumed she must
have connected to it from the first. But in truth there was no
such feeling. Maybe Lavinia Hathaway would come to feel
that way, but in 1946, Anne-Marie Parks did not. Instead,
she did not like Aurelia and she hated the idea of going to
the party.

It was not the first time this had happened. Her insides
had a habit of withering in anxiety whenever she was faced
with an event like this. The farm at this point was not the
great estate it would come to be in my lifetime, but it was
still considered to be a prosperous holding and the Hathaways
were a very respected family in the community. Nobody
would have missed the party if they could help it and the
weight of expectation that was implicit in the invite weighed
down on Anne-Marie from the moment her husband had
mentioned it to her over dinner. Because no matter what she
wore or how many hours she spent on her hair and makeup,
she always felt like the unwanted niece of her lawyer uncle,
the abandoned child, a product of other people's charity.

It was as if she had been branded and nothing could re-
move it. Not seducing and marrying the town doctor; not
moving into a house of her own, which was only slightly
smaller than her uncle's. Often she would wonder if this was
to be it. If she would live and die as nothing more than the
doctor's wife and her uncle's former charge. She would think
these things as she cooked, or ran her errands, and she would
suddenly be consumed with an urge to utterly annihilate
everything around her. Once she took the kitchen knife to
the soft pink curtains that hung over the window above the
sink. She slashed at them, not caring where she plunged the
knife, thrusting so deeply that the point scraped against the
glass, leaving long thin scratches on the pane. She eventually

stopped, the energy just draining from her, but once it was over she hadn't felt contrite or ashamed. She bundled up the material, composed an excuse for her husband and ordered some new curtains from a magazine she subscribed to. Why she felt like this she did not know. It seemed to her she had always been this way: always bitter and resentful because she did not count, and even now she did not know how to change this.

As she climbed the mound to the house, which was already strewn with lights, she began to prepare herself for the night ahead. She knew it annoyed her husband that she couldn't interact with their neighbors. He had known about the comments and gossip that started after their engagement had been announced, but only from a distance. To his face, at least, it was clear that all the men were secretly envious that he had managed to entrance a pretty nineteen-year-old. He did not know that the women had labeled his wife a harlot and a temptress; that despite the respectability of his name, to them she was still no better than his whore. Nor did he ever guess at how they stared at her belly after the first six months and noted with pursed lips and inward smiles that it had continued to stay flat. He did not sense their distaste, he only saw her isolation, an isolation he believed was self-imposed. That was why he left her at gatherings. After a few weeks into their marriage, he told her that if he stayed with her, she would never force herself to socialize. He chose not to acknowledge that whether he was with her or not, it made no difference.

So when they reached the door and were shown through to the garden, he immediately detached himself, leaving her standing on the back porch, cradling the flowers she had brought and staring at the islands of people knotted among the expanse of green punctured by white-clothed tables and multicolored streamers of silver, turquoise and gold.

She moved through these islands like a navigator through treacherous waters, slipping between the gaps she could find until she reached a small clearing that had not yet been invaded. She did not even try to see where her husband had gone. She came near one of the long tables covered with steaming hams and bowls of salad and rested the flowers near the paper cups and the punch bowl. Nearby stood a group of huddled men, whom she ignored. Instead she served herself a drink, and as she picked over the food she began to wonder how she would be able to get through the evening without taking a knife to something.

"Must just eat you up, Leo," one of the men near her said.

"He'll be gone soon, we all know he won't stay."

"What was he doing up in Oregon anyway?"

"Salesman."

"Walter knows he ain't no farmer. Blood or no blood he's seen you sweat over this place and he won't do anything that ain't in the interests of the farm. Ain't no salesman can farm."

"Yeah, but he did use to farm here, didn't he?"

"That was a long time ago, though."

"To be sure."

"You're the one who's been here. No one cares about that firstborn stuff. It's about what you done, not what position you were born into."

"I hope he knows that."

"He's a shrewd man, your pa."

"Yeah and a sick one. Sick ones stop being shrewd and start getting sentimental."

"Not when it comes to money they don't."

"And besides, if your pa does start to feel sentimental all's he got to do is start remembering why he sent him away in the first place."

"Come on now, Dan, everyone knows that were an accident."

"I don't want to talk about that."

"No…sure, Leo, of course. We meant no disrespect."

"Why, Anne-Marie, don't you look fetching?"

Anne-Marie turned to see her cousin, the girl she had grown up with, standing before her, a broad smile drawing a hole in her wide, pink flushed face.

"Thank you, Louise," she replied calmly, though she turned away briefly and slowly closed and reopened her eyes. She had not spoken with her cousin in weeks but each time she did it drained her. It ate up all her reserves to keep a neutral expression on both her tongue and her face, when secretly she wished God would just grant her lifelong wish and snap the girl's neck like a twig.

"So thin, though, Anne-Marie, if people were to look at you they'd think we were still in the Depression. You know I think you've lost weight again. You been losing it steadily ever since you left home, but I guess that's what happens when you have to cook for yourself. I noticed Lou is thinner than he was, too. Maybe you should talk him into hiring you a housekeeper, if he can afford it on a local doctor's wage."

"I wouldn't know. I don't question him about his finances." Anne-Marie turned to her plate. Louise cackled in laughter and put a hand on her shoulder.

"My God, what wife doesn't know how much she can push her husband for? You are a funny one. The very least he can do is get you some Negro girl in the place, preferably one from down south somewhere. They don't haggle as much as the ones up here. I insist you try, any more weight loss and people will start thinking something's wrong with you."

"I'm just fine," snapped Anne-Marie as her jaw ached under the strain.

"But maybe not," said Louise, cocking her head to her side and fingering the hem of Anne-Marie's dress. "Maybe the dress just makes it seem that way. Boy, you can do anything with a sewing machine," she said, dropping her hand away and smoothing down the cream silk that fell across her own waist and flared out at her hips. Suddenly she laughed. "Remember all those times I'd come home and find you just sewing away, always mending, always poring over your clothes and stuff. Why you didn't just ask Daddy to buy you something new I could never understand."

Anne-Marie stared at her cousin. She saw her cock her head to her side and gaze at her as if she were waiting for something, always waiting for something, and then finally smiling as she used to when she saw that Anne-Marie could not think of a way to respond.

"Daddy said you used to get that from your mother, that thriftiness." She bent nearer to her at this point. "Truth be told, I think he was glad that's all you got."

Anne-Marie cleared her throat and tried to turn away. Louise stepped back and frowned.

"Sorry, I forgot how you never mention your mother."

And she never did—never. I remember my father saying how he had asked about her once. My grandmother had gotten up from her chair and left the room without saying a word, and when he had asked his father why she was that way, all my grandfather could say was, "Some things just run through you so deep, all they leave is a hole."

And so it was with my grandmother, so that she became little more than a void in the disguise of a woman.

But while Anne-Marie may have refused to talk about her mother, almost everybody else did. They couldn't help themselves after her uncle's wife, a rotund woman who had an unfortunate partiality to loudly colored prints, had taken every opportunity at the store or in the street, to explain to her neighbors how her sister-in-law had turned up on their doorstep with a carpet bag, a spaniel puppy and a seven-year-old girl in a blue gingham pinafore.

Soon everyone would come to know that Eleanor Brown had left her husband, a teacher in San Diego, to come back to her home town. The rumor was that he had run up debts and their house was to be sold, though people suspected there were far more shameful indiscretions than these two meager facts. No one said so directly, but everyone knew they would divorce. People, including her own family, had assumed that Eleanor would stay in town under the supervision and support of her brother and create a new life, but it was not to be. In the early hours of a Wednesday morning, three weeks after she arrived, her brother came down to his morning coffee to find that not only had it not been made, but his wife also sat at their table, her head in her hands with a note laid open before her. While brief, Eleanor was certainly direct. The child was to stay with them until she could find a job and a home elsewhere. She left no forwarding address in case they chose to forward her daughter to her as well as her mail. So they were left with this little girl from San Diego whom they had only ever met once before and who was now to be staying with them for heaven knew how long.

At first Eleanor decided to keep up the pretense of parenthood and send them money every month. The amount always varied. Then after two years she sent forty dollars and a wedding photograph of her and her new husband. Her sister-in-law had humphed at this.

"At least she's not wearing white," she had said.

That was the last they had ever heard of her.

It was after this that they changed my grandmother's name. Her aunt had never liked it. She had thought it pretentious, flighty: in short, far too reminiscent of the traits inherent in her wayward mother. So they had taken it away and instead settled her with her middle name Anne, though they thought Anne Brown was far too dour so they had given her Marie as well. They had thought in doing so they were being kind.

So she had lived and grown up with them as Anne-Marie Brown, one of them, but always aware this was by their admission rather than her right, so that at any moment this could be taken away and no one would intervene. How much of this was of her own thinking and how much was gauged by their implication, no one will ever really know. What is known is that one day at the age of nineteen, Anne-Marie had placed the silver tray of honey roast chicken on the protective place mat in front of her uncle and when he stood up and scraped the carving knives against each other, over the clang of metal she announced there and then that she didn't want to be served any dark meat and that she was planning on marrying Dr. Lou Parks.

Her aunt had dropped her fork, her uncle had put down his carving knife and her cousin had shrieked with laughter.

"You can't marry Lou Parks," Louise squealed. "He's a hundred years old."

"Forty-nine," Anne-Marie had replied quietly.

Over the dimming candles and intermittent incredulous gasps and other noises, they had questioned her for over an hour, while the chicken shriveled up and the steamed vegetables began to wilt, until all they were left with was a cold meal and more questions than answers.

How had this happened? they wanted to know. Had she done anything improper? Louise at one point demanded to know if she had slept with him, at which point out of disgust or fright her mother had slapped her across the mouth and Louise had burst out crying, which had only made her mother start bawling herself. Her uncle sat there trying to compose himself, but he was hungry and he stared plaintively at the chicken and mourned the fact that on any other evening, he would by now be sitting in his study, fed and sated, not stiff-backed at the dinner table with his women crying.

"Don't you want to marry someone your own age?" her aunt asked her. "If you ever had any children, by the time they are grown up, why—" she turned to her husband, her hands splayed in a posture of both pleading and exasperation "—he'll be old enough to be their grandfather."

"I don't know if you've noticed but there aren't any young men left anymore," Anne-Marie answered coolly. "And the last thing I want is to raise some brat on my own while my husband gets his head blown off overseas."

Her aunt had opened and closed her mouth like a fish choking on air.

Finally, in an effort to impart some good on the proceedings, her uncle had asked Anne-Marie if she truly loved this man; if she was ready to spend the rest of her life with him, until death do they part, and, more importantly, if she really knew what this meant. She had leaned back in her chair and sighed, then looked at him with such tired contempt that when she dropped her head and turned away he had not dared to press her for an answer. For the very first time he had seen her naked in expression and suddenly he had an overwhelming desire to get the girl out of his house once and for all.

In that fact, he could not have known how alike in sentiment they were, probably the only thing, apart from blood, that they ever had in common.

Her family could not understand why Lou Parks wanted to marry her. A bachelor, with a taste for whiskey and a strong Presbyterian streak, he seemed the least likely person to fall for Anne-Marie. Her uncle couldn't help but question him over the validity of the relationship, when Lou, like a lovesick teenager, had come to his house the next day to properly ask for Anne-Marie's hand. Anne-Marie had bent over the upstairs banister, watching her cousin and aunt in the corridor below, trying to listen in on what he was saying, and she had smiled to herself at what she had accomplished, and even more that they would never know how she did it.

No one believed it would actually happen. They all thought it was a brief bit of madness that would be slowly weaned out before it could ever come to full destructive fruition. But even though the night before the wedding they had lain in their beds and wondered aloud if he would go through with it, the next day Lou had stood up in the church and never once faltered in his vows. Even their kiss had seemed sincere, as he cupped Anne-Marie's waist to draw her closer. Louise had made a gagging noise until she was hit on the arm to make her stop.

Her family was afraid of her after that, and she was glad. She saw how they greeted her and how anytime they said the words *Mrs. Parks,* their tongues seemed to slide over the letters as if, should they linger too long, someone would laugh at them and they would realize that they were the punch line to a joke she had been playing on them all this time. That wasn't too far from the truth and part of them suspected so. To them she was a stranger, capable of what…they did not know, nor did they care to find out. But Anne-Marie did, and she was waiting: waiting for the chance for her true self to emerge as an independent, not defined by who she was with or whose house she lived in. But the more she waited, the less likely it seemed that it might happen.

She saw her cousin look longingly over her shoulder and in that instant she took the chance to slip away. By the time Louise had noticed her absence, Anne-Marie had moved too far away for her to want to call her back. She wove her way through the garden. They called it a garden but in her mind it was no better than an untilled field, just long grass and bushes that sprawled down the back of the house in a wide arc and before she knew it, she had let it lead her away as it branched off to the left behind some trees. It was there, sitting on a bench, that she found Cal Hathaway. Later on in life he would say she was looking for him but she did not know it; that it was fate that had led her there. I am inclined to agree.

"I'm sorry, I did not mean to intrude," she said. He looked up at her then. He was reclining back on the white bench, a tumbler beside him and a bottle of scotch.

"Who are you? I ain't seen you before," he said curiously.

"I'm Anne-Marie Parks," she replied coolly and then held out her hand as an afterthought, but he'd already turned from her back to his scotch and her hand fell limply to her side.

"You from here?" he asked sharply.

"Most of my life."

"How come I don't know much of you then?"

"I don't know. Nobody knows much of me."

He looked her up and down. "Probably the best way," he said conclusively. "Soon as anyone knows anything about you in this place they all start wanting a piece. Well, they've had as much as they're going to get of me."

"Where you been? They— I heard that you had been away for some time now."

"Oregon. I'm a salesman there."

"Oh?" enquired Anne-Marie casually. "What do you sell?"

He shrugged. "Whatever needs selling."

This was how my grandfather was—cold, casual, unattached to anything and anyone except his daughter. He'd had enough of attachments at this stage in his life. All they ever seemed to do was bring him harm.

"I heard your daddy is dying."

"You heard right."

"I'm sorry."

"You wouldn't be if you knew him."

"I think you knew him and you're still sorry, or you wouldn't be down here away from everyone knocking back scotch."

In the dark she could see his gaze arrest in surprise. His hand hovered over the bottle before he poured a thimbleful.

"Want to taste?"

She drew herself up.

"Ah, now there's no need to be like that. A bit won't kill you and it's the good kind anyhow. My pa has good taste in liquor."

"How old are you?" she asked.

"I'm thirty-five."

"Well, it's a sorry state when a man of your age is hiding from a party thrown for him at the bottom of a garden, drinking stolen liquor."

Cal laughed. "You ain't very popular, are you?"

Anne-Marie put a hand to her neck and then dropped it in irritation.

"About the same as you from the sounds coming out of people. Who says I ain't anyhow?"

In the dark he seemed to smile. "Nobody is who likes pointing out other people's truths."

He stood up then and she saw how tall he was, the broad shoulders, the thin nose and square jaw, his long hands that were now cradling his drink. She would come to know how much he would like to drink and for a long time it would not bother her.

"What did you say your name was?"

"Weren't you paying attention? I told you it was Anne-Marie."

He shrugged. "Anne-Marie just don't seem to suit, is all. You don't look like an Anne-Marie to me." He licked his lips. "Anne-Maries are soft creatures. You ain't soft, you're hard and brittle and harder because you know you're brittle. Your name is a lie, Anne-Marie, but then so is mine. People call me Cal, have done all my life, but my name is Abraham. You know your bible—Abraham is the father of the twelve nations of God's chosen people, all-wise, all-knowing. But I ain't no Abraham just like you ain't no Anne-Marie, so what then is your name, girl?"

It was then, my grandmother said, that she knew it. She watched the swaying man try to steady himself on his drunken feet and even though he wasn't handsome, even though he was just some salesman from Oregon, even though she felt a creeping vine of disdain tug at the corners of her mouth as she observed him, it could not change her revelation.

"One day you will know," she would say much later. *"You will just know and all you can do is pray for the serenity to accept it and the courage to follow through."*

"My mother called me Lavinia," she said finally.

He smiled down at her, and as he leaned forward she could smell the rich yeast of his breath.

"See—" he cupped her neck in his palm "—didn't I tell you?"

★ ★ ★

That's as much as she would ever reveal about what happened that evening in the garden. My grandfather on the other hand was more forthcoming. He once told me how even though he had noticed the wedding band, even though she was just a slip of a girl with a bitter tongue and even though her face was twisted in contempt, he had still looped her up by the waist and pressed his mouth against hers. He was drunk, he was angry and he saw in her the same anger at everything. Perhaps it was an act of consolation or the comfort of two strangers who found in each other a sense of kinship. Perhaps I am being too sentimental. Perhaps it was only ever meant to be just a kiss.

Later, when her husband would decide to go home and start to look for her, she would appear next to the table with the punch bowl, and he would ask if she'd had enough and wanted to leave, and she would say, gladly.

On the ride home, my grandmother said, she wrestled with herself. She thought about Cal's words while she twisted her wedding ring. She conjured the faces of her cousin and her family, of the last time she ever saw her mother and finally of the pink curtain she had slashed to ribbons. The weight of it all, of all she knew and hated and all she wanted and was too afraid of, made her sag in her seat. For once her husband seemed to notice. He leaned over as he steered the car down the thin tree-laden lanes and, holding her hand he said, "Are you okay, Anne-Marie?"

And just like that she broke.

When I think of a time when things could have been different and then when something happened to make it so that they could never be, I find myself back at that garden party.

If it were possible to undo that one thing, then everything else in time would unravel with it and we'd be left clean and renewed with hope.

Before I went to bed that night I dialed Ava's number. It was late but I didn't care. In the end it was the answering machine that picked up. Usually I would not have left a message but this time was different. This time I said, "I'm going back. I thought...well someone has to look over things and I don't want Mom's stuff sold off to a pack of strangers or gossip-hungry neighbors. I was thinking...I don't... I wondered if maybe you may want to come with me—just to see what stuff you'd want to keep to remember them by.... No, why would you, right? I know. But I am going. I just thought you should know."

I put down the receiver and lay supine on my bed. I knew I would dream that night, but I did not care. In the silence behind my mouth I said to myself, *Let them come.*

As if they needed an invitation.

3

AT THE AGE OF SEVENTY-ONE, WALTER HATHAWAY had cancer of the colon. That was the only reason his eldest son had come back. He had been diagnosed in the office of an oncologist upstate, a specialist recommended to him by Lou Parks, who had gone to college with the man and had followed his career with a respect tinged with envy.

After a series of tests and weeks of waiting he had driven back up to the doctor's office, where after a few minutes of chitchat and polite conversation, the doctor had told him that not only did he have cancer of the colon, but that there was also nothing they could do to save him.

"Bullshit," said Walter.

He had picked up his hat and thanked the man, who, after taking a moment to recover, was still hastily trying to explain that with his symptoms Walter would be dead within a year. Despite the doctor's protestations, Walter left him with little more than a curt nod of acknowledgment. He refused to believe that death would be coming for him so soon, and so when he came home and sat before the dinner his daughter had made for him, all he'd said when she asked him where he'd been was that he had spent the day in a meeting with a supplier.

But then four months later he had woken up in a pool of his own shit and blood and saw death beside him sitting in a wicker chair. So he had lain back into his pillow, sighed and said, "Okay, you win."

It was then he began to talk about his eldest son and how to bring him home.

It was also the first time he had mentioned him in over sixteen years.

When he was laid up in his bed and the doctor had given him his medication, he gritted his teeth against the pain and curled his fingers into claws so that they dug tunnels in the sheets. Twisting in agony he beckoned to his daughter and told her, "Go find your brother."

"Sure, Pa, I'll go get him for you," said Piper. A few minutes later and she came back with Leo, who winced when he saw the state his father had become.

Walter closed his eyes and sighed irritably.

"No, not him. I mean your brother Cal. Get Cal."

Piper felt Leo stiffen beside her but she dared not look at him. She stared at her father but the old man had his gaze fixed to the ceiling, battling against the forces of his own body, and she saw then what she would become despite everything she was now and her back sank beneath the weight of her revelation.

"Pa?"

"Didn't you hear me, girl? You making me talk when I got no energy to talk. Do as I say!" he shouted and then doubled over into himself. Piper went to help him but he smacked her hand away. She looked desperately for Leo but he'd already left the room.

When she went down the stairs she found Leo standing on the front porch, his fingers splayed against the fringe of the roof that hung over them. He was staring out onto the drive. Without looking away he asked, "Is he dead yet?"

"What the hell is wrong with you? Of course not," said Piper.

He turned to face her.

"Well, by God I wish he were. I wish he'd hurry and up and go before he does something stupid."

"I don't want to hear you talk like that."

"That man up there is not my father."

"He may be more of your father than you'd like."

Leo lurched himself forward down the porch steps.

"What do you want me to do?" Piper called after him. He turned around, and when he did his face was half in shadow.

"Get a gun and end it. If it were a horse you wouldn't think twice."

Piper leaned back and clasped her hands over her skirt.

"Well then, don't ask me again," he said, his profile throwing up long shadows as he walked home.

After a while it seemed that the medication began to take hold. Her father was weak but quiet, as if he had resigned himself to his fate. Sometimes as she passed the hall that led to his bedroom she would hear his voice and wonder to whom he was talking. She mentioned it once to Lou Parks, who said not to worry, one of the side effects of the treatment was hallucinations. He asked her if she wouldn't want to move their father to some palliative care place that would help control his pain before he died, but Piper refused. She had nursed her mother in that same bed before she died and she felt it was only right to do the same for her father. Lou

Parks shrugged and touched the rim of his hat as he left her. She went to the kitchen to prepare dinner.

But then a few days later, Lou came into the living room, where she was mending linen, and said gently, "Your pa is asking for Cal."

"What?" she asked, startled.

He stepped gingerly into the room, cautious to avoid any mines. "Walter won't stop talking about the boy. He wants to see him."

"Could this be the effect of the medication?" Piper asked hopefully.

"No, more like the effect of dying and the regrets that come to you before you do."

"Oh," said Piper as she sat back in disappointment. "I see."

"Do you know where he is?"

"Cal? Of course I do."

"It's just what with Walter feeling how he did about him I thought…"

"I never stopped talking to Cal," said Piper. "I just didn't do it in my daddy's earshot."

"Well, it's up to you, of course."

"Yes, I suppose it is."

Later that night, Piper went down to Leo's house, a small honey-colored place he'd built half a mile down from the main house. She knocked on the door and walked in to find her sister-in-law wiping flour from her hands.

"Hi there, Elisa," she said. "Is Leo home?"

"Sure is, he's upstairs having a bath. You wanna wait?"

Piper nodded. "I think I'll have to."

The women sat in the kitchen and chatted while Elisa put the finishing touches to her pie. Then quietly Elisa said, "My sister is pregnant again."

"Oh, how wonderful," said Piper before she had time to

stop herself. Elisa smiled down at her fingers as she licked cherry juice from them.

"Yes, it is. I'm very happy for her. I do love playing with my niece and nephews. She was a little afraid of telling me, I think, on account of the troubles Leo and I have been having, but I'm glad she told me. She must feel so full of purpose."

Piper kept silent but she watched the back of the woman's head keenly. Usually she would reach out and touch her, but she could not afford to do so at a moment like this, not with what she had to tell her brother; not with knowing that she had approximately thirty seconds to say what she needed to before she was sent packing out of the house.

When Leo came downstairs, he nodded at his sister in greeting.

"I told Piper about my sister's baby," said Elisa as she dusted the pie in sugar. Leo gazed at his wife and then as if conscious of his sister watching, coughed into his hand and turned away.

"So you stopping for supper?" he asked.

"No, not exactly." Piper placed a hand on her stomach, willing the courage to come, but it would not. So instead she leapt forward anyway, hoping that its inability to show itself was merely a product of delay rather than a sign of total absence.

"I think we should send for Cal."

From the corner of her eye she saw Elisa's hand hover in midair and then gently resume shaking the sugar over the crust. Her hand beating against the sieve was the only sound in the room.

Finally Leo said, "Now what in hell gave you that idea?"

"Pa is dying. You should respect a dying man's wish."

The chair scraped on the floor as Leo seated himself level with his sister.

"You ever think that maybe you should respect the wishes of a man when he was sane and well, rather than hallucinating and sick? That in his right mind Pa would never ask for such a thing?"

"It's not just for Pa. Cal has a right to know."

"For what?" Leo snorted. "He didn't want to know for how many years now? Did he want to know after Ma died?"

"I think Daddy is ready to forgive."

"I think this is horseshit."

Piper stood up from the table and spread her fingers in a fan against the edge. She made herself tower over her brother.

"I believe we are better than this. I believe we are better than some people who would just let their own interests get in the way of doing what is right and I believe that even if Cal came back it wouldn't make no difference to anything other than Pa would finally stop asking for him and could get some peace before he dies."

Leo's jaw worked thoughtfully at this last part. Piper saw it and pressed her advantage.

"You have to trust that Pa would have recognized what you've done, Leo. You've been here, Cal hasn't. Maybe things were meant to work out differently to that, but they didn't. We won't lose anything by having him back. Once upon a time this is what you would have wanted."

Elisa's hands provided the background noise to the pause that followed Piper's words: the opening and closing of the oven door, the scrape of dishes in the sink. Piper willed her brother to show a glimpse of the boy she had known since childhood. She willed it so hard it was almost a prayer, and for a moment as he lifted her head she thought perhaps God had been listening.

"Whatever," said Leo and he left the room.

She knew better than to look at her sister-in-law for comfort when it came to this subject so she left and made her way back home. Three days later as Leo came in for lunch, she slipped a piece of paper and some money next to the arm holding his corn beef sandwich.

"What's this?" he asked.

"I need you to send a telegram for me."

"To who?"

"To Cal."

Leo slapped his tongue against his teeth.

"Will you?"

"I wasn't planning on going into town."

"Neither was I."

They stood there in their silent contest of wills, and as Piper felt herself falter, a shadow passed over her brother's face and he dropped his sandwich onto the plate. He hunched over as he stood up to leave and she made as if to touch him, but he gave her a look that forced her hand back to her side.

And then her father called for her. She was up the stairs in an instant and when she came back down, she saw the plate was now in the sink and that the money with the piece of paper was gone and she held on to the banister to steady herself as she leaned against the wall.

Did Walter have an inkling of what his simple request had done to the equilibrium of his household? Did he even care? It was a question she longed to ask, but she held her counsel. Instead she thought back to the last time they had all been under the one roof. It was the day of her mother's wake and she had been thirteen years old. She remembered how she had stared up at the blueness of the sky and at the good china laden with finger sandwiches and cakes from their neighbors and the house full of people, and she remembered thinking that on any other day, to any stranger passing by, how much it would have looked like a party.

She remembered her father sitting in his chair, when he was still strong and intimidating, surrounded by their neighbors and Leo, only two years older than she was, hovering in the doorway looking silently at the shadows Cal threw up on the walk as he stalked up the drive away from them.

She remembered all these things with color, and between the stairwell and the walls she gave up a shudder.

Whenever my grandparents talked about their courtship, they always gave the impression of a passion and romance that could not help but transgress all boundaries. In one sense they were being truthful, but in another how else could they have presented it? Because the simple truth, as Piper loved to point out and did so more frequently the older she became, was that while theirs was a respectable marriage, their courtship had been far from it, with the inconvenient fact that my grandmother was already married.

I have often been struck by the differences in the ways in which Piper and Lavinia laid out the early years of my grandparents' relationship, and indeed both their versions fascinated me because despite their differences they both illuminated an aspect of their partnership that neither myself, nor my siblings, nor even their own children, had ever witnessed: a time when it was my grandfather, not Lavinia, who had the power.

When my grandmother was still known as Anne-Marie Parks, she and Cal had begun their affair. At first, certainly from my grandfather's point of view, it was never meant to be serious. He had no intention of staying in Iowa—this was simply a way of passing the time until his father died and he could be free. And he liked Anne-Marie: he liked how she always twisted her hair in her hands on one side of her neck as she listened to him tell stories from his childhood; he liked that she smelled of rose water; he liked how she spoke the truth regardless of consequence or feeling; he liked that she was unhappy.

My grandfather used to have a thing for unhappy women. He could sense them a mile off and he was always drawn to them, because they didn't expect much and were always more than appropriately grateful for what they could get. But more than that, unhappy women, when you made them happy, relished the thing like a cat basking in a pool of sunshine: they unfurled, they blossomed and their smiles of incredulous delight at this transformation always gave Cal a surge of pride in his own abilities. It made him feel like a good person, before he remembered otherwise.

They would meet a few miles down the road from Aurelia, during the day so that Lou was out at the practice or when he had been called away for a series of home visits. Anne-Marie would park her car behind a turnoff into a clearing shielded by the long prairie grass and Cal would meet her there in his Chevy. They would go to secluded woods, sometimes on long drives to nowhere, where they would park in any cloistered place they could find. They would stay there for hours. My grandmother often said later that she lived for those drives, though she would never have indicated as such to Cal. She knew she could not push him, but she heard tales of Walter getting sicker and she would listen to Cal talk of Oregon and what he planned to do when he got back and she would wring her hair in her hands to stop herself from screaming at him.

She waited on those drives for the moment of inspiration

to come, just like it had with Lou. She knew better than to force it, but still she worried. She could not bear the idea of Cal going back to Oregon and she stuck in her house with her husband, looking up night after night over the dinner table and finding him sitting there at the end.

Irritatingly, he had grown kinder to her since the garden party. Since the night she had broken down sobbing and choking in their car he had been more tender, more concerned. She had tried to endure it as best she could.

So she sat there in the car with Cal waiting for a sign, keenly alert for whatever guise it may present itself as, while he stroked her skin under his hands and called her Lavinia.

And then finally it came.

Cal struck her so hard across the mouth that he broke the skin on her lip and she bled into her teeth. She saw him lean back, his face ashen, and he stared down at his fingers while self-revulsion contorted his features. Without a word she got out of the car and began to walk. It was ten miles from where she had parked her car. She waited for Cal to come after her but he didn't. She heard the engine of the car roar behind her but the sound faded away. So she walked the ten miles and in that time she thought over what had happened.

Now my grandfather was not a man who ever lifted his hand to a woman, nor would ever again, save once years later when he would strike his daughter so hard she would fall and catch her temple on the table corner as she went down. He would stare at his hand then in the same way as he had looked at it now with Anne-Marie. What shocked me when I first heard these stories was not only that my grandfather, when provoked, could lose all sense of reason and restraint, but also that these provocations existed in the first place.

Maybe this may seem strange, but if you ever met my

grandfather you would not have believed it of him. He was a man who was so temperate his perpetual state was placid. It was helped by his drinking surely, but never did his manner or nature ever tip those scales except for three times in his life. Once was when his mother died, once was now in a car parked outside Sunrise Wood and the last time would be in his kitchen in the spring of 1968. But at the time Anne-Marie knew nothing of this. What she did know was that she had said something that, without even realizing it, had flipped a switch in the man beside her, so that for a moment he ceased to exist. She hadn't even seen it coming; there had been no warning. One minute they were talking; the next, the back of his knuckles had slammed her lips against her teeth. So she went over in her mind what she could have said to set him off.

They had been talking about his father. He was the one who had brought it up.

"Doctor came over yesterday."

"Lou?" she asked.

"Yeah." He shifted in his seat. "They say it's not long now."

"Oh."

"He wanted to see me up in his room."

"Who? Lou?"

"No, Pa."

They fell silent. She curled her hand around the open lapel of his shirt.

"Did you go?"

"No, I didn't."

"Why not?"

His chest rose and fell under her cheek. Try as she might she couldn't hear his heart through the shirt.

"I haven't spoken to him in sixteen years."

"Well, you must have now that you've come back."

"No, not at all. I've seen him but I haven't said a word to him."

"Oh. Why?"

"I don't know. I kinda like seeing him suffer."

She lifted her head then and, curling a finger under his chin, she made him face her.

"Why do you hate your pa so much?"

"Doesn't everyone hate their pa a little?"

"I don't know my pa to hate him, and your sister and brother don't hate him." She added cautiously, "Julia doesn't hate you."

"That's because she hasn't been raised on hell."

"It don't look like hell to me."

He jerked his head away from her.

"Do you know about my ma?"

She shook her head.

"She died. A while ago now. She got sick, drank some contaminated water and she died in the same bed that he's dying in. She's buried on the farm. I lowered her coffin in the ground with my brother." He paused to lick his lips and then settled back into his seat and stared ahead again. It was late in the afternoon. Lou had been called away to a conference in another county so they had stayed out later than usual. Their skin took on mottled hues of orange and pale pink from the sunset pouring through the windshield.

"The day of her funeral I was nineteen and I left home for good. I went up the drive and I just kept walking. No one stopped me, no one called after me. I slept rough, hitchhiked, took a shower when I could, lived without it when I couldn't. I didn't even know that I was leaving when I was, but I guess my feet knew better. I knew my pa wouldn't give a shit. He told me as much, that he wanted me out of the place when Ma died. He said he didn't want me under his roof no more. I been thinking on that for years. It could have been any one of us, it just happened to be me."

He was still staring straight ahead. My grandmother knew that he'd almost forgotten she was even there. She didn't care. She sat there watching him, barely moving, her breath shallow and uneven. He heaved a great sigh and when he spoke his voice was flat in a low monotone.

"We had always done chores around the farm, but then when I got to be sixteen Pa started to really teach me the ropes. He was always talking about the farm and leaving it to me and Leo and how we should manage it, and what we had to do for it. He was sick with love over the place, all the more because he only won it from his boss due to sheer sweat. And boy, did he make sure that we sweated over it. He thought it would make us love it as much as him. And we did, I guess. We didn't really have a choice."

He narrowed his eyes as he remembered.

"When I got to be eighteen he started giving me more responsibility. I was glad of it. I wanted to do things right. And to be sure, I never saw any other life for myself other than the one he laid out before me. So careful to follow only in his footsteps, neither shifting to the right nor looking to the left. Dead center," he said as he sliced his hand slowly through the air in front of him.

"We used to use this pesticide during the crop dusting. And one time I was in charge of it. I'd seen it done a hundred times. Small thing, no-nothing thing. Only dangerous if you were careless. On one of the wheat fields near the stream we have a small stone well. Hardly a well, more like a built-up pool. Us kids used to drink from it in summer when it was hot and we were in the fields and too tired to go back in the house for water. During the crop dusting we always covered the well. And I remember…I remember putting the big stone tablet on top of it before I started the dusting. I remember it so clearly. I picked it up, and to be sure that thing was heavy, but I heaved it up on there all the same. I did, I know I did, I remember doing it.

"Ma used to come down to us. She used to help sometimes in the field when we had a lot a work to do. Not often, but she was always one to get her hands dirty. Ma, she grew up on a farm in Indiana with six brothers, she was—" he laughed "—she was a heck of a woman. Sometimes she'd try to tell Pa how to farm and they'd have these blazing arguments about it, real hammer and tongs. She didn't give a shit if he smacked her on the mouth and told her to hush up—she always had to have her say.

"One day she came down to see me and Leo when we were busy doing some chore and I can see her now, leaning against the well. They all said she had to have drunk from it, weren't no other way that she could have gotten how she did. But if she did…well…Leo said he saw her drink from it but I didn't see it. She got sick the next day, took to her bed a few days later and never got out of it. Piper nursed her the whole way through, and she was only thirteen. It didn't take long for her to die. She was gone before she knew it. Before we knew it."

He nodded and bit his lip, rocking his neck back and forth as he finished. She looked him up and down for a moment.

"She was young, you know. She was only forty when she died."

"Is that why you left then?" she asked.

He was struck dumb. He blinked in assent.

"God, I hate this place," he muttered. "I wish to God I'd never come back. It weren't by choice me leaving. That son of a bitch. I may not have been a kid exactly when I left but you know at the time I'd never even been out of the state? Farthest I ever got was Des Moines once for a state fair for chrissake!" He braced his hand against the steering wheel and began to chuckle to himself. She shrank back in her seat as he twisted his face this way and that, struggling with his memories.

"Son of a bitch. I'm glad it hurts. I see them all, our neighbors, all wondering why I'm back, wondering why he's asked me back here now. They don't know how to greet me. Before it was fine, I was the black sheep, a killer," he growled, "but now he's asking to see me like some prodigal son and they're confused. They can't figure it out, but I can. I know why he asked me back and I don't give a shit. He wants me to join Leo on the farm. Be a Hathaway again. Well, that's his vision, not mine. I'm waiting and just when he needs it the most I'll pull the rug out from under him, I'll let him die knowing it all went to hell with him. I'll have me a real good day."

"Oh, Cal," she said, touching his shoulder. "I'm so sorry." She paused.

"It weren't your fault. He should have known better. He should have known it was just an accident."

There.

A second later—was it a second later? Wasn't it less, half a moment, in an instant and his knuckle had slammed into her mouth? Her body cracked against the window with the force. He had screamed at her but at the time she didn't register. Her hand was at her lip in an instant, she was too shocked initially to feel pain, but she saw his knuckles ripple under her blood as he withdrew.

And that was how she found herself walking down the side of a road now, only eight and a half miles left from where she had parked her car.

What went through her mind at that moment? Was it anger? Was it hurt and betrayal? Was it shame at her own foolishness?

She conjured up the last thing he had said to her as he struck her. She hadn't realized it at the time, but she heard it clearly as she thought on it now.

"I put the lid on the well!" he'd screamed.

So no, none of these emotions went through Anne-Marie as she walked. She held her hand to her aching jaw and lifted the corner of her lips ever so gently in a smile. She was not angry, she was elated. She saw her opportunity.

I wonder now if I am being unkind to her. Perhaps too much has been colored by what I know would eventually happen to allow me to ever present her in a way in which she could have been innocent, or good. I am too used to seeing her as the villain. But, as she used to say, she was made, not born. Firstly by those who came before us in her life, and now years later by me in memory. I want to say that she didn't think those things, or feel those things, that it all came out later under duress with due cause. But that's a lie. It was always there brewing, it had to be. She took to it too easily.

Just like I did when my time came.

4

WHEN CAL CAME HOME, THE FIRST THING HE SAID
to his sister was, "Did anybody call?"

Piper paused in her stirring of the mixing bowl to take
stock of her brother.

"No," she said carefully. "You expecting somebody?"

"No," said Cal.

He drew out a chair at the table and sat down heavily.

"Where's Julia?" he asked after a moment.

"She's out back in the garden. I gave her some of my old
toys and stuff. She's having fun."

"I think we should be going soon," said Cal quickly.
Piper's wrist wavered momentarily, before she continued to
beat the spoon against the bowl.

"Before Pa dies?"

"Why does that even matter? Who cares if I stay or go
before then?"

"Pa will."

"Screw Pa!"

He drawled the words out in his rage, strangling them in his throat so that they emerged stretched with fury. He put his hands up to his hair and held his crown in his hands. Piper saw the blood on his knuckles.

"You want to tell me something, Cal?" she asked.

He stood up abruptly and went out of the kitchen.

"No," she said, continuing to stir, "I didn't think so."

Three days later he began to panic. He wondered if she would tell her husband. He had certainly given her cause to, and that busted lip would need some explanation. He prowled the farm waiting for Lou to show up. He told himself he didn't care. He could more than handle Lou Parks. He told himself that people could talk and his siblings could look at him with disgust and it wouldn't affect him. He would be gone soon anyway. He told himself he was used to exile.

But still he woke up in the night, his mind already crowding with voices tumbling over themselves to be heard first.

He tried calling her once, but he realized he had nothing to say even if she should answer. He saw that he had gotten himself into a mess, but he comforted himself with the knowledge that all he need do was bide his time until his father died and then he could leave. He counseled his heart to be patient, to be patient and to forget. Forget that he had struck her; forget her skin under his hands.

Forget that he missed her.

Piper saw the restlessness in Cal and she tensed. Against her will and much to her self-disgust, she began to wish her father would hurry up and die. She had tried to sound out Lou Parks on the subject. He would only shake his head and say, "He's holding on. For what, I don't know, but he's holding." Piper nodded in assent, but this only made her worry even more. She knew what her father was holding on for and she knew Cal wouldn't give in. She had hoped that her brother's resolve would melt, or that her father's strength would wane, but she saw now that neither would do as she wished and so one afternoon as she was washing her father's soiled sheets, she made up her mind and asked God to help her and then to forgive her.

Leo had stopped coming up to the house as much, so she went out to see him in the barn. She brought a plate of roast beef and mustard sandwiches as a peace offering.

"I already had lunch," he said as his eyes brushed past the plate.

"I've come to ask you a favor."

"Oh," he said, wiping his hands on a rag. "Shoot."

"I need you to talk to Cal."

Leo began to laugh as he turned away from her. She grabbed his arm and swung him around.

"Enough. You want Pa to go, then you listen to me. The only reason why he is holding on up in that bed is for Cal. That may hurt you but it's true nonetheless. The only way he will go is if Cal will speak to him."

"For what?"

Piper sighed and cradled the plate.

"I think he wants forgiveness," she said, looking down.

"For what?" asked Leo slowly. Piper sighed.

"For sending Cal away all those years ago. What happened to Ma could have been an accident, Leo. You used to think so."

Leo's voice when it came out was curdled with venom. "And now Pa does, too, that it?"

"I don't know," said Piper, exasperated. "All I know is Cal is itching to leave, you're itching for him to leave, Pa's itching to die and it's about time somebody started to scratch these things out before they do some real damage."

"Here's me thinking you were enjoying your little family reunion."

"Take Cal into town when you go and get the horse feed. Talk to him."

"And say what?"

"Jesus H. Christ, do I have to think of everything?!" She bit her lip and steadied her voice. "Do it this afternoon."

She made as if to walk away.

"Leave the plate on the bale," said Leo after a pause.

If you asked my aunt Julia what her earliest memory was, she'd tell you that it was of her mother's decapitation. She was lying.

Later on she would admit to her husband, Jess, that she didn't really remember anything too much about the accident, or her father picking her up at the hospital, or being covered in her mother's blood. She would say that she had the feeling the memory was there but that for some reason she just couldn't get to it. Some part of her wouldn't let it spring into life. That was the closest she ever got to trying to understand her own psychology.

Her first real memory was of her father's second wedding. She remembered the smell of the courthouse, how polished the woods were and her feet dangling as they scuffed along the floor while she waited for them to finish. She could recall her aunt Piper holding her, the pressure of her fingers on her waist and how Piper's body had heaved with Julia's as she gave a great sigh when her father had kissed her new mother. Piper would say that it was the first time Julia had ever met her.

But here she was wrong, because unbeknownst to her,

Julia had met the woman who would be her stepmother four months earlier, as she had lain sobbing on the dust floor outside the local feed store.

In the car on the way there she had sat in the back watching the views change in the windows. According to my father and uncle, she used to say that whenever she sat in cars as a child she always felt as if her mother were right there next to her, her head severed from her body, her hands limp, the top of her neck slewed with the bone creating a pyramid of blood and flesh at the top. How she could have known this—when she didn't remember the decapitation itself—is anyone's guess. Perhaps it was a dormant memory that occasionally sprang into life. Or perhaps it was simply her imagination of what the physical effects of a decapitation might be. If so, you would have thought that she would have envisioned a clean, neat severing, not the crude hewn state she saw. Whatever the reason, it later became a valuable weapon against her younger brothers. But a year before the first one was born, she sat in the back of her uncle's truck, so intent on not looking at the last surviving image of her mother beside her, that she did not hear the stilted conversation of the men who sat up front. All she knew was that suddenly the car came to a stop and with the unspoken promise she had assumed her father had made to her of licorice laces beckoning, she climbed out of the car, careful not to disturb the dress of her mother beside her as she left.

When they got out of the car she skipped ahead into the store, only to be severely disappointed. There were no jars of multicolored candy, no licorice laces in red and purple spools. The place smelled and everything seemed dull and boring. She felt she had been betrayed and so she did what she would always do in the face of disappointment. She threw a tantrum.

Her father was angrier with her than usual. Normally he

would gaze at her in a cool, collected way until he eventually gave in or she exhausted herself. But this time he slapped her on the back of her legs, hauled her up by the arm and dragged her out of the store, her legs curling underneath her as she tried to kick out in anger and frustration, and then quite suddenly he dropped her; he just let go and the slam of earth on skin made her sob stick in her throat. The silence for the both of them seemed eerie, but while she looked up at him, he was looking somewhere else.

My grandmother said that the moment she saw Julia curled up on the floor next to her father, staring at him obstinately, snot and drool spitting from her lips and nose, she knew she did not like her. It was not the mess the child had made of herself, it was the way she had looked from her father to her, and how when she had seen that his attention had been caught by someone else, her eyes narrowed and she spat out another spit trail that curled under her chin.

"I didn't know you would be here," Cal said when he finally found his voice.

"I was out getting groceries," said Anne-Marie.

Cal saw her lips covered in rouge and the swell of the jaw beneath the heavy makeup. He reached out to touch her and she shrank back, and glanced over her shoulder quickly to see if anyone had been watching. He snaked his fingers through his hair in frustration.

"I thought about calling," he said.

"I am glad you didn't."

She was so cold as she stood there waiting for him to finish, as if he were just another piece of nuisance she had to climb over before she could carry on with her day. It angered him, this aloofness of hers. It made him want to smack her again just to get a reaction. Suddenly he began to feel sick.

"I don't know what…I don't—"

She continued to stare at him, her foot rubbing against her ankle in impatience. Beside him he felt his daughter shift and her shoe scuffed against his heel with a small kick. He looked down at her and saw her glare back at him. Her knee was bleeding.

"Please don't talk to me again," Anne-Marie said finally.

He panicked. "Lavin—"

"Don't you *ever*—" She took a step forward and he saw more clearly the yellowish swirls near her jaw. "*Ever* call me that again."

She walked away, passing Leo as he came out with a bag of horse feed. Leo saw his brother standing there, his mouth open, looking at the doctor's wife and his niece sprawled on the floor, her left knee bleeding, her face bright red as she stared with hatred at her father.

"Cal?" he asked. "What are you doing?"

Cal looked down at his daughter and with one hand pulled her up. She cocked her bad knee for effect as she stood but he didn't seem to notice.

"Will you take Julia back for me, please?" he asked.

"You thought any more on what I said?" asked Leo as he cradled the feed.

"Yeah, I—I listened."

Leo paused. "Okay," he said finally. "Let's go, girl," he said to his niece.

What happened next no one really knows. There was to be a lot of speculation that surrounded the events of the next sixteen hours for some time afterward. Everyone had their own theories. Leo believed Cal had been planning it all along, Piper believed that the opportunity presented itself and Cal was too weak to say no. My grandmother believed it was destiny. I don't know what I believe.

Because it was so unexpected, so shocking, that it has

never really made sense. Trying to rationalize it now could only be accomplished through conjecture and imagination. All I know is that my grandfather was a man who felt things deeply. He hated that about himself. He tried not to grow attached, but he was simply a man to whom burdens came easily, and every time he tried to shrug them off, the weight of his guilt would burden him all over again. So here is what I think happened.

I think he was afraid. Afraid of who he was and what he wanted and what he didn't want to be.

I think he was tired of fighting for what he wanted, tired of fighting himself for wanting those things in the first place and tired of feeling guilty for all of the above.

I think he wanted to settle. I think he wanted it all to stop. I think he knew that life had a will of its own and for the second time he was willing to be borne along by it. I think he reasoned that he was a man, not a boy this time, and he could deal with things better.

I think he was sick of feeling like a failure.

Piper cooked dinner for herself and Julia that evening. She made a chocolate pecan pie for dessert that Julia wolfed down in sullen self-pity. She put her niece to bed and checked on her father, before going to bed herself at around eleven. Cal still wasn't home. The next morning she fixed breakfast, changed her father and gave him a sponge bath. She enlisted Julia's help in the chores, but gave up after her niece kept crumpling to the floor in mock agony on account of her "bad leg." She went to check on her eldest brother, but when she knocked on the door he didn't answer and when she tried the handle, it was locked. She assumed he was still asleep.

She went to bring Leo some lunch. He was down by the crops on the far side of the farm near the stream. When she gave it to him, he nodded in thanks before jerking his head to the left of her.

"See that?" he asked.

Piper turned. Against the well was the stone slab cover. Now broken, the pieces were splayed against the base of the well.

"What happened?"

Leo shrugged. "Don't ask me."

This was before she discovered that Cal had gone to speak with their father. This was before she would check in on Walter at six to bring him supper, when she would find him, eyes gazing upward and unseeing, his mouth half-open with a fly crawling across his upper lip.

This was before the funeral and the reading of the will, when things still made sense to her. But later on, after everything, she would recall this moment and wonder.

Anne-Marie was in the kitchen when she heard that Walter Hathaway had died. She was peeling potatoes for a stew. She listened to her husband talk of the man's heart failure and willed herself not to scream. She sliced the knife through the potato into her palm when he mentioned the funeral.

"Good God, woman, what is the matter with you lately?" her husband asked as he pulled up her arm, down which a thin trail of blood was already pouring. "First your jaw, now this. Your head is in the clouds, Anne-Marie."

"I'm sorry," she muttered.

The night before the funeral Anne-Marie pressed her husband's best black suit and a somber-looking navy dress with a high-buttoned neck that irritated her skin, and hung them both on the front of their wardrobes. Then when her husband was asleep she went downstairs, pulled aside the half pint of milk that she had left to curdle in the gap between the refrigerator and the wall and forced herself to drink it. She had learned the hard way in the past that feigning illness when your husband was a doctor was not a viable option.

She was sick all night. The next morning Lou gave her a glass of water, some Pepto-Bismol to settle her stomach and went to the funeral alone. She slept most of the day and dreamed.

It was after eight in the evening when her husband finally came home. She heard him wandering through the kitchen downstairs: she traced his movements by the opening and closing of doors. The way he hovered in the living room without a sound for a long moment told her that he was having a drink. She timed how long it took for him to come upstairs. If it was ten minutes, nothing out of the ordinary happened, if it was twenty the day had been stressful, if it was forty, hellish.

An hour later he came up.

He sat on the edge of her bed and stroked her arm with one hand while the other held a tumbler of whiskey.

"Are you feeling any better?" he asked.

"Mmm-hmm." She nodded, letting her eyes skip over the glass. "Tell me about the funeral."

He took a long gulp and then eyed the bottom of the empty glass thoughtfully.

After a moment he spoke. "I suppose it's already doing the rounds," he said.

"He just sat there, staring at the glass for the longest time," she said to me as I sat there next to her bedside. *This was after she had grown sick and they had all died and gone and there was only the five of us left.*

My body was all tensed up. I was so taut that my stomach muscles started to cramp up again. It took every piece of will in my body not to take the glass from him and smash his head in. I often marvel at the patience I had in my youth. How much of a blessing it would prove to be. I never fully appreciated it until I grew older." She had splayed her hands as she spoke. *"What you see here before you is a product of patience, Meredith."*

But at length her husband did speak and the story he told would change her life.

They had arrived at the church for the funeral. Cal and Leo were pallbearers. There had been a big turnout as was to be expected for a man of Walter's stature. Lou had sat near the front during the service, behind Piper and Elisa. Afterwards everybody had gone back to the house for the wake. Nobody had noticed anything different about Cal at all. He had seemed as normal as could be expected under the circumstances.

They had the speeches and the food and then Piper, Cal, Leo and the lawyer had gone upstairs into one of the rooms to have the will read.

Why they did this then, people couldn't understand. Some said later that it had been at Cal's insistence—that he had known what was coming and so wanted to get his hands on it all as quickly as possible. Others said he couldn't have, because when Leo punched and kicked him he didn't even attempt to fight back. Instead his face was ashen and gray, as if it had been drained of all blood. Piper would later whisper that it had been Walter's choice—he had wanted the will read out the day of his funeral. She would say that she thought he did so because he believed if it were done then, that Leo might be able to find it in himself to temper his rage. She was astonished, she would say, at how little the man knew his own children.

The first anyone knew of anything being wrong was when Cal came hurtling down the stairs. Leo picked up his brother as he fell on the bottom step and smashed his fist into his jaw. People roused themselves from their grief to pull him off Cal. Then all hell broke loose: Julia started screaming; the county sheriff, who was at the funeral and had been part of Walter's poker club, had flashed his badge and used his large overhang of a stomach as a dividing barrier between the two.

That was when Leo shouted, "You sneaky son of a bitch!" His finger stabbed the air at his brother's throat. "I knew you would try some stunt like this. What did you do? What did you do?!"

But Cal couldn't speak. He tried but his mouth opened and closed with no sound. Leo lunged for him again, but it was a feeble attempt. His wife came to his side and the men pulled him off screaming toward the door. He kicked out and caught one of the legs of the table that held a tray of casseroles. They all went crashing to the floor.

The townspeople were in their element. Julia was put to bed sobbing, Cal was taken upstairs to be washed, calmed and aided. Piper found herself enveloped in someone's arms; the casseroles were cleared, while others simply dispersed to their corners of allegiance. The lawyer looked on with horror, shaking his head and muttering in low breaths as someone passed him a drink.

Then, when there was no more carnage to be wreaked and then cleared, people began to go home. Some stayed to help, but mostly the flat plain of the farm became a barrage of taillights disappearing behind the bend.

That was when Lou stopped talking. He sat on the bed, lost in thought, and then stood up.

"Would you like anything?" he asked his wife. She seemed flushed. He knelt over her and felt her forehead but there was no fever.

"Some water, I think," he said as if to himself before turning to leave.

"What was it?" she said quietly to his back. "What made Leo act like that?"

"What else? The farm," he said. "As far as I can make out, it's all gone to Cal—or most of it anyway." He stopped at the doorway and looked at her. In the dark, the features of her face became a hole filled in by shadow.

"Do you want some ice?" he asked.

The instructions of Walter's will were fairly simple. After a few small bequests to friends and distant relatives, the bulk of the estate would be divided up as such: Piper was to receive a ten percent share of the farm as well as a thousand dollars outright. Leo was to have a twenty percent share as well as another two thousand dollars outright and Cal was to have a full seventy, the main house and all its contents as well as the bulk of Walter's savings. Walter had a reputation as a frugal man bordering on miserly, and though no one knew how much his savings were specifically, everyone could guess at them being more than substantial.

My grandfather would tell my father that Walter had dictated a letter a couple of days before he'd died, explaining why he had done what he'd done, to be read by the will's executor. Everyone would say later that it must have meant he had changed the will at the absolute last minute and so it wasn't really valid because he wasn't in his right mind, he was so sick.

People longed to ask what had been said in the letter, but the truth was no one really knew. None of the people present had been able to hear all of it, because midway through the opening paragraph, Leo had turned around and driven his fist into Cal's stomach. Piper would later say that she had no idea why she and Cal were present. From what they could gauge the letter was mostly addressed to Leo. It never mentioned Cal or her once.

That was what happened. But, of course, that wasn't what people would say.

She waited. She made her husband breakfast in the morning, she did her chores, she made her lists and she served them both dinner in the evening. The sun rose and fell on her patience and she bided her time listening and hoping that what she had done had been enough.

Here is a question I am forced to ask: did she really love my grandfather back then? Certainly, she did later, even to the rest of us it was evident. But at the time all those years ago, did she? Or was it simply an escape, just as Lou had been when she was a girl of nineteen—the next rung on the ladder? Or was it that my grandfather had seen in her all the things she had been waiting for someone to find, and in him she saw the potential to realize those dreams into a reality? Is that what you would call love?

Why, you may wonder, do I not ask the same thing of my grandfather?

Because there is a much simpler way of clearing that up.

Two weeks passed and in that time this was what Anne-Marie learned.

She learned that Leo had not been back to the farm since the day of the funeral.

She learned that Cal had not refused his share and that he had continued to stay in the main house with his sister and daughter. When the suppliers had rung up, it had been he who fielded their calls, and when the farmhands came down in the evenings, they said it was he who gave them their instructions during the day. Leo stayed in a hotel on the outskirts of town and Cal began to farm Aurelia.

Piper tried to see Leo. She was admitted into his room at the hotel. She started to tell him Cal's side of the story. She pleaded with him to see sense and come home. They could still farm the place together, each taking a share, she insisted. It would be a family business just like their father had wanted.

But when she next tried to call on him a week later, the man at the front desk told her he would not receive her and when she telephoned, she was told that Leo had asked not to be disturbed. She resorted to writing a letter, which she took to the post office and gave to Florence Baxter, who noted the name and address with an uncomfortable grimace. No one saw Cal outside of the farm.

And then one evening Anne-Marie and her husband sat down to dinner. The meat was overcooked and the vegetables wilted on their forks but they ate it nonetheless. When the doorbell rang, Lou pushed his plate forward and wiped his mouth on the napkin before going to see who it was.

She heard him before she saw him.

When he came into the room she saw immediately that he was different. Instead of the cheap salesman suits he usually wore, he was in slacks and a blue plaid shirt. His hair was lightened by the sun and she could see the faint discoloring line on his forearms that spending time out working in the fields had given him.

"So what can we do for you, Cal, that's so urgent I can't finish my supper?" asked Lou as he sat back down at the table to do precisely that.

Cal didn't look at Anne-Marie as he spoke.

"I've come to talk to you, sir, about a matter that has been plaguing my conscience for some time now."

"Why would you come to me about it? I'm a doctor, not a priest," Lou joked.

Anne-Marie saw the ignorance of her husband draw a blank across his features as he stirred his food with his fork and she allowed herself a brief moment of irritation.

"There's no real easy way of saying this so I guess I should just say it," said Cal. Lou did not look up from his plate.

"I believe I'm in love with your wife, sir," Cal finished.

Anne-Marie watched as her husband's fork paused underneath a heap of sweet corn. His jaw worked slowly as his mouth caught up with his ears.

"Did you hear me, sir?"

"Yes, I heard you." Lou put down his fork and, composing his hands in his lap, stared at Cal.

"What do you expect me to do about it?"

Cal flicked a gaze at Anne-Marie but she gave away nothing. This had to be his fight, she decided, though she would never forgive him if he lost.

"I don't know what you mean, sir."

"Well, Cal, you come into my house, interrupt my dinner and tell me that you're in love with my wife. I assume you've done all this for a reason."

"Yes, sir. I have. I've come to take her home with me, if you've no objection."

Lou stared at him, incredulous. Suddenly he laughed.

"Cal, even if I wanted to, I couldn't hit you. The way you talk I don't think I could live with myself as a doctor if I hit a simpleton."

"I've been sleeping with her," said Cal, "in the full sense of the word. It's been going on for some time now. I have known her and been with her knowing that she was your wife. But that's only in name, and now it's time for her to come home with me, sir. Seeing as how she hasn't been yours for a long time now, I cannot see how you can object to her returning to her rightful place."

For the first and last time in her life Anne-Marie would see a raft of emotions find life in the eyes of Lou Parks. The man who had been little more than a ghost since she'd come to live with him as his wife remembered his blood and let it course in shades of puce and purple throughout his skin. He was so still she wondered if when he finally broke his pause it would be to fly at Cal and try to kill him. She could see Cal bracing himself as he contemplated the same thing and all the while she kept herself still, wringing her napkin between her fingers under the table.

Finally Lou turned to his wife and asked, "Is this true?"

Anne-Marie nodded.

"And do you want to go with him?"

Anne-Marie paused and then nodded again.

"Well..." said Lou and he stood up from the table, went into the living room and shut the door.

Cal stared at where he had gone and then said quickly, "Get your things."

She was finished in twenty minutes. She had made a mental inventory weeks ago and made sure everything that was needed would be ready. She came down the stairs carrying her overcoat and a single suitcase.

"Do you want to speak to him?" asked Cal.

Anne-Marie gave him her suitcase. "I'll see you in the car," she said firmly.

Cal hesitated, but she had already opened the door to the living room.

In the car he waited for ten minutes drumming his fingers against the wheel. Eventually the front door of the house opened and in a moment she climbed in beside him.

Without saying a word they drove home and that was when my grandmother finally stopped being Anne-Marie

Parks, the local doctor's wife, and came to be known as Lavinia Hathaway: adulterer, whore, monster...victor.

That is where my grandfather used to finish this story. That was where everyone finished the story, but that was not the end.

As they stopped at some traffic lights, my grandmother said very quietly but clearly, "If you ever hit me again, I'll stab you while you sleep."

My grandfather nodded in answer and when the lights went green, drove on.

5

TODAY I PULLED OUT THE SUITCASE FROM THE TOP of my wardrobe and lay it open on the bed. Then I made myself a drink.

I packed some clothes, my diary and a list of phone numbers, and went about the business of trying to organize my life for the next few weeks. I made a checklist of things to do: people to call to let them know I was going away; to change my voice mail; to go through the fridge and throw out all perishables that would otherwise greet me with a noxious aroma on my return. I got to the end of the page and tapped my pen against the pad for a few minutes and waited.

I don't know what I was waiting for, but after a while I realized that my refusal to stand up and start getting on with things was less a willful act than an inability. Try as I might, I couldn't move. I sat there feeling the weight of my legs anchor me to the floor. Time passed and I knew I had things to do. I saw the list on the notepad staring at me with reproach, but my body refused to cooperate. For the first time in my life my head was saying yes, but the rest of me was saying no, and there was nothing that I could do about it.

And suddenly I was reminded of my mother. She went through an exacerbated version of this when my father died. She didn't emerge from her room for a month. After the funeral, she washed and cleaned the house, set out the breakfast things for the following morning, then went upstairs to her room and undressed before she climbed into her bed and then didn't get out of it again.

Piper came to attend to her with my uncle's wife, Georgia-May, but it was my grandmother who saw to me and my sisters. She moved us into the main house. There was no discussion, no preamble, she simply showed up at our home the day after the funeral and waited in the kitchen as we each packed a bag and then followed her up the long drive. She cooked breakfast, got us ready for school, watched over us as we did our chores and homework: she was faultless. During that month she took sole responsibility for our welfare. My grandfather helped, of course, but my father's death hit him hard. I think it if weren't for the fact that my mother had gotten there first, he would have taken to his bed just as she did.

The only thing that we really hated during that time was that we were not permitted to see Mom. That was Lavinia's wish. She batted aside our questions with such ferocity that in the end we stopped asking. Once Claudia snuck away, when Lavinia was busy with our grandfather, who had drunk all the whiskey in the house and then tried to drive into town for some more. Claudia walked down to our home in the middle of the afternoon, but whatever it was that she saw or heard there, it caused her to lock herself up in her room when she came back and no matter how much Ava and I pushed and pressed her, she refused to tell us anything about it. In the end, because I wouldn't leave her alone, she slapped me across the mouth and pushed me out the door. After that, at Ava's request, I stopped asking her. We've never spoken to her about it since.

That was such a strange time, living with my grandparents. That was the first time I really began to see what being a Hathaway meant. Instead of sitting down for meals in our scrubbed kitchen, dinner was a stiff-backed affair every evening at the long polished oak table with triangles of white cloth and china plates with patterns of blue swallows around the rim. Instead of the eight rooms I was accustomed to in my house, I now had twenty-two. The finest linens were on our beds, fresh flowers were in every vase (of which there were plenty) and various newspaper clippings, framed and placed on the walls, were interspersed with the customary family portraits.

Piper caught me staring at them once. She smiled and smoothed her hand down my braid. "Hard to believe sometimes," she said. "Things used to be so different when I was your age."

I was not the only one awakened to my social status by our time there. Claudia came to learn of our position in quite a different manner. Our grandmother's way of trying to help us in our grief was to talk about my father, not how my mother would come to talk of him, as a man, but as part of a legacy: a legacy cut short that we must now take up.

"Make him proud," she'd say. And Claudia would look up at her so eagerly, her brow became knotted with confusion.

"How, Grandma?"

"Remember who you are. Remember what your last name is." She leaned back and smiled. As if that were the key to everything. As if we had been born to a world of unlocked doors where everything that lay behind them was there for the taking. Claudia would come to think so and look what happened to her. But if we had been smart enough, we would have remembered our mother in her bed, utterly devastated by the loss of her husband, and known that our name was just a name: it gave us no magical protection; it had no divine right.

As I sit here in my chair, I wonder if this was how my mother must have felt immediately after my father's death. I can understand now, how during that time her body was acknowledging a fact her mind hadn't been able to process, which I believe was this: that she was afraid, more afraid than she had ever been in her life, of what was before her, of what she had to do and even more so that she had to do it alone. I know this because that is exactly what I am feeling now.

"We are all alone," my grandmother had told me once. "No one feels our aches with us, or our pains or our joys. We are like islands floating in a sea together but that's all, we are still just islands, so close we can touch each other, smell each other, but always from a distance."

It is strange that it is her voice I remember now, not my mother's comforting arms when we finally came home, or how she held us and buried her face in our hair and told us she would never leave us again. No, it is not this I think about; it is my grandmother's words instead. I hear them strung out through the notes of her voice as I sit at my desk. They go around and around my mind in a continuous loop while the light outside seeps from pearl to gray.

A few weeks after her Decree Absolute came through, my grandparents stood in the courthouse and were married. There is only one remaining photograph of that day. It would come to sit in a frame of dark wood on a small chest of drawers in the entrance hallway. My grandfather stands there stiffly, his arm wound about my grandmother's waist. He is squinting at the camera, though it is difficult to tell because the picture is so grainy. My grandmother is not looking at the camera: she is turned away, her face buried into her new husband's chest. To the casual observer she looks adoring, overwhelmed with love. In truth she was fighting a bout of nausea that had been plaguing her for days. It didn't take her long to figure out what had brought it on.

To say that my grandparents' marriage was a scandal would be something of an understatement, although the way it was expressed by the townsfolk *was* rather understated. Iowans by nature are polite at all costs and even though they may long to tell you what they actually think of you, something—be it the morals of church or their love of community—holds them in check. So to that end, despite the contempt they felt for her, people still nodded at my grandmother when they passed her in the street though their lips were pursed and they slid their eyes from hers. People still responded to her questions and doomed attempts at polite conversation, though as minimally as they could legitimately get away with. She always knew that once she passed them they would stare at each other and in low voices berate her and everything about her, starting from the day she showed up at her uncle's house in a pinafore dress accompanied by a feckless mother.

But for the first time in her life she didn't care. She didn't care when they noticed her stomach grow and their eyebrows lifted into crescents of surprise and then lowered in disapproval. She didn't care when her family refused to speak to or acknowledge her (the only people in the town who did so). She didn't even care when people pointedly mentioned Lou within earshot. None of it mattered; none of it could touch her, because for the first time in her life she was happy. Truly, unadulteratedly happy. She sang to her belly, she did her chores, and while her husband worked in the fields, she imagined the Aurelia I would come to know and live on, the farm we would love and live for; the home we would die and sin for.

Meanwhile Piper despaired.

Her brother's affair with the doctor's wife and their marriage had upset her greatly. As long as she would live, she would remember the night Lavinia came to the farm with Cal. Piper had sat at the kitchen table in her dressing gown, waiting anxiously for her brother to return. He had been gone for hours with no indication of where he was or when he would be back and with everything that had gone on in the past few weeks, the uncertainty made her nervous. So she waited up for him after she had put Julia to bed, watching the sunlight outside eventually grow dim and vanish. When she finally heard her brother's footstep in the hall at around ten o'clock, she leapt up and ran out to see him, but when she saw the doctor's wife standing behind him holding her suitcase, she took one look at the both of them and slapped her brother so hard across the face, the sound made my grandmother jump against a small rosewood table by the door and topple the flowers in their vase, so that the water spilled across the surface and dripped down onto the floor.

"For God's sake, Cal," Piper spat, "hasn't this family enough to contend with?"

Cal rubbed his face gently, massaging the blood back into his cheek.

"It's done, Piper."

Piper looked at my grandmother, who peered at her uncertainly from behind Cal, and curled her lip in distaste.

"Anne-Marie Parks?" she asked, her eyes narrowed to slits. She assessed my grandmother in one long, contemptuous look.

"It's Lavinia," my grandmother corrected.

"What?"

"She's coming to live here, Piper—she's going to be my wife." Cal looked down at his sister, who was staring at him in shocked horror.

"Her? She's married, to a doctor, to our *town's* doctor. For the love of God, do you know what people will say?" Piper screeched.

"Hush," said Cal, looking up at the stairs, "you'll wake the girl."

"You need someone who can be a good, *faithful* wife," she spat at my grandmother. "Someone who knows a thing or two about farming, someone who will be up with you from sunup to sundown. Not some prissy town maid whose only function is shopping and ordering linen from a catalogue."

Cal took a step toward his sister.

"You just watch what you—" But then he stopped, because my grandmother had already moved away from him. She came to stand before Piper, her eyes burning a hole in Piper's face so that my great-aunt leaned her head back and blinked. Then my grandmother stalked past her and went into the kitchen. She began to search through the drawers, opening and closing them, while Cal and Piper stood in the doorway, openmouthed.

When she took out the long kitchen knife and held it up so the light shone on the blade, Cal put his hands up and took a step back, but she was already coming toward them. They sprang away from her as she walked past and opened the door. She went out and stood on the porch and, holding the blade to the soft flesh of her inner arm, she drew the knife across it, so that her blood began to pour from the wound and splatter on the ground.

Piper stifled a scream; Cal stared at her, unbelieving. My grandmother held up the bloodstained knife and her arm from which her blood was continuing to fall. She looked Piper in the eye and said, "My name is not Anne-Marie and I am not a doctor's wife anymore. I may not have been born here but I will live and die here. I may not have any claim on this land but now I'm part of it, just as much as you. And you'd better get used to it, because I ain't going anywhere."

For a minute no one spoke. Piper held her nightgown across her tightly as if it were a shield. Eventually, my grandfather stepped forward and after a brief hesitation took the knife from my grandmother. "It's been a long day," he said to his sister. "She doesn't mean to scare you."

Piper dropped her gaze and then slowly turned and went back into the house. What she must have thought, how that made her feel, no one ever knew. Piper only ever really confided in one person and that was her childhood friend, Bella. Bella was Piper's closest ally. When together, they would finish each other's sentences and fetch cups of tea back and forth from the kitchen in a strange ritual that was a prevalent feature of their relationship. They were a closed book only open for each other. Piper didn't speak for days after Bella died in 1983 and I remember how every year on the anniversary of her death she would visit her grave and tend to the flowers there with Bella's husband.

Lavinia once said to Cal in front of my father, "If you want to know why your sister won't marry, all you have to do is look out there," and she nodded to the two women sitting closely on the porch steps, their heads bowed in whispered conversation.

My father said that Cal had looked up from the accounts

ledger frowning and said in a strange voice, "Darling, you got the strangest mind sometimes."

But after the night she arrived, Piper saw the determined ambition in her sister-in-law and it scared her. She stood by and watched her marry Cal despite the fear that held her stomach in a cold fist; she stifled her humiliation as she heard conversations fall away whenever she entered a store in town and then resume after she left. She balked as she saw the judgment in people's faces and though she longed to undo it all she was helpless. Leo would not speak to her and Cal would not listen. She was trapped.

A few days after my grandparents were married. Leo came over to get his things from the house. Piper saw the taillights of the removal trucks Leo had organized pass by in the drive, but when she went down to see him he refused to talk to her. In the end his wife came out onto their porch and stared down at her sister-in-law with icy disdain.

"My husband don't truck with no traitor," she said.

I suppose I can understand how Leo felt. He had worked his whole life on the farm and he had believed, right up until they heard the will, that he would continue to live and eventually die on it. But the share allotted to my grandfather was too much for him to bear. He may have been right, but even though everyone knew this and even though it had just been the two of them for so long, Piper refused to take a side. At least that was what she said. She didn't realize that in not taking a side, to Leo, she had in fact taken up with my grandfather. Leo was not a man for neutrality.

He left town and moved to Indiana, where their mother had been born and raised. Rumor had it (though it was eventually proved to be true), that he stayed with one of their uncles there who owned a farm. People thought he would contest the will on the grounds of their father's men-

tal incompetence, but he never did. He simply left town
and all the gossip and scandal with it. That was the last we
really heard of him for a long time. He would not speak to
my grandfather again for nearly twenty years and Piper for
ten. That was the first of the splinters in our family. With
hindsight you could take it as an omen, but maybe that's just
me being superstitious.

As for my grandparents, they rarely left the farm during
the first year of their marriage. It was at Cal's insistence that
they laid low. Lavinia's affair and divorce, and Leo's departure, had brought a fierce amount of attention onto a man
who, even when I knew him, was intensely uncomfortable
with any kind of spotlight, be it good or bad. My grandmother did as he wished. My grandfather hoped that the less
they were seen the more quickly they would fall to the back
of people's minds.

My grandfather began to concentrate on building up the
farm. He wanted to show his neighbors that he was just as
good as Leo, just as capable. He saw how aloof and wary the
other farmers were toward him and he knew the only way
that would change would be if he made something of Aurelia, or at least maintained it to the standard of his brother.
So they lived and they worked and Lavinia, his wife full of
so much ambition and pride, humbled herself and waited.

But she didn't mind because it was all hers. At last, a home.
She would say how different she felt on the farm compared
to Lou's redbrick house. She hadn't liked the farm when she
first saw it at the garden party, but as she worked on it with
her husband, walked on it and explored it, while her belly
swelled beneath her hand, she began to take strength from
it. Soon she knew it as well as if she had been raised there,
and every meal with her husband and his sister was always

peppered with her questions. Cal was flattered; Piper suspicious.

And then she began to talk to Cal when Piper wasn't around, about her thoughts and ideas for the place. While frustrating at first, she soon came to realize that their isolation was a blessing. It was a gift that allowed her to penetrate her husband's strict principles without the interference of outside influence. At first Cal might have thought her ideas were just fanciful dreaming. He would sit next to her at the table and let her words pour over him as he ate his food, or read his paper. My great-aunt always believed that at first he never really believed in what his wife was saying; he was just humoring her. It was a severe underestimation and perhaps for that reason, one day without even fully realizing it, he began to listen.

For the first time in her life Piper felt like she may unravel. In the space of a few months she had lost her father and her younger brother, her family was the speculation of gossip and rumor and, worst of all, now Cal was beginning to act on his wife's crazy ideas.

The first of which was about the house.

This part is really unclear. Piper never really spoke of it, nor did my grandparents. Whenever the subject was raised with my grandmother all she would say was that the old house was falling apart and needed so many repairs that it made sense to rebuild a new one entirely. Piper would snort if she was in the room and draw her lips together in silent disapproval. My grandmother would watch her as her face would draw to a close, until finally she would snap and say, "Piper, are you sucking on a lemon or something?"

Piper would look up, her features twitching in surprise. "I don't know what you mean, Lavinia, my tooth is giving me trouble, that's all," she would respond, and then she would go on with either her reading or her sewing, unaffected by the glare of hatred my grandmother focused on her from the other side of the room.

How my grandmother managed to secure the approval of my grandfather to rebuild the house, when she was already six months pregnant and he himself was just getting re-accustomed to the farm and all its responsibilities, remains a mystery. What is clear is that she persuaded my grandfather to use most of the money Walter had left him to do it. It shows just how much sway she once had over him.

They moved into Leo's old place while the house was being rebuilt and, as Lavinia made plans and nested, Piper took over the aiding of my grandfather in building up the farm. That's one thing I'll say for him, something which Piper was always grateful for and which may have just saved her: he gave his sister a far greater share in the running of things than Leo ever would have. She managed the accounts and the money, while he went about the practicalities of the farm.

But because she managed the accounts, she began to see how much my grandmother was spending. On more than one occasion when she would see architectural blueprints sprawled on the kitchen floor or swatches and materials draped over the sides of chairs she would tut, she would mutter and she would ask herself and the air around her when it would all end.

"Cal?" she said once to him as he sat at the edge of the kitchen counter, tearing a piece of beef with his teeth as he scrutinized the paper. "Do you know how much your wife is spending? Because I don't think she does."

"Leave her be, Piper," said Cal between mouthfuls. "She never had something of her own like this—she's just trying to make us a home."

"Well, does she have to bankrupt us to do it?" she asked angrily and stepped forward with a host of receipts in her fist. Cal batted her away with his free hand as she approached him.

"Daddy's money is running through her fingers like water, Cal."

"I'll make it back."

"You'd better hope you do," said Piper as she angrily peered at her brother. "Why don't you take this seriously?"

And he had looked at her wearily. "Because you do too much."

So Piper stayed up each night, balancing books and ledgers, holding her head in her hands as she saw the outgoings of her sister-in-law. As she passed the place where she had once lived torn down to form the tall pine erections of a house she did not recognize, but that would now be her home, she saw numbers pouring from it in a haze that made her stay awake at night and worry.

One night when she was staying up late, a mess of ledgers across her table, she heard her brother pass by her bedroom and called out to him. He peered around the corner of the door.

"Why you sitting in the dark for?" he asked.

"Cal, sit down," she said.

He perched with a frown at the foot of her bed.

"Look at this," she said and handed him a ledger. His eyes scurried across it and the blood began to drain from his face.

"Exactly."

She waited for a moment, savoring his uncertainty, his fear. Serve him right, she thought.

"Piper..." he began, his mouth a perfect O.

"I don't want to hear it, Cal—it is what it is," she said, and snatched the ledger back from him. He looked down at his empty hands, disconcerted.

"Now I been thinking on it and it seems to me the best way would be if I put in some of the money Daddy left me."

Cal stared at his sister. She pulled her braid down over her shoulder and stroked it as she talked musingly.

"'Course, if I do that it means by right I should have more of a say in what happens with this place. I mean it is my money after all, which is acting as a sort of plug for your wife's whirlpool of profligacy."

"What do you want, Piper?" Cal asked slowly.

And that was how my grandfather made his sister a business partner—much to his wife's hidden chagrin. Though in time even she had to admit Piper knew the business better than she did. It may have been my grandfather who talked about setting up a hog operation, but it was Piper who made it financially viable by waiting two years, saving up money from the harvests, investing in soybeans and maize. With Piper at the reins, Lavinia could not spend as much, did not have the unlimited access she had taken for granted, but because of Piper, the farm stayed afloat in those early years despite my grandmother's excesses, because she could do what her brother would not—and that was tell her sister-in-law no.

As a trio, they became a successful team. Cal was a physical and hard-working man, Piper had a great head for figures, while Lavinia was all about the presentation. She knew how to make a thing seem better than it was, so that other farmers looked upon Aurelia with new respect and even envy, while Cal and Piper provided it with the goods to back up the claim. Even Piper acknowledged as much, though her newfound respect did not mute her suspicions of my grandmother and her motives.

My uncle Ethan was born in 1947 before the main house was completed and it was said that my grandmother fell wildly in love with him. Apparently he looked just like her, although his hair was a deep dark brown rather than her russet hues. Julia, however, was said to be less than impressed with the new arrival.

But my uncle's birth did not just affect his family, it rippled far beyond the confines of Aurelia. Upon his arrival a new rumor began to circulate around the town that Lou had been unable to give Lavinia children and this was why she had left her husband. What else, they said, could explain how the woman fell pregnant at the drop of a hat with Cal while her stomach had stayed resolutely flat in all her years of marriage with Lou? My uncle caused not sympathy, but a suspicious empathy toward my grandmother amongst the town folk. They were cautious in their disapproval, no longer sure that they had wielded the sword of truth above her head. They began to wonder if perhaps her actions could be sympathized with, even justified. They began to feel guilt.

The family would move into the house on its completion just after Ethan turned one and Julia started going to school. Lavinia had the idea of throwing a party with all their neighbors to celebrate. She convinced my grandfather that it was a good way of rebuilding relations and showing everybody how well they had done in Leo's absence—proof that Walter had been right to do what he did. That swung it.

My grandmother said that was a day she would remember for the rest of her life. Honey-colored lights were strewn around the house, there was the smell of newly planted roses in the air and she stood on the porch, one hand resting against the columns, the other cradling her son against her hip as she watched the jaws drop on all the neighbors who had hated and secretly mauled her for years as they walked up the drive in varying degrees of awe, astonishment and incredulity.

Two years after their first child was born, they had my father: Theodore, Theo for short. The farm was beginning to show the seeds of prosperity that in time would make it legendary. Invitations both verbal and written began to arrive regularly from the people who had once scorned them. Lavinia noted the names and the regularity of their invitations, but my grandfather didn't care. At last, at last he was happy. He was home, and whenever he thought of his brother and the reading of the will, he knocked back a glass of scotch until the memory passed away.

My grandmother would look out onto her home while gently playing with the scar on her arm, and revel in what she would later describe as happiness. She thought it would go on and on, this feeling; she could see no reason why it shouldn't. None of them did. She was safe in the knowledge that this was to be her home, and just as she had vowed the night she first came to live here, she would spend the rest of her days on it.

She once told my uncle and father the story of that night. My father was thirteen at the time. When they heard it, they, too, went and got out the kitchen knife, went out to a field and cut their arms and spilled their blood onto the land. And so this tale and its actions trickled down the generations so that when my sisters and I turned thirteen, we too would do the same. What began that night in 1946 as a mere act of defiance would eventually become a sacred family ritual.

I remember when it was my turn to do it. Ava, Claudia, Cal Jr. and I stood behind the barn and my fingers trembled as I came to draw the knife against my skin, my body recoiling at the pressure of the blade. I looked at Ava, who winced as she saw me strain, and then Cal Jr. leaned forward and, whispering, asked me if I was okay. I shook my head and the knife drooped in my hand. He pried it gently from my fingers and I leaned against his shoulder, ashamed and grateful at the same time. And then in one sudden movement, he jerked my arm up and slashed the knife through the underside. It was so quick I didn't have time to register any pain, or even outrage; I could only look at him in astonishment as he held my arm above me coolly, and watch as the blood trickled down and seeped into the earth.

We did not understand then, the power such an action has. We shed our blood on Aurelia, willingly, to claim it, to be part of it, just like our grandmother: yield for us and we are yours. And so we are tied to Aurelia and to each other until the day we die. Somehow when I think of that, despite a sliver of horror, I feel less alone.

My childhood was filled with stories of my father. My mother focused on telling them to me in particular because I was only seven when he died. So whatever we were doing, no matter how small or banal, she would try and find a way of twisting the conversation to incorporate some story about my father and his life. This was a few years after his death, when she could finally mention his name.

Those stories were, of course, ones he told my mother himself, though in time I would come to know much of the truth behind my father's memories, from a completely different source. My father was an incredibly intuitive man, observing and detecting all the unsaid things that hung in the air of his memories while growing up on the farm, storing them in hidden vaults until a later time when he could draw them out and reminisce about them. He was a man who lived inside his imagination and memory.

This made sense when people described him as a child.

Theo was a golden boy: he had curly blond locks and milk-and-honey cheeks, but it was his temper that set him apart. While Julia was an extrovert and Ethan a simmering cauldron of emotions that always got the better of him, my father was temperate, placid—in short, exactly like his father.

To say that he was Cal's favorite would be going too far, because Cal spoiled and indulged Julia far more than he ever did the boys, but my father and he shared a quiet bond of kinship, the like of which he never had with his other children. Whether it be the way they both cocked their heads to the left as they sat and watched *Dragnet,* or the way they both walked, arms swinging, their bodies springing from hip to hip. Theo was Cal's boy and so, in contrast—maybe even because of it—Ethan became Lavinia's.

My uncle and his mother would come to share a complicated relationship, the seeds of which were sown in his youth. Lavinia poured all her energies into her eldest child. She watched him, she analyzed him; she questioned and prodded him so much that in the end she came to know him better than anyone, better even than he knew himself. One day when she had mused over the choice of colors he had used in a drawing he made her, Piper had snapped at her and said, "Jesus, Lavinia, they were the only crayons left in the box, that's all."

Piper thwarted her in every way she could. She was always encouraging the children to run off and play together away from the watchful eye of their mother. Lavinia recognized her attempts to undermine her and complained to Cal, who, naturally seeing nothing wrong with the notion of kids playing alone, lamented his curse that with two boys in the house he was still beset by the constant problems of women.

Almost as soon as they arrived, the children became a battlefield between Piper and Lavinia. Piper observed the way she made factions between them: her constant eye on Ethan, her dismissal of Julia, and she believed herself to be a neutral party, pouring balm on the oil fires their mother created. She saw the way Lavinia watched Cal and Julia together and her increasing irritation at the child's hold over her father, which caused her to push Ethan to try and be the same, but the boy just didn't have it in him. A solitary and thoughtful creature, Ethan was an introvert, constantly absorbing everything about him in such a way that he was perpetually affected by every aspect of his environment. It was a trait Lavinia preyed on. But Julia was different. She grew into a hedonistic, savvy creature, already aware of the ways in which to manipulate and control the men around her, beginning with her father and brothers. Perhaps you may have thought Lavinia would have seen in her more of the prodigal elements that could be molded into her own likeness. But this was the problem. The likeness between the two of them was too striking and she soon saw her stepdaughter as less of a child, and more of a rival.

The feeling was more than mutual. My father often said that his childhood was beset by arguments between his sister and his mother with Piper or Cal acting as an intermediary. They were at constant war and what my grandfather failed or refused to realize was that he was the battleground. In the end, it was Julia who took home more victories than my grandmother. She had only to wrap her arms about his neck and my grandfather would remember his three-year-old daughter in her blood-spattered dress and his mind would twist and turn to find a way to absolve her of whatever infractions she had been accused of.

It took several years, but eventually Lavinia learned her lesson. When she heard the way her husband talked of the impact of the death of his first wife and his relief that his daughter had been spared, she realized that direct confrontation with her stepdaughter would always be to no avail. No matter what, her husband would always take her side because for him, time had stopped in a hospital ward in Oregon. She watched over her sons and the farm and whenever she thought of their future and the land, a sharp thorn of remembrance pierced her reverie as she heard Julia's singsong voice carry out of the windows toward her. No matter that she was Cal's wife, or that she had given him two sons, she could not deny the unassailable fact that Julia was not only his firstborn, but that she had also faced death and survived. That one act held her above everything, even her clutches, and there was nothing she could do about it.

Never was this fact made clearer than when Julia became a teenager. Once, the family had traveled to the Iowa State Fair. It was 1955 and Julia was thirteen years old. A huge attraction, it covered about four hundred flat acres of wooden campsites littered with people, farmers, produce, food stalls and rides. It was a great place for families and even more so for farmers. With its huge emphasis on all things grown and reared, farmers from all over the state came to show off wares, make business deals and forge new connections with suppliers. That was why my grandfather went, but the rides and contests meant that the whole family could enjoy it, too. I would be taken along to these often as a young girl.

My father said that his favorite thing at the fair had been the butter cow. Every year they would produce a cow sculpted from butter like some latter-day version of the golden calf. My father would reach out his hand and try to stroke the smoothness of its skin before his mother caught him and smacked it back.

At some point after they had eaten, my grandfather had gone off to meet a supplier who'd recently advertised their new business. There was a talent contest later that afternoon and Julia had wanted to sing in it. My grandmother had rolled her eyes at this, but as usual Cal hadn't noticed and had promised to be back in time for it. Besides he wanted to enter the arm-wrestling contest himself, he'd said with a smile before challenging Theo to an arm wrestle in midair. My father had grappled with his father, laughing as he tested his strength with his idol. His mother was less than impressed. She soon took him and his brother by the hand and kissed Cal goodbye, while Piper listened to Julia jabber excitedly over what song she thought she should sing.

As they wandered about the fair and saw the largest rabbit and the sheep shearing race, Julia continued to dance around them, her arms splayed, her voice strangling Patsy Cline in a timbre that lacerated at the tight bonds of self-control protecting her stepmother. Lavinia held on to her sons and sucked in her cheeks, but her eyes still found the figure of her preening stepdaughter nonetheless. At one point, as Julia half pirouetted in the air in front of her, her stepmother could no longer resist her near murderous impulses. Lavinia felt her self-control snap and grabbed Julia, pinching her underarm violently between her finger and thumb.

"At least attempt to conduct yourself like a young lady," she spat.

Julia rubbed her arm and, staring over her shoulder, narrowed her eyes and mouthed the word *bitch*.

My father said that before he knew it his mother had smacked his sister with such ferocity, the ringing clap brought the people near them up short. Julia, who had been preening at the time and unaware of what was coming, had overbalanced and gone sprawling to the floor. She looked up at her stepmother in a mixture of shock and alarm before a glimmer of triumph raced across her features, for what she saw in front of her was a trembling tower of unbridled fury.

She screamed, raised an accusing finger at her stepmother and said, "She hit me! She always hits me! I didn't do anything. What did I do to you?!"

Lavinia swept down and grabbed the girl to haul her up, her nails digging into the pink flesh of Julia's upper arm so that she buckled and twisted in pain.

Piper came running. She had been lagging behind with Ethan, but at the commotion and Julia's screams she was behind Lavinia in an instant. She wrestled the girl's arm from her stepmother and as Julia crumpled back to the floor crying and twisting her arm in her hands as she doubled over, Piper stared at my grandmother with a mixture of fury and fear. Lavinia looked down at the child with a seething hatred that seemed to have burst its banks and was now coursing through her with heat. Her skin began to flame and her temples throbbed. She could not control it, she could not mask it—she looked at the girl and in her mind she knew she could not stand her; she could not wish her anything but harm. She knew then that this girl was perhaps the greatest enemy of her life and try as she might she could only see her childish form as a disguise, not an excuse.

It was the first and last time she ever lost her composure in public and it was also the last time she ever allowed anyone to know the strength of her feelings. She saw Piper inspect Julia for bruising and as she gently moved her arms, she found the small red half moons where Lavinia's nails had dug into the skin. She helped Julia to her feet and they both stood there, accusations flying from their eyes.

What did my grandmother do? What could she do? She fled.

She said she must have walked the whole length of the fair

but she didn't see anything. She was afraid of Cal's reaction and there was nothing she could say that could justify her behavior in order to abate it. She remembered the time in his truck when she had still been married to Lou, and how she had walked along the dirt road holding her hand to her lip feeling the same isolation, the same confusion, but this time without the bolt of inspiration that had made it bearable. And then she remembered her sons.

She knew where they would be. An hour later, she found them at the singing contest just as Julia was midway through her performance. She watched the infectious excitement in the girl's movements and how she played to the crowd, and she saw the waves of pride and amusement run through her husband's features. She came to stand by him and when he saw her he did not inquire where she had been, but put his arm around her and drew her in close so that in appearance, they looked just like the doting parents he believed them to be.

Julia didn't win, but afterward Cal took her to one of the stalls and bought her a whole box of caramels, her favorite. Lavinia watched them, waiting for the storm to come, but it didn't. Piper said nothing, though she refused to meet her eye, and the boys were lost in their own amusements. In the car Julia appeared to be normal as she licked her fingers happily as she ate the caramels, and everyone but her stepmother talked about what they had seen and done at the fair and how much they'd liked it.

Because they'd eaten so much they only had a light supper and as they'd done so much walking the children went to bed early. As Lavinia came up to say good-night, she hesitated outside Julia's room. The door was slightly ajar, and she could see that the child's small bedside light was on. Cal had bought Julia a small gramophone for Christmas and it was playing a Bill Haley record. Gingerly, Lavinia opened the door and went inside. Julia was lying in bed, the covers pulled down, her washed hair wrapped up in a towel. She saw her stepmother in the doorway and pulled the needle from the record so that the music was scratched into silence. Julia beckoned to Lavinia to come closer and, casting a quick glance over her shoulder, Lavinia did so.

In a small voice Julia said, "I just wanted you to know, that I made Auntie swear not to tell and neither will I." She paused, watching her stepmother for effect. Lavinia willed her face to show nothing. Julia frowned and then continued. "I won't ever tell Pa what you did."

Here is where the discrepancy lies. Julia would later say that she meant it. That this was her way of making a peace offering, holding out the proverbial olive branch. She was only a kid she'd say, how could she have had any malicious intent? But Lavinia would feel differently. To her this was the child's way of throwing down the gauntlet; letting her know that it was she who had the power.

My father believed his sister. He said that by the time they could recount this memory too much had been done by either side for them to think straight, but to his mind Julia was never clever enough to be that calculating. When he said this to my grandmother, she gave a little smile and simply replied, "The greatest trick the devil ever played was to convince people he didn't exist."

Years later when she was forced to tell me about her life, my grandmother made a confession to me. What she said was this:

"I would not have done anything differently, you know? Not really. It all had to be done for the good of the family even if they couldn't see it at the time, but I could. I always could. I don't regret

anything and even the things I might have cause to regret I was proven to be right in all along."

I was seventeen years old when she began telling me the history of her life, of the things she had done, of what she had made. I believed I was ready, I wanted to know, I felt both privileged and terrified.

"What do you mean, Grandma?" I asked. "What are you talking about?"

She had turned away and stroked the sheets with her papery hands.

"Lou, you were the only thing I looked on with any regret. But then I saw, I knew it was the right thing. I knew. You told me so yourself."

Later I learned that not only was she referring to her first husband, but also to his funeral.

Lou Parks died of a stroke in his office at his desk while reading his newspaper. His secretary had gone in to inform him that the next patient was waiting and found him with his face buried in the sports section.

When my grandmother heard of his death she had shaken out the tea towel she was holding and had said, "Well, at least he died with little interruption to his afternoon routine." At this my great-aunt bit down hard on her bottom lip.

But despite her laissez-faire attitude, that night my grandmother had a nightmare. She wouldn't say what it was, only tried to fall back to sleep. But the next night she woke up screaming and then the night after that my grandfather woke and found that the bottom of the bed was covered in dirt. He raised the covers and saw that the soles of his wife's feet were muddy. She had been sleepwalking.

"Nonsense," she had said, "I don't sleepwalk. Theo, how many times have I told you to pick your toy cars up off the stairs?!"

But later, when Ethan had come down in the middle of

the night to get a glass of milk, he had found his mother standing in the hall. The moonlight dappled on her hair and in the dark her white nightdress made her look like a ghost. He had screamed and dropped his glass but still she did not move. My grandfather and great-aunt had come down the stairs with Julia complaining from her bedroom and Theo rubbing his eyes as he plodded after them.

"How long's this been going on?" Piper asked as she came to stand with her nephews and brother in a half circle around my grandmother.

"A couple of nights maybe," said Cal. "What should we do?"

"Well, don't wake her, it's dangerous," said Piper. "Just lock all the doors and make sure she can't get out and injure herself."

"Why's she doing this?" asked Ethan.

"Maybe she feels guilty," said his aunt.

"Piper," Cal warned.

The next day at the scrubbed kitchen table, Lavinia, attempting to rub the stiffness from out of her joints, saw the same crescent of witnesses from the night before holding onto alternating mugs of coffee, hot chocolate and milk. They all turned from what they were doing and stared at her when she came in.

"What?" she asked.

When they told her about happened, she unexpectedly gave a great sigh and sat down at the table. Cal sent the boys out to play. Piper looked at her with curiosity.

"Maybe you should go to the funeral," Piper said.

"I don't think—" began Cal.

"I wouldn't be welcome," Lavinia answered.

"By whom?" asked Piper. "Lou ain't got no family. It's his friends who are doing the funeral. What are you afraid of?

You weren't afraid when you left him, or when you had an affair with my brother, so why are you afraid now?"

And that Lavinia could not answer.

The truth was there were times when she wondered whether she had made the right decision. What if this was not a product of her fate, but a decoy away from it? Was this who she was meant to be? A farmer's wife...stepmother... mother? They were all suitable roles in themselves but had she ever wanted to play them? She didn't stab the curtains anymore, but sometimes she would look through them out onto the green and the flowers and the flat horizon beyond and she would feel...weary.

"I am not afraid of anything," she lied.

So she went. She sat in the white church, outside of which years before she had iced her cake never knowing the name Cal Hathaway. In the stifled air she listened to the hymns and the eulogy and stared at the coffin in which lay the man she had once thought of as her ticket to freedom.

Piper came with her to pay her respects to Lou for everything he had done when she had nursed her father and mother before their deaths, but she watched her sister-in-law whenever she could. The woman barely moved an inch the whole way through the ceremony. She half whispered the prayers and her voice faltered during the singing. When the service ended and they came out into the air, she was so pale Piper thought she would faint.

She drove her home and for the first time in her life, my grandmother genuinely fell sick. She lay in bed for a week and no one was allowed to visit her. Cal was frantic with worry; no one could tell him what was wrong, but at the same time no one could tell him how to make her right.

"Just let her rest," one doctor had said.

"That's the problem," said Cal.

Then one morning he woke up to discover she was not there beside him. He flung on his overalls and stalked through the house and then the garden until eventually he discovered her forty-five minutes later on the edge of the cornfield.

In her hands was a clump of dirt. She was fingering it, letting it crumble and watching the dust fall on the wind.

"Lavinia, what are you doing? You scared me half to death," he shouted.

She did not answer him, only stared at the seemingly endless field of cornstalks.

"I had a dream," she said softly, half to herself almost. "I was dreaming and then…and then I woke up. Yes, I woke up." She paused and then smiled. "I think I'm better now," she said, and after a pause he took her by the arm and led her home.

As she passed the house, the boys were outside, dressed and ready for their chores but clearly perplexed at the absence of their parents before breakfast. Julia sat on the porch cradling a glass of milk, watching them.

"I found my way before you came to me, Cal," she would say in the future at the end of that story. My grandfather would laugh and turn away. I'm not sure he ever really understood what she meant.

I'm not sure she even wanted him to.

JULIA

The Devil and All His Forms

6

AFTER MY MOTHER HAD ALREADY HAD MY TWO sisters, she had decided that that was it; she would not have any more children. Don't mistake me, my mother loved her daughters and she was a good parent to them, but my father didn't care about having a son and after two incredibly diffi-cult pregnancies (she almost died with Claudia, from the blood loss), Mom had a categorical fear of childbirth. So she and my father did something that as a Catholic she felt guilty about, but not guilty enough to stop: she began using birth control.

And then one afternoon while her daughters were playing, she sat on our porch swing and in the relentless haze of the afternoon sun, she fell into a sleep in which she dreamt that she was drowning. She said she must have been holding her breath because she could feel her lungs straining, the insides burning and palpitating at the slow suffocation of oxygen. She reached out her hands in the dark mass of water but instinctively she knew she was too far from the surface and that made her panic even more. Then she put a hand to her legs and the sticky wet feeling there reviled her, so that she opened her mouth in anguish and swallowed a lungful of water. She woke up gasping as her body heaved with exertion. She was so focused on breathing that she didn't realize for a moment that her hands were covered in blood and when she looked down she saw that it was coming from her lap.

Before she knew it she was lying in a hospital bed, her legs in stirrups raised above her head. She was embroiled in a struggle to keep hold of a child she hadn't known she was carrying and probably wouldn't have wanted if she had. But that was the charm, you see: I was an ambush.

"I had to love you," she said. "I was fighting so hard to keep you, I didn't have enough time to choose not to."

My mother was in the hospital for three weeks. She was just over four months pregnant. Her periods had been slight and irregular, but she had none of the nausea and cravings she had with my sisters. After she was released, the doctor said she had to have complete bed rest to ensure that I was delivered safely, so for the next five months my mother became intimately acquainted with the pattern of her bedroom ceiling. She read and she listened to music and in the evenings when he came home, my father knelt beside her and told stories to her growing stomach.

He told the still forming version of what would be his youngest and final child the story of the farm. He told me how it grew, about the hog operations and the deal with a major supplier that had cut their outgoings by twenty-five percent; about how the Gainses' farm to the left of us had been sold and how my grandfather had bought it and added six hundred acres onto our land. He talked to me about growing up in a tall white house with his brother and sister. How he had swum in the stream and built a swing rope so they could dive into it in the summer. He told me of the time he had played Zorro with Ethan and had used the poker irons as a sword, accidentally scoring his brother with it as he had tried to scratch the immortal *Z* into his chest. He told me how Ethan still had the scars even to this day.

He told me about visiting fairs as a child, and riding horses with his sister along the flat plains of Iowa. He told me how I was to be born into a state of farmers and prairie grass and that as a kid he had gone to see the cornfields on the farm and had been overwhelmed by how tall they were so that it seemed to him the very sky gleamed with the colors of the sunlight hitting the heads of corn.

He told me about the house I would be raised up in and the sisters I would meet, about how proud he had been to grow up on a place like Aurelia and how I would be proud, too. He talked so much that my mother's dreams were filled with the figure of a yellow-haired boy riding beside his father in a thresher, washing a chestnut-colored colt and falling asleep next to his mother with a milk moustache.

And then one time when I was restless and kicking so hard my mother winced, he told me the one story of his youth that no person was ever allowed to speak of because my uncle had forbidden it, but he told me anyway.

He said: "Child, don't you ever tell nobody about this, but since you're kicking up a storm how's about you hear of a real one? You're coming to a place that is filled with tornadoes every summer and when we were younger your uncle and I got caught up in one. A pretty big one, too. There was your uncle Ethan, me and there was also this girl. Her name was Alison but everyone called her Allie."

Ethan's first love, Ethan's only love, was Allie Lomax. A slight girl whose father was a clerk in the county court and whose mother was infamous for her pound cake and machine-gun-rattle laugh, he had met her the day of the Iowa State Fair, when he was only eight. She had wandered away from her parents at the fair entrance by a selection of candies at one of the food stalls. She had looked in wonder and greedy anticipation at the spirals of pink cotton candy and sweating chocolates, and as she contemplated all these things before her she did not see the small boy with dark hair and eyes so brown they looked black, who was standing behind the large glass jar of red-and-white-striped candy canes, staring at her as if he had never seen anything like her before in his life.

She had turned to ask her parents to buy her something but they had already begun to move away and she was annoyed.

"Here—take this."

The boy reached out from the other side of the table and handed her a candy cane. Alison looked at it distrustfully.

"Take it," said the boy.

"You have to pay," she said sullenly, arms folded, eyes narrowed.

"Oh." He frowned and his wrist wavered. "I don't have any money."

"Then that's stealing," she said, drawing her chin up in righteous indignation before turning on her heel and walking away.

"No, but—but I want you to have it!" the boy yelled, but she was already running after her parents.

"Thief," she cried over her shoulder.

In those fifteen seconds my uncle's life changed. Later, he would recount this story many times to himself in memory and then many years after that, sobbing brokenly over it when drunk.

That would be how I would come to hear it for the very first time.

For five years, since that day, Ethan spent his time haunting the steps of Allie Lomax. At school he searched every hall and sports field for a glimpse of her long brown hair hung in its ponytail, or the sound of her voice high above a crowd and whenever he found her he would stop what he was doing and find a place so that he could watch her and drink her in without notice or interruption. That lasted until his brother found him and asked him what the hell he was doing. "Get off me, squirt," he would shout and punch my father in the stomach before stalking off in a hotbed of simmering fury.

One night at dinner, he pushed his casserole around his plate, brooding because he had seen Allie wear the varsity jacket of Jimmy Galloway at recess.

Julia, who was sixteen by then, set down her glass of Kool-Aid and, ignoring Lavinia's retelling of her argument with the assistant at the gardening store over the correct way to treat American Beauties, said loudly, "Jesus, Ethan, why don't you stop being such a freak and just ask her out on a date? That way I don't have to watch you mooning like some lovesick pup over every meal."

My grandparents spoke at the same time.

Lavinia: "Julia, will you please learn some manners and not interrupt me?"

Cal: "Who's he asking on a date?"

Ethan scowled over the rim of his plate, his eyes boring into the winsome smile of his sister.

"There's this girl at school—"

"Jules," growled Ethan.

"Julia, I'm sure this is all incredibly interesting," drawled my grandmother, "but your father and I were already in the middle of another conversation."

"What girl?" asked my grandfather, staring back and forth between his daughter and his son with a grin already creeping across his mouth. Lavinia put down her fork and wiped her mouth with her napkin.

"Cal, are you finished?" she asked, already whipping away the plate from underneath him.

"Wha— Oh…is there any pie?"

"Yes and custard," she said over the harsh scraping of food into the trash can.

"Cut me a piece, would you?"

"And me," said Julia.

"I thought you said you were on a diet," said Lavinia to her stepdaughter before dropping the plate in the sink.

"You—" Julia began.

"Ethan, is there a girl at school that you like?" asked Cal.

Ethan glared at his plate and strangled the length of his fork with his fingers. He never spoke about Allie back then. He hated talking about her: she was his, his alone. She was not for sharing and no one could make it otherwise.

"Yeah, there is," said Julia, momentarily distracted as she rescented her old prey. "Her name's—"

"I'm warning you," Ethan said quietly still staring at his plate.

"All-iee—" Julia began leaning forward and stretched her lips to overenunciate the vowels "Lo-max."

Ethan stood up, put down his fork and in a swift movement balanced the plate of food on its side with his wrist and hurled it at his sister's head. Both she and her father ducked but the casserole and greens hurtled across the table before the plate shattered on the wall.

"Ethan!" Lavinia shouted.

"Jesus Christ, boy, what the hell do you think you're

doing?!" Cal roared, staring at his son, who, apart from two red circles on his cheeks, was completely calm.

Cal stood up and undid his belt. Lavinia put her hand on his in an instant.

"To your room, Ethan," she said.

"No way, boy, you don't go around breaking plates in my house like you're some big shot—" Cal began but Ethan was already halfway up the stairs. He could hear his parents arguing below.

In his room he threw himself on his bed and vented all his rage at the ceiling. The white swirls seemed to take on pinpricks of black so that a swarm raged above his head and then the door opened and his mother came inside. That was when he realized he'd been holding his breath.

"You owe your father an apology."

"Fine," he said.

"And you'll do extra chores as punishment after school."

"Whatever."

"You will sit up and address me like your mother when I speak to you," Lavinia snapped.

As if on autopilot Ethan heaved himself off of the bed and sat up, his eyes finding the dresser to his mother's left.

"Who is this girl?" his mother asked.

"I don't want to talk about it."

"I don't like secrets in my house."

He sat in silence.

"If it's a secret, it isn't a very well-kept one if Julia knows about it," said Lavinia nastily.

Ethan felt his face begin to crumple, but he drew in a deep breath and kept his eyes firmly on the dresser. His mother took a step toward him.

"What have I told you about showing your feelings to others? You should never have let her know how much it means to you—now she has a hold over you. You know that—how many times have I told you that?"

Ethan nodded.

"You will stay here until you are under control again and then you will apologize."

"To Jules as well?" he asked.

"Julia," Lavinia corrected. "Yes, your father insists."

She turned to leave.

"Does this girl know about your feelings for her?" his mother asked as she reached the door.

"No," Ethan said to the floor.

"Good," his mother said before she opened the door and left.

Four days after that night, when it was the end of the school day, Ethan finally got lucky. He lingered behind the rest of his last class as always, because that was the class he shared with Allie. He stood by his locker, which was five down from hers, and using the slats of the front as both a shield and a view, watched her as she retied her ponytail and loaded her school books into her bag.

When he and the other kids went out of school into the courtyard for the school bus everyone craned their necks and looked up at the sky. The whole mass was a bruise of dark gray. The air smelled of rain and the clouds seemed to bear so heavily over the school and its discolored building that Ethan felt himself running for the bus even though it was not due to leave for ten minutes.

He found his brother and sat next to him. "Storm's coming," Theo said.

They got off at their stop, about three quarters of a mile from their house, and they started walking, until Theo turned around and said to Ethan in a low voice, "Don't look behind you."

"I don't know why I said that," my father said to my mother's stomach. "Trying to tell Ethan what not to do was always a guarantee that he would sooner or later find a way to do it anyhow."

So Ethan turned around and though he kept walking, his steps began to slow and though he turned to face the front, he couldn't help but continue to twist his neck so he could see behind him.

There, as if in a vision, she was walking behind him, her ponytail swinging out from behind her, her back laboring underneath her khaki-colored canvas bag. Lightning forked to their left and above them the thunder cracked.

"Sure is getting windy," said Theo but Ethan wasn't listening. He kept looking behind him. His face soured and he gave a great sigh as he pulled the front of his hair down over his crown with his fingers.

"Why is she here?" he asked angrily.

"I think her aunt lives down around here," Theo replied.

"How the hell do you know that?" spat Ethan, grabbing his brother, who promptly shrugged him off.

"Everyone knows that the Lomaxes are related to the O'Brians. Tammy is her cousin, you mouth-breather."

"What did you call me?"

"I said 'mouth-breather,' what are you deaf, too?"

Ethan grabbed Theo in a headlock, who then both kicked out and tried to punch his brother in the nose.

"Say it again. Say it again, squirt."

Ethan's arms were so tight around his brother that Theo's face was fast turning from scarlet to crimson. Theo threw out a vicious kick to Ethan's ankle, which made him overbalance and fall to the ground, still holding on to Theo as he did.

"Mouth-breather!" screamed Theo, who was now lying on top of his brother and kicking wildly.

"Why were you fighting?" asked my mother.

"I dunno. We were always fighting, we're brothers, that's just what you do."

"I'm glad we don't have any boys yet then." My mother sighed.

"Yet," said my father, smiling as he stroked her stomach.

They were so busy fighting as they tousled on the sandy path that when Theo rolled back over Ethan, twisting his arm and holding him by it so that he was now standing over him, he didn't immediately register that Allie had stopped walking. When he did, his first thought was that she was looking at them, so he pulled Ethan's arm harder, as his brother bit back a yelp of pain. But she was not looking at them. She was looking at the plains behind them.

"What's that?" Theo asked, letting go.

Ethan swung himself up into a sitting position, cradling his elbow. He kicked Theo on the shin and when he saw that he was hopping and holding on to it in pain, he was satisfied enough to look at where his brother had been pointing.

In the distance the sky was an encroaching force of black, but it was not this that he was seeing.

"Is that a dust cloud?" Theo asked eventually, wincing as he brought himself upright.

"No," said Ethan, standing. "It's not."

Barely visible in the darkness, they saw a thin funnel rising up from the ground to meet the sky.

"You mean the other way around, honey."

"Yes, technically, but when we first saw it that's what we thought. I mean, we'd never seen an actual tornado that close before."

"Whoa," said Ethan.

"Cool," said Theo.

"We gotta get outta here and quick. Now."

"Hey, wait a minute—"

"You want to outrun a tornado?"

Theo stuck out his tongue as he grinned. "Fun to try."

And then finally Ethan looked at Allie. Not the way he usually looked at her, not coveting and imagining her, but seeing her and her bags with the books already spilling out onto the ground beside her as she gazed in horror at the horizon.

"Hey," he called out, but his voice failed at the end so he shouted at her again. "Hey!"

She turned to face him.

"That's a twister," he said, pointing.

Her face crumpled. "Yeah, I know that," she said dryly.

"Yeah, well…well, what are you doing here anyway?" Ethan said defensively.

"He was never good with girls, you know? Just couldn't relax, he was always so tense. Intense. If you're a boy in there, and you need girl tips, don't ever go to your uncle, that's all I'm saying."

"Theo, please don't give dating tips to our baby. It's not even born yet."

"I'm staying with my aunt tonight. My parents are away visiting my grandparents," she shouted back. She had to, the wind was like a roar in their ears, their hair whipping around their heads in crazy halos of gold and brown.

"Well, you can't go there, you'll never make it in time, it's too far down the road—it'll lead us directly into the path of the twister," Ethan shouted back. He seemed to hesitate for a moment and then he started to walk toward her and picked up her bag by its strap.

"Jeez, Ethe, look at that!" cried his brother from behind.

The sky was forked with lightning, white lines that splintered the encroaching dark in intersecting patterns. The funnel stood out to them now; it was moving in a diagonal form across to the right of the path ahead of them.

"We'll never make it back home before…" Theo trailed off slowly.

"Oh, my God," Allie whispered.

Her hands were cradling her face and Ethan allowed himself to imagine that it was his hands holding her and comforting her and suddenly he felt his spine straighten.

"Come with me." He grabbed her by the arm.

"Where are we going?" she shouted.

"Ethan!" called Theo.

"Theo, grab the bags and let's go," cried Ethan over his shoulder as he hauled Allie by her wrist, straining against the winds that were buffeting them with hard invisible blows.

"We went into the thicket, through the tall grass which was like wading through water, what with the winds. I knew where he was going—we'd been down that way loads of times before when we used to go exploring. She was hollering her head off but he wouldn't let her go, just kept dragging her on with him while she cursed him out."

"Where did you go?" asked my mother.

"There was this abandoned farmhouse. Totally derelict. It had one of those old cellars that you can get into from the outside with those slat doors raised up over the floor. Anyway we used to go in it sometimes and mess around and stuff. It was about ten minutes away, but it was straight on and it was a good idea in hindsight because it was farther on from the tornado, which was heading in the opposite direction. Otherwise if we kept on going home, we'd have ended smack-bang in the face of it. To be honest I don't know if that place would have stood up to the twister. I've seen more of them since then and they can demolish a sturdier building than that if they want to, but we was kids, what did we know? And besides, Ethan wasn't really in the mood for an elective vote."

When they got to the cellar, Ethan pushed Allie inside

through the crumbling whitewashed slats and down the stairs. By now she was both sobbing and shaking, and as she was dragged past the last step she wrenched her wrist away from him and went to the other side of the cellar. The only light in the room was from a small grubby windowpane on a concrete ledge just above ground level on the farther side of the room. The floor was covered in dirt and the walls were black. Theo crashed in after them and dumped the bags to the floor. He braced himself against his knees as he tried to catch his breath.

And then Allie took a step forward and smacked Ethan right across the mouth.

"You're crazy, you know that?!" she screamed. "You grab me and force me to come here, you didn't even ask me. You've no right to do that. When we get back to school I'm going to tell everyone how you kidnapped me and brought me to this awful place and Jimmy Galloway will beat the crap out of you."

"Okay then, why don't you go face the twister by yourself if we're kidnapping you?" Theo shouted back. Allie stopped and stared at him disconcerted.

"Yeah, go on," he sneered. "Door's that way."

"Theo!"

"I was a kid and she was being a brat."

She eyed the door and then the boys.

"I wouldn't like your chances," said Ethan quietly. He hadn't moved since she slapped him and the side of his mouth was red. Gently he dropped her bag beside her and then emptied his book bag and laid the satchel on the dirty floor.

"You can sit on that if you like."

"Or go to hell," volunteered Theo. "Just a suggestion."

Ethan sat down on the dirty floor and hugged his knees to his chest. Theo paused for a second and then did the same.

Allie stood there, caught between her anger, her disgust at the cellar and her fear of what lay outside.

"We were there for two hours in the end. Ethan didn't say a word. At the time I thought he was stupid, I mean he'd been hankering after her for ages and then he gets his chance and nothing. Zilch. But actually it worked. 'Cause she sat on the satchel after a while and stared at him all guilty or whatever. I think she felt bad about panicking and smacking him one, though she had a good hand on her for a girl. So anyways eventually I got bored and went to look outside and whaddaya know? Clear sky, not a breeze, just dead flat. It was all smoky gray like how the sky looks after you put out a large fire or something, so we started to walk back and we didn't see anything. It was like the twister never happened. Then we got back on the path to the farm and the nearer we got, the worse it was—trees everywhere, whole path was littered with branches and leaves, was like a forest shed itself all over the road. We had to clamber over what we could and then when it got to be too much, we took a detour the long way around, but we got home all the same.

One of the smaller cornfields was totally decimated and the barn was half-smashed in, but when we got to the house—"

The house was untouched, but before they could even climb the mound, Lavinia—swiftly followed by Cal and Piper—was running down to them. Lavinia shook Ethan so hard Theo heard his brother's teeth rattle even though he was half-smothered in his father's arms.

"They must have been terrified."

"And angry."

In the kitchen Theo explained what they had done while their mother checked them over, Cal poured himself a shot of bourbon and Piper rang Allie's aunt to tell her she was okay.

"The roads are blocked so I guess you'll have to stay the night for now, Allie, until your aunt and uncle can get over to pick you up," said Piper, rejoining them from the hall. "They're all fine, not too much damage by the way. They'll call your parents, too."

"Oh, thank you," she said, cradling a glass of milk.

"Where's Julia?" asked Theo.

"She stayed behind for cheerleading practice and they all hid in the school gym. She'll stay the night with a friend in town until they sort out the roads," said Cal. "She's okay, full of tough stuff, like my boys," he bragged and ruffled the mops of their hair.

"Dinner," said Lavinia.

That night Allie stayed in Julia's room. Ethan didn't talk to or look at her all through the meal and he went to bed without saying good-night to anybody at all. His father put it down to shock.

But in the middle of the night, he was woken up by the pressure of a small hand on his chest and the next morning when Allie's aunt and uncle went to get her, she kept her eyes to the floor as they thanked my grandparents and the boys.

They climbed into their car to drive off, and Ethan watched them as they left, before putting a hand to his mouth on which a small purple bruise had already formed. He choked back a smile. Then he saw Theo watching and whacked him on the shoulder, and his brother promptly punched him in the stomach before Piper caught them both by the ears.

He did not see his mother's eyes on him or how they flitted back to the disappearing taillights of the O'Brians' car. Even if he had, it would have meant nothing to him...then.

"Will you tell me some more about your sister?" my mother asked one night when she was eight months gone and my father lay beside her, munching on a sandwich and reading the paper by his foot.

"What do you want to know?" he asked as he turned the page with his toe.

"I don't know. Anything really—" she shifted and then amended her voice "—anything you want to talk about, that is."

My father polished off his sandwich and then wiped his fingers on his shirt, before licking his teeth thoughtfully with his tongue.

"Did you like her?" my mother asked.

"Yeah," he said softly. "Yeah, I did. So did Ethe."

"When did you stop liking her?"

"It wasn't really that simple. I mean..." He trailed off and sighed. "When your father ran out on you and your mother when you were a kid, did you stop loving him just like that? Did you think, well he's done this bad thing, so that's it—no more love for him ever?"

"No, not at first," my mother replied. "But I did eventually."

"Well, that's because what he did meant a lot of hardship for you and your mother. He hurt you a lot."

"So did Julia."

"Yes but...what she did, it wasn't meant to hurt us, it was just... Oh, hell, I don't know, I've never understood it. I don't think any one of us ever have."

He paused.

"Except Ma."

"Why?"

"Because she was waiting for it. She'd been waiting on something like that for years. Sometimes I used to think that..." He stopped and stared at the wall ahead, and then he shook his head, his great mop of blond hair swirling in a wave.

"Never mind. What's done is done. That's what I say."

"And your pa, what does he say?"

My father went quiet and put his hand on Mom's stomach. Apparently I gave a kick.

"He doesn't say anything anymore."

Julia spent her life on the farm, living in the fantasies that her mind had created. Her whole world was a product of imagination and so whenever she was faced with reality she found it an unwelcome and even hostile intrusion to the series of reveries she constructed in which she was rich, admired, loved and famous. She took singing and dance lessons and forced her family to sit through an endless parade of recitals despite the fact that, while no one would ever acknowledge as much to her face, Julia had no ear for music and no talent for dancing. In fact, the girl had no performing talent at all, but it didn't deter her. She didn't care. Her real talent was the strength of her self-belief, so much so that her ferocity could make other people doubt their own.

Years passed and my grandmother watched her intently for any sign of a chink in the girl's armor, but as time went on she saw, much to her dismay, that the surfaces of Julia's resolve were still smooth and gleaming. When she believed in something, neither contradiction nor refusal would be tolerated. If her father told her she couldn't have a dress, she found a way to convince him that her reasons were more important than his for refusing her. If she insisted on singing the national anthem at the Fourth of July fair, even though Mrs. McClusky knew Rita Pessel was a far more gifted singer, she found herself falling for Julia's rationale as to why she was the obvious choice. She would then spend the entire performance wincing, until she finally gave up the ghost and closed her eyes in pain as Julia attempted and failed to find that elusive top note on "free."

Julia only had to want something for it to be hers. This was her greatest talent, and even though she never fully recognized it, it was far more valuable than that of singing or dancing.

It was a talent that would allow her to seduce Jess Thorne away from his long-term sweetheart Caroline Lumas, and convince him to marry Julia when she was just eighteen.

As if in a replay, one night in June, Lavinia experienced an uncomfortable sense of déjà vu. She found herself at her dining room table with Cal at the head and the boys and Piper on either side. There was a bowl of mashed potatoes in the middle, a chicken-and-mushroom pie and a jug of sweating ice water on either side. She saw all these things and thought nothing of it, but when her stepdaughter came in bearing a roast ham on the silver tray and set it down before her father in such a way…Lavinia felt the hairs on the back of her neck rise. She knew it before the girl even said it, and for a second, the walls could have melted and all the people with them and she would be staring into the face of her cousin, wearing a red-checked house dress just before she told them that—

"Pa, I'm getting married."

Lavinia opened her eyes, startled that she had somehow closed them.

Cal turned to face his daughter, his face arranging itself in such a way that it could start smiling at the joke she was so obviously playing on him, but she stayed silent.

"Did you hear me?" she said finally.

"Julia—what did you just say?" asked Piper, bracing her hands on the table.

"I'm getting married. Look." And she thrust forward her hand on which sparkled the blink of a diamond underneath the lights.

She stared at everyone around the table. Theo watched her for a second and then went to help himself to a piece of pie.

"Theo, we haven't even said grace yet," admonished Piper. He set the dish down with an irritated clunk.

"Why isn't anyone saying anything?" Julia pouted. "For goodness' sake—in polite circles I believe the word you're looking for is *congratulations*."

"Julia, let me get this straight—you're getting married?" asked Piper, incredulous. Julia put her hands on her hips and tossed back her flicked red hair.

"Yeah, I think that's what I said like half an hour ago."

"But what about college? And who is this man, I mean you've never even brought a boy home here, how can you be marrying someone?" Piper insisted. It seemed she was the only person besides her niece who had found her voice. Theo sat back in his chair bored and was eyeing the mashed potatoes, Ethan was watching his sister, his face a mask devoid of expression, and Cal…well, Cal was utterly still, frozen, as he gazed on his daughter and all that she was telling him.

"I'm not going to college anymore—well, not this year anyway. Me and Jess were thinking of traveling to Los Angeles for a bit actually—he's got family there. His uncle's a music producer or something and you know how talented he is? Remember in May when he played that gig at the Oden theater? And—"

"Jess Thorne?" asked Piper. "You're marrying Jess Thorne?"

"Yep," said Julia proudly, and a smug look of pride flashed across her mouth.

"But isn't he with—" Piper trailed off and stared at Lavinia, who sighed and said it for her, "Caroline Lumas."

"Not anymore," Julia said with a raised eyebrow. "Not for quite a while, no matter what else she's been spreading around town."

"I'm hungry," said Theo. "Food's getting cold."

"Daddy, ain't you going to say anything?" asked Julia sulkily. "Can you hear me? Are you even in there? Your only daughter has just said she's getting married and you're struck dumb?" She folded her arms and surveyed him in disappointed indignation. "You do realize what I'm saying, don't you?"

Cal stood up very slowly, letting his napkin fall to the ground, and in that moment, Julia shrank back, wariness slicing through her arrogant calm.

"Daddy?" she asked, taking a step backward.

"You ain't getting married to NO ONE!" he shouted, stabbing a thick digit at her. "You're going to college and you're going to finish your schooling, like we planned." He smashed his fist down onto the table, making his glass jump.

This was what Julia had been waiting for and what she could more than handle. Lavinia watched her husband play into the girl's hands and sighed in disappointment.

"Well, that ain't in my plans no more, Daddy. My plans are about going to California and marrying Jess!"

Cal grabbed his daughter by her arm and shook her like a rag doll as she smacked him on his shoulder.

"Look at you, answering back, lifting your hand to me." She raised it in an arc but he caught it at the elbow and batted it down behind her back, which made her yelp in pain. "I knew it, by God, I knew it would come to something— stepping out at all hours and your grades slipping. But marriage?! Over my dead body, girl," he screamed into her ear, her hair flying as she thrashed under his grip. He leaned into her. "And yours!" he finished.

Sobbing, she freed herself, or more likely, Cal let her go, and she ran crying her hatred for him up the stairs and into her bedroom.

Cal sat back down as he heard her bedroom door slam and wiped his brow with the back of his hand. He stared from the impassive face of his wife to the horrified one of his sister and promptly began to start dry heaving.

Lavinia watched the food wilt under the hot lights and even hotter temper of her family and took in a deep breath. Ethan stared at her solemnly; Theo kicked the table leg in frustration.

"Am I right?" asked Cal as he finally composed himself. "I am right, ain't I?"

Piper shrugged, Lavinia arched an eyebrow.

"What the hell's gotten into her? I just—I just don't understand it." He stared at the table, his eyes running back and forth along the edge as if trying to decipher the answer among the wood grains.

Lavinia pursed her lips and took Ethan's plate.

"Well, I suppose the pie will still be good even if it is lukewarm," she said.

Cal looked up at her, startled. Slowly and carefully she picked up the silver knife and caught his eye as she sliced it deep into the heart of the crust.

My father would come to remember 1961 for many reasons. It was the year that JFK was inaugurated as president and my grandmother sighed in annoyance because she had voted for Nixon, her reason being that "he had just wanted it more." It was the year he was forced to sit through *The Old Man and the Sea* and *For Whom the Bell Tolls* in English class because his overemotional teacher had changed the syllabus after Hemingway had shot himself; the year Charlie Brown successfully flew his kite for the first time and the first American soldier was killed in the Vietnam War. That part, the part where this fact slipped into and through his consciousness with very little disturbance, he would remember years afterward with incredulity at his innocence.

My uncle would come to remember 1961 as the year he first bought *The Fantastic Four* comic book, the first time his father started to give him more responsibility on the farm, the first time he successfully mastered riding a horse backward, and the year Allie Lomax fell asleep in his arms as they lay underneath their tree one afternoon after school. It was also the year when their relationship was still secret. It had been at Ethan's request. He didn't want anyone to know about them. He had a tight feeling of panic just below his lungs whenever he thought of anyone finding out about them. I suppose perhaps he thought if people knew, they would start spoiling it—a paranoid but prophetic idea.

But despite their differences, both boys would remember 1961 for one thing in particular and that was Julia. It was the year Julia turned eighteen and had a huge party in the spring that Theo wasn't allowed to go to because he was considered too young; it was the year she announced over a roast ham that she was getting married, and it was the year that she eloped.

After the argument at dinner, Julia took to her room. She refused to come out and speak to my grandfather even though he raged at her, slammed his fist against the door and threatened to kick it down. She said she would not come out until Cal had agreed she could marry Jess, but for the first time in my grandmother's memory, Cal refused his daughter. He walked past her locked room with a stiffening in his

features and a heavy step, but he did not speak or call out
to her. Piper brought Julia food on a tray, but she refused to
eat and each time she took the tray away bearing the now
cold dishes, she scraped them into the trash and asked my
grandmother the same question: "What are we going to do?"

My grandfather didn't speak at meals anymore, only glared
at the empty chair that was Julia's place and wolfed down
whatever had been put before him. He was irascible, distant,
and whenever my grandmother woke in the night she would
find him lying on his back staring up at the ceiling, his
face a hard mask. This lasted for three days—Julia's hunger
strike, my grandfather's inner war—until on the morning of
the fourth day my grandmother rose from her bed, dressed
herself in a long green wrap dress and, carrying her gloves
and bag, went into town, to the house of Julia's best friend,
Betsy Turner.

Betsy, even when I came to know her when she was married with twin boys, was a flighty, excitable woman with
absolutely nothing between her ears. She was kind, though,
and whenever she used to see me or my sisters in town she
always smiled and said hello, though her smile would falter
when she saw our cousin Cal Jr. Then she would nod and
look down at her feet as she left. I believe this was guilt—for
what people still accused her of even after—but I'm getting
ahead of myself. Needless to say, she always was and always
would be a simple girl with a simple mind and my grandmother had a field day with her.

This part my father did not know. This part no one but
myself and a raving woman with glassy colored eyes, as she
lay in her bed and poured out her secrets, would ever know.
My grandmother went into the house of Betsy Turner, to
find out about Julia's relationship with Jess in the hope that
she could somehow convince them both to see sense. Betsy's

mother, who opened the door to my grandmother, had been with her daughter at the time because, she said, she didn't want Betsy's good name being dragged into Julia's mess. Betsy's mother had more reason than most to fear any sort of sexual scandal being associated with her daughter: Betsy's grandfather was Michael Banville, the town preacher.

My grandmother sat on their hard sofa and watched Betsy squirm and twist her fingers under the glare of her questions. But Betsy's answers were less than sufficient for my grandmother. They were barely polysyllabic. All she would say was that Julia and Jess were in love and that he had proposed. She insisted Julia had been secretive with her; she didn't want anyone else to know. She stared at the floor the whole time she spoke. Ordinarily, my grandmother would have pressed on Betsy like a board that was bound to crack under her weight, but that day she didn't need to. Her own mother was more than happy to add her feet to the cause. She pulled Betsy's fingers apart when she buried her face in her hands, and hit her daughter on the back when she took too long with an answer.

"Answer the woman," she said through gritted teeth.

Lavinia suspected the woman thought if Betsy were as truthful as possible, my grandmother would be lenient with her reputation and not accuse her of being involved in Julia's sordid affairs. She pondered this idea as she gazed from mother to daughter and leaned back in her chair.

"Daphne," she said gently, "would you mind awfully if I had a glass of your blackcurrant cordial? I am absolutely parched and I remember you bringing a large jug of it at the last church fair— Oh, it was just refreshing. I'll have to get that recipe from you...if you can bear to part with it? Would you mind terribly?"

Daphne bit the inside of her lip. While she did not want

to leave her daughter alone to incriminate herself, neither did she want to pass up the chance to indulge in my grandmother's flattery. So Lavinia watched the woman wrestle with her fears and her wants and waited for her to choose.

"I'll just be a minute. I'll be right back," Daphne said, rising quickly from her armchair.

While she was in the kitchen, my grandmother slid one leg over another and said softly, "Do you know Julia's starving herself?"

Betsy looked up at my grandmother, meeting her eyes in surprise before dropping them to her feet.

"They used to do it in my day when I was a young girl, that sort of thing. Hunger strikes. Sometimes they would have to force-feed them." My grandmother played with the hem of her skirt, which had come loose, and wound it around her finger. She watched the girl from the corner of her eye.

"They'd push a long tube down their throat into their stomach—they'd have to or they would die. They were so serious about their causes, those women. I hope Julia isn't the same about Jess. I hope he's worth it if she is. He must be quite a man if he's worth dying for, don't you think?"

Lavinia watched a wet dark spot form on the floor below where Betsy bent her head.

"Malnutrition can do such awful things to a girl. I used to be married to a doctor, you know—and the stories he would tell me. Damage your insides something awful, shrivel your organs, stretch your skin so it's like cracked paper, dry up your womb so it's like a prune, withered and shrunk—but there's no use talking to her, she's so stubborn, so sure. If only I knew what was going on inside her head I could convince her that maybe—" my grandmother watched the hands in Betsy's lap tremble and released the curled hem "—he isn't worth dying for. No one is, except your children."

"Here you are," said Daphne, and she gave my grandmother a tall frosted glass of cordial. She was so busy smiling at my grandmother she didn't notice her daughter shaking in her chair.

My grandmother reached out and took a long drink from the glass.

"Thank you, Daphne," she said after she'd finished. "That was exactly what I needed."

Between sobs that both exasperated and bewildered her mother, Betsy revealed as much as her body would allow. Lavinia left the house both satisfied and purposeful. But as she wandered down the street, a growing sense of unease began to plague her. The thing had to be done carefully, delicately, especially because of Cal. She ran her gloves through her hands. Cal would have to be managed.

What she learned was this: Julia had always had a crush on Jess Thorne, ever since freshman year. He was popularly considered to be one of the most handsome and talented boys at school. Everyone thought he'd be a great musician and he was always talking about his uncle in California. He had so many ideas and plans to travel and Julia loved to listen to him. She hung around him and his friends as well as on his every word, Betsy said. She was besotted.

But for a long time, Jess was not. Jess had been with Caroline Lumas since ninth grade and it was a relationship he was happy to maintain. How then, my grandmother asked, did Julia convince him to marry her? Daphne Turner looked at my grandmother sharply when she said this.

"What do you mean *convince?*" she'd asked, but she received no answer because just then her daughter swept ahead with her tale.

There had been a night when they had all gone drinking down by a creek on Bull Tucker's land. Bull was a meathead but a good friend of Jess's and they had rung up a crew of girls and boys. Caroline had been away on a class trip to Washington, D.C. They had grabbed some cans and taken a blanket and whiled away the hours. Betsy hadn't really noticed anything until she saw Julia leaning over Jess, who was reclining on the blanket. She was talking and he was playing with the curls of her hair, but, added Betsy, they had thought nothing of it, they were all pretty drunk.

Julia had grown more secretive after that. She had watched Caroline and Jess constantly, her moods fluctuating whenever she saw them. If Jess held Caroline, she slammed her locker door and lost herself for hours after. If he was alone or bored around his girlfriend, Julia smiled and teased him. Caroline noticed Jess's mood swings and Julia's attentions and apparently there had once even been a "scene" between the two of them in the locker room after gym class.

Betsy had had no idea what Jess and Julia were up to, until one day Julia ran out of math class crying. She had been dreadfully sick in the washroom and had had to go home. Lavinia sat up as she had heard this—she had remembered this incident. Piper had picked the girl up from school and had nursed her. Julia hadn't come down to dinner and was quiet the next day. She had dismissed it at the time as nothing out of the ordinary.

After that, Betsy said, Jess got more fidgety and anxious. Now he was chasing Julia in corridors and ignoring Caroline. Julia had been sick again one morning in school but she had insisted on not going to the nurse. When Jess heard, he tried to talk to her but she brushed him off. Then two days later, he broke up with Caroline in the parking lot of the diner near school. And then a week afterward, Julia came into class with a huge smile on her face and, pulling Betsy into the girl's washroom, had showed her the diamond on her left hand.

"I see," said Lavinia at the last. "Clever girl."

"I don't think she's been clever. I think she's been very stupid, hiding all this from everyone until now. Why didn't you say anything sooner?" cried Daphne, shaking her child. She had thought Lavinia had been talking about her daughter.

"But why Jess?" Lavinia persisted, though it was more to herself, than Betsy. "Of everyone, why him?"

"Because he's going places," Betsy said. "And he'll take Julia with him."

And that was when Lavinia smiled.

How Julia would tell it, was that when she heard the house was quiet, she came downstairs and got a sandwich. She could track the movements of her family in the house from her bedroom and she knew their routine well enough to know when they would usually be in and out. She had mostly been going down in the middle of the night—three, four in the morning for reserves, but as she had heard her stepmother say goodbye earlier that day, the boys were at school and her father was with her aunt in a business meeting with a new supplier, she decided to risk the venture. Grabbing what she could, she left and went up the stairs just as her stepmother pulled up into the drive.

She was in her room when she heard the front door close, and she heard her stepmother go up the stairs and knock on her room.

"Julia, are you ready to talk yet?" came the muffled voice

through the wood. Behind the door Julia gave her step-mother the finger. Then she heard Lavinia go into her bed-room for ten minutes and then she came back out and went down the stairs into the hall. For a few moments there was nothing, but then she heard her muffled voice seep through the walls. At first she said she didn't listen. She knew she would be talking about her, she was all anyone talked about now except when they were in front of her father, so for a while she didn't pay much attention, but then she heard something that made her sit up.

"But what shall we do if she finds it?" she heard Lavinia ask. "Maybe we should just be on the safe side and put it in the bank."

Julia rolled off of her bed and put her ear to the floor.

"I just don't think it's wise to leave it here. We're not always in, she could just grab it at any time and be gone and no one would stop her. You know we have nearly a thousand dollars there. That'd set her up in California for a good while. We should put it in the bank, Cal... I know you want to trust her but she's clearly not thinking straight at the moment—she's liable to do anything with that Jess boy. Why wouldn't she, especially if she has money to do it?"

Julia rolled onto her back and stared at the peach-colored wallpaper. Her parents had talked about keeping a stack of money in the house in case of emergencies before. Why, she did not know—did they think they could just pay the bur-glars off if they came? But her aunt had said that her father had lived through the crash and the Depression and he was afraid of banks. He liked to have ready reserves in case he needed it. Her stepmother had thought the idea was more likely to encourage burglaries if people knew about it, not prevent them, and had been adamant about it, but evidently her father had gotten his own way. If he could, he would have kept the whole of their money under the mattress, but the compromise apparently was a thousand.

She heard Lavinia finish her conversation and go out into the garden. She looked out from her window and saw her in her pruning gloves and straw hat bent over the azalea bush. Quickly she stole into her father's bedroom, lifted the mattress and removed the brown paper bag there. Then she went back into her room, checked the window again and then stealthily crept downstairs and called Jess.

The next night while my family slept and my grandfather choked his pillow into his mouth to stop his wife from hearing him sob, Julia crept downstairs, down the drive and to the entrance of the farm, where she found Jess Thorne parked in his T-bird and waiting. In the morning, my grandmother listened carefully at the door of her stepdaughter's room and then, trying the handle on the pretext of attempting to reason with Julia face-to-face, she found it unlocked and the closet half-empty. My great-aunt half fainted in her chair and my grandfather threw a bottle of scotch, which burst on the wall.

"We'll never see her again," he said in despair.

And that was how Julia left home for the first time.

To my knowledge, she's always believed that it had been all her own idea.

7

ON THE PLANE TO IOWA I HAD A DREAM. I DREAMT
I was in the big double bed I had shared with my sister Ava
in my grandmother's house after my father died. My grandmother was saying good-night when, uncharacteristically, after
she had pulled the covers over us she hesitated and then had
asked, "Do you want me to tell you a story?"

Ava had wriggled herself into a semi-sitting position. My
grandmother had twisted her wedding ring around her finger
and looked from the door to us and back again.

"It's just...did your— Do you get a bedtime story at
night?"

Claudia, who was lying in a single cot bed that had been
put in our room, said swiftly, "We're too old for stories."

"You're never too old for stories," said Ava, conciliatory.

"I was never told stories as a child," my grandmother said,
smoothing the edge of the bed down in order to give her
nervous hands something to do. "I used to make them up in
my head, and then of course I read books, but no one ever

read *to* me. I remember, though, my father had been a teacher of English. He must have loved stories. Maybe that's where I get it from—my liking to read. Do you want something to read?"

"No, thank you, Grandma," said Ava.

"Very well." She drew herself up and threw an analyzing glance around the room as she prepared to leave.

"You know," she said as she got to the door, "this is just as much your home as the house you live in. More so—your father was born in this house. He grew up here, he took his first steps, said his first words. This is your home because it had always been his. You don't have to feel...well, you don't have to feel out of place. If you want to read, you can read, if you want to be read to, you can just ask. This is your home, no matter what happens outside of it or wherever you go, this will always be home for you." Her face was half in shadow from the dark of the room and the light of the hall. I thought she would say something else and I raised myself up on my elbow, leaning into Ava to hear, but then she turned away and closed the door.

At Des Moines International Airport I got my bags and then caught a Greyhound at the bus depot. I was exhausted. I seemed to slip in and out of dreams as my body rocked on the twists and turns of the highway. Whenever I did wake and I saw not my beloved Manhattan, with its thin streets and crowds of people toppled by a swarm of buildings that rose and defeated the skyline, but Iowa with the weight of the heavens on the flat square buildings and pockets of trees lining the long caramel-colored roads, I felt sick and curled into myself.

Oh, God, I thought, I'm here, I'm really doing this. Over a decade had gone by and none of it had changed. I could be coming home like any other normal person, ready to see my family, sit down for dinner, open a bagful of presents and sit in our living room on our couch and remember my childhood and feel at peace. But when I finally got off the bus and went to a taxi stand, my legs could barely walk. Everything seemed to be an assault on the senses. It was too much of home, too much to remember all at once, the smell, the look: I could no longer pretend.

And when the car pulled into the street of the house I had often stayed in as a child, where I watched *Cagney and Lacey* reruns over a plate of raisin cookies and fruit juice waiting for my mother to pick me up, I thought my head would explode with all that I was feeling.

I got out and paid the driver, and after I took in the rose-and-white clapboard house, I walked up the steps to the screen door and rang the doorbell.

I said a prayer when I pressed the buzzer. I had my eyes closed at the time so when I heard the main door open and saw her behind the screen door staring at me as if I were a ghost she had forgotten could still haunt her, I realized for the first time how difficult this was really going to be.

"Meredith?" she said, her tongue forming the word warily, hesitantly, wondering if her mind and eyes were deceiving her. Half hoping, I thought.

"Jane," I said. "Is that you?"

"Oh, God," she said and put her hand up to the screen. "It's you, it's really you."

When I knew Jane, she was in her early fifties, her hair was semi-permed around her head and she always wore primary colors, and never any prints. She met my mother in a grocery store, not long after my father died. I don't know how exactly, but the two struck up a conversation and through Jane and her friendship, my mother began to create a small but necessary life for herself away from Aurelia. Jane was a widow, too—her husband had died in Vietnam and she had never remarried and never had any children. She worked in the hardware store and loved to hike. I remember how the halls of her house were always cluttered with camping equipment and walking boots that I used to frequently trip over. She was a private woman, kind but she never gave herself away. I used to spend so many afternoons in her house and if you asked me I could tell you what cookies she ate, when she did her grocery shopping, how she liked her coffee, but about her life—aside from these meager facts—I knew nothing. It's funny, but I realize now how little we really used to interact with people outside Aurelia, outside the family even. We talked, we played, we even made friends with them but nothing concrete, nothing lasting. They were not one of us and we were not one of them. They were black-and-white; we were color.

Though she had aged, and the halls no longer had the remnants of a recent hiking trip lined up against them, in the fundamentals she was still the same. Her eyes were still the clear blue behind the horn-rimmed glasses she was now obliged to wear, her hands, though wrinkled and mottled with brown liver spots, still had those long tapered fingers that were always so deft and capable. And that mouth, on which a smile had always played lingeringly in the corners, now came forward in greeting to my cheek.

"I never thought I'd see you again, Merey," she said as I came and sat in her kitchen while she watched me.

Shit, no one living has called me that in years. As soon as she said it the hand holding my glass of water trembled. I set it back on its coaster.

"So when did you hear then?" she asked.

"A few weeks ago," I said, clutching my hands together on the plastic cloth of the table.

"My God, I never thought of everyone that it'd be you who would come down here once they did find out." She stared at me, her hands running through the gray of her flaxen hair.

"I...they said it's going to be sold. I thought— I thought I should come down and make sure that it...um...that it goes well and that Mom and Dad's stuff, that the important stuff doesn't get mixed up in all of that mess."

"That's really good of you, Merey," she said carefully. "That'd mean a lot to them, especially to your mom."

My mom. The last time I saw her was when she was being lowered into the ground in a coffin. Ava kept telling me to come home, that she was sick, getting sicker. I put it off and off and off, and then one day there was no need to be afraid of the phone ringing anymore.

My throat was suddenly dry. "I was hoping...I mean I know I showed up here unannounced and everything, but I thought if it wouldn't be too much trouble, if I could just stay one night and then I could get a motel or something—"

She was shaking her head. I sank back in my seat.

"Oh...okay, I—"

"I wouldn't dream of letting the daughter of Antonia Hathaway stay in a motel on her own while her home and all its contents were dispersed to the winds. You'll stay with me, child." She rubbed her hand over mine. "Gracious, are you cold?"

"No." I withdrew my hand from hers as if I'd been bitten and she leaned away from me.

"You must be tired. Shall I show you to your room? We can talk later about everything. You must have questions."

She leaned her head to the side and I saw her face fall. "Don't you?"

For a moment I couldn't speak. "I am quite tired," I somehow managed to reply.

"Okay, well your room's upstairs and all ready. The usual one. Do you need to me to show you? Have you forgotten where everything is?"

"No, no, that's fine," I said, standing up, and then I stopped.

"What do you mean it's all ready?"

She looked up at me, and I saw her eyes flicker and then fall to a blank.

"Oh...I—I don't think that's something we should get into now."

"Did—did someone...?" I trailed off but her gaze was unflinching and gave away nothing.

"Okay," I said. "Okay."

My uncle Ethan should have been concerned that his sister had run away from home but he wasn't. In fact he was glad. The house was understandably in an uproar, with all its focus on finding Julia and bringing her back, which suited him just fine, because it meant he could carry on seeing Allie Lomax with no one to suspect as much. Even his brother had left him alone, so overcome was he by the change in their father, who worked until long past dark as their mother stood at the kitchen window staring into the blackness, muttering as to why he wouldn't come home.

So as he made his way down to the field behind the O'Brians' farm, swinging his hands along the heads of the sunflowers that had sprung up, he allowed himself an unexpected burst of happiness, because now he could concentrate solely on Allie and know that no one, not his brother, or his mother especially, were watching him. Silently he thanked his sister for the first and most valuable gift she'd ever given him: the chance to be invisible.

That night he made a vow to Allie. As she sat underneath their tree and curled herself into him, her legs entwined with his, he whispered to her that he wanted to marry her.

"Don't think you should be mentioning that word in your family, not right now." She chuckled.

"I don't care. When it comes to my time we'll do it properly in front of everyone. You'll see. I'll make you a good husband, Allie cat. Do you promise you'll say yes?"

"Do you promise you'll ask?" she whispered.

"Of course," he said, delighted. "You have my word."

In the morning I woke to find Jane at my bedside laying a breakfast tray on the whitewashed table.

"Oh, you didn't have to do that," I said.

"Hush." She turned the corner of the tray so that it balanced properly. "Get something down you. I'll bet you haven't had decent cooking in a long while."

"Does take-out count?" I asked ruefully, taking the tray, but looking at the fried eggs, hash browns and curling bacon, I was suddenly both glad and uneasy at the same time.

Later when I was dressed, I came downstairs and found her in her living room in her old rocking chair, listening to the radio. I stopped in the doorway. She looked up and laughed at my expression.

"Hasn't changed, has it?" she asked, throwing a glance around the room. And it hadn't. The chairs were still the same honey-colored flower pattern in the exact same arrangement I would throw myself on after school. The wallpaper was the same, the radio playing jazz and blues softly in the background was still next to the small gray-fringed TV set on top of a clothed table in the corner. She set down her book and said gently, "Why don't you come here and tell me what you've been doing with yourself since…" She stopped and then thinking better of it, turned up her lips and then put her book away. "This must be very hard for you, Merey," she said after a brief pause.

"Yes," I ventured, feeling my way around the words. "I haven't been back since Mom died."

"And had no plans to, I'm sure."

I frowned.

"That wasn't a reproach, more like an observation." She put her hands in her lap.

"You were never coy in my house all the days I knew you—I see no reason why you should start now. Sit down."

So I sat on the couch opposite her.

"Have you seen it? The farm, I mean?" I asked the floor.

She gave a long sigh. "I have. It's changed—well, that's a bit of a lie. It still has the same things, the house, the drive, but to say it's falling apart is to put it mildly. It's the same picture but wrong. He really did a number on it."

"Cal Jr.?" I said, looking up.

She licked the corner of her lip. "He was a sick man—well, you know that. As soon as he got the place, he started to ravage it. He blamed it, he punished it and when your mother died—" I winced "—and your sister finally left, he punished it some more. God knows what was going through his mind when he did the things he did. But I believe he knew what he was doing when he destroyed it. None of us could understand why. You all had your troubles, but your family was the envy of so many."

I bit my lip.

"Of course we knew about his mother and the problems there, but still, your grandparents gave him such a good home and we knew they would have raised him right…but from the way he carried on you wouldn't know it. Those parties—" she shuddered "—and the stories of what he got up to. And of course he drank—well, that's how he died. But the stories of what he used to do up there…we all knew, but none of us could ever understand it, how he could hole himself up there doing those things for as long as he did. It was like he thrived on it."

I looked into her eyes and the pity and pain there made me want to run.

"I'm not here to try and make things right, you know?" I said. "I know that can't happen. I just— I just want to make sure that things are done properly. Someone has to."

She gave me a weak smile. "I'll help you as much as I can, Merey," she said over the strains of Nina Simone.

"Thank you, Jane," I said. "Thanks a lot." I stood up. "I think I'll take a walk, do you want something in town or groceries or something?"

"No." She patted the radio top. "I'm just fine, you know."

I turned to go, but then I paused.

"Jane," I said.

She looked up at me. "Yes?"

"I am really grateful for you putting me up at such short notice… Well, I mean without me asking you to before I came. And it's really good of you to be this—this kind to me about things, but can I ask you for one more favor?"

"Of course," she said, leaning forward. "What is it?"

I took in a sharp breath.

"Please don't call me Merey."

For a month, my grandfather did nothing. He worked until the light gave out and only turned in when it was so black he could barely see his hand in front of his face. He ignored his sons and sister, he barely spoke to his wife and on one occasion he drank so much he fell asleep in his thresher and was thrown head forward into a ditch. The doctor told him he was lucky the thresher hadn't toppled over and fallen on top of him. My grandmother had slapped him in her fury; he had done nothing but grunt.

Later on that day, she had come back to his side and taken his hand in hers and apologized.

"But you frightened me, Cal," she said. "You can't do this. She is only one child, you still have two others and she's not much of a child now if she can run off and leave you like this with no thought or care for her family. It's cruel and she doesn't deserve your unhappiness. You'll see. You will come right enough eventually in time."

"I owed it to her mother to keep her safe," he said to the ceiling. "I failed her."

Later that evening, coming out on the porch, Piper found Lavinia staring into the night. The woman was so still, the only thing that stirred around her was the breeze playing with her dress. But then she heard Piper's step and turned.

"We could look for her in California," said Piper. My grandmother's voice when she next spoke was dripping with scorn.

"Oh, yes—just take off half a year and go up the California coast until we spot her and then drag her back, do we? That's if she isn't married, in which case we have no rights at all. Besides which I think she's pregnant."

"Surely not?" gasped Piper. "No, she would tell me."

Lavinia's mouth inched into a smile. "You have no idea who she is." She turned away. "None of you do. If she doesn't want to be found she doesn't want to be found. There's nothing we can do but get on with our lives. Cal will come through this, as will the boys."

"And you'd say the same if it were one of the boys, would you?" asked Piper angrily. "Jesus, woman, call yourself a mother."

"I am a mother, Piper, and do you know what one of the great skills of motherhood is?" She hugged her arms, her hair curling about her temples in the stray breaths of the evening winds. "Adaptability."

"Well, I made my mind up there and then," said my great-aunt much later. "The next day I went to find Jess's parents. His father was upset, as you can imagine, and his mother— well, she was always a bit fragile if you know what I mean, but they told me everything they could think of. Apparently Jess had written to them telling them he was happy and he was planning to marry Julia and that they would have some special news for them soon but not yet. He didn't say where they were, but he hoped when he'd made it big to have his parents come up and stay with them, and by then no one would think about how it all started. He also added as a postscript, to say sorry to Caroline."

"Thoughtful, isn't he?" his mother had said. Piper had kept her counsel at this.

Then a few weeks later she came down the stairs at break-fast carrying a large brown suitcase and told her brother she was going on a holiday.

"Are you nuts?" Cal asked. "Harvest's due to start soon. We need all the hands we can get. And who's going to do the books and balance the ledgers?"

Piper laid a small piece of paper with the name of a respectable firm of accountants on the table.

"It's about time we started using proper businessmen," she said. "You know the accounts are just growing and growing. We need shrewd investors and people who can manage this thing for us properly. Besides," she added firmly, "I haven't had a holiday in I'm ashamed to say how long, Cal, and I'm not asking, I'm telling. I hope to be back in a month."

"A month!" Cal exclaimed. "Jesus…" And he went to the sideboard and took out a bottle of whiskey.

"No," said his sister, swiping the bottle from his hands. "Christ, Cal." And then because she could think of nothing else suitable to add, she said, "Grow up."

It took her three weeks to find them. She had gone to Sacramento, where a friend of Jess's lived, and she'd been given his telephone number by his parents. He had balked a bit when he had seen Piper on his doorstep, but he had given her Jess's forwarding address, which had led her to the fifth floor in a block of apartments in L.A. where she had found her niece, who opened the door with its peeling paint, in nothing but Jess's oversize Des Moines Demons T-shirt.

The place was furnished but shabby and there had been nothing to offer her aunt in the way of refreshment but cupcakes.

"Is this really how you live, Julia? Doesn't Jess mind?" Piper had asked, fingering the cupcake with trepidation.

"No, no, he thinks it's all romantic, like we're heroes in some novel. And he thinks having cupcakes for breakfast is really sweet," Julia had said, shaking out her hair. "I think I'm going to dye my hair, you know? Blond like all California girls. Get rid of that lingering farm trace once and for all."

"So there's nothing I can do to persuade you to come home?" said Piper, crestfallen.

"Why would I come back? I'm never coming back. Daddy doesn't want to know about Jess and I can't stand that bitch any—"

"Julia, please." Despite her feelings for my grandmother, Piper's sense of propriety prevailed. Julia shrugged.

"So you will marry?" Piper asked softly.

"Done and dusted," said Julia, fingering the gold-plated band on her ring finger.

"We're going to have a honeymoon once Jess gets set up. We'll go traveling all over once he starts getting gigs. It'll be so cool."

"And in the meantime, what'll you do for money?"

"Oh…" She eyed her aunt carefully for a minute and then shrugged. "I figured that out before I left. Besides Jess's uncle got him a job in the studio helping out the sound technicians. Jess kinda hates it." She laughed. "He doesn't get to do much but lug around amps all day, but it's fine—he's going places. I know it. Next time you see him, his face will be on a billboard."

"And is there…?" Piper's eyes fell to Julia's stomach. "Is there nothing else?"

"I thought there was," said Julia after a pause. "But the doctor says no. There will be soon and it doesn't matter. We married for love." She bit into a cupcake and the pink icing smudged across her nose. She giggled. "And cupcakes. He just loves my cupcakes."

Piper didn't tell Cal she'd been to see Julia, although she saw Lavinia watch her eagle-eyed all through dinner when she came home. All she did say was that she'd received a letter from Julia telling her that she was married and that Jess had gotten a job. Cal had gone silent and then left the room.

"That must have been a great comfort, to know she was safe," said Lavinia.

"Isn't it to all of us?" challenged Piper.

"Of course," Lavinia replied, her head bent over her sewing. "So ingenious of her to know where to send it to you when you were away on holiday. She has powers of detection that not even I could have guessed at."

Piper excused herself from the company of her sister-in-law and followed in the wake of her brother up the stairs. And aside from a letter on Thanksgiving and a card at Christmas, Julia did not try to get in contact with them again.

And so they went on. For a year afterward the farm still prospered, my uncle still held the silk of Allie's hair in his hands on their secret afternoons, my father rode his chestnut mare through the neighboring fields and my grandfather began to reach out again for my grandmother as they lay together at night. He never mentioned his daughter.

And then over time, things returned to normal. My grandfather, from his grief at his eldest's departure, poured himself into the farm. He could barely be torn away from it. His every waking hour was concerned with its welfare and he urged and encouraged his sons to do the same. Once he turned to my father and uncle and picked up a clump of yellow earth. "Look," he said and he turned his face to the fields. "You can do anything with this if you nourish it, if you love it even. Make it soft with your care and it will yield so much for you." He took a satisfied breath and let the dust crumble in his hands. "It will always be here even after we are dead and gone. Land will always last." And so my father and uncle began to see Aurelia as more than just their home, but their birthright. They worked in the fields and watched with awe as the saplings of wheat grew under the toil of their calloused hands, and my grandfather saw the change in them and was proud.

"It's always been there," he told my grandmother one

night in bed. "It happened with me just the same around their age, though Theo's a bit younger."

"Blood will out," my grandmother said contentedly.

"Reminds me of me and Leo," he said to the ceiling. "How we used to be over the place." And a shadow passed over his eyes.

"Hush now," she said and put a hand on his chest. "No more about that."

My grandmother told me that for that year, she remembered her happiness as a vivid thing, almost in the same way as when she had first come to the farm with Ethan growing under her heart and her husband's hand in her own. She saw her husband and sons labor on the place with fervor and she was satisfied. She saw her future clearly as if it were written on the sky: how her family would grow and live here and marry and raise their own families on it. She saw how the people of the town now looked on her with new, if wary respect as tales of the farm's prosperity grew and at last the road was a smooth one on which all she had to do was travel.

She should have known better than to be so untroubled in her contentment. Even she would say as much in time.

It started with a phone call. My grandmother picked up and the line went dead. She looked at the receiver in bewilderment and then set it on its rest. Then the next day it happened again, except this time my father answered. He was sweating from target practice with his father, who was teaching him to shoot beer cans with his rifle on the fence near the rose garden. His manner was abrupt because Ethan had beaten him in shooting more targets, but his irritation increased when the line again cut off after a few seconds. He opened the larder and started to slice himself a hunk of bread, which he ripped apart in his teeth, when Piper came into the kitchen and raised an eyebrow at his feral state.

"Get a plate for that, Theo," she said.

"Fine," he said and pulled one from the cupboard.

"You all right?"

"Yeah," my father said. "Just...what's the point in phoning someone if all you're going to do is hang up?"

"I don't know, Theo, that's strange behavior indeed."

"I'll say," he said. "Going to watch *Dragnet*." And he went into the living room.

But his words had an effect on my aunt and when she casually mentioned the incident to my grandmother, who then told her of her own experience the day before, she felt a sense of uneasiness make the back of her neck prickle.

"If it weren't for the farm and the business I would have told Cal to make sure that our phone number was unlisted," my grandmother said as she polished the rosewood desk.

My great-aunt lingered around the house waiting, for what she did not know exactly, but her instincts were telling her to do so and my great-aunt was always a firm believer in instincts.

And then sometime after lunch not two days later when she was alone, the phone rang and she answered it. This time the person on the other end spoke, and when Piper heard who it was a wild joy broke through her, and without meaning to she began to laugh.

One day Piper came to her brother in the barn where he was conversing with his foreman. She drew him aside and said, "Cal, I want you to take me to lunch in town, I have some business to discuss with you."

"Lunch? What's wrong with home? There's still some of

that beef from yesterday Lavinia cooked. You could make a stew or something."

"You're not listening to me, Cal. I don't want to cook, I want to be treated. We have some things to discuss about the hog operation and for once I'd like it to be somewhere nice with good food where I don't have to wash up afterward."

Cal stared at his sister and after a moment he shook his head.

"All right then, be ready in half an hour."

"Hmm." Piper sniffed. "Best if you bathe first."

Piper decided to drive, but as they turned off Highway 5 and began to get onto the main road that led to the opposite county, Cal shifted in his seat. Then when she parked outside a motel and turned off the engine, he stared at his sister, who was looking at him with a hardness he had not seen in a very long time.

If you were passing by the red pickup truck, you would have seen through the semi-opaqueness of the window the flailing arms and stabbing fingers of two people in the heat of an argument. If you were of an inquisitive, prying mind and had stayed, you would have seen that this tug-of-war took over half an hour before it was resolved. Then you would have seen a tall woman with graying brown hair get out of the car and slam the door before going toward the motel and knocking on the door of one of the rooms. You would have seen the door pull back, but whoever opened it would have been obscured as they stood behind it. You would have seen the woman enter and the man in the pickup truck go still, staring straight ahead at the window, on which its lace curtains would be pulled over by a female hand.

By now you would have thought, whatever the drama there was, was over and you may have gone on, but if you were to wait just ten minutes more, you would have seen the lumbering gait of the man as he stepped out of the pickup truck, walked to the door his companion had just entered through, before he paused and then began to pound his fist against the wood.

Lavinia was a woman who did not like secrets in her house. At least not those kept by other people. She knew when a secret was being kept from her and whenever she discovered this she would do her best to root it out. Secrets were weeds and she would not permit them to flourish unless they were guided by her hand and hers alone.

So when she observed Ethan's solitary walks in the afternoon, his quietness afterward, his susceptibility to dreaming, she did her best to coax the truth from him. The business of Julia had meant that for a long time her energies had been spent elsewhere and she admitted she had allowed her grasp on her eldest son to slip, so busy was she in dealing with Cal. But now that things had begun to settle, she could concentrate on her next battle—regaining neglected territory.

So one day when Ethan was late back from school she asked Theo where he was.

"Dunno. He doesn't tell me this stuff," said Theo with a shrug.

"Hmm," she said and, carrying a basketful of laundry, she went up to Ethan's room.

There she closed the door and carefully but methodically began to go through her son's things. She checked his drawers, she ran through his closet but she found nothing. She placed his folded clothes on the edge of his bed and went out of the room.

The next evening when once again Ethan came home late, Lavinia said to her son, "What's keeping you after school?"

Ethan had practiced this in his mind many times. He spun

her a story of an after-school science club that he had been afraid of telling anyone about, because people who went there were generally considered nerds and were beaten up.

"You think your father and I would beat you for joining a science club?" his mother asked, her eyes narrowing.

"No, it's just that…well, you might mention it to one of your friends and if they mention it to their kids then they'll tell everyone at school and then well…" He tailed off with an emotional flourish. Lavinia could not suppress her feeling of pride and then irritation that he should dare use the instruments she had taught him against her.

"Very well then," she said. "I won't tell your father."

Ethan practically beamed at her before dashing off. She looked after him and it was then she began to worry about exactly how her son had managed to acquire a secret this important, of which she still had no clue.

She watched him, biding her time until one day, as she went down to the barn before dinner to call after Cal, she found that not only had her husband gone out without telling her, but that her eldest son was walking out of the barn, his arms swinging.

"What were you doing in there?" his mother asked.

"Oh." Ethan saw his mother and colored. She observed this with icy disdain.

"I…uh…I just, I was doing some chores for Pa before I came in. I don't want to fall behind what with the club after school and then he might start asking questions about why I'm not keeping up with things at home, which wouldn't be good. Anyway," he added cheerfully, "I'm done now. You coming back?"

Lavinia looked over the top of his head to the barn. Out of the corner of her eye she saw him fidget.

"Of course," she replied, and they walked back together.

Half an hour later, she, Theo and Ethan were gathered at the table. The food was laid and the places set but neither Piper nor Cal were there.

"Well, really," she said after ten minutes. "They might have telephoned if they were going to be late. Did any of them say anything to either of you about something keeping them tonight?"

"No, Ma," chirped the boys simultaneously. "Not a thing."

Just then the front door opened. Lavinia could hear a crowd of footsteps.

"My God, about time. Food's getting cold, not that I guess that mattered to you or you would have had the decency to..."

Cal came in first followed by Piper. My grandmother stared from one face to another. Their expressions were alien to her in a way that made her fingers clasp the edge of the table. And then Piper moved aside and at first all she saw was a halo of cropped blond hair.

For a moment no one could speak, but then quite unexpectedly Theo leapt from his seat and threw himself into the arms of his sister.

"Julia!" he exclaimed.

Ethan got up and went to his sister, who smiled and put a hand on his shoulder.

"You're so tall," she said to him.

Lavinia looked at each of them. She saw her husband and sister-in-law gaze at her sons in happiness; she saw her step-daughter standing in the doorway and then finally she saw the suitcases by her feet.

"Aren't you going to say anything, honey?" asked Cal, staring at his wife. But she was not looking at him, she was staring hard into the face of a ghost.

"You're back then?" she somehow managed to ask.

"Of course—" and the ghost became flesh and laughed "—I'm home."

After I telephoned the lawyers to let them know I was in town I borrowed Jane's car and went for a drive. I knew where I was going, as did she, because she paused before dropping the car keys into my hand.

"Be safe," she called after me.

It was easy, my hands were on autopilot. I followed the route, wondering at first if perhaps I may have forgotten, but it was like I was being led by an invisible thread that pulled me back along the streets and roads of my childhood through the familiar lanes, past the fences I would jump in my youth and along the fields I had driven past, run through, laughed in.

When I came to the fork in the road, the trees lining it either side were still just as tall and verdant in the flesh as they had been in memory. I stopped. Just a little farther, I thought. Just a little more. My foot hovered above the gas pedal, my fingers clutched the wheel. The minutes dissolved and then suddenly the clouds broke with rain.

Beside me something shifted, and out of the corner of my eye I saw him pull a cigarette from his mouth and blow a funnel of smoke from his lips.

"Miss me?" he asked. I started to shake.

"Always," he answered for me and smiled.

No one noticed that my grandmother did not speak at dinner except for Piper, but she did not draw attention to it. Lavinia merely sat as the torrent of conversation and questions circled around her like a fog that would not lift.

Julia, the new Julia, thinner with blond frosted hair and

pink lipstick, told them how she had lived with Jess in California and for a while things had been really good. He had even started playing gigs in bars in the evenings and they had thought it was only a matter of time before things improved.

But they did not. Jess's uncle was arrested on charges of embezzlement from the studio: several bands were suing him individually. He was bankrupted and disgraced. As his relative, Jess immediately lost his job.

"So unfair," said Julia, shaking her head. "I mean Jess had nothing to do with it. He isn't smart enough to embezzle anybody. I guess he was just tainted by association. Well, that's when things really started to go wrong."

Jess went through a "black cloud," as Julia described it. He couldn't eat or sleep; he missed some gigs and was thrown out of a club for turning up drunk and throwing up on an audience member. He tried to hold down a series of jobs but he hated them. All he wanted was to be a musician but nothing seemed to be happening. And then one night he met a man in a bar who needed a bassist.

"Jess has always been a front man, but at that point anything musical would have done, so he thought why not? Thing was, they were going to go touring across the west coast in this guy's van. It seemed like a great chance and we had Jess's car so we could go with them."

Except the places they played in were holes and the band members were on drugs or alcohol or both. One of them made a pass at Julia and Jess broke his nose. That was it: he was slung out of the band in Portland, Oregon, with only twenty-two dollars and half a tank of gas. They went to a motel and Jess had lain down on the bed and stared into space for six hours.

"He was so lost, he couldn't see his way out and all I kept thinking was how much I wanted to come home."

So Julia called home, and when Piper answered she convinced her to wire her some money for two plane tickets. Piper agreed. At first, Julia said, she was afraid that Cal wouldn't forgive her, but then Piper talked to him and he came to see her at the motel she was staying in.

"And the second we saw each other it was like…it was just like at the hospital. You coming to save me all over again." And she smiled at her father, who held her hand.

"I know it's what your mother would have wanted had she lived," he answered.

"So where's Jess?" asked Theo.

"He's with his parents for now," said Julia airily. "He wasn't sure about coming over until…well, he thought this should be a family thing and I agreed. It's so good to be back in a nice house with everyone." She smiled around the table until her eyes rested on Lavinia. Turning to her father she put a hand on his arm and said, "I know I was stupid and young but I've been through… We—Jess and me—have been through so much. We were so broke and things were really hard. We just want to be somewhere safe and happy. And I've told him so much about this place, so much, I know he'd love it here just as much as I do."

"Well, we'll talk on that later," said Cal as he patted her hand. Julia's mouth dropped, but she sighed and then rested her head on his shoulder.

"You're right. We can deal with all of that later."

And Cal bent down and kissed the top of her hair.

That night when everyone was asleep, Lavinia put on her shawl and went out of the house. She walked the trail of the land until she got to the barn and sat down heavily on one of the straw bales. She could not sleep, even though her body was weary and her mind would not stop, though she was sick of her thoughts.

She removed the shawl and rocked her body back and forth, clenching her fingers into her arms until from somewhere deep inside a howl of rage emerged. She started up and beat her fists against the wood of the barn walls, screaming and spitting as all her hate burst its banks and overwhelmed her. Her fingernails scraped splinters into the flesh of her cuticles but she felt no pain. Eventually she sank to the floor sobbing in outrage, until disgusted, she clamped a hand to her mouth and sat there curled like a stricken fetus waiting for her monsters to be shut up in their cages once more.

After a long time she became very still. She sat there, overwhelmed, looking without seeing until her eyes sharpened into focus. On the floor, peeking from under the straw in the corner that she had kicked and loosened in her fury, she saw a flurry of white. She moved the straw away with her hands and groped under it until she found herself pulling out a small stack of papers. In the dark she peered at it until she stood up and went outside and held them up to the light from the moon.

She recognized what they were at once and she drew the papers into her chest. She held on to them until she was home and in the light of the kitchen she read the declarations of love from Alison Lomax to her eldest son, her blood smearing across the sheets as she turned each page.

In the morning, the foreman saw the small streaks of blood on the barn walls and was puzzled. But then he took a sponge and a pail of water and in a few minutes the traces of blood were gone. When he mentioned it, no one had any idea how the blood had gotten there and as there was no sign of injury to either his men or their animals, he had forgotten it by the end of the day.

8

SOME THINGS WERE PLANNED AND OF COURSE
some things were not. Opportunities presented themselves
all ripe for advantage, if you had the inclination and the will.

Who knows what path we would have taken if she had let
them carry on as they had? Perhaps some things that eventually happened would have done so anyway; all the key players
would still have been the same. But then again, maybe not.

It is this hypothetical that haunts me in the waning hours
when my mind bends only to the one road leading to the
past. Or the past that could have been.

I wonder if my aunt and uncle would have felt the same?
If years later they, too, had lain in their beds and pored over
the acts that led them to their present and how different
it was from how they had once imagined it to be. I know
what it's like, that incessant need for retrospect. Twisting
your body back and forth, hoping that in doing so what lies
before you will twist with it and change. It's so compelling

and like all compulsions a slow poison, so that before you know it, you've allowed what destroyed you once, to destroy you twice.

My father said that as a boy, because his windows faced toward the east, he was always woken at dawn by the sun lighting up his room in a rush of white fire. He would rise out of bed and go to the window and look out, as he stretched, into the distance of blue sky, yellow stalks and red barn. As he did, he knew that one day when he was a man he would go out among those things and live and work there until the sun dipped below the horizon and the world turned to dark. It was a foregone conclusion. For most people who were brought up on farms in those days it was a logical step that the land that had sustained them as a child would also be the source of their revenue and employment as an adult. It was second nature—and only brought them trouble when it was questioned. Depending on the farm, they counted themselves lucky.

But not so for Jess Thorne. Jess had lived in a single-story house a few blocks from Main Street. His father was a mechanic and his mother a homemaker. His whole life he had dreamed of getting away from them, and from what people said of him, his guitar became a ticket on which all his hopes and expectations were based. So when he came back and stayed in their house and slept in his own bed while his wife slept in hers miles across town on a farm, I can imagine how he would have felt like a failure. And worst of all, how everyone around him was probably thinking the same thing.

Jess had tried California: he had had so many hopes when he got out there, but everything had turned sour almost from the start. When you look at what happened to him, it seems that as soon as he gained some distance from the one place he thought had been holding him back, he seemed to move further away from the only thing he actually wanted. There had been some moments of relief: I would come to learn that although he had been angry at first, finding out that Julia wasn't pregnant after all became something of a blessing. Their lives had turned into such a mess that I doubt he could have handled a kid on top of it. But the question he must have been faced with on his return was what to do next. They couldn't go back, but they couldn't stay as they were. All Jess knew was music and Iowa and he had failed at the first and was out of place in the latter.

Jess had dreams: everyone knew that, but it was Julia who determined their future. When she entered his bedroom that morning she found him lying on his bed as lost and bewildered as he had been in a motel room in Portland. She knew there would be protestations when she told him of her plans for him, there always were. But he could think of no alternative and their situation made him feel as if he had no choice. This was a lie, but Jess was afraid of the hard thing. But that didn't matter to Julia, as long as she got her way. And this was how, despite his childhood dream, Jess Thorne came to live and work on Aurelia.

My grandfather commissioned the building of a house for them on the farm after a month. He welcomed Jess over the threshold into the main house while it was being completed and gripped his hand so tightly that a muscle in Jess's cheek quailed.

Lavinia watched the erection of the house's foundations and Julia's trips to stores nearby with her aunt and she said nothing. Not when Julia showcased the new china she'd bought on their dining table; not when Cal complained at night of how unsuitable Jess was for farming, yet still insisted that his foreman find him a good position among his hands;

not even when as a present for coming back he bought Julia a white Thoroughbred from Kansas who pawed the earth when he came out of his horse box and she, laughing, threw her arms around her father's neck as Jess summoned a smile to his mouth.

She was as silent as anyone had ever known her to be. She said nothing, only watched and waited.

Though it was bound to happen eventually, Ethan was still afraid when he suspected that Allie had begun to tell people about their relationship. He noticed the way people began to look at him in class, the newfound respect that lit up the boys' expressions when they passed him by and the curiosity of the girls. But when Jimmy Galloway slammed a ball with both force and fury into his face during a game of dodgeball, he bit the bullet and asked her outright if she had said anything.

She didn't seem contrite. If anything, she was spoiling for an argument.

"I'm sick of lying to everyone. It's ridiculous. It's not like I have anything to feel ashamed of," she said, and stared at him, challenging him to contradict her.

But when she asked him over to her house for dinner he really grew afraid. Drawing her aside under the bleachers during recess he tried to voice his concerns, but she wouldn't listen.

"Mom's making a pot roast," was all she would say in reply.

So with that he was forced to tell his parents that he had been invited to her house for dinner. He mumbled it quickly between forkfuls of chicken salad. Cal had winked at his wife over the heads of his children. She didn't wink back.

Piper ironed his shirts and drove him to Allie's home and,

over the polished woods of her living room, he watched her with blue ribbons in her hair as she sat in a cream dress next to her father and his heart swelled with love. He was so busy enjoying himself he didn't realize how happy he was until he came into the hall of his own home and caught his mother coming out of the kitchen bearing a basketful of laundry. At the expression on her face he felt the breath steal out of him.

"Did you have a good time?" asked his mother.

"Of course," he said, and then winced.

"Your father and I would like to return the favor," she said. "Could you invite that girl over next week for Sunday lunch?"

"What? I mean...pardon, ma'am?"

"Are you deaf now, Ethan?" she snapped.

He recoiled.

"Do as I ask."

The next Sunday, promptly at one, Allie arrived at Ethan's home. She marveled as she stepped inside.

"I always wanted to come here," she whispered. "Everyone said how beautiful your home was but—" She stopped when my grandmother and grandfather came into the hall.

At the table, my father sat in his chair, concentrating solely on wolfing down everything placed in front of him. Sunday lunch was his favorite meal and to give credit to my grandmother, even in my day she did it with style. There were always mounds of creamy mashed potatoes, steamed vegetables, roasted parsnips, a roast meat and roast potatoes cooked in butter and rosemary. It was the one meal he lived for and the only one you could never have any hope of having a conversation with him during, but for once Theo was not alone in his silence. My grandmother was noticeably reticent throughout, while my grandfather peppered Allie

with questions and stories and feeble jokes that made my
father choke on his crackling.

Afterward, when they were alone, Allie would say how
much she liked my grandfather. Ethan would frown at his
shoe and mutter something about how embarrassing he was.

"Embarrassing? At least he made an effort with me," she
snorted.

"What do you mean?" Ethan asked.

"Oh nothing, just..." Allie stopped and searched his face
but Ethan, as ever, was a blank.

"Nothing," she finished.

Jess and Julia moved into their home on the farm in 1964.
It was a square, redbrick building with white shutters. Julia
had had it fashioned that way and when Cal saw it he commented on how much it looked like their first home in Oregon. But when he looked over at his wife he let his voice
trail off into nothing.

Jess started to help on the land and he soon became pretty
good at it. Well, as my father would say, good enough not
to warrant any complaints but never good enough to elicit
any praise from my grandfather. While no one would ever
say as much, Cal could never quite get over how Jess had
come into the family. He had rewritten that entire event so
that even though it had been Julia who had run away and
not contacted him for over a year, Jess was somehow still to
blame. In my grandfather's mind he had driven her to it, it
was he who led her on, and Cal saw his efforts on the farm
not as an example of his honest nature, but as a product of
his guilt.

Julia, however, was once more his golden girl. It was as
if the shock of her elopement and their year apart made
him need to draw her even closer. He would not talk of

her elopement except to criticize Jess, and Julia let it be that way. She would walk into the white house from her own and sit at the table utterly comfortable with her surroundings, despite the hard hatred of her stepmother whenever she glimpsed her stepdaughter curled up on her settee, or baking Cal a pie using the contents from her fridge. Julia treated all as her rightful domain; the shock of California and being ripped from her comfort zone to a level of living she had only encountered once before, when she was too young to remember it fully, had taught her a valuable lesson. It was better to be queen in her small sphere, than insignificant in a larger one.

Of course, my grandmother noticed.

She took every one of these occurrences and built them up as slights to be recorded and remembered. She dipped into her legendary reserves of patience and let them feed her, rationing them for a long period of endurance. How long this would have to continue, she did not know, but a few weeks before Thanksgiving she got her answer.

Julia came into the living room, Jess's arms shyly wrapped around her, and blushed with her eyes, though her skin remained smooth alabaster, before announcing that she was pregnant.

And a year later, on the 11th of July 1965, Cal Jr., my cousin, was born. Julia said she named him after my grandfather so that he would be as strong, as kind, as devoted. My grandfather cried there and then in the hospital room. Tears of pride coursed down his rough cheeks as he held his first grandson in his arms, utterly unashamed.

And so my grandmother drew herself inward, made a pact with her soul and stretched out her already thinning patience a little bit more.

★ ★ ★

Did Cal notice that she was not happy? Not likely, she would say later. She was too good at hiding it. Silence in her marriage was not a weapon; it was a source of respite. The quieter she was, the more secure Cal felt in his emotions. Instead of her pouring all her feelings and desires into him, he began to do it instead. Now it was he who would lie in bed next to her and tell her of his plans for the future, his ideas for the farm, his wishes for his family.

It was he who told her that whenever Ethan talked about his future, he always mentioned Allie's name. It was he who told her that he would have to rewrite his will now that Cal Jr. was born and it was he who told her the most damning thing of all. He told her that he wanted to make peace with his brother.

At this, Lavinia sat upright.

"What on earth makes you think he'll listen to you? He hasn't spoken to you in nearly twenty years, Cal—he's never even tried to get back in contact with you."

"I know that—don't you think I know that?"

"So *why*?" She rang out the last word in repressed fury. Cal did not look at her.

"Because if it had been the other way around, wouldn't I have done the same? Pa gave me the land but his wishes could only have been carried out if I took it. And I wanted to take it even though I knew it shouldn't have been mine."

"So what?" his wife sneered. "You think by telling him this it'll make a difference to him? You think he'll forgive you, do you?"

"No, I don't, but I think it's about time I did the decent thing and asked."

Lavinia stared at her husband, unseeing, unbelieving. "What has gotten into you?" she said at last.

"I've just been thinking these things over, that's all. Family is family. I realized ain't nothing more important. Nothing."

And he leaned over and turned out the light.

He did not speak about this with her again. Though she probed him, he became unusually reticent. He had seen her disapproval, perhaps even guessed at her outrage, and so had drawn inward, closing his mouth and thoughts to her. It drove her mad.

"Why are you shutting me out?" she had raged at him one night when they were alone. "I'm your wife."

"Do you tell me everything?" Cal had replied. "Of course you don't, nor would you if I asked."

"Someone's put you up to this. Someone's been turning you against me."

"Lavinia, you're being hysterical."

"I'm not. You don't think I don't know what goes on in my own house? A husband and wife shouldn't have secrets."

"You didn't always used to think that way," Cal said softly.

"Wh-what do you mean?" my grandmother asked, disconcerted.

"I mean…well—Lou," he said and then looked her in the eye. It was dark and my grandmother said later on, that it was just as well, because in that moment she let her face reveal how much she hated him.

They did not speak much after that. Not for a while. Cal knew he had overstepped a boundary, but an innate stubbornness would not let him come to his wife and admit his error. Though he did not know it, it would not have mattered to her if he had. My grandmother later told me that after that night, she knew Cal was not to be trusted. He was too malleable, too easily swayed. His thoughts were only what other people put there, his views what others before him had expressed. His only autonomy was in choosing his influence, but there was no doubt in her mind that he was merely a product of that influence. She knew those words were not Cal's words, such thoughts would never occur to him, but she did not know whom to fully attribute them to and this worried her greatly. *There are too many snakes in my house,* she thought.

One Saturday morning she came down the stairs to find her family at the breakfast table. Cal had already gone out to work but Ethan was there, hunched over his cornflakes, Theo over his waffles. Piper was standing next to Julia, who was balancing Cal Jr. on her hip, and the two women leaned against the oven, each of them clutching a cup of coffee. Everyone glanced up as she walked in.

"Good morning," Piper said.

Lavinia stared at her family and saw all their dirty secrets and she made herself a promise.

"What was it, Grandma?" I asked. "What did you promise yourself?"

She laughed. "Never you mind, girl, never you mind. All you need to know is, I kept my promise. It took a while but I kept it all the same. That's the thing about me, girl. People always thought different but I can be true to my word." I had folded the blanket up under her hands.

"I don't doubt it, Grandma," I had said.

I suppose the time has come to talk about my eldest cousin. It is hard to think of him as an innocent child. In my memory there is no room for him in this light. I cannot see him as the pictures have shown—as a smiling baby in a blue onesie, or a curly red-haired child in jeans riding up on the thresher with my grandfather. An innocent, a blank with none of the monstrous imprint that he demonstrated when I came to know him, he existed at this stage as a source of joy, and a hope for the future. My uncle was eighteen and my father was sixteen when he was born. They played with him, they threw him up in the air and caught him again to make him laugh. His father, Jess, though intimidated by being wholly responsible for another life on this planet, was attentive and tender in the early years and Julia played the role of doting mother to outsiders, though history has it that Piper was more responsible for the actual practicalities of child rearing. As for my grandfather…well, my grandfather spoiled him rotten. He adored him, and Julia even more now for making him.

What did my grandmother make of him initially? What else could she make of the firstborn son of Julia but another rival? Most of all she saw him as an unstable catalyst. With his birth the dynamics in her family had changed in a way she did not like. Now Cal was hell-bent on reconciling with his brother and to her that meant that, if it went according to plan, Leo and his family could easily troop back on the farm and start taking an active hand in it. He had had a share in the farm and its profits all these years but aside from a check sent to his place in Indiana quarterly, Leo had never tried to have anything to do with Aurelia, and Lavinia wanted it to stay that way. But Cal had other ideas. And now with the arrival of my cousin he seemed to have finally found an incentive to bring those ideas to fruition. She saw her plans fray, the edges begin to disintegrate, and she watched on, finding herself for once unable to stop the slow descent with my cousin as its champion. Through him, her husband suddenly found the driving force he had been lacking. He bounced him on his thigh and stroked his face with his finger and saw in his grandson's youth all the possibilities he had dreamed of creeping up on him and he was energized.

He had big plans.

He wasn't the only one.

It is at this point in the fall of that year, a few months after Cal Jr. was born, that Georgia-May Healy enters our story. Her father bought the old McGregor place next to our farm. It was a good bit of land that boasted a successful dairy operation, one of the few farms around us to do so. When her family moved in, Lavinia and Piper went over to the farm to pay their respects. They were welcomed over the threshold by Georgia-May's mother, who took their offers of sweet wine and apple cinnamon pie with both relief and gratitude.

They went into the kitchen, the only room in the house that was fully unpacked, and as they sat over the red-checked tablecloth and sipped their iced tea, my grandmother cast her eye over the daughter of her neighbor.

"How old are you, Georgia-May?" she asked over the rim of her cup.

"I'm nineteen, ma'am," replied the girl. A slip of a thing at that age, Georgia-May was a petite girl with pale blond hair and even paler skin. Translucent, my grandmother described her: a quality that would come to be a hindrance, as well as in the end perhaps something of a blessing.

"I got a son near your age," my grandmother said when she saw Georgia-May. "He's in his last year at school. His name's Ethan."

"Oh," said Georgia-May, lowering her voice slightly.

"Georgia-May's going to be a teacher," said her mother, who smiled proudly.

"Ethan will be a farmer," replied my grandmother. "When you're moved in you should come over and meet him," she said, looking at Georgia-May, whose skin blushed a deep crimson so that her face slipped into fire before the color dissipated. My grandmother looked after her with renewed interest. Piper flicked her a look beneath her lashes.

On the way back my grandmother thought aloud: "Shy little creature, isn't she?"

"Who?" asked Piper.

"Georgia-May."

"Oh, I guess."

"Sweet, though, but very shy." She stopped and cast an eye around the Healys' land.

"I wonder what they'll make of the place," she said. "Let's give them a year."

"To do what?" asked Piper, but my grandmother had already started to walk ahead and when Piper caught her up, she did not answer her.

Things carried on as much as before. The beginning of 1966 was a quiet period. Cal Sr. went away on a trip for two weeks without telling Lavinia where he was going or leaving her with a forwarding number, but she bit back her anger and did not question him when he left, or when he came home one night looking tired and asking for supper, which he only picked over. She suspected that he had gone to see his brother, but from both his heavy silence and snappish manner with Piper, she guessed it had not been successful.

She went over to the Healys' farm often now and acquainted herself readily with Georgia-May's mother. Both my grandfather and great-aunt were shocked. My grandmother had no real friends nor had she ever shown a desire for them, but she soon became a regular fixture at the Healys and vice versa. My father said that he would enter the living room and find the two women sitting there, barely speaking, just bent over their sewing or reading, and he would wonder why they needed each other for company when together they were still so solitary. Maybe that was part of the attraction, but only on Mrs. Healy's side. No, my grandmother had other reasons for cultivating a relationship with her neighbors.

"Who are you taking to your senior prom?" she asked Ethan as she sat in her garden, three months after the Healys had moved in. He lay out on the grass next to my father, who was ripping blades to bits in his hands.

Ethan peered at her, though he had to squint because the sun was in his eye.

"Allie, of course," he said suspiciously.

"Well, not 'of course.' What if she didn't want to go or she fell ill, what then?"

"Then I wouldn't go."

There was a pause.

"I think that's very foolish of you," his mother said softly.

"Well, it's my choice, isn't it?" he asked angrily, brushing a fly from his arm.

"Don't raise your voice to me."

"I wasn't raising my voice."

"Yes, you were."

Ethan sank back into a gloomy silence. My father turned over onto his back and put his arms over his eyes.

"I don't know why you're so sensitive about such issues, Ethan. It's not healthy the way you're so defensive about that girl. I hope you don't act the same way around her. It would make it very difficult for her to talk to you about anything, especially if it were something you might find unpleasant. Not a particularly nice footing to be on in a relationship, I can tell you."

"I didn't ask for any advice from you," Ethan said between gritted teeth. His mother flashed him a look but let it pass. My father rolled over onto his side and closed his eyes.

"Is she going to college?" asked Lavinia.

"Who?"

"Alison."

Ethan frowned against the sun and then raised himself up. "I hadn't...I mean— Why would she?"

"Well, surely it's one of those conversations the two of you would need to have, unless...she didn't feel that it was a conversation she could have with you." She watched the impassive expression of her son. She gave a snort. "Come now, Ethan. She's a smart girl, isn't she? She lives in town, not on a farm, and she's got to do something with her life. The Healy girl—Georgia-May—is going to become a teacher, you know? Enrolling in the local community college. But Alison never did strike me as a girl who would be content with something like that."

Ethan stood up so quickly his face blocked the sun over his mother and all she could see was a hole of shadow where his face would have been.

"You don't know anything about anything."

"Ethan, this is highly dramatic, don't you think?"

"You don't know her, you've no right to—to..."

"To what?" Lavinia put down her book and cocked her head to the side, seemingly confused. "I don't understand this. These are perfectly sensible questions. Questions that if you have failed to ask will still need answering, though by that time the damage may have been done. With whom are you angry? Me, because I thought of it, you, because you didn't, or—" she leaned forward "—her for causing them in the first place?"

My father had turned over now and could only see the

sandaled foot of his mother behind the heaving form of his brother. Her voice flowed out over the winds rippling through the garden.

"Did you think because college wasn't something that applied to you that it also wouldn't to her?"

"You don't know anything," he repeated again. "We don't talk about that stuff. There's no need," he added half-defiantly.

"Well, that's good," said my grandmother. "I know how much you hate surprises."

They glared at each other before my uncle moved past her to go up the porch steps and inside the house.

"I might go to college," my father said after a minute. His mother peered at him as if she had forgotten he was still there.

"If you and Dad think it's the right thing to do, ma'am," he added quickly.

"What would you study, Theo?" she asked with a smile playing at her mouth.

"Dunno yet, but—" and he seemed to struggle with himself but then he pressed on regardless "—but I wanna see things. In the world, I mean. There must be more than just this," he concluded and threw his arm out at the lawn.

"Yes, there are, Theo, but that doesn't mean they are as good. And if you want to go to college you're going to have to give your pa a better excuse than just wanting to see the world."

My father leaned back, heavy thoughts furrowing his brow. My grandmother went back to her book.

Days later Ethan borrowed the truck and went into town. He spent four hours there and when he came back he looked flushed but content. Then one evening he drew his father aside. Though behind the closed door of the study their soft baritones could be heard through the wood, try as she might my grandmother could not decipher what they were saying…but she could guess. That night while her husband slept peacefully next to her, my grandmother stayed awake and plotted. She went through all the scenarios, all their likely conclusions and also their possibilities. It was nearly dawn before she was finished, gently closing her eyes as Cal stretched beside her and roused himself from sleep.

She did not ask questions, she did not pry; she let it come to her.

She observed my uncle anxiously, wondering when he would do it and then when she saw him come down the stairs not a week later, wearing a freshly laundered shirt, with his hair combed back, she knew.

My uncle went to the house of Alison Lomax, where he found her in her living room, reading a magazine while lying on her stomach.

"Is there somewhere private where we can go?" he asked her.

She took him to the garden, where they sat on her father's handmade bench. Leaning into her, Ethan took the ring box out of his pocket. The weight of it settled naturally on his palm as he watched her, though her face had been drained of all expression. As he looked at her, he was full of hope, delight and expectation and when he opened the box to reveal a single diamond dropped on a bed of white gold, he believed her acceptance was inevitable. Hadn't they already discussed this time and time again? Hadn't they planned their future together? Hadn't he dreamed of it for years, his mind pouring over the fantasies day and night: in times of despair when in need of hope, in moments of joy if only to exacerbate it; when bored, when wistful, when drunk with love and desire? He was a man now at eighteen. There was no need to wait any longer and after his discussion with his mother he realized that if he didn't act soon, life might get in the way.

Alison, I cannot blame you. You did not know, I think, the hold you had over Ethan Joshua Hathaway. You did not realize you were his star, shining out in the darkness to him: his only guide, without which he was lost.

The first my grandparents knew that anything was wrong was when they got a call at one-thirty in the morning. Cal answered, and afterward told his wife that Sheriff Patterson was coming to the house in ten minutes. She blinked at him—for a moment neither of them able to move—and then they got up, dressed and stole quietly down the stairs so as not to wake anybody and sat in the kitchen where they saw the sheriff's car's headlights cast white circles up the drive when he arrived. Cal opened the door before he had walked up the porch to knock.

He didn't bother with any preamble.

"It's Ethan," he said. "He's been in some trouble. It was Alison Lomax who called us. Told us that he had come over and apparently there was an incident. Told us she thought he might do something stupid. We just thought it was some lovers' tiff maybe, you know what the young-uns are like. Anyway, we kept an eye out and his truck was found in the ravine. He's at Mercy Hospital now, doctors say he's stable, but he looks worse than he is."

"What?" asked my grandmother. "How did this happen?"

"Your guess is as good as mine, Lavinia," he said. Patterson was a good friend of my grandfather's. "But when we got him to the hospital we called up the Lomaxes, told them we were going to need to talk to them about what happened. One of my boys went over there while I was still at the hospital. Told me that there had been some almighty row. Paul, her father—well, as one of my boys described it, his face looks like it met with a couple of fists. You need to come over and see your boy. I don't like what I'm hearing, Cal, not at all."

When they did they were met with a sorry sight that would keep my uncle in the hospital for weeks. Aside from a severe concussion, Ethan had broken three ribs, his leg in four places (with a metal rod in it to keep it together), his nose and two fingers on his right hand.

That would all mend, that was not what worried his parents. What hurt them was that he wouldn't speak. Not a sound came from his lips to tell them what happened. He was a wall of silence. But he was not the only one. When the sheriff came over again some time later, he told them that none of the Lomaxes would make a statement about what had happened at the house. The doctor who saw Paul told Patterson that whatever had happened, the attack was a brutal one, and judging by the cuts on Paul's knuckles, someone else was worse off, but no one would speak. Not when Patterson tried to grill Paul over his injuries, not when he asked his wife why she was shaking, not even when he saw Allie in her bedroom, her mother stealing into the room and curling an arm around the girl, who was bent over into her mother like she was five again, her hair spilling over her face revealing the red marks a tight grip had scored across her neck.

For an event with so great a need of an explanation, not one person involved could have been less forthcoming. Hatred hung in the air and yet they bound themselves together in their refusal to talk. Patterson couldn't understand it. Truth be told, even for a policeman with all his years of experience, it unnerved him.

"Well, it can't be anything to do with Ethe," protested Cal. "He adores Allie. He was even going to ask her to marry him." He glanced quickly at his wife. "He told me about it himself. He borrowed some money for a ring. They'd spoken about it before."

"I don't know, Cal," said Patterson. "It seems a lot more serious than just some proposal going wrong. There's bad business going on here."

"Ethan's suffering, too, you know," ventured Lavinia.

"That's what worries me," said Patterson.

Yet Ethan never spoke of it. Not a word or even a moan passed his lips. They took him home, with his broken bones plastered, and showed him to the study they had converted to a makeshift bedroom until he was more mobile. Even after countless one-sided arguments, pleas and recriminations, he would not speak and his father and mother raged as to why he had driven their truck through two roadside fences and crashed into a ravine. And why Alison's father had cut his knuckles on his cheekbones.

Desperate, Cal even went to the Lomaxes' house to enquire as to what had happened, but Alison would not see him and when her father answered, Cal could not conceal his horror at the mess of chartreuse and navy that swelled across the expanse of the man's face.

"Ask your son," Paul said, when my grandfather found his voice. "I'll not do his dirty work."

No one knew what had happened. My father tried talking to his brother, but it was no use—Ethan was closed to the world and he saw no reason why he should open up the connection again.

"Do you think he tried to kill himself?" Julia asked aloud one time. Cal turned in horror and stared openmouthed.

"Why the hell would he do that?"

"Maybe he was unhappy," said Julia and then as an aside added, "God knows we've all had that feeling in this house."

She went to her brother to try and talk to him as well, but she had no more luck than anyone else. She stared down at him and, running her hands through her dyed brittle hair, sighed and said, "You'll have to talk sometime, Ethe. If not to us then to the police."

The sheriff knew Cal well and he was as lenient as he could be, but even he began to run out of patience. "We need to talk to him," he said on Cal's porch a week after Ethan was discharged from hospital.

"He won't say anything," replied Lavinia. "He hasn't spoken since the crash."

"Doesn't matter, we need to hurry things along now. Alison's leaving for Georgia in a few days, we need to get everything about that night straight."

"What do you mean leaving?" my grandmother asked.

"She's going. Family are rushing her out quick sharp. Staying with some friend of the family down there 'til she starts college in the fall. Anyway she's not saying much, either, but we got to know. One of them will break soon, but without meaning to worry you, I think something pretty bad happened there."

He paused and looked out into the sun. "Look, if it were just a case of your son getting drunk and smashing himself up we could try to overlook it. Not like he's the first, but this is a bad business and I don't like bad businesses festering in my town." He spat on the ground and then changed tack. "Your boy, he was never prone to violent outbursts or nothing, was he?" he asked.

"'Course not," Cal shot back.

"Hmm, well—let's hope someone cracks soon," Patterson replied and he kicked a clump of dirt with his shoe.

Days passed. Both Piper and Lavinia tended to Ethan, even Julia began to help. Theo found he could not go in there and face the silent vacuum that had replaced his brother. He avoided that part of the house and though it was noticed, no one commented on it. Then in the second week of Ethan's silence my grandmother somehow contrived to find out the routine of Allie's mother and one afternoon she ambushed the woman as she searched for new bed linen in Kacey's department store.

"I have nothing to say to you," she said frostily, putting the linen back on the table.

"Please," Lavinia said, stepping in front of her. "Please, he won't speak. He won't tell us what happened. You must understand—"

"You ask for empathy for that—that—" Alison's mother broke off in disgust.

The two women faced each other, a silent battle raging in their faces.

"What did he do?" Lavinia finally asked.

In the middle of the night, Lavinia gently got out of bed so as not to wake Cal and crept downstairs to her son. He was wide-awake, staring into nothing when she opened the door.

Closing it behind her, she stepped into the room and approached the foot of his cot.

"I met Alison's mother in a department store today," she said. "I asked her what happened that night."

There was no flicker, no trace of life behind the glassy facade of his features.

She stretched out her hand and opened her palm.

"She gave me this to give back to you," she said and then paused for effect. "Was it because I asked if she were going to college that you decided to ask her to marry you? Did you really have no idea what she had planned or had you just not bothered to find out?"

Silence.

"It must have been a shock, I can understand that, but what you did, Ethan, or at least what you tried to do— Did you not know or just not care that her family were only a few rooms away? Or was that all part of it? Punishing her for her refusal of your proposal. Did you feel she had led you on? That she behaved like a little tease. I can imagine how you would have wondered if she could do this to you, what else she had done, but still…even I was shocked at your methods of retribution."

She dropped the engagement ring onto his lap.

"She won't talk. She's refusing to. They think—well, they think it's out of love or fear or maybe even both. She won't see anyone, has cut herself off from everybody. They think it's out of shame. Her mother said you've destroyed her. That must make you proud."

He dropped his gaze from the ceiling to her face.

"I will not speak of this to your father. Alison won't speak of it to the police. I will compose a story that you will tell to the sheriff by the end of the week. There will be no more room for these errors anymore, Ethan. I hope you unleashed your beasts to the full because that will have to last them a long time, do you hear me? I am not having you jeopardize everything I have worked for, because you can't control yourself. Have you any idea what your father would do if he knew? You'd never be able to get out of that bed again for a start."

She rubbed her hands together and then pulled at another blanket resting on a chair and shook it out to settle over him. His eyes were boring holes in her. Just before the blanket fell down, Ethan reached out and snatched the ring from his lap.

"If you want to take it back—to the jeweler's, I mean— you can," she said quietly as she smoothed the blanket out. "Or maybe not. Maybe you don't want to give it back. If that's the case it's okay." She leaned over him and stroked his hair. "You can always keep it to remember her by."

A few days later just like she said, Ethan made a report to the sheriff. Patterson then went, by all accounts to the Lomaxes' place, where he was finally permitted to see Allie. She sat across from him and listened to what Ethan had told him and at the end, all she had done was nod. Without waiting for the sheriff to speak again she had risen heavily and gingerly made her way upstairs.

Her mother had called out to her from the bottom and had pleaded with her "to see sense."

But she did not. And by the end of the month, she had left for Atlanta, Georgia.

My uncle gradually began to heal and a month after Allie's departure he finally spoke and asked my father to bring him a glass of iced tea. There was a general sigh of relief when my father reported this. They assumed that Ethan was getting better.

But he had changed, and though they only realized it gradually, they saw the ways in which he was different. He was solemn, quiet, prone to being alone even more now than before. He threw himself into working on the farm when he was well enough, but he had no passions, no notable pleasures. He seemed to view the world in a filter of gray but he did not complain. My father tried to talk to him, to cajole him, but my grandmother would catch him wheedling my uncle and she would draw him aside and tell him to leave well alone.

"I'm handling it," she'd say.

"But look at him," my father protested.

"It doesn't matter, leave it to me," she insisted before turning from him.

My father waited, but his brother made no progress toward being the boy he had grown up with. Something in him had broken and died.

From that time on Ethan refused to ever let another person mention Alison's name around him again, as his brother once learned to his cost.

Theo came home limping from the barn one afternoon holding his side while his face winced with pain, and his mother, noting what he told her, barely said a word as she bandaged him up.

"Now you'll know for next time," she'd said to him. "I told you—leave it to me."

Two days after I had arrived in Iowa, I sat in my makeshift bedroom on the window seat and hugging my legs, stared at the sky, which was black except for the moon burning a white hole among the clouds. I had forgotten the sky could look like that. In New York you are surrounded by so much electric light and neon you have no need to look up and seek the stars.

I thought how the moon would be shining on the husk that was now Aurelia. How its light would find the withered rose garden, the dead cornfields, the empty homes…

Its inhabitants are now scattered but I can still feel the pull of the farm, like an invisible cord routed around my navel. Whenever I feel like I am beginning to forget, it tugs ever so gently, making me wince with nostalgia. It is a constant throbbing ache, a wound that weeps beneath the hasty bandages I have pulled over it. It is a fight that will stay with me my whole life, but it is also one I know I will never win. By now, having lived with it for so long, I am scared of what I would be without it.

9

I LOOKED DOWN AT HER AS SHE FINISHED SPEAKING
and waited for her to continue but she turned her head from me and
faced the wall. For weeks I had debated telling Mom what was happening, what she was telling me, but I never did. I was afraid, both
of what Mom would do if she knew, and also what I would do if she
stopped. I longed to know the truth now, to fill in all the holes that
she had made, and she was the only one who could help me. At least
that was how I justified it to myself.

"Why did you do it?" I asked her.

Her breath rattled out of her throat.

"Because it was the only way to keep it. To make sure it went to
who it was supposed to."

"But she had just as much right, Grandma. It was just as much
her home."

"Oh, she didn't give that for the place, not a thing. She would
have run it into the ground, she didn't know anything about farming
and as for that husband of hers—he couldn't stand up to her. He was
so weak, always dreaming about being a musician, always hoping

*for that piece of luck that would swoop down and save him. Huh,
fool. Sweet dreaming fool." She turned to look at me and her eyes
were struggling to focus, but she battled on. "It was for the good of
the farm, for you, for all of us."*

"And Julia, Grandma? What about her?"

"Oh—" she waved a hand "—she never counted."

In 1968, my aunt cut her hair and wore it in a bob that
curled underneath her ears. She took to wearing the latest
fashion, like miniskirts, paisley prints and slim-fit pants. She
would totter around the farm looking completely out of place
as her son lagged behind her. She spent her days poring over
magazines, shopping, driving into town to look at more
shops and planning her next expedition. She hung around
her father's kitchen while Piper fed and played with her son
and she would stare out the window, absorbed in her own
mind.

It was around this time that she and Jess began to really
argue.

She would burst into my grandparents' home in the early
hours of the morning clutching Cal Jr.—who was half-asleep
on her shoulder—her hair askew, crying or raging or both, at
the ineptitude of her husband. No one ever knew what the
arguments were really about; Julia was never clear. Instead
she would list a damning indictment of Jess and all his faults,
starting with his ridiculous pipe dreams about being a musician. My grandmother noted with inner satisfaction that the
very trait that had allured her to Jess, had now become one
of his worst faults. Life is hard, isn't it, Julia? she thought.

In the end Jess would always come for her and there would
be tears and recriminations but they would eventually rec-
oncile. My grandfather scratched his head, unable to understand. "Why doesn't she just leave him?" he'd ask his wife

and sister. "She knows we'd take care of her and the baby. She knows it. She don't need him."

"She loves him, Cal," Piper would soothe, but Lavinia knew better. For once she could empathize with Julia; she knew why the girl brought these middle-of-the-night dramas into their home, why she stared out of windows, why she took to wearing daring hemlines and outrageous clothes.

"Oh, I knew, I knew what was really going on inside of her, but even I could not have seen where she would let it take her. Always surpassing expectations, that girl."

But she did not share these thoughts; she knew they would neither be welcomed nor listened to. But, to put it this way, whenever my grandmother went to Julia's redbrick house from then on, she would always inspect the kitchen windows for knife marks.

This part...well, this part is vague. I guess no one in my family really wanted to talk about it that much. It was seen for a long time as an embarrassing stain on a history that was already patchy. But due to the prosperity of the farm and its reputation, people were willing to, if not forgive, at least gloss over the murkier parts. So I will try to remember what I can and to make sure it is accurate, but even my grandmother was reluctant to speak of the finer details, unlike anything else before or since. I doubt it was out of any sense of propriety toward Julia, but rather because of what it did to my grandfather: something not even she expected, or could ever fully overcome.

Julia was twenty-five when it started. And though her name was mired with shame and disgrace all the years I grew up, I cannot help but pity her. Where was I at twenty-five? I was living in Italy in a rented apartment in Umbria that I shared with two English girls and a German boy. I was studying sculpture at the International School of Art; driving around the winding cobbled roads on my moped; eating in small cafés and for the first time in a long time, I felt my life was one long route of unencumbered possibility, at least in the daytime. At night, well that was a different story. I may not have been completely happy, but for all intents and purposes I was free. Julia did not even have that.

At twenty-five Julia had a three-year-old son and six–year-old marriage with a man she had probably never loved and had never really tried to. She woke up on the farm, she went to bed on the farm. She played the roles of wife and mother and knew that this was all there was for the next twenty-five years and the next lot after that. Though she tried, she could feel her life slipping away from her—the promise, the dreams all bursting in midair and settling down on her as an aging farm wife. This was never what she had had in mind.

So she became restless. And the town she was raised in, the one I was born in, was never one for the restless. It was a place for those who either wished to settle, or needed some safe stopover until they could leave. And she could not leave, but neither did she wish to settle. Boredom is a dangerous thing.

She began looking for other ways to overcome the ennui. It wasn't to be found at home, so she found it elsewhere. She was still good friends with Betsy, who had dropped out of Iowa State College and had been working in a clothes store one town over ever since. Betsy was single and she and Julia would go out on the weekends with her friends from the store to bars for some girl time. Jess did not stop her: perhaps he knew better by then, than to get in the way of Julia's wishes. But that was how it started, innocent drinks in bars on weekends so that she didn't want to scratch her eyes out.

No one knows when she found the first one. No one ever

asked, but pretty soon she began to step out on her husband. At first with random men out of town, but then it crawled closer to home. They used to throw parties with some of Betsy's friends, and of course Julia would go. Though no one would ever tell me exactly, from the half-whispered things I overheard over the years, the things she did during that time were not considered to be...well, anything that my family had encountered before. She moved with the times and she didn't care where it took her. By all accounts, she was more than happy with any kind of experimentation, just so long as it was fun, just so long as it didn't have anything to do with being a wife or a mother. She wanted to feel like a girl again—free, unencumbered. She was lying to herself, but as she'd spent most of her life lying to others, it was only a matter of time before she, too, fell under her own spell.

So like a secret drinker, my aunt was, initially, very good at keeping her secret life hidden from all fear of rebuke or discovery. She was very careful for a long time, but her ability to fool those around her only enhanced her arrogant belief that she was untouchable. She had gotten away with so much in life and this, she felt, was the last straw. If she could do this, she could do anything. She started to believe in her invincibility.

It's not that hard to see why. At the age of three she had survived a car accident that had decapitated her mother; she had stolen from her father and run away from home to find she could return as the prodigal child. She did things that no one would ever suspect her of even knowing, let alone living, and she did them without suffering once in consequence of her actions. She was charmed.

And then one evening, my grandmother went to the home of Mrs. Healy. A card party had been planned and she came over bearing a tray of homemade macaroons and settled herself in the Healys' large pistachio-colored kitchen as she helped her friend set up. The Healys were having repairs done to their roof and the workmen were directly outside the window. Mrs. Healy went into their lounge to arrange the bridge table while my grandmother made a pitcher of iced tea.

What happened next she believed was divine providence.

The men were mumbling together outside on the veranda. At first she barely listened, but as their talk grew coarser she couldn't help but overhear what they were saying. They were talking as men do, about a woman they had slept with. In disgust my grandmother realized they had taken turns with her one after the other, even at the same time, and they were discussing her and her performance under hushed tones, crude jokes and abstract hand gestures and winks. Even though they were talking quietly, in the silence of the kitchen, where the only sound was the pouring of iced tea into a large glass jug, their voices carried. She winced as they delved into particulars and then she caught something she was not expecting. What they said next she would repeat to my grandfather word for word, though she hardened her features when she did so. Some have said that it was too much, that there was no need for her to tell him the truth so vividly, but I think she did it because any loophole she provided, Cal would have clung to like a man drowning. And so the phrase those men threw out about my aunt has come down through the generations to mine, still intact, as an epigram of both shame and betrayal.

They laughed at their own joke. Their hoarse chuckles drifted through the kitchen, refracting off of Mrs. Healy's pristine surfaces.

For years after, people would ask why. My father, even my uncle: people did not understand. Was she influenced? Was

she coerced? Did they force her into it—but that couldn't
work because she went to those parties and bars time and
time again and lied so smoothly before and after about it that
no one could be in any doubt that she was in control.

So why? Why risk everything? Why do those things and
have them done to her? Boredom couldn't be it surely, no
one could do that just because they were bored. This was her
home, had always been. How could she turn against it so?

Why?

As my grandmother answered, "Why not?"

Though she saw before her what she would do, she could
not help but feel wary. She would not relish this task; there
was no way of accomplishing it without clearly showing the
dirt on her hands. It would be a pyrrhic victory but a victory
nonetheless and this spurred her on. Daring: you couldn't
beat Lavinia Hathaway for that.

So she observed her stepdaughter closely. She would document later the times she went out with Betsy Turner, when
she came home and where she said she would be. She began
to gather things together. She even hired a private detective,
but first she took the name from Mrs. Healy of the repair-
men she had employed.

"They did such a good job on your roof," she had said.

"You think?" Mrs. Healy turned around and observed her
roof plates. "If you say so."

Looking back, there were signs, but no one saw them. My
grandparents and great-aunt didn't have a clue about things
like that back then and my uncle was a solitary recluse so
would not have cared even if he had realized what was happening, while my father had a more pressing concern on his
mind than noticing the despondency of his sister: the draft.

He was eighteen and while he had been accepted into

Iowa State College, my father had no idea what he wanted to do with his life. Ostensibly he was going to college to study history, but this was met with little fanfare in his family. What was he going to do with a history major? they asked him. How was that going to help him on the farm? Because there was never any doubt in their minds, nor really in his, that he wasn't going to end up right back on Aurelia. He had never thought of a future outside of it, but that didn't mean he wanted his whole life to have been centered on it.

The time was approaching for when he had to register for the draft, and he thought about it often. Ethan was no longer a serious contender after the injuries he had inflicted on himself the night he proposed to Allie Lomax. For the rest of his life my uncle would be plagued by pains in his bones whenever there was rain and his left leg was forever held together by a metal rod. Besides, he did not share my father's hankering to pursue a life outside of Aurelia, even if it were only temporary. He had tried a dream once and it had failed him, so he did not dream anymore.

But my father did, and what he longed for was adventure, experience, all the things you want when you're eighteen and on the brink of finding the world. Did he know about the Quaker who had burned himself in protest of the war, or the march of five thousand people in Illinois led by Martin Luther King Jr., or Muhammad Ali's conscientious objection? Sure he did, but that was miles away. My father would describe growing up on the farm as sometimes feeling as if you were part of a different country. He knew these things occurred elsewhere but they did not immediately affect him here. The newspapers reported them dutifully and the TV showed the same pictures across the country, but in the streets, on the farms, in the community, the events of the day were muted. So, yes, he did know all these things, but did he feel it? No, he did not.

What he felt was that somehow his home had changed. His brother had never been the same since Allie, and his sister was always so unhappy, so vicious in her boredom, and he saw his father's worry and his mother's unnervingly quiet observation of them all, and this made him want to leave even more. In vain, perhaps he thought that it would eventually go back to how it used to be given time, and that he could seek a life elsewhere until it did. But my father was never one for spontaneity. He did not have the willful spirit of his sister or the purpose, however misguided, of his brother. He was a follower, my dad—a good man, but a follower nonetheless.

My father did not know when his moment would come, but he knew that it would be soon. As the days went on he became restless. He did his chores around the farm and he went through the routines of his day as before, but he was not like before. Though the sky was clear, he could smell rain, he would later say. Something was coming, and back then he still believed that it was to do with him.

But Lavinia was making plans. She looked up at the clearing and saw the paleness of the sky and thought how splendid it would look against an array of black and gray.

And then one day my father woke up and realized he was leaving. He woke earlier than usual, showered and dressed, and went down to the kitchen, where he made himself a cup of coffee. He was soon joined by his father and his brother, who sat at the table while his aunt fried eggs, bacon and mushrooms in a large pan.

His hands clasped around his mug as he sat and he was overcome with the feeling that all this—the plate with the blue swallow pattern set down before him with breakfast, his father talking over their chores as he scanned his paper and his brother silent as ever beside him—was for the last time. It would not leave him, this notion, and so he walked through his morning as if in a dream, as if it was the lie and he would soon wake up and face the truth.

Which he did, around lunchtime. He came into the house to find a circle of women facing him. Their faces were blank, but then his mother came forward and handed him an envelope. He knew what it was before he opened it and suddenly he felt light, almost heady as he gripped the paper, his fingers playing at the corners.

"What's the matter?" asked Ethan as he came in behind my father.

"I've been drafted," he said.

Everyone was somber after that. They had known it was coming, it was happening everywhere else. Though they had never talked about it, now that the news was not just on the TV sets or in their papers but in their home, it finally came to roost with them that death could once again come to Aurelia and come for the young.

But my father did not think of these things. He was scared and he was nervous, but most of all he was relieved. Here was his chance, he thought, here was his chance to see the world, to escape and go somewhere, do something other than farming, live a little. Yes, it was war, but what did he know of war? What did he know of how it would be like—what he would see, what he would do, what he would let happen? There was never any question in his mind that he wouldn't come back, and though he had no idea about army life, he wasn't afraid of hard work and he would just muck in like all the others.

But now that her son was going away, possibly to die,

something happened to my grandmother that rarely ever happened to her. She lost her patience.

For months now she had collected information on her stepdaughter. The detective she had hired had been instructed to get the names, descriptions and if possible, photos of all Julia's activities, evidence that my grandmother now kept in a large brown envelope and which she documented in the early hours of each morning before the house awoke, so she could pore over them. Yet still she did not expose her. She had been waiting for the opportunity to present itself to her, for despite her hatred for Julia, this was one task in which she did not wish to appear to be directly involved. She knew that whoever came to my grandfather and laid the photographs and accounts under his nose, would incur not only his wrath, but also his hatred for destroying the love and belief in his daughter he had once been convinced was unconditional. It would not just be Julia's weakness that came to light, but Cal's, and that was a dangerous mission. But when she learned of her youngest son going to war and looked out onto the farm to see Jess talking to the foreman, or Cal Jr. toddling through her house with Julia's voice calling after him, she saw her hopes fade and the visage of Julia triumph over her. At this point my grandmother believed that should my father go to war he would undoubtedly die. Theo was too good; she had always known this. She had not taught him the art of self-preservation because she was sure he would never stoop to the lengths that it required. And the notion that one of her children would die in some godforsaken place abroad, while her stepdaughter continued to pollute their farm with her brats and all their claims, stood on the boards of her self-control and broke them.

So she scoured the names of the men whom her stepdaughter had been with, looking, searching, for inspiration.

"I was looking for something new, something I hadn't seen or thought of, something different. And then I realized, why teach a dog new tricks when the old ones work just fine?"

And that was how my grandmother came to find herself at the house of Betsy Turner for the second time.

It was a gamble, irrational even, and far beneath her usual careful handling of such things, but Theo was due to leave for boot camp in a week and my grandmother was resolved that he would not be alone when he went.

So she found out the address of Betsy's apartment, which she shared with another girl, and caught Betsy just as she was on her way out. She didn't say much, she simply pulled out the brown envelope and handed it to her.

"I believe this is more to your taste than mine," she said. Betsy took the package from her, bewildered, and as my grandmother turned to leave, she heard the girl open the flap to peer inside before letting out a moan of horror.

"Mrs. Hathaway, Mrs. Hathaway, please!" she called out after her in desperation, already running after her and coming to stand in front to block her path, her arms flung wide.

"Just ripe for a crucifixion."

Even though years had passed since Lavinia had sat on the couch of Betsy's mother, nothing had changed. Cowering in fear, if anything, Betsy was even more pliant, even more willing. To her surprise and disappointment, the girl was far less of a challenge than before. And much more cowardly: she immediately blamed Julia.

"And where would she have had the chance to do these… these disgusting things if it hadn't been for you?" my grandmother shouted, holding up the photographs to Betsy's whimpering face.

"She would never have even thought to go to these places, be around these people, if you hadn't introduced her to it."

"No, I never, I never introduced her to anything. It was Julia she…she just—"

"My God, look at this filth!" my grandmother said as she rifled through the photographs like a deck of obscene cards. "Can you imagine what people will say when this comes out? Your poor mother has no idea the rotted thing she has given life to. Admit it, you made Julia do these things, you led her on, didn't you?" She crouched low and craned her neck up into Betsy's face, her eyes serving as a flashlight of accusation under Betsy's chin. "She never showed any signs of this sort of depravity before she resumed her friendship with you—and God, look what happened the last time? Ran away from home to get married to a man we'd never even met!"

"Please, please, you have to believe me—I never did any of this. I mean I was there, but…but I didn't—"

"Who? Who will believe you?" my grandmother interrupted. "She's a mother and wife. If this comes out who will believe that she would willingly jeopardize all this without your influence?"

It was a bold lie. Everyone knew Betsy had no will of her own; the idea that she could have manipulated Julia into doing anything was a laughable concept, but struck by terror and shock, Betsy was in no fit state for rational thought.

"Couldn't—couldn't you just…if I make it stop, if I don't see her again…?"

My grandmother scoffed in righteous indignation.

"You think I can keep this from my husband? Her father? You think when he finds this out there won't be an uproar? He'll be looking for someone to blame and since you were the one providing her with—"

"I did not—"

"—opportunity and God knows what else, you'll be the first one he'll blame. There's no way of escaping that."

Betsy looked at my grandmother, stricken; the photographs lay on the coffee table underneath her shaking hands.

My grandmother gave a sigh and her shoulders slackened.

"I know what my stepdaughter is like. I've seen the way she is around Jess, those clothes, that attitude.… I could sense things were wrong but she'd never come to me about it. If only you, her friend, had come forward and told me what she was getting herself involved in. Then I could have saved her, stopped her. I would be able to say to anyone if they'd asked that you had come to me as a friend in an effort to save her from herself. Or even to Cal if you didn't feel you could talk to me. He'd have listened to you under those terms. All what must now happen would have been prevented. Foolish Betsy, you were so foolish. I don't understand it."

There was a silence. Betsy's red-rimmed eyes were darting around the photos.

"Are there any of…of me?"

"No, none actually." My grandmother picked them up and put them back in the envelope. "It could all have been avoided," she said wistfully.

"What about now?"

"It's too late for Julia, she has sunk to such depths. No, I'll have to tell Cal, though God knows I wish I didn't. I don't want to be the one to bring this to him, but what choice do I have?"

There was a silence.

"Well, why don't I tell him?" asked Betsy hesitantly.

My grandmother looked up at her, feigning surprise.

"What do you mean?" she asked.

Betsy wrung her hands in her lap. "I could—I should have come to you before, I see that now. I made a mistake but I want to correct it. I can make it right. I'll go to him and I'll tell him everything, like a friend would, just like you said. I do care about Julia," she added. "I don't want to see her doing these things anymore. Not with her boy and everything. But she won't listen to me and I went with her to keep her safe, make sure she wasn't hurt. Stuff can really get out of hand at those places."

"So I've seen," said my grandmother softly.

"And you know how stubborn she is. She would have gone anyway, so—so I went to try and keep an eye on her but…there was only so much I could do, you know?"

"Of course I do. It must have been awful there."

"It was… Jesus—" her voice broke "—it's been driving me mad keeping all this in." She licked her lips, her mascara-laced tears pooling at the top. "Do you think if I spoke up now it would be too late?"

My grandmother regarded the girl for a few moments and then reached out a hand and smoothed it over her wrist.

"You know I believe you, Betsy," she said gently. "You tell it just like that and there isn't anyone who won't believe you. Besides—" she gave her a little smile "—I always think it's never too late."

Betsy came to Aurelia on a Tuesday at lunchtime. Julia was out shopping. Betsy knew this because she had asked her to meet her in the food court of the mall to ensure she would not be at home when she called. So while Julia waited there for her to arrive, Betsy knocked on the large door of the great white house on the mound and shattered the man called Cal Hathaway Sr. who opened it to her.

He was home for lunch. My uncle and father watched as the two went into the study and raised an eyebrow to each other.

To see Betsy turn up at the house and ask for their father was odd enough. But neither of them in their wildest dreams would have expected the shouts and screams of their father that started up in the study, swiftly followed by the sound of crashing furniture bleeding through the walls.

Their mother was down in the study before they were, and though they hovered outside the door and could hear the muffled shouts of their father and the placating tones of their mother, as yet they still had not learned the truth.

Betsy came running out and slammed straight into my father, who attempted to hold her shoulders to steady himself.

"Is everything okay?" he had asked.

Betsy was flushed, her eyes darting wildly, her breath erratic.

"I done my duty, don't anyone say anything different. I done my duty," she repeated before fleeing.

My father and uncle looked into the study and saw that it was a mess. The chair was overturned and books and papers were strewn across the carpet, on top of which was an array of small photographs. My father picked the one up near his foot. When he saw it he covered his mouth with his hands.

"Is that…?" Ethan asked over his shoulder, but just then my grandfather let out a scream so loud, that even though they were adult men, my uncle and father both jumped back. Cal's face had turned red with the strain, his fists raised up against his hips. He looked unlike anything they'd ever seen before, wiped clean of memory and association.

And then he stalked past them. Their mother followed him as far as the door, but she stopped at the threshold. He was in his car and was gone.

He would go to the house of one of the men who had been with his daughter. He had needed to know it wasn't true; that it was a lie, a false rumor started in a bar when drunk under the need to perform some kind of act of bravado with his friends. Not his girl, not his child, who had been ripped from the bloody car of her mother in a cherry-patterned dress. Not Julia.

"Yes, Julia," the man had said.

"You are sure?" Cal could not believe a man would uphold that sort of lie to a father's face. He would quail, his eyes would flicker, his body would betray him even if his tongue did not. But he was a rod, giving nothing away, because there was nothing *to* give away.

So he had driven back home to get his rifle, and then had walked out to the paddock and shot the white Thoroughbred he had bought from a horse farm in Kansas twice through the head.

She had screamed. She had clawed at the front door demanding admittance. This was not the tantrum of youth designed to overwhelm obstacles, this was beyond control. This was the true meaning of fear.

Theo had been the one to cave. My father—still hoping.

As soon as she was inside, she had run from room to room, slipping past the arms of her brother and the desperate hands of her aunt, who was both berating and pleading with her at the same time. She saw no one, recognized no one.

But Lavinia saw to it that she acknowledged her.

And she did by flying at her so she could dig her nails into her face. Ethan held her back but she kicked and bit, so that Theo had to help him. She was an animal. My grandmother called it her true face.

Among the curses she threw at her stepmother like stones that bounced off of her proud battlements she reared her head back and hawked a globule of spit at her, just missing her face.

Lavinia spoke.

"Anyone would think I made you get on your back and spread your legs. Come, I'm interested, what's the reason you're going to give me now?"

But my aunt was screaming for her father. It hurt everyone's ears to hear her—well, almost everyone.

"He won't come," my grandmother said. "He's disgusted with you. You've soiled his love for you. Nothing but trouble, he'll never come to you again."

Julia reeled in her brothers' arms. Murder, any sentence, any penalty, anything just so long as that woman was rotting in a ground she could piss over.

Piper pleading, begging, holding the clawed hands of the niece who was more like her daughter, though she had always pretended otherwise. But what was the use in pretending now? Though she wanted to rebuke her sister-in-law, she knew her brother, she knew the truth. God had turned his face from her, she saw now, as Julia slumped forward in agonized defeat.

But then the stair at the top of the landing groaned under a familiar weight and they all looked up. He had no eyes for anyone but her. He saw her looped in the arms of her brothers, his sister hunched over her, his wife straight-backed, blocking her path. It was like a play, but he had seen the blood of the white horse course its way in rivulets onto his land and knew this was no fantasy onto which a curtain would drop. This was real.

Just like his hatred.

No, never, he could never abandon a child. He could never let a child of his throw long shadows up the walk into exile. He was not his father.

But it was so easy.

And, among the black glass shredding any love he had for

her, any memory he cherished, a sense of vindication that she deserved it.

Bitch.

So he came down to her and they all parted.

He came close to her. She stood up now, but though the words tumbled from her mouth, his ears were closed to her. This body had come from his body but he had seen, had heard, what it had allowed itself to do. Polluted filth. He saw them all over her, he saw her swallowed by it, consumed by it. His firstborn, his clean daughter, nothing but dirt.

God, he needed a drink. He went past them to the kitchen but she broke free and followed him. She was shouting and crying in turn, trying to overcome the noise of his search for the scotch. And then her hand, that small hand that had hung around his neck twenty-one years ago in Oregon, on his arm…

His body knew what to do before he did.

His hand smashed itself into the side of her face, feeling no pain though it was already throbbing, just sending her crashing to the side of the room, and she caught her head on the kitchen table as she went down. And then her eyes wide with shock. Broken, she knew it now. Nothing between them.

He stared at his hand in revulsion as if it had been contaminated by her. His other was empty. He still had not found the scotch.

Piper now, here on the floor beside her niece, looking up at her brother while Julia clutched her temple where a small trickle of blood was already winding its way down her face.

No words, just half words, half-formed sentences that flared and died on the tongue before they even found the air. Cal…at last the thick-necked bottle cooling the palm of his hand as it ran down his throat. Nothing existed for him outside the amber liquid. He didn't want it to.

And then a step. My grandmother standing by the doorway as her sons tentatively came behind her, horror finding new ways to etch itself across their faces. Their father oblivious to all of them: the crumpled figure of their aunt, the long milky legs of their sister sprawled on the floor, all but his bottle. This was the last image my father would take with him before he went to war the following week. This and the sight of Julia's horse when he found it by the stables, its long legs folded over on the floor as its unseeing eyes bored into the hay bale in the corner, its brains and blood splattered on the wall and floor.

When our mother thought we were old enough, she would tell my sisters and I that our aunt had done a wicked thing, that she had been a bad wife and mother and had disgraced our family and her husband and that was why we were not to speak of her, not ever, and especially not to Cal Jr.

"But he mentions her all the time," said Ava.

"What?" my mother asked. "When?"

"Yeah, when, Ava? He's never mentioned her to me," I said.

"No, but..." She trailed off and dug her fingers into her palm, a habit she had of doing when uncomfortable. She used to come home from exams with bloody half moons all over the apples at the base of her thumbs.

"He talks to me a lot about things. He—he likes talking to me, I think."

"Well, it's just—you shouldn't," our mother said. "He was badly affected by what she did to his father. That's why—well, that's sort of why he is the way he is a bit. Things happened after—and he was a child, but well, there's no need for

you to know that, just be careful if he brings her up again."
She resumed her folding of the pastry in the bowl. "And
never mention her to your grandfather."

But years later when I would sit by the bed of my raving
grandmother, she spoke Julia's name often and it was here I
learned what my mother really meant when she had alluded
to Julia's "disgrace" and what it did to Cal Jr.

But even though I know the truth, I cannot forgive him
for what he would do, any more than I can forgive myself
for letting him.

AVA

A Diseased Tree

10

IN THE AIR-CONDITIONED MEETING ROOM OF Dermott and Harrison, I thought about the last time I had been in a lawyer's office. It had been at the reading of my mother's will. I was nineteen and it was toward the end of the summer before my sophomore year. I had been house-sitting in New York, waiting until term began, when we were all summoned to Iowa by the lawyers. It had been the first time I had seen Claudia since…well…and I remember when I walked in, already ten minutes late, how shocked I had been at how much she had changed. Ava had refused to look me in the eye and Claudia had dropped her gaze to the table when I entered. Neither of them would sit next to each other, so I had made my way apologetically to the end of a long polished table to the only empty chair, which was between them. There we had been, a triumvirate of pain and recrimination, while the voice of the lawyer droned on above our heads, reading aloud the final words of my mother, who had hoped for such a different outcome for her daughters.

But this time it's different.

This time instead of a graying man in a forlorn suit, I got a peppy brunette with raspberry lipstick and heels that spiked across the hallway as she came out to reception and proffered an elegantly manicured hand. She was all cool smiles and crisp suits. I was there in jeans and a blazer and could not have felt more out of place, or more nervous.

While she went over the "issues at hand" (her phrase, her opening phrase I should say. Not "how are you?" or "would you like some coffee?" Preamble not a strong point), I sat there utterly unmoved. Because what she was saying had nothing to do with the Aurelia I knew. Those digits and terms meant nothing to me, or how I felt about the farm I was raised on. I did not recognize them and I could tell that neither did she. There she was in full flow, her fingers snapping at papers, manila files openmouthed on her desk. She thought she knew what she was talking about but she didn't. Then again, from the looks she threw my way, I could tell she felt the same about me.

"Look," I said, leaning forward during the first available pause, nearly twenty minutes after she had asked me to sit down, "I don't want the Queen Anne dresser or the antique pearl necklace or any of that stuff. You can keep it or sell it or whatever. I'm not interested. I'm just here because—" I felt myself falter and the words slipping away, me desperately clinging on "—because I want to make sure the important things—the really important things to me, that is—aren't caught up in all of…of Cal's mess."

I leaned back. She gazed at me, those raspberry lips parted just a little.

"Of course, but for our sake we want to ensure that you know everything you need to," she said.

"Trust me, darling," I drawled, "knowledge is overrated. Just tell me when I can go and get my parents' stuff."

Much later, I was picking over the plate of mac and cheese Jane had made for me when she called. Jane had tried to ask me about my meeting with the lawyer when I first got home, but I wasn't very forthcoming. What I did do when I came back to the house was sleep, on top of the covers, still clothed. Every little thing over this place is such a battle. A painful, ridiculous war that once again I am not equipped for. When it comes to this, all that Hathaway blood seems to clog up in the veins and starve me of some much-needed spirit. But not her, no. When I answered the phone to her I could tell those particular machinations were working just fine.

"So there you are? Finally," she said when I answered. "Thanks for letting me know FYI, Meredith, that you'd decided to take it upon yourself to deal with the farm. That was a pretty piece of unilateral thinking."

I stared at the floor openmouthed, brain scrambling.

"Don't think just because you're up there that it's all up to you, you know? I'm getting on the next plane and we can *both* do this together. While you and Ava might like to forget the fact—you're *not* the only descendants left and other people, other equally significant people, might also like a say. Don't say I didn't warn you, a courtesy, you may like to note, you didn't offer me."

And then she hung up. I was speechless and suddenly shaking with mirth. My shoulders heaved before the laughter had even reached my mouth. God, I thought, what a thing it is to be back.

"What was that about?" Jane asked when she came into

the kitchen and saw me shaking my head back and forth against the refrigerator door.

"Oh, no more than I should have expected." I was in the grip of my laughter now. I moved positions and came to lean against the sink.

"Just—Claudia's coming home."

Claudia. Her hair once a mixture between blond and brown before she started dying it, her eyes dark, her nose like my father's, her legs like my mother's. Their first child, a true combination of both. They had looked down on her when she was born and cried. She was the reason my father decided to return to Aurelia.

Claudia, the eldest, my eldest sister. Should have been my gold idol but instead was one of the clay gods. My early memories are filled with visions of her, her white two-piece with red sunglasses sunbathing on our lawn, her strawberry-smelling lip balm I used to steal and sniff until she caught me, the endless red licorice laces I would find around our house half chewed. My sister: scathing, watchful, ambitious. Destined to leave Aurelia from the moment she set foot on it, but she had always believed it would be on her terms.

Claudia Marie Hathaway. We used to call her Clo.

At a quarter to three, two days after her phone call, a white taxi pulled up on Jane's street. Jane was sitting in the living room smoking cigarettes as she people-watched from the window. I was on the couch reading, my legs over the armrest. We were sitting in comfortable silence before the swift puncture of heels on stone steps rose in volume and then just before the sharp rap of knuckles on wood, Jane said, "Your sister has arrived."

So I opened the door and there she was in front of me.

At first all I could see was deep dark red lipstick,

burgundy-colored, the only part of her that was really exposed because the rest of her was shrouded in a mottled dark fur coat and a black felt hat slanted at an angle that covered most of her face. I stepped aside in greeting; in acknowledgment she entered, careful to take in, with a downward glance, my jeans and rumpled shirt. The first thing I could think of to say to my sister, who I had not seen in over a decade, was "You don't have any bags."

"No," she said casually, as Jane stepped into the hall, "they're at the hotel."

No, of course, I thought, no Greyhound and hope-against-hope for her. It was never her style anyway.

"Jane," she said, arms outstretched, mannequin-like. Jane stepped in and out of them as seamlessly and as perfunctorily as possible.

We stared at each other for a moment, not really knowing what to say. I couldn't really bear it.

"You can shut the door now, it's kind of cold," Claudia said officiously. I looked up. She still hadn't taken off her hat.

"You look well," she said finally as I moved inside.

"I've been feeding her up. You should have seen how she was when she first came," said Jane, stepping forward to take Claudia's coat. So that's the effect of fur, I thought. It makes servants of those not wearing it themselves.

Claudia obliged Jane, shrugging the dead skin from her back, and I saw she was wearing a jet-black suit dress, neatly tucked at the waist with a gold-colored belt, and gathered at the shoulders. She always was about the detail. Whereas I—

"Is Ava here then?" she asked sharply.

"No, of course not, why would she be?" I asked, incredulous. She looked at me with disdain.

"Well, you are, and usually where you go she follows and vice versa."

"That was a long time ago. We're both grown up."

"Or grown apart," she added with a flourish.

"Speak for yourself," I snapped and then because I couldn't help it, I reached over and whipped off her hat. "And take this ridiculous thing off. You're not at New York fashion week. This is Iowa, remember?"

"I wouldn't know," she said in a low voice, eyes fixed on mine. "It's been a while."

"Well, try and remember."

"Tea?" Jane offered quickly, already walking into the kitchen.

"Green?" asked Claudia, following.

"No, brown," I answered scathingly. She turned around and swept her eyes over me. Usually as kids this would be when she knocked me over or pinched me, tempting me into a tussle she knew I would not win but my hot temper could not resist. I have a lot to thank her for, my sister. She taught me the art of battle from the moment I could walk. And I thought, wouldn't it be easier if I could just push her as before? If she could just throw me in a headlock and we can fight and sweat until all that is between us is spent? It would not be like it would with Ava: ours is not a fight to the death.

"I had hoped we could be civilized about this," she said.

"Well, yours wasn't exactly a civilized phone call, was it?"

"What did you expect from me?" Her nostrils quivered though the rest of her was in complete control. "I might have thought the two of you would have had the good grace to—"

"The two of us? Oh, you mean me and Ava? Us two, conspiring against you? Well, Ava didn't tell me about the farm. The lawyers told me about the farm. They contacted me after going through her and finding, surprise–surprise, a brick wall."

She blinked, disconcerted.

"Why wouldn't they try to contact me?"

"Probably because your last name isn't Hathaway."

"Neither is yours," she added maliciously.

"Legally it is, though, isn't it, Mrs. McCulley?"

I noticed from the corner of my eye that Jane was behind us poised next to the kettle.

"So how did you find out?" I asked suddenly.

"My husband discovered it at an annual fundraiser."

"Pardon?"

"Yes," she said, resuming her clipped tones as she stared down at a manicured hand, splaying her fingers. "John went to a law society ball as part of a fundraiser for victims of some kind of leukemia, I forget. What I can't forget is that one of his old friends happens to be a partner at the firm of Dermott and Harrison and over canapés and scotch, he managed to find out about the dissolution of the estate of one of their former and best clients, a case that was proving particularly troublesome as the owner had died and the last living descendants either refused to have anything to do with it or couldn't be traced. He managed to find out enough for me to start making some calls and lo and behold what do I find?"

"I'm surprised you told him enough in the first place to let him."

She raised her chin in defiance.

"I'm not here to go through that again."

"Neither am I," I said. All of a sudden I was tired.

For the first time since she arrived, for a second, the ice thawed around her and she softened her mouth.

"Why are you here?"

I could have told her, about Ava, about all of them, all the things I have kept hidden for years. I could have drawn her into my confidence, maybe this could even be the tool that undoes all the threads of bitterness she has allowed to form around us ever since the day when she sat in a pickup truck and was driven away by our uncle. But even I am at least self-aware enough to know the difference between a courageous moment and wishful thinking.

"I felt like coming home."

She twisted her burgundy mouth into a sneer.

"Yeah, right."

It's ironic that Claudia should be so contemptuous of the idea, when if it wasn't for her, there is a very good chance I would not have known Aurelia as home at all.

Theodore James Hathaway had gone to war in Vietnam in 1968. He was seen off at the bus depot by his parents and brother, who all hugged him individually but, aside from his mother, could not meet his eye. Nor did he wish them to. Though he knew as he sat down and the bus moved from under him that this could be the last time he ever saw his family, he did not wish to prolong their goodbye. The specter of his sister haunted them as much as any vicious spirit, her name burning on their tongues and in their minds in their efforts not to mention her, or the terrible scenes that had preempted the last week of his stay. He had leaned against the window and sighed. His companion had shot him a look of pity.

When he was shot by a sniper in the knee and right shoulder and discharged a year later he did not go back to Iowa. Instead, on his release he sent his family a letter, which he wrote on a train to New York telling them he would forward an address when he had one. It exhausted him to try and

balance the tone between cordiality and falsifying an emotion he was not yet ready to feel. They received the letter
and a month later another telling them that he was working
as a clerk at Syracuse University and the address of his new
basement room in a block of apartments. His mother sent
him a care package, his aunt a knitted sweater for the New
York winters, and so began for two years, the dance between
avoidance and denial between my father and his family.

Theirs was a careful balance between what was expected
and what was uncomfortable, all behind a mask of cold cordiality. They did not berate him for not coming home at
Christmas and he did not ask why they did not visit. They
did not push him for further news of when he would come
home, and he glossed over the painful parts of their letters
when they alluded to the aftermath of Julia's actions. They
did not probe each other, they did not test their sores and,
aside from when he remembered where he had come from,
my father learned once again how to be happy. He began
to build a life for himself in New York, even started taking
night classes in history. That was how he would eventually
come to meet my mother, running into her in a hallway
where she had signed up for classes in Italian language and
literature. They had crossed paths on the way to their lessons
and engaged in that oh-so-awkward he-goes-to-the-left-
she-goes-to-the-left, he-moves-to-the-right-she-moves-to-
the-right dance, until my mother let out a peel of laughter
at their collective clumsiness, and for the first time in a long
time my father felt real warmth. He did not ask out the
brown-haired girl in the yellow smock dress that day, even
though her laugh struck a match in his soul, but he made
sure to be in that corridor at the exact same time on the exact
same day for the next two weeks so he could see her again.
One day as she walked past him and smiled, he scratched the

back of his neck and finally asked her out for a coffee. That was it: no great romance, no thunderbolt, just the tender embrace of a gentle thaw where his heart used to be. My mother did not realize the effect she had had on him until the same thing started happening with her.

The life of Antonia Magdala Pincetti had always been in a state of flux. Her father couldn't or wouldn't hold down a job. He went through a veritable succession of careers—salesman, barman, chef—but the longest stretch of employment was as a clerk at the Italian embassy in Washington. This lasted for fifteen months and both she and her mother, Angela, believed that at last they had found the security they so desperately craved. But then her father began to take time off from work, until he stopped showing up at the offices altogether and then one day Angela received a telephone call telling her that her husband need not come in on Monday, though it was doubtful by then whether he'd ever had the intention of doing so.

As a result, Antonia moved around constantly. From Baltimore to Washington to New Jersey, until she came to New York when she was fourteen. Two weeks after arriving, her father got a job interview with a travel agency. The interview was at 2:00 p.m. He left at one sharp. Wearing his job-hunting suit, he gave Angela a kiss and borrowed twenty dollars for gas. He took their car, a weathered yellow jalopy, and waved goodbye to her through the window. They never saw him again. And my mother never forgave him for it.

Individually my parents were blighted with memories they longed to forget, yet when they were together, they were suddenly able to paper over the cracks their past had made and, astonishingly, let it hold. My mother told him she loved him on their fourth date. Three months later they were married and she fell pregnant with Claudia on their honeymoon in Quebec, where they had bought a blue-and-white-speckled tea set that I used to play with as a child in make-believe doll parties. My maternal grandmother, who died before I was born, and twenty of their friends were in attendance at the wedding. None of Theo's family made it to the ceremony, though they sent them a set of very expensive silverware as a wedding present. Lavinia had picked it out.

My mother could not understand it, but there was a small, nearly imperceptible but still noticeable change that crept into my father's voice and face that stopped her from ever questioning the facade of his relationship with his relatives in Iowa. She herself knew what it was like to carry the burden of home and so she let the matter rest, never calling into question why the halcyon tales of his childhood past stumbled into an impassive wall whenever he spoke of his family in the present. But even she would eventually reach her limits.

You see it was at her request that they came home. They were living in a tiny flat in Queens and my father had spun her such gold-threaded tales of life on Aurelia that when she looked down at my sister and at the meager contents of their flat, she couldn't see why they were pursuing a life of hardship, when there was one of ample prosperity just waiting for them to come back and claim it.

But my father dragged his heels. Though he indulged her in everything (which was not hard because my mother never asked for much), he stalled at this. It was hard for him to tell her that he was afraid to go back. She may have seen the peeling paint of their living room and the oversize closet they turned into a nursery and pained at these things, but when he thought of Aurelia, he did not see the house on the mound but the blood of a white Kansas Thoroughbred running in streams across the dust floor of the stable. Home was not home to him anymore. A lot had happened since he'd been away.

For the first time since they had known each other my parents argued. All she could see was what they did not have and all that they could with my father acting as a barrier in between. But how could he tell her of the scene that had occurred just before he left? That his sister was the town whore, who if she'd been a common streetwalker, would have commanded more respect? That he had watched as she had been taken away by his aunt to where he did not know, only he was sure that she would never come back. She was to be, as my grandmother later put it, "shunned." Quickly tales of her wantonness had spread around the town. Cal, at Lavinia's insistence, took out a restraining order against his daughter. There were threats she would come back for her son, but Jess—passive, unsure Jess—who had not come to the house since that night, came out of his self-imposed isolation and threatened to kill her if she ever stepped foot on Aurelia or near Cal Jr. again. For once Julia cowered before the seemingly docile musician she had once coveted, perhaps realizing for the first time that her poison had spread through more lives than just her own.

For Jess was wounded badly. Humiliated, deceived, disgusted. It was more than what his wife had done; it was what he had given up for her in the first place. He had made himself into the type of husband and father that in the end was acceptable for nothing more than a whore. Those were his words. So he began drinking heavily, until the house, as my grandmother noted whenever she came to visit, was littered with bottles. There was barely any food but there was more than enough liquor. He could hardly look at his son anymore. Piper took care of him. She was afraid, she said, to leave the boy with Jess, but his grandfather could barely look at Cal Jr. any more than his own father, so she could not have him to stay in the house as she would have liked.

A few months after Julia had gone, just before Christmas, there had been an "incident." Cal Jr. had ended up in hospital. There had been a grave fear that he would not survive intact. He had had a broken arm, cracked ribs and a mass of contusions to his head that left him unconscious, and in intensive care for a week. He was only three years old. The police had been called as he was placed in intensive care and Jess, when they found him, was slumped at the wheel of his car two and a half miles away outside a titty-bar, his knuckles covered in his son's blood, snoring loudly as he clutched a bottle of Jack Daniel's to his chest. He was charged with grievous assault but my grandmother persuaded the police to drop the charges. She gave Jess five thousand dollars and a legal document that forfeited all of his parental rights. He left town and they did not hear from him again, though his parents had gone to see Cal Jr. in the hospital. Afterward his father had had to excuse himself to be sick. Jess would never come back to our town. My grandfather had threatened to lynch him if he did. At the hospital he stabbed his finger in the air at Jess's father over the bed of his comatose grandson, and then drew it in a line across his neck.

Nobody informed Julia of what had happened.

But Julia did not try to claim Cal Jr.

Though no one in the family was allowed to contact her or have anything to do with her (even Piper, who raged and howled at her brother, but was told she would be turned out if she so much as breathed his daughter's name again), Julia did not try to assail the walls of silence her family had built against her. It led some to believe in time that this was the opportunity she was looking for. She got to leave, to finally escape her marriage and her son. Though she lost everything she had, in some quarters there was a deep-rooted bitterness that perhaps in the end, she had still won after all.

In the end, to everyone's surprise, it was my grandmother who proposed that Cal Jr. come to live with them in the white house. My grandfather had been reluctant at first but Lavinia insisted. She hired decorators and remade a room for him especially. She nursed him when he came out of the hospital, and she attended to his every need. Her sister-in-law did not know what to make of it. Until that moment Lavinia had never shown any interest in her grandson, but it was as if none of that had occurred. She took him to her as if he had always been her own and my grandfather, out of his own deep-rooted guilt, did not question it; he let her have her way and an exhausted Piper did not try to intervene. I think losing Julia had hit her the hardest out of everyone, though no one would have cared to find out. I remember how even as a child whenever she dared to mention her niece's name to me that lick of love would still slide into her voice and mouth. She had been the child Piper never had while she was there, but none of those rights existed once Julia had been sent away from the farm. If the two remained in contact no one knew it, but losing her broke my great-aunt in a way nothing had before or ever would. She grieved for her until the day she died. But even when she asked for her as she was dying, my grandfather would not allow his daughter to come and visit. As far as I know, no one ever told her that Piper was dead, though I'm sure somehow she would have discovered it and mourned the death of the one person who had truly loved her from a stranger's distance.

As for Ethan, he had married none other than the daughter of his neighbor, Georgia-May Healy, a sweet but plain girl who was as unlike Ethan and, more importantly, as unlike

Allie as it was possible to be. At first Theo would not believe it until he saw the wedding photo. But there his brother was, dressed in a suit so black it looked like he was attending a funeral. He was frowning at the camera. The sight of Georgia-May clutching onto his brother's arm in nervous excitement made my father shiver when he saw it.

My mother could not understand his reaction. "Don't you like her?" she'd asked, but he had shaken his head unable to explain. He could only say that during Ethan's proposal, his brother had raised the point that at least in marrying him she wouldn't have to change her initials. After that my mother did not need to press him further. My father recognized instantly that when Georgia-May's father died the dairy farm would be joined onto Aurelia's ever expanding estate. The Healys had more than survived the first year Lavinia had estimated and she had been delighted at the opportunity to align the two farms. My father had not liked the thought but it would not leave him, no matter how many times he had batted it away.

Yes, he had grown up in a tall white house on a mound and run his horse alongside the wheat fields there, but those days of careless happiness were gone. And not one bit of this did he reveal to his wife, not until it was too late. I cannot help but think that if he had she might have been able to provide him with the strength to withstand the difficulties of their lives together and the weariness that being poor can bring. And his resolve would not have waned and he would not have allowed that treacherous seed of hope to plant a vine that strangled his reason with the idea, the small dangerous fragment of an idea, that even though all these things had happened, perhaps Aurelia could still be a new kind of home for his daughter, who never knew what it had been like in the past and so could not know any better.

★ ★ ★

When he came back in 1971, he came as if he had only been away for the afternoon and not four years. He walked up the drive and into the house knowing, as always, that in the daytime the door would be unlocked. When he pushed back the door, the only person who sat there, as ever, as if she had been waiting for him, was Piper.

Older, more lined even in four years, but still Piper.

Except she did not look up when she heard his step. She must have thought he was Ethan.

"Hello?" he said. She looked up then, slowly, cradling a cup of coffee, her pen poised over a crossword. For a moment nothing, and then a slow dawn of recognition lighting up feature after feature from the eyes down.

"Theo," she breathed midhug, drawing in a large sniff as she pressed her nose against his shoulder. Yes, it was him, the boy who had left after that awful time was here now as a man—his blond hair grown long and crowded against his ears and neck, his body lithe and still strong, but most of all alive. Here he was and he was not alone.

My mother was waiting in the hall, dressed in white and holding my sister, who was still a baby at the time. Long brown hair, big brown eyes, young, naive, hopeful. She cast her eyes about the place she had heard of so often from my father, who had unknowingly wooed her not with the dinners he took her to, or the flowers he bought her, but the tales of his childhood and the near reverence with which he spoke of his home—the one thing she had never really had and always longed for.

Piper stopped short when she saw them as Theo led her out into the hall. She took in my mother and her child clutched against her chest, and for the first time my father saw the fissures that had formed long cracks along his aunt's composure because just then she crumpled. And out of joy or fear or sadness or all three, she held on to the top of his shirt and burst into tears.

"So this is what I think we should do," said Claudia, who, after sipping at her coffee rather than brown tea ("Instant?" she asked in disappointment as Jane had set down the mug beside her), had decided to pull herself together and take command.

Out came the long list of thoughts she had been compiling ever since she had heard of the farm's demise. I watched her coffee get cold.

"And I was thinking of hiring someone to—"

"Hiring someone? Why would we need that?"

"Well, that's the beauty of letting someone finish their sentences, Meredith."

"Look, I know what you're going to say—"

"The gift of foresight?" She leaned forward and narrowed her mascara-heavy eyes into slits.

I let myself throw her a dirty look half-mixed with condescension, the ones I used to practice over a table very similar to this one.

"Listen, there won't be enough for you to box up and take away. The farm is gone and anything that is left will be auctioned off to pay back the heap of debts Cal left on the place."

"Aurelia," she said.

I blinked. "What?"

"You never use its name. It's 'the farm,' or 'that place,' but it's actually Aurelia. That's what it's called. Anyone might think you'd have an aversion to it."

I waved a hand in front of her to signal how pathetic I found her attempts at psychoanalysis.

"Pretty strange. After all if anyone should have an aversion to the place it should be me," she said, and lifted the cup of coffee to her lips.

She did not know. She had left by then and Ava would never tell her and neither would I. I wouldn't even let myself believe it had happened for years.

"So when can we go over there then?" she asked.

"Sooner the better."

"Fine, I'll pick you up tomorrow morning. I suppose it might be too much to expect you to be awake before ten, so shall we say eleven-thirty sharp, just to be on the safe side?" She flicked me a scornful look before rising stiffly from her chair and smoothing her dress over her thighs. She paused for a minute.

"Do you think if she'd had any idea she could have stopped it?" she asked.

"Your mother did the best she could. Ain't no one could have predicted how far things would go," said Jane soothingly. Claudia looked down at her and then flicked her eyes at me before heading out. We did not correct her, but we both knew whom Claudia had meant and that it was not about Mom.

My grandfather's favorite saying when we were younger was "And the meek shall inherit the earth." He loved it because he thought it was talking about people like him, farmer folk, one of the last few classes that could still make money but could never earn as much respect and prestige outside of the farmland circle. But then when his grandchildren came along he would say it in such a way that we knew he was talking about us: specifically that we would be the inheritors of the earth he had stretched and built and added onto by marriage, work and corrupt means and what was now the most prosperous holding in our county.

And so we were all born, our mouths open wide to swallow all that he had laid out for us. Ava and Charles, Ethan's only son, were spread across the year of '73: Charles in the spring and Ava in the fall, closely followed by me by way of a near miscarriage in '75. My grandfather had three granddaughters and two grandsons all crowded onto his beautiful property. We gave him satisfaction, knowing there were many who could potentially take up the mantle of work he had continued. We made him feel like he had a family again. We helped close up the holes Julia had made.

And of my early childhood, I was happy, I confess it. I never went without. I had a lovely home and sisters and cousins to play with amongst the tended gardens my grandmother had nurtured to burst with a multitude of buds in the summer months. My memories were the average memories of any girl who grew up on a farm in Iowa. My father taught me to ride horses, holding the reins and leading me in wide arcs while he clucked and encouraged my back to straighten, my legs to tighten. I rode on a thresher with him during the day, eating berries from a basket on my lap. I ran through the rose garden with my sisters in games invented and taught. I loved my mother, I loved my father. I was safe and warm. I assumed we all were.

When he was two Charles was taken away for testing and Georgia–May was told that her son would never grow past the mental age of seven. She told my mother this in hushed tones on our back porch. But she was not ashamed, nor did it stop her love for her son. If anything it strengthened it. She gave up teaching and dedicated her every waking hour to nurturing her child. As for Ethan—he never took any interest in Charles. When people first found out about his condition and apologetically asked after him and the family, he looked at them with distaste, as if they were stupid for expecting anything else.

"You deal with it," he had told Georgia-May in the doctor's room upon the diagnosis, before heading to a bar. Lavinia had tried to explain away the latter as grief. My father had snorted in disgust.

But out of all that came a flower from a pot of dirt, which was this: that Georgia-May loved Charles more than I've seen any mother with her child, because Charles needed love more than anyone and she knew what that felt like. Hers was a barren marriage with a husband who saw her only as a thing impairing the cool lines of his vision. She had known about Allie, to some degree everybody did, but no one outside of Ethan and Lavinia knew what had really happened the night of his proposal or the depth of the effect it had upon him. She looked upon my parents' marriage with envy and in her darker moments begged and pleaded with her husband to touch her, but he only returned her efforts with a raised fist. She stayed with him, though, despite everything. She was a good woman but never a strong one. She was built for married life and she did not question, only lamented the lot that had befallen her.

Seven—for seven years we were happy. Well, at least I was.

I was too young to notice how my uncle and grandfather constantly drank, too young to let the icy thaw of my grandparents cast a chill around me when Lavinia leaned forward to kiss her husband in the afternoon and caught the stray wisp of alcohol on his breath. I was far too young to understand the strange dynamics of my grandparents' relationship with Cal Jr. or to realize that Charles was different. When my youngest cousin smiled up at me, the thatch of brown hair falling across his eyes in blind happiness at the smallest things—a look you gave him, or gently trailing a blade of grass up and down his wrist—I never saw him as anything other than my cousin who loved water sprinklers in summer and who you could always, always play with because he never grew tired, and who adored us all even if we did not deserve it.

And Ava, my companion, who genuinely liked me, who was my best friend. I made her laugh and she made me care. With her I always felt like the older one. I was the one who fought Lucy Stevens when she called her stuck-up and broke my tooth on her foot when she kicked me. I was the one who stepped in the middle when Claudia blew up at her for whatever she had borrowed without asking. I was the one who braided her hair on our living room carpet watching cartoon reruns. I was so young, too young. Too young to know I was happy and too young to know this could not last. My life appeared to be following a set path and I could not see why it would ever change. Who would want it to?

I asked all the questions in the world but the important ones.

It's strange when I look back on that early part, how the happiness was a haze. It never had the gift of clarity, it was all a delicious blur just slightly out of focus, like the feeling you get when you try to look directly at the sun. For those seven years, despite the undercurrents, despite the tensions that I stepped across and yet was untouched by, mine was a charmed existence.

I had not one but two homes. I had the small yellow house, with the white framed windows and shutters and dragonfly knocker, which was utterly redundant as no visitors ever knocked—our door was always open. But as well as this, I also had the large white house with the tall columns, a place of luxury and finesse. I had the best of both worlds right on my doorstep: my loving, comforting home and the physical embodiment of grandeur that was the Hathaway name, right at my fingertips. I had cousins I played with across a sprawling mass of both tended and untended land, perfect for games, perfect for sunbathing, perfect for running under sprinklers in bathing suits in summer.

I had my mother and father, who adored us children. I was never hungry, never without, never lonely. I was never alone. I was always surrounded by noise and activity and work. Such a stark contrast to my life now. Now, I have chosen a place that hems me in, that is filled with the ringing of silence, but back then my life was full of color, and a tumult of voices rising and falling in laughter and shouts.

And then he died.

Dad, if you had lived, perhaps things would have been different. You would have sensed what was wrong the night before I left for college. You would have coaxed and cajoled it out of her. You would have told me what I did not want to believe. You would have made converts of us all and he would have been punished.

You'd have killed him, I suppose. Even you had your limits.

My strong Pa, who never needed to strike us, would only have to give us a look and we'd know we were in for it, our long legs hiking us the hell out of there. Red checked shirt, long blond hair. I cannot remember you. I only remember the feeling of you. In my head you have been immortalized in seven-year-old aspic—taller than you would have been, stronger, more handsome, good.

Mom told us all about you, but the things I wanted to ask I'll never know because she would not ask you herself. Like, were you happy on Aurelia for the second time? Could you bear the change in your brother, who had been laid up in a bed after proposing to his girlfriend and had, in spirit at least, never gotten out of it? Did you mourn for the loss of your sister despite what she had done, because you saw the drinking of your father and the years of age finally fall onto the hunched shoulders of your aunt and long for the days that were now only a memory? Did you see the eyes of your nephew on your daughter and wince? Did you know even then, but how could you? Not even I, her closest confidante, knew.

Pa, my darling Pa—what things were in your mind on the day death came for you? Did you argue with him that he was too early? Or did you look at him and feel peace? When they found you in the field your legs were crumpled underneath you from your stroke, your eyes closed, lips parted, soaked through from the downpour that had held sway over the heavens all afternoon. Had you tried to cry out in pain or for help, or were you only attempting to catch the last few drops of rain you would ever taste, in your mouth?

I feel I am doing this memory a disservice. There should be more here surely? All other things have been relayed with painstaking precision and detail, but this—one of the most earth-shattering events of my life—has been rushed through, skimmed over, barely registered.

Even though I know he was thirty-three at the time and that his gravestone says his death was on the 27th of September 1982, I don't actually remember those few days after he died. I don't remember hearing about his death, I don't remember anything about my family's initial reactions to it, nothing. When I used to talk about my dad, remember him even, it was through the borrowing of other people's stories, other people's memories. I don't think it was the same for my sisters, but that's how it was with me.

Aside from my mother's self-imposed isolation when we went to live with my grandparents, the episode of my father's death is a blank where the truth presses, but never quite makes it past the edges. Even the funeral itself is a haze and then at the wake, which was held at home, I removed my hand from my mother's grip as soon as we were inside and ran to hide under a large oak table facing the wall, with a white cloth peeking out over the edge so that the world was cut into two triangles.

My mother left me alone, as did my sisters. While they were comforted, I sat cross-legged with my back pressed to the wall watching the various legs of the adults pass in front of me. I wanted to stay underneath that table forever. If I stayed there, I thought, then nothing could happen to me, nothing else could change, there just wasn't enough room.

And then somehow, Cal Jr. saw me. There was a knock on the top of the table. I looked up and as I did, he crouched down and knocked twice against the table leg.

"Can I come in?" he asked, half-smiling.

I paused and then shrugged indifferently.

He slid underneath the table but he had to curl his legs beneath him as there was so little room and I, obstinately, refused to move.

"Cramped in here," he said.

"Not for me."

He settled himself and then went still. I eyed him cautiously.

"You gonna stay here all night?" he asked.

"Maybe."

"What good will that do?"

"I don't know."

He sighed.

"At least you had your father for a good few years. May not be much but it's more than some."

I bit the inside of my lip.

"At least you got memories of him, at least he was there for you. You being ungrateful hiding in here when you got more than most. Some people ain't got nowhere to hide. They got to bury their pain deep down, so deep that whenever they look inside themselves all they see is the darkness left behind. They don't get sympathy or cucumber sandwiches. They don't get to grieve. They get to lie and pretend and never question. Do you get what I am saying? Do you, huh?"

His voice was soft the whole time that he spoke, but there was such menace and pain in his tone that I began to feel afraid. He prodded me with his forefinger between my ribs when I did not answer him, but I did not move. Instead I closed my eyes and willed him to disappear. He leaned against me, his breath on my ear, his hand now on my knee. I squeezed my eyes shut and let the inside of my lids go red with the effort.

I could feel him watching me, could sense his eyes scurry up and down my face.

"Brat," he said finally. And then he unfurled himself and slid out from underneath the table and left.

When I was sure he had gone, I slowly opened my eyes. The world beneath my table seemed starker, as if the softness had been pressed out of it. I wrapped my arms about my middle and pretended my hands were someone else's as they rubbed my stomach in comfort.

Before my father died, I don't have memories about anything of that time as much as feelings. It's strange but when I look back on that episode of my life it's the sensation of warmth I conjure up, not the images that tell me I am in a good place in the past. I never felt warmth like that after the wake. I guess that is what it means to grow up.

I think I need a minute to stop now.

11

BEFORE MY FATHER'S DEATH I USED TO PLAY THIS game called "Thirteen at the Table." Using my parents' tea set from their honeymoon, I would arrange thirteen of my dolls and bears around a makeshift picnic cloth and we would all sit down for tea. And then the first of them to rise up would die in an awful way and we would have to guess which one of my bears and dolls had committed the murder in question. I, of course, would act out the death noises and the voices and the conversations. Claudia would say I sounded like something from *The Exorcist*.

Sometimes I would try and include Charles but he was no good at the game. He would look at me with a blank smile or, even worse, laugh. More often than not, I would rope Ava into my games to play the role of the victim. She would fall down theatrically onto the floor, her arms splayed in a pose reenacted from a movie while I voiced the dramatic noises of her make-believe death.

Once Cal Jr. found us. We were outside in the garden with

Charles. Ava had just been poisoned with strychnine (I got the name off of a TV show) and I had directed her as to how she was to die. She fell to the floor writhing in slow soundless motion while I parroted the caws of suffocation and slow death that were gripping her limbs as she slid silently down. She collapsed onto the grass, her arms above her head, her long hair spilling brown onto the green.

I did not see him until the last minute. I had my eyes closed as I vocally demonstrated her death but when I opened them, Cal Jr. was standing above her looking down. He was about eighteen at the time, and Ava would be ten in three months. He saw her there and even though his shadow fell across her face she did not stir.

"Cal?" I asked uncertainly when he would not move, only bent his head to take more of her in and then suddenly he swooped down and lifted her up all in one movement. He was very strong, my cousin, and Ava was such a slip of a thing; while Claudia would be all curves and I was tall and lithe, Ava was delicate, weightless, her clothes often had to be taken in by Mom.

She yelled, of course, as did Charles, but with excitement. Cal had gone running down the garden laughing, holding her higher as she screamed with terror and delight. Charles and I were chasing him, not sure if we were players in a game or heroes in a tragedy. And then he stopped and swung her around and around until she was dizzy, her hair whipping about her head, her legs fast in his arms. We started laughing; we realized it was in fun. We had figured him out.

And then he dropped her.

"Ow, Cal, that hurt," said Ava and she slapped his foot hard. Her face was flushed and she pulled her hair off her brow as she rubbed her thigh. I knelt down beside her.

"What did you do that for?" I asked and stood up to show

him I was angry. He wasn't looking at me; he had turned away, staring at the rose garden.

"You hurt her, butt-wipe," I yelled, trying to attract his attention, but when I touched his arm he shrugged me off.

"She kicked me," he said.

"No, I never," said Ava, standing up. "I hate you."

Cal whipped his neck around and grabbed her by the arm as she made to stalk off, Charles and I flanking her. But just then instead of us needing to rally to defend her against his attack, he sank to his knees and in a mock voice started crooning to her for forgiveness, like one of those Italian singers you see in old movies where heroines stand by lamplight before men in tuxedos.

Ava didn't want to play along, I could tell, but her lips twitched and though she pursed them together in fury, her cheeks relented in laughter as Cal rolled his eyes and contorted his face with the effort.

"Come on, Ava," I said eventually, grabbing her arm.

"Ah, Merey, it was just a joke," he called after us but he did not follow. And though I did not respond, Ava turned to give him a smile.

When Pa died I stopped Thirteen at the Table. Suddenly death was not so funny anymore. It was not something I could invite and banish away at will. I learned that there were some things that would come into your life and you would not always be able to fight them. They could pick you up and throw you around like a rag doll and you could plead and reason, but that would not be enough to stop them.

So the picnic blanket was packed away and the bears and dolls no longer met for tea.

The next day Claudia came for me on the dot of eleven-thirty. I was sitting outside on Jane's porch cradling a whiskey in one of her tumblers.

When Claudia saw me she rolled down the window and frowned.

"Jesus, Mer, it's not even the afternoon yet. Get in."

Her tone was so authoritative that I was up and halfway down the walk before I realized why I was out there waiting for her in the first place. I stopped. She slammed her finger against the horn.

I leaned down against the window and she shot me a look of irritation before rolling her eyes.

"I don't want to hear it—just get in the car," she said.

"I'm not sure if this... It's a bit soon, isn't it, to star—"

"Look, you were the one who said that the farm is going to be auctioned off soon, and you were the one who high-tailed it over from New York so we could go over Mom's stuff and make sure that not everything was dispatched to the winds and all traces of our lives and our parents' lives were gone forever. Right? Then stop pissing about and get in the fucking car, Meredith."

She hadn't lost her touch, my sister. I was there in the car beside her before my head had caught up with my body. Childhood autopilot. When she wanted to, despite my attempts at rebellion, she could flick a switch in me and make me inwardly cower. I had assumed that this was a thing of the past, but as we sped down the familiar roads in her rented car, once again, I was proven wrong.

When we got to the trees I knew so well, I braced my hands against the window and seat respectively.

"You're going to have to stop," I said.

"What do you mean?" she asked, staring straight ahead.

My body realized what was happening before I did.

"Oh, God."

She was so far up the lane I could see the bush lines part and a flurry of speckled white slipped into vision.

I leaned right across her and threw up.

★ ★ ★

After my father died something shifted in my grandparents. I don't want to say that something broke, but it did fracture and the fissure ran a course through their relationship, like rivers on plaster.

The strange thing was, the fissure was in my grandfather, not my grandmother.

Like all things, Lavinia took the death of her youngest child in her stride. She did not cry in public, and she did not cover her face in a veil at his funeral. She did not even break her routine once he was buried. She dusted, she cleaned, she cooked. She wrote thank-you notes to those who sent flowers and cards of condolence. She exhibited no signs at all of grief. She called it stoicism. Others called it cold.

While my grandfather's drinking worsened and my uncle retreated even further into silence, my grandmother was a model of normality. It was she who, when people asked how a man as young and healthy as my father could have died of a stroke caused by a brain aneurysm with no previous symptoms, answered them with the cold facts of the postmortem. It was she who soothed their shaking heads of disbelief and fielded their questions and concerns.

All this I saw when we lived in her house during that time. And I knew then, for the first time, that my grandmother was the one in our family who was the rock against which our waters broke. And yet we were not grateful. We did not want her strength, we wanted to see her body racked with anguish, to watch her pain and know that it cut through her carefully tendered links of self-control.

In other words—to know that she was like the rest of us.

As for my grandfather, he would fall into long lapses of silence around us, sometimes only punctuated by a brief smile that flickered and then died on his mouth before he knocked back whatever drink he was holding. He withdrew utterly from his wife through the medium of compliance. Anything she wanted, she got, anything she asked for, he did without question. It was robotic. My grandmother observed this but she did not raise the issue. She refused to acknowledge anything else was rotten in her home outside of my father's death. It was in everything she did and said, from how she would smile at neighbors who passed her in the street, to refusing our school to allow us any time off to grieve. Perhaps she even came to believe it a bit, because anytime anyone asked after us all she would say was, "Fine, we're just fine, aren't we, girls?"

Despite everything, this small habit of hers is something that has stayed with me. I use that word all the time whenever my life feels anything but. If you ask me a question and I use that as a response you know that despite my outward calm, something inside me shivers.

Which is why as if on autopilot, as I was gasping after heaving my guts up all over her, while Claudia screamed at me asking what the hell I was doing, saying my name over and over in varying degrees of anguish and disgust, before I could stop myself I was saying, "It's okay, I'll be fine. I'll be fine."

At the nearest gas station, as Claudia cleaned herself up in the bathroom, I stood outside, my arms folded across my chest. Despite my earlier nausea, my body felt okay now, numb, but otherwise normal. This, I knew, would anger my sister, who if she had to have her expensive dress covered, however involuntarily, with my vomit at least wanted to know that I had suffered for it.

Which I had, but not in any way she could obviously discern, so what use would that be to her?

Eventually she came over to join me, her dress smudged and in serious need of a dry-clean despite her concerted efforts. Through clenched teeth she asked, "Are you okay?"

"Fine now, thanks," I said gingerly.

"Great, glad to hear it."

"Look, I'm sorry—I couldn't help it."

"I'm sure."

"I didn't do it on purpose, Clo," I said, suddenly really angry. "I mean for fuck's sake, it isn't all about you, is it?"

"Or you," she suddenly screamed at me. "You think I like being back any more than you? You think I want to be here? That I get some kind of kick from it? I know what you're thinking, who gives a shit when it was all my fault anyway? Little Miss Bitch got her comeuppance, right?"

Her nostrils were pinched and white, her cheeks blotched with color. For a moment I didn't recognize her and then I did—far too much. She was panting with exertion. Suddenly she drew herself up and held her hand against her chest to steady her breathing.

"You're not the only one with memories you'd like to exorcise, Meredith," she said in a low voice after a while. "Sorry to rip that precious idea from your head but your pain is no more special than anyone else's. We all have our demons here, so you'll just have to get over yours like the rest of us. We are going to go down to the farm and we are going to sort through Mom and Dad's things like we planned before everything gets auctioned off. No excuses, so suck it up." She glared at me and then sighed. "And next time I'll bring a change of clothes, just in case."

Arrogant presumption. Perhaps the reason why she is so angry with me is because I cannot so easily forgive myself the way she has for her mistakes. Maybe she's made of sterner stuff than I am. Maybe she's more like our grandmother than she'd like to admit. So am I in some ways. It's so easy to lay all our faults at Lavinia's door, isn't it? Any bad trait, any negative feeling we say comes from her, from her line, her genes. We don't like to think they may be things inherent in us rather than just inherited. Scape-goating—we're good at that in my family.

Or maybe she's more capable of dealing with her memories because she doesn't have to remember as well as I do. Maybe she does not go over things again and again in her mind, looking for clues she ignored right up until it was there in her face and even then her mind scrambled for a way to deny what was slowly burning its way right through the bone.

We lived with my cousin for a whole month as children and in that time I never noticed anything amiss. If anything during that time, I came to see my eldest cousin as a victim rather than a predator. I saw how awkward my grandfather was around him. How he barely ever looked him in the eye; how he would always find an excuse to leave a room if he suspected the two of them would be left alone together. And I saw Cal Jr.'s resigned attitude to his coldness. He would look at me when I watched him with a questioning eye and shrug, as if to say this is my life, this is just how it has always been. I felt sorry for him, I felt like he needed a champion. I began to court his approval.

To my sisters and I, Cal Jr. was older, aloof and the source of a subject that, from the hushed tones of our family, was both taboo and yet enticing. He was mysterious, like a foundling, looking nothing like the rest of us with his shock of red hair and pale blue eyes, so pale they could be diluted, except when he was angry and then they would suddenly color. We sought his attention as kids. He was the eldest, the strongest, the most difficult to please and so the most pleasing when we finally secured his favor. If he laughed at a joke, we were funny; if he scorned us we secretly wondered if there was something in us that was wrong. He had a way for such a long time of making you wonder about yourself rather than about him. But it was Ava on whom he focused his attentions the most. I could not see it for a long time, and even afterward could not understand it, but I do now. Now that I'm old enough and have seen enough, I understand how such things can happen in those ways. There were times when I saw him look at Ava and I would wince ever so slightly. Yet I did not try to keep them apart, I did not warn her, and, more importantly, I did not question her. He is my monster because of what I know now, but back then he was my cousin and though I feared him, I also loved him.

Strangely it was always our grandmother he turned to, our grandmother in whom he confided, leaned on, learned from. Piper was always hurt and surprised at their relationship, constantly cajoling, even wheedling him for that same needless affection that he threw so readily on Lavinia. She could not understand it; even more so she could not understand why my grandmother took it. It was a question she was too innocent to answer. Even after all she had learned she could not sense a power struggle when it was right under her nose.

On her bed, her breath rattling, suddenly out of nowhere, she interrupted my reading aloud and said, "Don't trust him."

"What, Grandma?" I asked, dropping the book and leaning farther in so she did not have to exert herself.

She closed her eyes in frustration and for a moment I thought she had slipped back into whatever blank she had stirred from, but then as I folded back the page she said again, "Don't be fooled. I'm not. He's not capable of love. But he'll take care of the place, he won't let it go. He needs it. He knows he's nothing without it."

"What are you talking about Grandma?"

"Obsession, that's all it is. He has to have it, but it's better than nothing. Get away from me!" She struck my hand as I went to rest it on the covers and then she looked at me and started laughing, really laughing, as if her body would erupt with the joke that was on all of us.

But she was wrong. Cal Jr. could love. I remember when he was about fifteen he had a pet once, a kitten given to him by Piper. He adored it, connected to it with a softness and protective possessiveness that no one had thought him capable of. And then one day, quite by accident, he broke its neck. He had held it so tightly against his chest in the crook of his elbow that its fragile vertebrae had snapped. To his credit he was inconsolable for days afterward, it even made him ill. My grandmother nursed him and when he was better again we never spoke of it. That should have been a warning to us all about the dangers of our cousin, who was so destructive even when he was trying to be good, but it wasn't—at least not until it was far too late.

In those few weeks of my childhood after we'd moved back home with our mother, our lives slowly began to resume a newfound sense of normalcy. Our house was tidy and clean, we did our home chores before we went to school and we helped out on the farm when we came home. Ava took up dance lessons; I tried and failed at piano. Our mother insisted on trying to implement structure and order into our lives. We became governed by routine. Every spare moment seemed to be accounted for, as if she were afraid that any gap was the chance for disaster, that every pause would be an invitation for crisis. Or perhaps she just thought that to aid us in our grief we should be kept busy so we could not dwell on the death of our father. But how could we forget, how could every moment not be colored by his absence? From our school plays, when we looked out into the audience and only saw our mother where once there were two, to the simple quotidian acts of each day, such as setting out places on the table for supper and realizing you'd laid too many plates. I remember seeing Claudia staring at the extra place mat, stricken, the plate still in her hand, and then as she heard our mother's footsteps, hurrying to put away the offending item before she saw it.

And of course every Sunday we still went to the tall white house for a big roast dinner, which my grandmother and Piper would cook, and there we would watch our grandfather and uncle drink until their faces turned red and their mouths grew slack, while everything in my grandmother tightened to make up for their slow descent. Cal Jr. would be there, sitting across from us beside our grandmother. He would change allegiances per the day. One day he would talk to Claudia, making low jokes and snide looks with his eyes that he knew Ava and I were meant to see and burn over. Other times it would be me and, just like my eldest sister, I entered into his contract of favoritism because being on the inside was more attractive than being on the outside. But with Ava he would never use her against us—instead when it was her turn, he was kind, attentive. He made her laugh, coaxed conversation from her. In short, he knew how to play to our weaknesses: mine and Claudia's were a propensity to be in the spotlight; Ava's was to be loved.

Even though they were both heavy drinkers, my grandfather and uncle still managed to run the farm as efficiently as they had before. That is, they made harvest every year, the numbers did not slip, our lands still provided and our farm as a business was still revered. But as people, their alcoholism changed them irrevocably. My grandfather became a muted drunkard whose light could only be turned on in his mind by a tumbler being placed in his hand. My uncle became altogether far nastier a creature. He never touched Charles, but we all knew he beat the shit out of Georgia-May. In the mornings as we would go off to school she would come over to our mother's house and Mom would bathe her and patch up her back from his belt scars and plead with her to leave him, but she never would.

Mom even went to Lavinia once. She found her in the rose garden, her straw hat tied with its dark green ribbon resting on her shoulders. She told her of the buckle marks on Georgia-May's back and how if Theo was alive, Ethan would never have been able to get away with what he was doing. Lavinia had looked at her tiredly and said she would speak with him, but it was for nothing. Ethan was beyond her control now and she knew it. So long as he was good for the farm, our grandfather would never cut him off, but the days when she could manipulate and coach his mind into her way of thinking were long gone. The alcohol was too strong a component in making his mind as hard and unrelenting as it made his gut slack and soft. She had no more luck with him than she had with her own husband and truth be told most of her energy was taken up with Cal Jr. Ethan was a lost cause now. With him she could only wait until he was no longer of use. It was on her grandson's shoulders now that she rested all her hopes.

Which we could all see. When we were young, the two of them were as thick as thieves. Always going off for walks together, gardening, talking, hushing their conversations when someone else intruded on their time together. And that's what it felt like for us—as if we were an intrusion. We would all learn, my sisters and I, that they were the kind of people who found you, you weren't to find them.

So Georgia-May stayed and was beaten and Mom and Piper nursed her. Ethan at least did not go whoring; his only satisfaction was taken from inflicting his fists and belt and shoes all over her body. He wouldn't touch her in any other way now, save to mark her—but never the face, always below the chest and never the arms in summer or the legs. You could tell the seasons on our farm by the location of my aunt's bruises.

My grandfather knew. Lavinia told him, but he said nothing, only drank some more. She began to seriously doubt whether there was a man left in there, or just the cool amber liquids of various spirits where a soul used to be. I remember him as kind; drunk but kind. And meek—he would lift you up on his lap and let you crouch there so long as you didn't disturb his drinking arm while you played. His body was a fairground, like a sleeping giant for playful Lilliputians.

But there must have still been something there that none of us suspected, because of what he did when Claudia was fifteen. It was as if for all those years, he had been scrambling in the dark, patting the walls anxiously with his hands and then finally, miraculously even, somehow he found the switch.

It started with a letter. I never read it but my grandmother did. After much scouring of the house she found it wedged behind a radiator in the downstairs toilet. She found it the day my grandfather announced at the table over the Sunday roast that his nephew, our second cousin, would be coming to live and work on Aurelia. His name was Jude; he was the child of his brother, Leo, and had been named after the patron saint of lost causes. Piper later told us it was because he was finally conceived when Elisa was forty-one so that his birth was considered almost miraculous. Elisa had apparently

NELLE DAVY

turned evangelical the older she had gotten and the more shriveled her womb had become.

Off my grandfather went on a great tangent over the dining table, peppered with digressions, musings and vague references to feuds and histories that I would come to learn in greater detail years afterward at my grandmother's bedside. At the time I simply let his words rush over me in their semidrunken torrent as they always did at the table when he decided to speak, which was not often. I did not listen much and so cannot repeat what he said. At the time I did not realize how much this had meant to him: it had just seemed another ineffectual event that would have little to no effect on the alteration of my immediate family's lives. Ignorance is bliss, my grandmother used to say, and I've come to agree with her. That evening I was utterly and happily unaware of the seething resentment stirred up by my grandfather's declaration. While Leo had eventually learned in part to forgive or forget the grudge that had stopped him from ever setting foot again on Aurelia, he had never been able to fully embrace my grandfather as a brother, until now. His suggestion that Granddad take Jude in and let him have a more active hand in observing Leo's stock on the farm had washed over me in a haze of boredom and inertia. I remember wondering why Granddad had bothered to have Jude over in the first place. If this man was so important, then how come we had never met him? But then I did not think of Aurelia as a business, it was just my home. I did not monitor its input and profit, even though the money from my father's share was all that kept my little family afloat since my mother did not work at this time. The bliss of childhood: to see clothes mended and food appear and never feel the need to question.

I do remember this, though, how my grandfather's eyes kept flickering back and forth to Lavinia the whole time he spoke and though none of us would find out until Cal Jr. told us weeks later, they had the most terrific argument when everyone had gone. The first one they had had in years, it was a screaming match where suddenly everything between them came vividly back to life and forced them to realize that something else, something other than themselves, had been dead all along.

My sisters and I were confused, we didn't understand the significance of what we were hearing. I remember that Claudia had asked, when our grandfather had finally stopped his long and winding spiel about family and forgiveness and bridges (there had been many a metaphor on crossings), "But Granddad, who is Uncle Leo?"

"Oh—" and he started to smile as if she had told him a clever joke "—oh, of course he's not your uncle, not *your* uncle, no, but you see that's what he's always been called by…by the kids who used to sit at this table—Uncle Leo. I forgot." He started to chuckle. "I forgot…" And then a flush of remembrance dragged the smile to the side of his mouth so that his face became lopsided and then he shook himself. It was Piper who intervened.

"He was your father's uncle, Claudia. He was our brother."

"Where is he?" she asked. "How come I've never met him?"

Piper and Cal looked at each other and for a moment there was an uncomfortable silence.

"He died quite recently. Cancer, like our daddy," Piper said. "That's why he got in touch with your granddaddy. He and his wife used to live on a farm owned by our mother's folk, but this was their first home and, well, we thought it best when your grandfather heard about our brother's death and everything that happened…" She turned to her brother for help, but my grandfather's face was closed in quiet grief.

"We thought how nice it would be for Jude to come back again, for his father's sake, since we could not do it for him while he was living."

I had looked down at the rose-leaf dinner plate and played with the food there, circling it this way and that with my fork, my leg listlessly scraping against the wooden floor. Surreptitiously my mother leaned against me and pinched the flesh under my knee to make me stop. I was always scuffing my shoes when I was a kid.

My grandmother turned away as I looked up in pain and picked up her teaspoon to stir her coffee. Her hand was trembling. My cousin Cal Jr. sat beside her. He heard the gentle clatter of her spoon against the cup, and then, he reached across the table and picked up the silver coffeepot, dropping it unsteadily so that it chimed against the milk jug and the sound made me rub my tongue across the front of my teeth. Our grandfather flashed him a look of irritation before clearing his throat to recommence his speech.

"So much has happened in this family. So much loss and fighting. This is going to be a new start for us Hathaways. Get this family back to how it once was," my grandfather said as he pounded the table and looked at all of us. Piper stood up as he towered over her, a maniacal grin spreading and then sapping at his cheeks, and motioned for him to sit down.

"After Theo and everything...you girls...lost two already and so young..." He trailed off and began to sway on his feet. "This means a lot to me," he said more to himself than anything else. "A hell of a lot."

"We know that, Cal," said my grandmother, watching him while she continued to swirl the spoon around her drink until her hand grew steady.

"No one will ever replace your father," he began again

in an effort to compose himself as his eyes found my sisters and I. "He was a wonderful son. But we need some fresh blood in this place—" Cal Jr. bent his head and a thin red streak appeared on his cheek as the blood colored against the skin there "—and Jude will give us that."

"And we'll do everything we can to make him welcome," said my mother.

"Yes." He smiled at her gratefully. "Yes, I know you will."

And then he looked at all of us and we smiled back at him. Cal Jr. kept his gaze on his plate.

On the walk home, I had lagged behind with Ava while Claudia held on to Charles's hand, barely concealing her irritation as Mom escorted Georgia-May. Ethan had gone into town in his truck. We all knew he would not be home until the early hours and that Georgia-May would be over the next morning as ever, while my mother got the bowl of hot water and salts ready. Thinking on this now I have a crack of horror winding its way through my memories for the first time about my aunt. Even though I know now that she would escape with her son, back then her beatings and the tender nursings of my mother for all her injuries was so normal to me, so routine, that I was almost nonchalant when on the weekday mornings, Georgia-May would bare the crimson and purple welts on her back to my mother's hands while I crunched on my cornflakes.

"Are you excited?" Ava asked me.

"I don't know," I said.

"I am. It'll be nice to have new a cousin to play with. I wonder what he's like."

"I don't know, Ava."

"I hope Cal Jr. won't be jealous."

"Why would he be jealous?"

"I don't— He just, he asked me if I was going to…uh…"

She trailed off, her brow furrowing as she concentrated on what she was saying. I looked away from her into the distance.

"I can't wait," she said excitedly.

I stifled a yawn and kicked a piece of gravel on the dust path. "Neither can I."

It was less than a year after my father died when Jude came to Aurelia. My days consisted of waking up in my whitewashed room covered in *E.T.* posters, going to school, doing chores on the farm and playing with my sisters and—occasionally when my mother felt strong enough to allow me to have them over—my friends, who would bring their sleeping bags and blankets and we would camp out in the gardens. Our favorite spot was the clearing with the stone god fountain, where we would pitch up our white sheets and tell ghost stories with flashlights under our chins. I was never short of friends as a child. Nor would I have been even if I were the dumbest, ugliest or most unpleasant. Every family wanted to align themselves with us. Who wouldn't want to be tied to the most prosperous family in the county, even with their mottled history? But my grandmother was more discerning. She watched the children my sisters and I brought home with a careful eye, asking after the families of those she did not know or recognize, making notes of the behavior of the offspring from those she did. And then a few weeks later we would learn of her decisions.

"Does that Galloway girl ever wipe her nose?" she asked as she sat in our kitchen while my mother served her tea. Or, "It's a shame the Mackenzies have done so badly this year. I saw that same dress on Mary not two years before and now it's ended up on Grace." And so bit by bit, we would come to learn the lives of our neighbors and more importantly, who should stay our neighbors and who were worthy of becoming our friends.

Claudia was better at it than either myself or Ava. She knew her worth as a Hathaway. Her friends were a coterie of the farming equivalent of blue bloods, with herself at the center. She quickly sniffed out who was a farmer and who was a "land owner," as she called it, casting the former out into the social wilderness.

"You can be friends with whomever you like," Mom used to tell us deliberately within our grandmother's earshot.

My grandmother would stop what she was doing and look at my mother, before saying carefully, "As long as you know what to like."

I didn't really understand the significance of what this meant back then. I knew I was privileged. I knew and liked the way people would look at me in the street or in class or at fairs when they came up to me and I said my name. But I still didn't really know what it meant. I should have been paying more attention to things around me, but I was a child who was caught up in the stories and worlds in my mind. I lived in my head and expressed myself with my hands. Always drawing or scribbling, taking things apart and then trying to put things back together again. That's how we went through two toasters and a burst water pipe under the kitchen sink, for which I got a spanking, one of only a handful my mother ever gave me. I flitted from one obsession to another, constantly questioning, constantly seeking, but never at home. Home bored me because it seemed uneventful.

"Nothing ever happens here," I would complain, lying in the grass kicking my bare legs at the hot air. And to us kids it never did. However Cal Jr., as I remember him, never seemed to want to go anywhere or do anything else. Every day after school and every weekend he was at home.

None of those raucous beer-swilling, cow-tipping days that seemed to form the spare hours of his contemporaries. He kept to himself and to his home. The two seemed to satisfy him. But Claudia found the farm as stiflingly boring as I did. Though it was beautiful, though we loved it, we were crushed by the utter banality of it. For aside from my uncle and grandfather's drunkenness and despite the savagery of Georgia-May's beatings, nothing did happen: at least not to me and Claudia. With Ava...now, there was a different story.

I want to say that I have tried to remember, but hindsight only makes the past a murkier thing, not clearer. There was a period just after we lived with my grandparents until she was about fifteen when she was prone to black moods. She would not speak, she would not really eat; she could not bear to be touched. Mom put it down to the hormones of puberty. Her moods could be incredibly fickle, sometimes so affectionate her hands were almost intrusive and Mom would sometimes slap her fingers for how she would hug or coil her arms around us, while we shrugged her away uncomfortably. Other times she was so dismissive, we would not understand what we had done.

But when she was herself, when she was Ava again, she was so different: prone to girlish moments of throwing her arms about herself in a dancing hug when overly excited, playing with her hair and tugging on it hard when concentrating. She was the Ava who soothed and listened to me as we grew older together, who retreated as I blossomed, until by the time she was fifteen she was a quiet, unassuming girl: pretty, loving, gentle. She had come through to the other side, as Mom used to say. That was what we had thought.

She never shirked away from Cal Jr., she didn't avoid him, she didn't cower before him. She defended him, she explained him, she was closer to him than any of us, not because they had anything in common, but because he made her that way. He chose her to confide in whenever he needed to, made her seem special, outside of the rest of us in only this one but crucial respect. It was one of the ways I see now that he groomed her and one of the ways in which we unthinkingly allowed him to.

But I digress.

Jude arrived in the middle of March 1982 on a Friday night. We did not see his arrival; Piper came around to the house and told Mom he was here and that the whole family was to be formally introduced to him at Sunday dinner. When the day arrived, dutifully we trooped over there in our clean smock dresses and our hair tied up with ribbons. Mom had gone into town looking for a present to welcome him to Aurelia and she had found a wooden tobacco box with intricate carvings on the lid of a glade with the wind running through it. Inside it we put in little cards and messages of welcome, while she had observed our spelling (Mine: perfect; Ava's very good; Claudia—well, she needed a few drafts. "If you paid more attention to your schooling than to your looks you'd do better," Mom had said).

We walked over with Georgia-May, Charles and Ethan. Charles held hands with Ava and me, while Claudia carted Jude's box in its wrappings of purple tissue and silver string. Charles was thirteen then, and Georgia-May had been looking into schools that could help him since he wouldn't be able to move into junior high as Ava had done. She had ordered books and tapes about how to school him at home. After all, she had trained as a teacher herself and she had even enrolled at night classes to learn how to teach those with learning disabilities. I don't know how Charles would have fared without his mother. She did more than keep him alive. If she could have breathed for him she would have. When she had gone, and things started to come out, we learned that she had never cried out when Ethan beat her, not even when he broke her ribs or split her lip with his shoe, in case she should wake her son. Maybe that was why when he got so drunk that night when I was sixteen and held her at knife-point right before Charles's eyes, she broke and finally left him, because she could not bear for her son to know and be damaged by what her husband did to her. We always thought that she was what saved Charles, but in the end without even meaning to, he had been the one to save her.

Piper opened the door and we saw by how smart her new dress was and how her braid of silver-streaked hair was so tight and smooth against her head, that we were right to be formal for the occasion.

When we entered the living room, Cal Jr. stood by the window biting his fingernails, my grandfather was pouring a drink and Lavinia sat, her hands clasped over her lap, on the long sofa next to the man who was my long-lost second cousin.

He had the most beautiful green eyes I had ever seen.

As we entered, Ava and I took one look at Jude, his curled brown hair, his blue jeans and white shirt rolled up to reveal his lithe and strong forearms, and then turned to each other and bent our heads in a sudden pique of stifled giggles. Mortifying. Claudia shot us a scathing look and tossed her hair back off her shoulder.

He came forward, hand outstretched, toward my mother, a wide grin showing perfectly white teeth and I could feel myself blush. I turned to look at Ava but she was staring deliberately at the floor.

As my mother introduced him to all of us, he smiled and shook our hands. I remember how calloused his palm was in mine and how big. Immediately I liked him. He set me

at ease at once and though he bent his head to try and make
Ava look at him, he didn't draw any attention to her, just
shook her hand timidly, enveloping it in his own before
moving on, and when he opened our present he leaned back
to smile with a grin of surprise. I could see how touched
he was as he gently discarded the purple tissue and held the
tobacco box in his fingers with a great big smile. That was
it—I was smitten. I was suddenly glad that Granddad had
done what he had. I could finally see what he had meant by
a new start.

Cal Jr. had been sitting on the cream sofa beside our
grandmother eyeing the bottom of his empty glass when
we had first come in, but then he had stood up and paced the
room, his hand straying across ornaments, sweeping along
the rim of the mantelpiece. He was always in the corner of
our eyes, emerging and then disappearing in an array of sudden inexplicable movements. My grandmother had stayed on
the sofa, listening as my grandfather talked to her, I forget
about what. Her eyes followed my cousin's listless movements.

"So have you always been a farmer, Jude?" my mother
asked.

"Uh, yeah, I guess," he said and rubbed the back of his
neck with his hand. Cal Jr. was beside the antique dresser, his
index finger tracing the rim of a Dresden shepherdess doll.

"I mean I never was that school smart and my whole family was farm folk, so…I never really thought about what I
wanted to do, I just did what I knew."

"And if you don't mind my saying so, you're a lot younger
than I expected you to be," my mother ventured.

He smiled a dimpled smile. I felt my insides dissolve just
a little.

"My mom had me late in life. Very late," Jude said. Cal Jr. came to stand by the door frame. His nails traced the lines.

"How old are you?" I asked. My mother shot me a furious look.

"Merey," she admonished. Jude smiled and shook his head. "How old do I look?"

"Forty-seven," Claudia deadpanned.

Jude's eyebrows lifted up and he pursed his lips into a whistle. I saw Cal Jr. shoot Claudia a smirk.

"Ouch," said Jude.

"Claudia." My mother's voice slapped her into straightening her spine as she stood.

"No, it's okay. Guess I need to lay off the beer for a while." And then he inclined his head toward me and winked. "I'm actually a very old, apparently, thirty-two."

"That's not that old," ventured Ava, half-doubtfully.

Jude let out a belly chuckle. "Thanks, kid."

Piper's voice called us all in for dinner and I turned to my grandmother and said, "How come you're not cooking today, Grandma?"

For a second there was a brief hush. I saw Jude's eyebrows furrow in disconcertment though his smile had not yet slipped, before my grandmother gave a small, gentle laugh.

"I had a terrible migraine this morning. Piper kindly offered to take over. It's a bit of tradition for me to cook the Sunday meal, Jude. I'm afraid I've let you down somewhat."

"Not at all, ma'am," he said. "I'm sure there'll be plenty more Sundays for you to cook for me. I'm sure you're wonderful."

"Thank you," said my grandmother softly. We turned to walk into the dining room and as was custom, Cal Jr. stood to the side to accompany my grandmother. But she did not look at him. Instead she was still gazing at Jude and then sud-

denly as if in some sort of silent communication, he crooked
his elbow and she slid her hand upward, looping it so that
she could take his arm. The two of them walked past Cal Jr.
without even a glance.

My cousin hesitated, still staring after them as they went
into the dining room and then Piper offered her arm for him
and he took it, after a slight pause.

The meal was a good one. Jude told jokes and was genial
and interested in everyone. Granddad didn't drink as much,
which was both a relief and yet so anomalous that it made me
feel uptight with tension. Cal Jr. barely spoke, but then neither did my uncle, so no one noticed much. Claudia twirled
the food around her plate in mock disdain and with bored,
contrived posings that made Jude chuckle into his napkin.
Mom whispered fiercely into her ear, which made Clo purse
her lips so hard they turned purple. In short the meal was a
success, or as much as it can be for our family. We seemed
to get along.

After Piper's pecan pie, which made us all lean back in our
chairs and rub our stomachs to ease the sweet discomfort of
overindulgence, Jude cleared his throat and our grumbles of
conversation died away. For the first time that night, I saw
him look marginally uncomfortable.

He cleared his throat. "I just wanted to say how thankful I
am to all of you for welcoming me into your home," he said,
craning his neck in our direction but not looking anyone in
the eye.

"It's your home too now, Jude, was your grandfather's,
God rest his soul, and your father's after him. And it's just as
much yours," said Granddad emphatically. My grandmother
licked her lips and flicked him a look from under her lashes.
Cal Jr. scraped his fork against the china rim of his plate.

"Well, thank you, sir, and I'm glad you feel that way," said

Jude. "I know there's been bad blood between our families in the past, but I hope to put an end to that so that we can be together on the land that is and always will be our home. Finally we can be as God intended—happy and healthy, hardworking and free. I look forward to getting to know all the members of my family and working together again just as I'm sure Walter Hathaway, the reason we are even here in the first place, would have wanted."

"Hear, hear," said Piper, raising a glass.

"Hear, hear," repeated Granddad.

"Hear, hear," we said, some more clearly than others.

"To new beginnings," said my grandfather.

The lights bounced off of the crystal in our hands.

"To new beginnings," we all echoed.

That evening, as we dispersed and went our various ways, I found Cal Jr. around the side of the house smoking.

"If Granddad catches you..." I said.

"He won't give a damn," he said angrily. "So—" he flicked the match into the hibiscus bush "—what did you think of our little prince there? Interesting that he didn't arrive on a white horse but a battered old pickup, though judging by tonight who could tell?"

"I like him," I said, wincing at his tone. "He's nice."

"He won't last," Cal Jr. muttered.

"Pardon?" I said loudly. Cal Jr. looked at me, but did not answer.

"Are you jealous?" I asked, lifting my voice to show my disdain.

Cal Jr. laughed softly and then began to cough, smoke spluttering out of his nose. "Merey, Merey, Merey. I thought you were the smart one."

I was affronted. "I am."

Cal Jr. laughed again.

"Tell Ava I want to see her," he said.

"Fine, whatever." I turned and went into the house. I found Ava standing with Jude and Mom.

"Cal Jr. wants you. He's by the side of the house," I said breathlessly. I was irritated and annoyed by the conversation I'd had, so I did not stop to tell her anything else or even to look at her. She left us silently, quickly, and I stepped forward into the circle to fill her place.

The arrival of Jude to the farm was a like a new breeze in a stale room. His presence was felt everywhere. It was as if he had lived here on Aurelia all his life. It was only a matter of weeks before he acquired the respect of the foreman and other farmhands, proving that not only did he know what he was doing, but that he was also prepared to work as hard as any of them. I soon heard tales from my mother over dinner of things she had learned that day about Jude. How he had asked to see the business model for the farm. How he spent hours pouring over accounts and ledgers well into the night. How he quietly questioned my grandfather on the practices of the farm, which the old man was all too happy to talk about and to which he would patiently listen. His eagerness to learn about the farm and everything in it was all too clear.

"He's just so eager to learn," enthused Piper one day to my mother, who had gone to the main house for lunch.

"Hmm," murmured Lavinia.

And I soon became accustomed when cleaning out the stables, or feeding the horses in the mornings before school, to seeing his tall frame striding through the fields, alert and ready for the day ahead, my grandfather matching his step with Jude's as he walked beside him.

We were all suddenly conscious of this new person, this

new intruder in a world that I now realize was always so closed and so isolated. It's strange but even though our grandmother prided herself on making our name known throughout our town, consorting with what she thought were families and people of equal stature, our farm was like a strange microcosm where we receded from the outside world. Unlike the homes of our friends, which we would traipse through with comfortable abandon, every guest was monitored, every invitation carefully thought over and approved. We were so used to this confined existence, so complicit in it, that Jude's arrival was like a tear in the fabric. Ava and I would walk down the road to our home from school and see him riding a horse, or eating with the farm hands and shyly wave at him before hurrying on. His presence seemed so alien, so strange. We had only ever lived with those we had known our whole lives, and though we knew he was family, he was this strange new entity from a world we ventured into yet I see now, never really believed we were wholly part of. Life was Aurelia, home was Aurelia. It was our past, present and our future. That was how we were trained and we did not question it. We knew of our father going to war, or our mother, who was not raised on a farm herself, but these seemed like strange dreams. Our farm was like the world when people still thought it was flat. And when you left it, it was as if you had simply sailed too far and fallen off the surface into the void.

Both Mom and Georgia-May did their best to be welcoming as they had promised my grandfather. Mom was always enquiring after him at the main house, where he lived along with Georgia-May, who always brought Charles with her. And Piper, I remember, used to fuss over him and exclaim how much he reminded her of her second brother in a voice that always dipped on the last with an expression I could not define, but which tugged at my heart anyway. I think he was such a novelty, like a new toy, we almost did not believe in him, believe that he was here to stay, or that he was truly part of us. There was an element of distrust and yet at the same time, this willing curiosity about him, this need to know him and make him our own.

He was a like a fresh breath that stole away the dust motes that had lingered around us for too long. Piper became more jovial, more active; Granddad stopped drinking so much, he sweated less and even lost weight. He proudly held out the waistband of his jeans to his granddaughters at a Sunday dinner two months after Jude first arrived, happily patting the newfound looseness around his gut.

My uncle and my cousin however, had a somewhat different response. Ethan never really bothered with Jude. I remember overhearing my mother's conversations with my aunt when they would talk of how Jude would pay them visits, bringing a six-pack of beer and a friendly temperament as he would try to strike a friendship with his immediate cousin and the only man on the farm similar to him in both age and background. But my uncle would simply take the six-pack and drink the beer, barely speaking to Jude, letting his doomed attempts at conversation rise and fall into a silence that was agonizing for anyone else but the drunkard next to him. He would leave each time, his brow furrowed in consternation, and Georgia-May could see that he was bewildered by my uncle, who had so much and hated it all.

In the end he would come to the house, less often than before, but instead of beer, he would bring a toy airplane for Charles, or flowers for Georgia-May. He would stop by always when Ethan's truck wasn't parked in the yard and just talk to her and play with her son as she shyly wrapped her clothes about her tighter to cover up her bruises and he politely deferred any questions about the visible collapse of her marriage.

And as for Cal Jr., as far as I remember, they never spent any time together at all. I don't seem to be able to recall an incident when the two of them would converse alone, or share a joke or even really sit next to each other. At each Sunday meal, Jude would either sit near my mother, or Piper, or right next to my grandfather, and though he would always circle the room so that you thought he talked with everybody, you never saw him alone with my cousin. Perhaps I am wrong, after all they did live together and there must have been moments when they were forced to share each other's company if only by the laws of close proximity, but never in public, never it seemed, if it could be avoided.

Do I think this was on Jude's part? No, because he always wanted to try everything, everyone. That was one of the first things I noticed about him. In a life of such rigid routine and tradition, he would always try to implement new ideas, new dishes even, from suggestions of a different kind of dessert at the table, which my grandmother would receive with widened eyes and a tight smile as she stared unseeing at his enthusiastic recount of his latest brainchild, to how the farm was beginning to run. You could find him standing with my grandfather in the cornfields, one hand on his hip, the other waving energetically into the distance as my grandfather listened carefully, intermittently nodding at whatever Jude was saying. And then the next thing would appear, a better harvester, a new piece of land carved out for a different form of crop, so that all around us, small almost imperceptible changes accrued and accreted with time. And soon it became normal to see him riding about the farm, to find traces of his hand in new paint on the barn and new dishes at the Sunday dinners.

One time when the two of us were alone sitting on my porch after my mother had invited him for dinner and Ava was helping her wash up, while Claudia was upstairs doing her homework, I asked him if he was happy here.

He looked at me and smiled.

"You know what, I think I am."

"You sound surprised," I said and he eyed me perceptively.

"It was a surprise, Merey. But a nice one."

We liked having him there, most of us. We began to realize that the new, the outside was not necessarily a bad thing. Could even bring good, could elicit change.

"We were fine the way we were."

"Says who, Grandma?"

She snorted. "Says me, of course."

But Lavinia was wrong and she knew it. She saw her last remaining child descend into irretrievable ruin, she watched our mother struggle in her widowhood, she saw her grandson's recalcitrant relationship with his grandfather and she knew that my father's death was only the latest and most violent wound on a body that was already mottled with scars. In the middle of the night when she would lie in bed and remember that her youngest child was dead, mingled with any sense of grief was anger that, because of his sudden and horrific departure from this earth, a void was left that my grandfather had unilaterally and dangerously filled. I suppose she was right. Would my grandfather have ever contacted Jude if his son had not died? Of course not. Just one in a series of catastrophic effects from a morning when an otherwise fit and healthy young man had closed his eyes and touched his temple as he felt the stirrings of what he thought would be nothing more than a bad headache. At first.

But if my father's death had affected anyone the most, apart from his wife, it was Claudia. When we lived with our grandparents, she barely spoke to Ava and me and she hardly left our room, which meant that we never went in there until it was time for bed. And whenever we did infiltrate her eye line, she would snarl and lash out at us, resulting in many arm burns, scratches and raised voices, to which Piper had to intervene and act as peacemaker. Ava was devastated and I... well, I did not know how to compute my father's death. But Claudia was none of these things. Instead she was something I've never been able to fully understand: she was livid. When we came home to our mother, Claudia was livid that she had even taken to her bed in the first place; she was livid that our father had not been buried on the farm like our grandparents had urged our mother to do, but instead was taken to Arlington National Cemetery; she was livid that she had to share her grief with her two sisters, and, most of all she was livid that there was any grief to be had in the first place.

Claudia learned a lesson she would never forgive life for— that bad things can happen for no reason other than they can, and so she stopped trusting in adults and stopped believing in God. She announced this at the dinner table six weeks after my father had died. My mother had put down her fork and stared at her child with such a mixture of fear and horror that I could feel the air crackle around us with shock.

"You don't know what you're saying," she had said.

"Yes, I do." Claudia was glaring at our mother, her head hunched beneath her shoulders but her eyes full of hate.

"If there's no God, Claudia, then where do you think your father is?" Mom asked quietly.

For a second Claudia's lip trembled and then she leaned forward and screamed down the length of the tablecloth, "With the worms!"

Mom thought it would pass. She did not know how to deal with her grief let alone her daughter's and she believed that whatever was going on inside of Clo would eventually heal, because all things did with time—that was what she had been raised on. Although she could not understand it and although it made her body ache with soreness, she had to believe that our father's passing was part of God's plan. Claudia would come to know this in time.

But time went on and still Claudia was the same. It was that period that really colored my relationship with my eldest sister. She was a horror to live with. Sullen, uncommunicative, vicious—we ended up in more fights during those few months than in any other time of my life and from then on we were constantly battling each other, quick to take offense at what the other had said, eager to read insult in any spoken word or cause injury whenever we could. She treated me as a punching bag for her frustrations, but I quickly learned to fight back so that our mother was constantly pulling us apart, scolding us for ripping apart another dress, ribbon, toy.

And then one day we pushed her too far. I don't even remember what had caused it, but I do remember that Claudia had punched me in the face and, reeling, I picked up the only thing available, which was a china figurine of a shepherdess, and hurled it at her head. It caught her temple before ricocheting off the wall, snapping the head off. Claudia started bleeding, there was complete confusion, my mother came running in amongst all our shouts and cries and then stopped dead in the middle of the room.

We didn't notice the look on her face at first. We simply crowded around her, reaching out for comfort, but she suddenly thrust up her hands as a barrier and immediately we shut up. She knelt down on the floor and picked up the head of the figurine, which had bounced and rolled away from the body, and cradled it in her hands. She didn't speak but she did start to shake her head, and the more she shook it the more her face crumpled. Claudia and I started backing away from her, watching her body as it began to tremble. The final eruption of her sobs only came when we had fled up the stairs to our rooms.

My grandmother came over to the house an hour later. It was Ava who called her. She swept into my room, still wearing her gardening gloves, and pulled me up into a standing position from my bed by my arm.

"Let me look at you," she said, turning my head this way and that by my chin. She drew herself up. "I've seen your sister. She'll live. Now I'm going to ask you the same thing I asked her. Do you want to destroy what's left of your mother?"

I think I was so shocked I swayed, because she caught me by my shoulders and shook me so my mouth fell open.

"Then I suggest you start behaving yourself, my girl. Your father would whip both you and your sister for today's little performance. That figurine was an anniversary present from your father—the last anniversary, might I add, that they had together before his death, God rest—and you and your sister broke it over some bratty argument. You were brought up *near* a barn not *in* one. Remember that." She sighed. "I've heard about the behavior of your sister. I'll be dealing with her, don't you worry, but if you provoke her again you'll have me on your tail, understood?" I nodded and then, apparently satisfied, she turned to leave.

"No supper," she said as she reached the door.

I don't know what she said to Claudia but after that, for a long while, Claudia began to have visits up at the house with our grandmother. I don't know what happened there, Ava and I were not permitted to join her, but every Wednesday between five and six o'clock, she would go there to see her. Whatever occurred there must have had an effect on her because over time we stopped fighting as much as we used to. Not completely, mind you, but she began to ignore me and so in acknowledgment I left her alone. In a way I guess that was when Ava and I really began to bond. Claudia didn't really seem to want to spend too much time with us after those visits. I used to think she hated us, but maybe it was just because she didn't trust herself to confide in us or us to understand what was happening to her. I didn't ask. We didn't have that kind of relationship.

I lay awake all night, thinking. When I dressed myself in the morning it was with that strange drugged feeling of seeing the dawn from the wrong side. Claudia came for me again. She stayed in the car waiting while I gathered my things and made to leave. Jane stood at the door to see me off. We didn't speak.

She drove slower this time and as we pulled up to the forked road I stiffened but she kept driving. Rows on rows of green trees lined the drive so that the road looked like a long hollow in a wood, and then as it curved to the right they parted and with a slam that stifled the air under my heart, I saw the tall white house on the mound and heard the crunch of the gravel as we veered off the road into the drive. The car was relentless as it moved underneath the sign, which as I swung around to look at it was still standing tall, still proud to bear Aurelia's name, still thinking it was a name worth bearing.

At the bottom of the drive she stopped the car, turned off the engine and we sat there in silence. The grass was yellow and threadbare, the drive unkempt and knotted with patches of crabgrass, the flower beds once so carefully tended, now withered to nothing. Only the house seemed to have remained at least relatively untouched, but we could see the windows boarded up with mottled planks of honey-colored pine and dark oak making it still seem dejected, ailing, unlived-in and empty.

And what did I feel when I saw the place that has haunted me for over a decade? A place I have loathed and loved and longed for in turn? Instantly I regretted everything. I was so sorry, so much more sorry than I thought I would ever be. Aurelia was gone, a husk now of its former self, a gaping wound of the Hathaways. We were gone, our time was truly over and nothing had ever brought it more home to me than seeing the place we had built and near worshipped now nothing but a desiccated waste.

I looked over at Claudia and knew from her expression that she was thinking the same thing. What would Lavinia say, I wondered, if she could see it now and know what all her planning and scheming had come to? It seemed to me standing there that the one truth we had never been able to acknowledge until now was that the farm was never really ours, it wasn't even our grandfather's, it was always hers and without her, it was nothing. I bit my lip until I felt the skin crack. As if she could sense it, or perhaps was feeling the same, Claudia suddenly moved and switched on the engine and turned the car down the lanes toward our old house.

"I just wanted to see it," she said huskily, almost apologetically. "I just wanted to know."

12

I THINK I WONDER FAR TOO MUCH WHAT OUR lives would have been like had our father lived. I often think that had he been alive so many things that happened would not have, and so many things that should have done, finally would. Since the day he died my life has split into two, the one I should have had with him and the one I eventually ended up with.

When I was around the age of nine I began to grow restless. I was constantly fidgeting, picking things up, putting things down and my school work began to suffer because I could not concentrate in class. My school counselor had stopped seeing me three months after my father's death but at this latest development she resumed her sessions with me. My mother was frantic with worry. There was no immediate negativity in my social behavior, but it became clear to her that I was not happy…but not in a way that I could express. And then during one particularly heated conversation when I was slumped over the kitchen table, my arm flung across my school books, my mother asked me, "What would your father say if he saw you now?" and I told her, "I don't know. I don't really even remember what he looks like."

It wasn't that we did not have photographs of him, because they were everywhere, but the fact was when I closed my eyes at night and conjured the faces of the people I knew so well, my father's was a pink fleshed void. I could not see the features that were so entrenched in my own. I could not picture him, I was starting to forget.

My mother's lip trembled and then without a word she left the room. Two days later, when it was the weekend, I woke up to find Jude sitting at the edge of my bed.

"Merey, do you know what time it is? Why aren't you dressed for breakfast?" he asked me. He was wearing this pale blue shirt and the sunlight made a halo around his head so that in the blurry haze of midsleep he seemed to be this soft, welcoming apparition.

"I get tired a lot lately," I answered.

"I have something for you, but I need you to get up in order to see it."

I moaned and then pushed myself upright. He brought out from the side of the bed a white bag with pink tissue paper. I took it and opened it, laying the items out on my bedsheet. It was a piece of soft brown dirt that took my fingerprint as I pressed it in my hands and a bunch of strange brown carving tools. But strangest of all was a picture of my father that I knew from memory used to reside in a brown leather photo album, now in a photo frame.

"Do you know why we remember things, Merey?" he asked me. "Familiarity. The repetition of seeing them or feeling them makes them ingrained in our minds. I think you need a little of that familiarity." He took the clay. "I am going to show you how to use this—" and then he picked

up the brown carving tools "—and use these. And after this,
you will be able to see your father every time you want, with
or without a photograph."

I don't think he knew what he started in me that day.
What it would lead to in my life—my love of form, of yield-
ing the most wondrous of objects from a piece of clay. Or
what it would it do to my memory. Because he was right.
After that day I could picture my father and every last feature
on his face down to the smallest detail. Except now he comes
like the rest of them without warning or invitation. They
have taken form and now they can control it themselves and
now I shut my eyes so I can block them out, even when I
feel their cold breath on my face.

Jude once told me why his mother had named him after
the patron saint of lost causes. I had thought initially that she
was mean.

"No, no," he said, laughing. "It's a good thing. She meant
that she wanted me to have hope in my life, that when things
go wrong, really wrong, there's always a way out if you try
hard enough."

"She could have just called you Hope," I'd said. "There's
a girl in my class called that and her sister is called Prudence,
which means sensible. That's kind of dull, though, I prefer
Hope."

"Well my mom didn't want to make life *too* hard for me,
Merey," he'd said wryly.

I loved Jude so quickly after he arrived. He made the gap
in my life that was left by my father's death less of a violent
chasm and more of deep crack that ran across every milestone
event in my childhood. God, I was so thin and gangly then
that he used to pick me up and swing me around and I'd
use him like a climbing frame. I loved him like a brother,

like—my mother said half-mournfully—I would have my own father had he lived.

I cannot think of him even now, even after all I know, without smiling.

What made me love him the most, though, when I was young, was how devoted he was to Charles. He adored him and I realize now looking back that Jude always paid the most attention to a person when they appeared to be vulnerable. He looked out for the needy, the weak, and obsessively stepped into the role of being their personal hero. From the blue bird with a broken wing that he nursed and sang to and loved as he gently cajoled it back to health, to my thirteen-year-old cousin whose mind had stopped at seven years old and who found in this man, who had appeared into our lives as if from a dream, a feeling of adoration and trust that he had never seen displayed in any other adult male.

To see them together, to remember that, is a joy. Because there was so much love between them—Jude's patience, Charles's delight at the simple affection he received from him, the gentleness and protective circle of strength that this man built around my cousin made him flourish, made him special, made him wanted in a way I had always taken for granted with my own parents.

Their favorite game in the summer was to play soldiers. They used to have these fluorescent-colored water guns that sprayed long streaks of liquid that melted on the grass amid shrieks of excitement and whoops of laughter. Georgia-May would watch them as we lay on blankets, soaking the heat into our skin, arms slung over our eyes if we forgot our sunglasses so that there would be a long red burn along the path from our elbow to our wrist. Sometimes Ava and I would join in with Jude and Charles. We would be the airplanes, our arms flung out in a seesaw, cutting through the shoots of water in our pink and yellow bathing suits.

Claudia would just lie on the blanket in her two-piece, which at the age of fourteen she was vainly trying to fill, desperately pretending to ignore us, until she could take it no longer and, muttering, swiped up the blanket and stalked past us into the house, her mouth jutting out in a furious pout of barely concealed outrage.

Mom rolled her eyes as she slapped her feet on the porch steps into the kitchen. Jude shrugged his shoulders and laughed.

When Ava and I went in to get some iced tea, she sat at the table flicking through a magazine.

"Clo, why don't you come back outside?" asked Ava as I tried to steady the jug and pour the drink into the glasses and not on the floor.

"'Cause you're making too much fucking noise," she spat, though she dipped her voice several octaves below normal on "fucking," as the door was still open.

"We're just playing," I shot back. "Jesus, like you're so above it."

"Actually I am, thank you. It's called being grown up." She flicked another page over in eminent disdain.

"Well, Jude's like way more older than you and he's not *above it*," I said over the clang of pulling a tray from the cupboard.

"Oh, please—you're so stupid, Meredith. He's only doing it 'cause Charles is a retard." She leaned forward and sneered at me before smoothing her hair back up into a ponytail.

"Mom better not catch you using that word, Clo," said Ava quietly.

"You're just pissed because he won't look at you no matter how skimpy your bathing suit is," I spat.

"Like I'd even want him to. His last girlfriend was probably a mongoloid or something."

"Claudia," breathed Ava, throwing a glance over her shoulder.

"Look, he's not some saint. Do you really think he'd give that—" and she snapped her fingers "—for Charles if he wasn't different? If God came down and made him all better the next day, give it a week and Jude would get bored and lose all interest and then maybe I'd get some goddamn peace whenever I wanted to fucking sunbathe."

And with that, her eyes following our astonished expressions, she walked out of the kitchen and up the stairs.

It's funny I remember that now, because I have wondered over time if maybe Claudia had a point. I realize that even though Jude would often set himself up as the protector for the meek, he never once reached out to Claudia. He never sensed her pain or her anger, which is in every memory I have of her since the day our father died. To him, she was just this arrogant, irascible teen, which she was, but that was all he ever saw or would see. I know now that even though Jude was good, he wasn't always very smart, at least not when it came to people.

Once when I was at art college I had to present a piece that was personal to me. My tutor said that it should reflect some aspect of my past or home. He said he wanted me to do this because he didn't feel that my sculptures, while technically good, had anything really to say. He wanted me to get in touch with my emotions.

I struggled and struggled. At one point I remember drafting this incredibly long letter to my tutor telling him that I simply could not do what he was asking. In the end though, after two aborted attempts, one miniature emotional meltdown and another long middle of the night draft, I came up with my piece.

My tutor held it in his hands and turned it slowly so he could drink it in, a quizzical look on his face. It was of three girls in various poses, either reading, staring into space or lying down with an arm over their face.

"What is it trying to say?" he asked eventually.

"Nothing," I answered, "it just is."

"But are they friends? Are they related? Have they had an argument? Who are they?"

Even now I don't think I know. My whole life I have always had my sisters. That is the luxury of being the youngest. And so, of course I took their presence for granted and so allowed myself to be irritated by them. Ava least of all, but from the moment she hit puberty Claudia and I were at constant loggerheads. Though we never allowed our mutual resentments of each other to spill over quite into the unbridled fray we had exhibited after our father's death, our relationship was one of constant war and the need not to be beaten.

Even when I could empathize with her, I never took her side, and with Ava's strange and increasingly withdrawn behavior during that period, our mother often wanted to tear her hair out.

From the age of fourteen Claudia became a beauty, there was no denying it, though I was seething with jealousy. Thank goodness I was still in elementary school so I did not have to see how boys fawned over her, but there were always phone calls from various classmates, notes she would accidentally-on-purpose drop on the floor or in the hall so she could present us with the latest in her long line of conquests. Often though she found them absurd and would read them out to us in a sopping voice and with a cynical rolling of her eyes, which would make us howl at the absurdity of this perfect stranger and his foolish love.

Mom would rage at Claudia about her clothes, she was almost a cliché of a teenager on that point, from her ridiculous hemlines, to her overzealous use of makeup. She was so confident, so self-assured, that she was frightening. Though I had waged a war with her ever since I could remember, if I was ever really in trouble, ever really afraid and in need of someone to fight in my corner it was Claudia I went to, though I know it made our mother worry.

During that period after Jude had already been here over a year, I remember how close he and my mother were. She would rage at Claudia and there would be the raising of voices and the banging of doors, and the next minute she would quietly go into the kitchen and close the door and I would hear her from the doorway on the phone to him, gently pouring out her fears and inadequacies. I suppose now that I look back on it, my mother was so alone. She was always strong for everyone, but with my father gone there was no one there to be strong for her and Jude was the only real friend she had on the farm who she could talk to. Georgia-May had her own problems and Piper, while sympathetic, was not exactly nonpartisan. Perhaps because she saw how well Charles and I had responded under Jude's care and help, she believed the same result would happen for Claudia if she confided in him, but if anything it had the opposite effect.

Once when he was in our kitchen, Mom had just made him a corned beef sandwich on rye and Claudia had come in, her hair dripping wet from the shower. She took one look at him and tossed her hair back like a horse's mane. It was so long and heavy with water that it caught one of Mom's little china doll ornaments and sent it crashing to the floor. Jude had choked on his mouthful and I'd burst out laughing while Mom started to shout at Clo for being so clumsy. She had turned bright red, and ran back up the stairs with Mom following, demanding that she come down and clean up the mess. But Jude and I knew there was no way in hell that she was going to show her face in that kitchen for as long as she could help it.

"Well, I'm sorry, Jude, I just don't know what got into her," said Mom when she came back in, and the look of innocence and bemusement on her face only made me laugh out loud even more.

Later though when he was gone, Mom had demanded that Claudia come out of her room and apologize for her behavior. Claudia flung open the door and leaned against the door frame shooting daggers at Mom.

"I did not raise you to have the manners of a field hand, Claudia," Mom admonished. "I want you to go down to the house tomorrow and apologize to him as soon as you are back from school."

"I would rather die," Claudia muttered through her teeth. Ava and I watched from the end of the hall, but the two of them were too engrossed to see us.

"What has gotten into you?" Mom asked, shocked.

"Don't think I don't know why he's here all the time, don't think I'm stupid," Claudia yelled. Mom took a step back and then she saw Ava and I staring at them openmouthed.

"I haven't forgotten, even if you have," Claudia finished victoriously.

Mom looked at us and then at her, before pushing her back into her room and closing the door. There were no raised voices, but they were in there for a long time and in the end Ava and I grew bored of trying to eavesdrop and dispersed.

The next day when we were outside in the garden doing

homework, Ava sat up on her calves and said to Claudia, "Clo, why don't you like Jude?"

"Who said I didn't like him?" she replied with an edge in her voice.

"Well yesterday...with Mom..." Ava trailed off.

"It's not that I don't like him," said Claudia, her head bent resolutely over her books, "it's just I already had one father and I don't need another."

"What are you talking about?" I shot back defensively.

Claudia put down her pencil and looked at us both. "We're it now. We're all we have got. Anything could happen to any of us. We owe it to Dad to make sure that we stick together. No outsiders, no intruders. Grandma always says how important family is, and now we're all the family we've got."

"But what about Grandma and Piper and..." Ava began, but Claudia raised a hand to stop her.

"Of course we have them, but...I just mean that it used to be the five of us and now it's four. Dad isn't here to protect us anymore, so we have start protecting ourselves. That was all I was doing yesterday." She picked up her pencil and turned a page of her book. "Trust me, you'll thank me one day."

As I looked at my tutor's face, I realized that I had failed in his assignment. He wanted me to illustrate a moment in my past to show depth or some sort of emotional gravitas, but the truth was that when I looked back at my life with my sisters all I could see was how—even though we lived together, ate together, had only a stretch of hallway to separate us for most of our lives—there was always an ocean between us in terms of understanding: what Claudia knew, what Ava kept hidden, what I refused to believe.

Who were they? Were they friends? Were they sisters?

I ask myself this question over and over again. I loved my

sisters—I did—but despite this love the answer I come up with is always the same.

They were liars.

I sat by the window looking out at the expanse of flat land and afternoon sun. She had been quiet for a long time and when I looked over at her she was staring in the distance at a spot near the corner of her vanity table.

"How long has it been since he died?" she suddenly asked me.

"Who?" I asked, confused.

"Ethan. I can't remember. I try but…" She shook her head and stroked the blanket over her.

"Two years ago," I said softly.

"How did he die? Did he kill himself?"

I hesitated. "We don't think so."

"He blamed me, all his life ever since Alison, he blamed me. Did I force him to marry Georgia-May? Did I force him to be a bad father to his son? I made so many excuses, so many allowances, and then when Jude came, he just rolled over like a dog. After all my efforts, all our plans. It was so disappointing."

She caught my eye and glared. "What? Oh, you pity him, I suppose. Cal always said I was so hard on him, but he would never be hard enough. He did kill himself, you know," she said suddenly and I flinched. "It was just the longest suicide I have ever known."

Three days after I turned ten my uncle received something that was long overdue. Ethan had been in the fields one day in early August, with his father threshing the corn. He had been standing next to him kicking dirt with his shoe while Cal's voice droned on above him. He felt a small tap on his shoulder, and turned around, but before he had time to register who was in front of him, or what they would want, his nose had been broken and he was on the ground howling in pain clutching onto his face, blood streaming down the back of his throat. He was in too much shock and agony to make out what was being said among the array of shouts and voices above him; he could only rock back and forth on his back moaning into the arch of his hands.

At the time he might have still believed that he was the victim, until he finally managed to open his eyes and saw that out of the crowd of men around him, including his father and cousin, none were reaching down to help him.

And then Jude leaned down.

"If you ever touch that woman again...listen—listen!" He grabbed the thatch of hair to jerk Ethan's head to attention. "I will finish you," he added, then lifted my uncle's head and smacked it back into the ground.

When we came home from the school that day, the first we had heard of anything wrong was the harried way in which our mother welcomed us into the house, just as she was heading out. To Claudia she said, "Look after your sisters. I'm needed at the house," and moved quickly past us, not stopping to welcome us home as she usually would.

We had no idea what had occurred between our uncle and our cousin for nearly two hours until finally Mom returned home, exhausted, and sank gratefully into a chair in our living room while Ava made her some tea.

She stretched out her legs and curled her toes upward as she threw her head back and raised her eyes to the ceiling.

"Mom?" said Claudia and the urgency of her tone made our mother register us properly since first thing that morning.

"Your uncle beat your aunt last night. Jude found out— doesn't matter how—but he broke your uncle's nose."

"Oh, my God, what?" laughed Claudia in shock and excitement. I sat up on the carpet and curled my legs under my knees.

"Really?"

"Yes. Your uncle is fine but Georgia-May and Charles are up at the house with your grandparents."

"So what's going to happen now? I mean…is Jude in trouble?" I asked.

"No, he's not. Georgia-May showed your grandparents what Ethan did to her. Your grandfather threatened to call the police on your uncle, but your grandmother and Jude talked him out of it."

Apparently my grandfather had stood over the circles of chartreuse and plum on Georgia-May's back and, referring to his daughter for the first time in over a decade, asked what he had done to be cursed with such monsters for children.

"It wasn't supposed to be like this," he said.

"Oh, my God. Did Grandma go nuts?" asked Claudia.

"No, she—she was on Jude's side actually. She's with Ethan now, getting some things for Georgia-May. She's told him he's going to have to see a counselor for…well, you know how much your uncle drinks. I've never seen her so angry."

Angry, she was incandescent with rage.

He ruined everything. With one fell swoop he had undone all those years of work and allowed himself to be so easily and readily usurped in a matter of minutes, when she had worked so tirelessly for him since the day he was born. And she saw then that he would never inherit the farm. And she had no more children to present as an alternative.

"What did she say?" I asked.

My mother debated inwardly for a moment and then she relented—because she wanted us to know, I think, that she felt the same way about her own children. That should have been a warning to all of us—and to most of us it was.

"Your grandmother told Georgia-May that if it had been her, she would have stabbed him in his sleep."

You'd have thought then that Jude's fate would have been sealed with my grandmother by that act, but you'd be wrong. She didn't like it, but it wasn't enough for her to stick the knife in just yet. My uncle had been circling the drain long before that incident and in a way it was the wake-up call she needed to recognize that there could be no future with Ethan at the farm's helm.

And then, as with all upheavals, there soon came a period of quiet. Georgia-May did not come to us in the mornings with as many bruises as before. Things seemed to get better, more peaceful. We settled into a family, Jude became less of a novelty and more of a fixture. We seemed complete. Well, almost.

It is strange but that whole time Cal Jr., who had always held himself on the periphery of our lives, withdrew even further into himself. He became like a ghost, to be found always alone and haunting the solitary untended places on our farm. No longer did we see him on walks with our grandmother around the rose garden, or working the fields with our grandfather. He was here, he was always here, and yet his presence felt all the more acute because paradoxically it was through his absence that we became more aware of him. When we would go over to the house on Sundays, he appeared once while we were waiting, drinking in the lounge as was our custom, and then somehow he would disappear and you would only just realize as you were being called into dinner. But suddenly, as if by osmosis, he would be there among you again and then you would wonder if perhaps you had forgotten him, forgotten he had actually been with you all the time. But you never got to ask him because his silence at the table removed him from view, so that you could see the dishes and the white cloth and the talking mouths in front of you, but somehow with a trick of the light you always missed him. He would slip away in the gap. Your eyes let him.

Once I was out down by the cornfields. I batted my hands against the sides of the cornstalks, enjoying the rustle that stirred against the air. And then I saw a flash of a light blue checked shirt and stopped. My hand was still resting against the shoots as I peered ahead wondering if it was a field hand, but then I saw his red hair and I called out to him.

"Cal Jr.? Cal Jr.?"

There was a silence. I looked and then walked toward where I thought I had seen him but there was nothing. "Cal?" I asked, my voice dropping in my uncertainty. There was no noise and then for a moment I thought perhaps I had been wrong. But then a violent tremor went through the field as if someone was thundering toward me. The maize shoots began to tremble and the rustle, which I had so loved a minute before, became a cataclysmic torrent of noise. I screamed and ran, not pausing for breath until I had gotten to the water fountain.

When I saw him next, it was on my way home from school the next day. I looked over at him and stuck my tongue out violently. His hand, which had been raised in a hello, drooped and then fell.

"Merey, what did you do that for?" asked Ava and I told her of what had happened the day before.

"I don't think it could have been him. I saw him drive off to town to get horse feed around then."

I stopped and stared at her. "I am sure he was there. I swear it was him."

Ava's brown eyes met mine. "Really swear?"

And her confidence filled me with doubt.

He haunted me then, just as he haunts me now. Only Jude isn't around anymore to keep him at bay.

As we made our way down the drive, Claudia and I looked at each other in shock when we passed the place where our uncle's house used to be and found that it had been torn down. The car jerked to a stop.

"You don't think...?" Claudia breathed quickly, but I didn't answer. Neither of us had contemplated the notion that Cal's revenge on the farm would be anything other than it as a business. The fact that he could have torn down our homes and already dispersed our things without us knowing had never occurred to us. A stupid assumption I realized now. Why shouldn't he feel the need to take these things? Though we had not wanted them we had always assumed that because they were ours that was all that should matter. We were still underestimating him as much in death as we had done in life.

I jumped out of the car and looked at the place where my uncle and his family had lived, where I had gone calling for my cousin to play after school and where I would often find my uncle on the front porch drinking with a vigor that would soon outmatch his own father's. It was here one night when I was fifteen and he was so drunk he could barely stop himself from sliding to the floor, that he had told me the story of the one woman who could have kept some semblance of the humane about him. That was how I came to know of Alison Lomax.

The place was covered in brown grass strewn with bits of debris. There was no trace of what had been there, which considering the memories may not have been such a bad thing. I ran back to Claudia and she drove quickly to where our house should be. Julia's former home, which had stood half a mile down from ours, had long been demolished on our grandmother's insistence when Cal Jr. had come to live in the main house. We held our breath when we got to the road that used to be covered in verdant bushes that served as a property line, but over the rims of the green we could see the white peak of our roof and as we swung round the bend, it came into plain view: our honey-colored house, almost exactly as I remembered it—untouched, windows still intact, even the dragonfly knocker was there, though there were cobwebs around the base. Claudia stopped the car and parked it by the front. I let out a sigh of relief and turned to face her, but her eyes were pinched black and I recoiled.

"What's wrong?" I asked her. She turned from me and gazed ahead.

"Back home, hey? Finally allowed now that everyone's gone." The bitterness rode through her voice so harshly it made the notes strain. I shrank back, awkward. "Oh, don't worry. I'm sure I got what I deserved. Mom was nothing if not fair, right?" She smiled at me then, showing the whites of her teeth.

"You can't be angry with Mom, Claudia."

"Can't I?"

"What you did—"

"What I did? What about her?"

"Was she holding a gun to your head?" I asked her. "I remember the stuff you said, how you made him sound, what he did to you? You set him up."

"I didn't know what I was doing," she spat.

"You knew well enough *how* to do it, though." I stopped and then inexplicably grabbed her by the shoulders. "You're so defiant even after all this time. Don't you ever look back and hate yourself for what you did? You think she wanted to do what she did? You left her no choice, Claudia. You're lucky she didn't beat the shit out of you, you'd have deserved it."

"Oh, banishment is so much more feudal. Just tapping into her Italian reserves," she snarled in my face. Then she lowered her eyes. "Take your hands off me."

I let her go and sat back in the leather. We fell into silence, neither of us wishing to be the first to break it. She tapped her nails on the steering wheel, I sucked the breath into my cheeks. And then she opened the car door and turned to me.

"Let's get this over with," she said.

13

A FEW DAYS BEFORE CLAUDIA TURNED FIFTEEN, Piper went into town to choose a birthday present for her. But when she got to the store she began to feel light-headed. It was only for a moment and seemed to pass so she steadied herself and resumed her shopping.

But then when she was only a few miles away from the farm, the light-headedness returned, only this time it was swiftly followed by a searing pain that made the muscles behind her eyes tighten. She swerved from the road, turned off the engine, flung open the car door and threw up. When she eventually returned home, she went straight up to bed and did not have supper. Just before she went to sleep, her sister-in-law came to visit her bearing a mug of hot water with lemon. Piper stared at her from the corner of her eye as she set it on the bedside table.

"There's no need to look at me like that, Piper. If I'd wanted to poison you I'd have done it before now," said my grandmother sharply. "I'm sure with a bit of rest you'll be fine."

Piper sighed and turned over on her side. Lavinia paused and stared at her back. Then against her better judgment she asked, "What is wrong, Piper?"

"How long do you think we'll do this?" Piper asked suddenly.

"What do you mean?" Lavinia asked coldly.

"This—working ourselves to the bone? Isn't it time for another generation to take over, for another one to take up this task? How long do we keep ourselves chained here?"

"I don't think you are yourself," my grandmother said slowly. "Give yourself until tomorrow. Things always look better in the morning."

"Lavinia," began Piper and the two women held each other's gaze for a long moment.

"Good night, Piper," said Lavinia finally and she turned out the light as she left.

"What do you want in life, Merey?"

"I don't know…to see the world I guess? Maybe go to college and do an art degree or something?"

She reared her head up like a cobra at that, her long hair spilling down her white nightdress so that she took on the visage of some horrifying phantom.

"You're all so stupid. You think it's so much better out there, so much more exciting, so much easier. You have no clue. You throw yourselves into exile. Don't you know what happens when you try to go? You come to the edge of the world and you fall off."

"How would you know?"

"That's what happens, Meredith—haven't you learned that by now?" And she leaned back with a soft laugh.

"I used to tell Claudia that, on those days when she would come to the house and we would sit and talk. You know, when I had her come up to see me when your father died. We would sit and tal. And out of everyone, she knew the most about how much this place meant to us. She would never have left it if she had the choice."

I stiffened. I knew what was coming but I did not want it, not yet.

"But then she would have done well wherever she was. She was always lucky like that."

Because of Piper's illness we missed going to the house that Sunday, so it was nearly ten days before we saw her again. She missed Claudia's birthday party on the Thursday but seemed to be fully recovered by the weekend so we dutifully made our way over to the main house for Sunday roast as normal. But when I saw her sitting in the living room by the window with a soda water in hand conversing with my grandfather I was visibly shocked. She seemed so thin and pale. Her skin beneath her eyes was wan and the rest of her face took on a chalky pallor. I stopped in the middle of the room and stared at her. Jude came from behind me and gently steered me away to a corner of the room.

"She hasn't been very well," he said softly.

"She looks like she is dying," I muttered.

"She isn't dying, she's just…" He bit his lip thoughtfully. "She's just tired."

And he shook my shoulders in gentle reassurance and left to talk with my mother. Cal Jr., as if from nowhere, suddenly appeared at my side.

"He's wrong, you know, it's a lot worse than that."

"What would you know?" I snapped.

"Oh, yeah, I only live here. Not that anyone seems to notice." He rolled his eyes and leaned down to whisper to me, "Wait and see."

My grandmother came into the room, resplendent as ever, and announced the meal was ready and we dutifully followed her into the dining room.

As we sat and watched our grandfather carve the meat and serve the plates down the table, Ava said, "It's good to see you looking well again, Aunt Piper."

Piper gave her a halfhearted smile.

"Oh, she wasn't at death's door, were you, Piper?" said my grandmother. "She's a lot tougher than she looks, Ava."

"Yeah, it would take a divine force to stop your great-aunt in her tracks," said my grandfather jovially.

Piper blinked rapidly and chewed the inside of her mouth. "And what would it take to make you stop, Cal?" she asked quietly. Immediately, we all stilled in our seats.

"What do you mean?" asked my grandfather unconcernedly, still finishing off carving a slice of the meat onto a plate, but when she did not answer, he turned and frowned at his sister.

"Piper, are you sure you're well enough just yet?" asked my grandmother silkily.

Piper licked her lip and then laughed. "Ignore me. I'm still…recovering."

I looked over at Cal Jr. and watched him hide a smile behind the rim of his glass.

"Your mother was very close to Jude, wasn't she?" my grandmother asked me. "As were you? Did you miss him when he left?"

I was tempted not to answer her, but I knew from experience that if I didn't she would bait me until I lost my temper and then laugh at me for the same.

"Yes."

"He was crying when he left, did you know that? Tears of anger, of anguish. So humiliating for him…" She broke off in a malevolent chuckle. "And I thought to myself, you suffer as you tried to make me suffer."

She caught me looking at her. "I couldn't let him get away with it. I couldn't let him actually do it. After all these years, after everything I have done, lost, sacrificed—my God." She choked on the last part and began to cough painfully. Her hacking rasps filled the petrified air.

Three years after he had first arrived, and two months after that Sunday dinner with Piper, Jude decided to organize a New Year's Eve party on Aurelia. He had persuaded my grandfather to throw it because aside from that one time way back when they had first moved in on the farm, they had never thrown another large party. Oh, they had dinner parties and small select guests to private soirees, but not a loud-music, bright-lights, colored-streamer affair for everyone. My grandmother didn't like to. She didn't think such affairs were dignified, but it was more than that. She wanted to make Aurelia exclusive, a place that people would give their teeth to set foot on. She thought to share the place would make it less valuable.

But Jude was a grown man and he didn't need or wish to play by my grandmother's hierarchical rules. He invited neighbors, suppliers, businessmen my grandparents knew or wished to know. He threw in a whole mix of people under the blanket of fairy lights and rum punch. A week before the party, after coming back from town after one day shopping, my grandmother stalked out to the cornfield and demanded in front of my grandfather for Jude to bring her the guest list. He had burst out laughing.

"What for?" he'd asked.

"Because Claree Tyler couldn't help but thank me over and over again for asking her to our New Year's party in the hardware store while her brats were running amok with the chicken feed. It was excruciating. I don't want people thinking I truck with those kinds of people."

"What kind of people?" Jude asked benignly. "Widows? Because that's what she is."

My grandmother had turned to her husband. "Cal, you understand what I'm saying here. We have a name to protect and this party is going to rest on and more importantly reflect that name."

"Well, I mean—" He'd rubbed the back of his neck and looked at the floor while his wife shifted her weight to her other foot in irritation. "Who is coming to this thing, Jude?" he had asked.

"Oh, well, there ain't no list so to speak. Just who takes my fancy. This is a good town here, good people. I promise there won't be anyone at that party who I wouldn't want to know."

"Well, maybe you're just not as discerning as you should be," said my grandmother tightly.

"I like to think of it as being open-minded," Jude said, grinning.

I had such a good time at that party. I got to show off to my classmates the home I had, the one they had heard of and revered and finally now all got to see with their open mouths and wide eyes when I showed them what we took as our right. My grandmother was almost regal in the way she parted crowds and took presents and offered glasses of punch. My grandfather, after some initial anxiety, actually looked like he was enjoying himself. He was jovial, generous, his laughter a boom during the lapse in conversation around us. But Jude was something else. He teased me and my friends, made those who would never normally be associated with my family more at ease, oiled those who usually were as if he had known them as long as my grandparents had. He was so comfortable and he made everyone else feel the same. Even Claudia forgave him whatever grudge she had held against him that night. I saw the two of them share a joke as they leaned against the columns on the foot of the landing's stairs. Claudia, a vision with her hair spilling over her left shoulder and fringing the top of her dress, smiled down at him. They looked striking, even though for once she didn't seem to be aware of it. I saw her touch his shoulder and cock her head to the side, laughing. He clinked his punch glass against hers in response.

And then at the end when we had the fireworks display, I thought I would burst with happiness, watching the rockets punch an array of colors into the sky with hisses and crackles and booms that filled the air and covered the sounds of drunken incredulity below.

For my sisters and me, the party was a success. When we came back to school in January, our classmates were still talking about it and for a while there on the street, a whole new cast of people who we hadn't even known existed before, would smile and nod at us with the glow of both memory and newfound respect.

Do you know, I think that party was one of the proudest moments of my life? When I first really appreciated the family I had standing behind me and I had thought how clever Jude was for orchestrating that, and how much he must have loved us and Aurelia to do it.

It should have made my grandmother love him; it should have made her accept him as one of us. It certainly cemented the bond he had with my grandfather, who the morning after, with the ravages of the party wreaked across his home, had smiled and wondered aloud why they hadn't done this more often.

But it didn't.

"Do you remember the party?" she asked. We were sitting in the glade near the garden on the white chairs. I had taken her for a walk. It was a good day for it. She had been quiet that day and restful, so Mom had told me to take her out for a while, when she was still in a compliant mood.

"What party?" I asked.

"The New Year's one that Jude threw."

"Yes, I remember."

"Do you remember who was there?" she asked, looking at me, and I saw in her face a sharpening of memory. She did this sometimes. She could fool you into thinking she was back, but it was only an echo of a voice that had already faded.

"Do you?"

She sighed. "Cal was so naive, so naive. A party—that's all. Just a party." She smoothed her hands over her lap.

"It wasn't?" I asked.

"It wasn't."

Among the people at the party had been Mike Grayson and Laurence Caulfield, owners of G&C Foods Limited, a food produce company whose main profit was comprised of the main brand cereals they distributed. They had recently bought a large farm corporation in a neighboring county that would now be put to the directive of producing enough cereals for their growing demand.

I did not know they were there, I did not meet them. But my grandfather did.

They met on the 31st of December 1985 on Aurelia and they met again a month later in the head offices of G&C

Foods Limited. And then once more a few weeks after that, and this time Piper was there.

And that is how my grandmother came to do the one thing I have never been able to forgive her for, and what I am sure is the event that has made her spirit haunt my dreams and memories in perpetual unrest. I don't believe in the God of my mother, or the heaven and hell that were thrust upon me on Sunday mornings, but I do believe somehow that our unfinished business in this life will hold us like an anchor, tying our atoms together in a forcible bind that relives our pain.

A hell of a different making.

And that is where I think Lavinia is, because of what she did to Jude—and to Claudia.

And for what my mother then had to do and never really forgave herself for, even though she would never undo it.

I would discover the truth about my sister during my grandmother's confessions, and after she instructed me to set fire to all her papers as she neared her end, I would find the letters Claudia had written to her after she'd been sent away: letters full of anger, of remorse, of bitterness and hatred. Of a desperate need for love and conciliation.

I did not burn these letters.

I buried them under the floorboards of our attic, convinced I would never see them again.

And then years later I would change my mind and take them out of the ground.

And me, the nonbeliever, would exorcize the ghost of Claudia's childhood.

My house was filled with photographs. My father loved them, loved taking them, loved showing them off, and after he died my mother maintained this hobby of his as a sort of memorial to a passion he would have continued had he lived. When you walked into my house, on the right-hand side of the wall was a row of black-and-white photographs in dark wood frames: my father in the field with his brother beside him staring off to the right and his father standing over him with his hand on his shoulder. I remember my father was squinting into the camera because the sun was in his eye. After that was a picture of him and my mother on their wedding day, his blond head bent over her veiled dark one with her smiling up to the camera. Then came pictures of him and my sisters up at the main house: Claudia's first birthday in the large dining room, sitting on my grandfather's knee before a pink-and-white iced cake; Ava on a white bed in a cotton baby dress laughing at an invisible photographer; me in Piper's arms watching my sisters and Charles play; my grandmother and grandfather walking through the rose garden, my grandmother a few steps ahead. As the walls led up the staircase you could see us grow up and get color from our original beginnings of black and white, but though the people and the expressions changed, the setting was always the same. It was always on the farm. The one constant was Aurelia.

After the New Year's Eve party, my mother put up a large photograph that would rest above the staircase as you turned left down to the bedrooms. It was on a starched white background with a bronzed gold frame. It was taken half an hour before the guests started to arrive. Piper had insisted.

"All of you, all together," she'd said, using her hands to bat us all out to the front of the house, while we genially grumbled and fidgeted about standing out in the cold, caught up in a mixture of both excitement and trepidation. My grandfather let me go through the door in front of him and

smiled. It was a nervous twitch of the lips and he sighed. I
ran my hand down his arm in comfort.

That's me in the middle. Claudia is to the left in the soft
blue gauze gown she had finally agreed to wear, even though
the hemline was about an inch longer than she would have
liked. Ava is behind Charles to the right-hand side of Cal Jr.
in white. My mother is standing next to Jude holding his
arm with Georgia-May on the other side and in front with
her husband is my grandmother in that emerald-green silk
she so loved with the pearls my grandfather had bought her
for Christmas a week before. And then Ethan, standing on
the top of the porch landing in his suit, leaning against the
white column. He was drunk, but not too much for him.
He is almost upright.

Those photographs were more than just a depiction of
our lives and history; they were a testament to our home.
And that was what was drummed into me every day, every
moment of my childhood: this is who you are; this is where
you are from.

This is all there is.

This is what should have happened.

Jude would have aided my grandfather in selling the farm.
It would have been a shock to all of us, as for my entire
life certainly, I was raised with the unshrinking belief that
whatever happened or whatever changed, the one constant
was my home.

I wonder how I would have felt? Terrified, upset probably, but in a small way relieved? Would I have seen it as
an opportunity to break away, to start afresh? Maybe we
would have left Iowa, maybe we would have gone back to
New York where my parents first lived and where I would
eventually have ended up.

Perhaps my mother would have married again. Perhaps Jude would have...

But maybe that's just fanciful.

Cal Jr. would have had to make a life of his own. Maybe he would have gone and found his mother, maybe he tried to do that anyway and failed. I never did learn of what happened to Julia and neither, I think, did my grandmother. She was gone, and that was all that mattered to her.

Piper could have got a small house with a nice garden and lived out her retirement. What happened with Ethan would have happened anyway but perhaps Georgia-May would have had the courage to leave sooner.

Strange all of this, all this wonder. We might have been free.

But she would have languished. She would have been devoured by a bitterness whose dark flame would have entered the rags of her soul and consumed it. It might have killed her, emotionally it certainly would have. And never as long as she continued to live, would she have forgiven any of them.

How could they? She would have raged, how could they do this to her?

For in the end, it was all for her, wasn't it?

It started with the phone ringing after we had all gone to sleep. The sound woke us from our beds, made us turn our heads from our pillows and stare at the alarm clock in disbelief. Could that really be the time? Who could be calling? Was something—

Finally my mother went down into the hall and lifted the phone off the receiver. "Hello," she said. Ava and I tentatively made our way to the top of the stairs. We were not afraid; we did not know.

"What did you say?"

The door was unlocked when Claudia and I went inside the house we had been raised in. It slid open with no noise

as we surveyed the powder-blue-and-white paint of the hallway, the wood of the floors under their sheen of dust and the
white steps of the staircase. It was eerie how silent everything
was, how still intact—as if the place had been waiting for us.
For a minute neither of us would step inside.

I looked over at Claudia and saw that she was trembling.
I smoothed a hand down her arm. She jumped and stared at
me—frightened? Was that what I saw?

"I will if you will," I said, gesturing.

Even though it had been over ten years, there were still
faded squares lining up the walls where those photographs
of us had once hung, where paintings that were my mother's
favorites had been placed over small tables bearing an array
of ornaments and china figurines that she had so loved in
her lifetime.

We made our way cautiously through the house, not
touching anything, just peering round corners, keeping our
steps small, careful not to disturb even the air.

*"What? Slow down. I don't understand— Lavin— No I...
Are you serious? Are you sure? It—it can't be, there must be some
mistake...."*

I came to the entrance of the kitchen.

*"What's going on?" I asked Ava, who shook her head as she
stared at Mom.*

*"I'll be right over," said Mom, sinking against the wall as she
bent over herself. "Did you call the police?"*

"It's so neat, isn't it?" said Claudia from behind me.

"Yeah," I answered. "Ava packed everything up after Mom
died... I don't think the place has been touched since."

I went into the kitchen and, as if to prove my point,
opened up the cutlery drawer. Woodlice scuttled over the
knives and forks.

"Hmm." Claudia cleared her throat. "Where did she put everything?"

"I don't know—the attic I guess."

I looked around. The furniture was covered in great white dust sheets. I suddenly had a vision of Ava, coming back here after the burial, how she would have ransacked the place, cleaning, tidying, locking it up for a slow and quiet death. She had had to come back alone. Claudia and I hadn't helped. Hadn't wanted to. And I had not been able to understand how she could still come back. I had seen it as proof of her lies and by default, of my innocence.

Claudia went up the stairs and I followed her. The hallway was as bare as downstairs but the doors were all closed. Her room had been at the end on the far right next to the bathroom, which she had hogged for ages every day before school. That had been one of the major adjustments we had had to make when she had gone. Ava and I would line up outside the door before realizing that she was not there.

When she got off the phone, she hugged her face in her hands and then slowly drifted her fingers down to cover her mouth. And then she saw us.

"What the hell are you doing there—get back to bed right this instant. Go on." She came at us, waving her hands forward, her snappish manner making us flee into our rooms as she continued to shout at us from behind.

"But what's going on?" I protested as she pushed me into my room with Ava, herding us out of sight.

"Just get in there and not one peep out of you for the rest of the night. Not one or so help me God I'll take a switch to you both!" And she slammed the door behind her.

We stood there staring at the door, listening to the sounds of her running into her room and the violent thuds of movement that seeped through the walls.

Suddenly Ava turned away from the door to face me.
"Where's Clo?" she asked.

I watched from the stairwell as Claudia made her way across the landing to her room and stood before the door. I waited on the second step.

She cradled the handle in her fingers and then there was the sound of the latch being released and it swung open.

We heard her leave. We waited a few minutes and then we came out of my room and hovered at the top of the staircase. "Look," said Ava, pointing over my shoulder and I saw that the door to Clo's room was ajar. I went inside and looked around. Her bed hadn't been slept in.

"Do you think she's hurt?" asked Ava. "Do you think...?"
"Shut up," I said.

Claudia disappeared inside her room and I made my way up the stairs to join her. The pale pink of her wallpaper with the small white daisies winding their way down in chains was covered in patches of brown mold and everything was draped in the same dust sheets as downstairs except her bed, which had been stripped except the mattress and a knot of pillows piled in the middle.

She crossed the room and opened up the window, letting air circulate into the room that had not breathed since she was sixteen years old.

"Do you want to talk about it?" I ventured.

"No, not anymore," she said with her back to me still facing the window. "I never thought I'd see this room again. If Mom had her way I never would."

"Mom did what she thought was right," I said, suddenly overly conscious of my voice.

"No—she did what was cruelest."

"You're blaming the wrong person, Clo," I said gently, and then she threw a glance at me over her shoulder and something there reminded me of how we used to be, how once there had been more than just blood between us. She summoned a smile that died as soon as it reached her lips.

"So did Mom."

Two weeks before my mother received a phone call in the middle of the night, my grandmother learned something quite by accident, and so tugged at a thread that would send my sister to live with the aunt and uncle of my mother in Massachusetts for the rest of her teenage life.

And this would not have occurred but for two events: My mother had gone out of town on a holiday with Jane for the weekend to camp in the Driftless Area in northeastern Iowa, and my sister had taken the opportunity to get drunk.

I can trace it all back to that night because of what my grandmother would later tell me. Have to tell me.

I had been at a sleepover. It was at the home of Mary-Louise Draper. I remember how her room had lilac-painted walls with pictures of white clouds on the ceiling and I had envied her collection of snow globes that her dad bought her from all over America because he was a salesman. I had particularly coveted one from New York, with its Empire State Building shining beneath the flurry of glitter when I shook the dome. As we lay in our sleeping bags on the floor, in a place of encroaching darkness, I thought how I would love to sleep in a city whose amber-colored lights sparkled in the night just like that one.

Ava had stayed at home. Claudia was supposed to be watching her but my eldest sister had other ideas, the main one consisting of her invading our father's liquor cabinet. I say it was Dad's because Mom never drank save for Christmas and weddings and even then all she had was one glass of champagne, which she would sip and leave half-full. However that night, Claudia had decided that the best way of putting our mother's absence to use was to devour the entirety of the cabinet's contents.

Which she did, in her room, dancing to the radio, pouring Ava shots that she then drank herself anyway when Ava sniffed at the glasses and left them on her dresser. Claudia then gave them both a makeover, which our mother would have scrubbed off her face with holy water had she been home.

Claudia pouted and preened and sang and garbled her way through her drunkenness. Evidently alcohol made her loquacious: moved her from a surly try-hard to an overtalkative desperate. I'm sorry I missed the transformation. I would have taken the opportunity to tease out her secrets and then when she was sober used them to goad her. My sister's temperament was like a dartboard when we were younger and nothing gave me more pleasure than hitting the bull's-eye.

But I was not there. Ava was.

Somewhere between her descent into inebriation and Ava's exhaustion, Claudia eventually was left to her own devices. This was sometime after a quarter to one in the morning. Until then Claudia was safe from herself.

"I found her by the stone well sobbing, howling like some animal. Oh, you never saw your sister like that—no, you didn't. Such hate, such anger—I knew what that felt like more than anyone, but when she realized I was there she tried to shut herself up. Stuffed her fist into her mouth, glaring at me for being there—for seeing her in her weakness. She always was about the presentation. Do you remember when she got sick at the Fourth of July fair and threw up on her dress and then slapped Piper for taking her to her mother? 'I don't want anyone to see!' Do you remember?"

"Yes, I remember," I said, the book I had been reading to her open in my hands.

"And I could see then that she wanted to slap me for just being there. She was humiliated for being so exposed. If she had been my child I would have trained her better, but then even I have had my moments. I suppose. And to be fair to your sister, I was just another wave in a torrent of bad luck she'd had that evening."

She looked over at me and gave a knowing look and I realized that what she was telling me was a story that somehow I already knew.

"She'd been drinking—she stank of whiskey and Jude had been there. I could see before she even told me. He'd stubbed out one of those Virginia Slims he used to smoke. I could smell it on her. She'd made a fool out of herself over him, of course, and he'd rejected her. What was worse was he was kind about it. She told me he had tried to hug her afterward, even suggested they could be friends. Foolish boy."

She stopped when she saw how I was looking.

"Oh, what, couldn't you guess? You didn't think your mother would send her away if she had been innocent, do you? For God's sake, Meredith."

"I don't want to hear any more," I said, standing. "I never wanted to be part of this and I only ever did it because you—"

"You did it because you were curious. And you didn't mind when it was about your aunt and uncle, did you? But now that it's closer to home you're developing a conscience? It's that fickleness of character that will get you in the end, Meredith. Some things you can't turn back from and change your mind about. Why do none of my family ever have the courage of their convictions like I did?"

"Did Claudia?" I shot back.

"Claudia had fear and pride—that served well enough. You know, it had quite escaped me, her crush on that man. I started to feel then that I was truly getting old. But I think now, it was only because I wasn't meant to know it until I was meant to know it, if you understand my meaning. And that's how I know that what I

have always done was right, Meredith. It was all for a greater good."
She lifted her head from her pillow in her urgency, her eyes boring
into mine.

"I knew then how I would do it and that she would help me,
and she did help me. Don't be fooled into thinking she was just
some ignorant puppet. After all, she never stepped out of character,
did she?" She leaned back into the sheets and sighed. The world
was listening because just then a stray wind rippled the curtains and
mirrored her breath.

"Hatred—it always comes down to that, doesn't it? But I've
found that it's always at its most potent when it's laced with love."

My sister got drunk and went out looking for Jude. She
found him by the well and there she tried to kiss him, but
he did not reciprocate. He gently but firmly told her that
nothing like that would ever happen between them and that
he was sorry. She had slapped him across the face and tried
to attack him but he had held her by her wrists and tried to
calm her down before the tears came.

And then my grandmother, on one of her regular late-
night walks, had found her slumped against the well.

And then two weeks later, we got a phone call.

On the second of March in 1986 at two-thirty in the
morning, the police were summoned to Aurelia, the home
of Abraham Hathaway and his wife Lavinia. They were there
to investigate a claim of attempted rape. The victim was
their sixteen-year-old granddaughter; the accused, her thirty-
three-year-old second cousin. The attack was alleged to have
taken place on their farm between the hours of 11:00 p.m.
and 12:00 a.m. The victim had been so hysterical it had
taken them two hours to calm her enough for her to give a
statement. Her mother, who lived half a mile away, had been

unaware of her daughter's whereabouts until she was noti-
fied by her mother-in-law, who had found her near the barn
when she had been on one of her regular late-night walks.
After half an hour of gentle preliminary queries the victim
was taken to the police station to give a formal statement
and then to the hospital for an examination. She returned
home just after six that morning. Her alleged attacker was
remanded in a custodial cell pending further questioning.

Twenty-four hours later he was released on bail.

Three days later the victim and her family requested that
all charges be dropped. They did not give a reason, but
when told the matter was now one for the state, the victim
withdrew her statement and the police were forced to let the
matter go and the suspect walk.

They did not look on this kindly.

We stayed up waiting for them to come home that night,
Ava and I. We lay in Ava's room and heard the front door go
at six-thirty. There were no voices, but there were noises in
the kitchen and over that, the sound of Claudia's steps on the
staircase as she went into her room. I lay there beside Ava,
tense, desperate. And then I threw back the covers and ran
as soundlessly as I could out of the room. I stopped at the
landing, pausing to look over the rail for my mother. Ava
opened the door to her bedroom, but then I ran down the
hall and grabbed at the handle of Claudia's room, pushing it
open with such force that as I stepped inside and hastily shut
it behind me, she had already given a half-shout of surprise.

"Shh," I said, putting my hands up to stop her. She stood
there before her closet, her hair messy and fallen about her
face, her lip cut, her eyes rimmed with red and her face
streaked with dirt. She was wearing a large brown jacket,
that looked like it belonged to a hobo.

"What are you wearing?" I moved to touch her.

"Get away from me," she said, whipping herself out of reach.

I stared at her, uncomprehending.

"Get out of here," she said, drawing herself up, "or I swear there'll be trouble."

I took her in. She clutched the jacket tighter. Her hands looked raw and bruised. Her eyes bore into me, her teeth were slightly bared over her lip. She looked feral.

I backed away from her and stole quietly out of the room.

That day when we came home from school, my sister and I were taken to stay with Jane.

"Is this about what's happened to Claudia?" Ava asked when after two hours of TV and no phone call from our mother, Jane started laying out three places on the table for dinner.

"Your mother just thinks it best if you were to stay with me tonight."

"Is she hurt or something?" Ava asked, standing in the doorway. Jane hovered above, laid down a fork and then gave a small shrug.

"She'll be fine."

"Why won't anyone tell us anything? She's our sister, we have a right to know," I asked angrily.

Jane moved and busied herself over the stove.

"Your mother knows better than you both what's best for you. Now don't make things harder for her. Just behave. Come and help me with the vegetables."

I stood there for a minute and then turned on my heel.

"I'm not hungry," I said and went back into the living room and turned the TV set on again.

I could see Jane from the corner of my eye throw Ava a

pleading look for compliance. But Ava knew where her loyalty was, so she came and joined me on the sofa. Jane sighed and returned to the kitchen and Ava and I refused to join her, until finally it was for time for bed and we went up to our rooms in silence. Our stomachs groaned from hunger well into the early hours of the morning.

The next day after school, our mother picked us up and we were relieved when we saw her small yellow car waiting for us, though her face when we got in, instantly silenced all the questions I had been dwelling on the night before. When we arrived home Claudia was in the garden, curled up on a swing chair. Ava and I hovered by the kitchen, but Mom caught us both by the shoulders and turned us around to face her.

"I want you to leave your sister alone, do you hear?" she said in a whisper. "You're not to question her about anything."

"Okay," I managed to say.

"Now go get ready for chores. There's a lot to do around here."

And then came dinner, possibly the worst meal I'd ever eaten at our house. Claudia sat at the head of the table silently watching our mother choke down every mouthful, while Mom kept her gaze firmly on her plate and away from her eldest, who was eyeing every movement of hers like a bird of prey waiting to swoop. Ava and I sat across from each other, daring to give furtive looks to these people locked in a silent battle that was raging across the macaroni and cheese we willed to go down our throats.

"Finish your food," Mom said when Ava moved her fork into the center of her plate.

Ava looked at her, her eyes wide.

"I'm serious. We don't waste food in this house. Finish."

And we did, right down to the last stone-cold mouthful…
in silence.

"Your mother knew."

*The next week, when it was my turn to nurse her, I came in and
shut the door bearing* The Blithedale Romance *under my arm.
As soon as I came in and sat down, before I even had a chance to
open the book, she said, "She knew all along. I found out she went
to see Jude after he was released on bail."*

"If you start on this again…" I warned.

*"She confronted Claudia in front of me—she didn't have the guts
to accuse me outright. Truth be told, I don't think she quite realized
my part in it. She thought your sister had thought up the rape al-
legation and the plan all by herself and that I had known but not
confessed because I had wanted to get rid of Jude. It was that night
when you came to the house with Ava looking for us—you had been
afraid because your mother and sister had had that terrific argument,
remember?"*

*Remember? There was a crack in the plaster on the kitchen wall
from when Claudia had thrown a chair at Mom's head. Ava had
cowered in the living room and thrown up all over the floor at their
screams. I ran into the kitchen between them, their hands batting
me away as they tried to get at each other amongst the cacophony
of rebukes and accusations. My mother wild with rage; my sister
incandescent with righteous indignation.*

"Did you do it?" Mom had screamed. "Did you do it?"

*"It only took your mother two days to accuse your sister, but she
suspected from the start. The night she came over to the house the
way she looked at her I knew that she was not fooled, nor would she
be. No one knows someone like a mother knows their child. And
she knew and she was so disappointed."*

I leaned right over her and hissed, "Shut up. Just shut your poisonous mouth!"

She stared at me, startled. "Did you know Jude came back to the farm after the attack?" she asked.

I blinked.

"No, I didn't think so— Did Ava not tell you then? She knew. Cal Jr. told her, but evidently she didn't tell you. Why was that? She does like her secrets, doesn't she, Ava? There's a whole host inside of her, like parasites just eating away. Crack her open and who knows what might come out?"

I sank back into my chair.

"He stood in our kitchen screaming at your grandfather. Most of what he said was sense, the rest just personal attacks. He never quite learned the way around your grandfather, but I think he just lost all control, you see? How often does it all boil down to that? He was like a madman screaming, blaming, hurtling out truths disguised as insults, and if it's one thing your grandfather was never able to handle it's an ugly truth. Like the fact that I was an adulterer and his daughter was worse than a whore and his only living son was a drunk who liked to torture his wife. He took your sister's side, of course—refused to believe any of it even with Piper's sense and your mother's quiet interest."

"Is that why you dropped the charges?" I asked her, I couldn't help it.

"Well, I couldn't have been sure of your sister if we'd gone to court, and anyway we didn't need the scandal or the expense. We just needed to clear a path. And though what came after was regrettable, it wasn't unbearable. Your sister always did complain about living on the farm." She smiled wryly. "Oh, don't feel too sorry for her," she said, staring at my face. "Another Julia in the making she was, mark my words. I know that girl in a way your mother never did. I was the one who counseled her after the death of your father. I was the one who taught her how to push down her anger and hatred,

to use them when needed, as she would eventually come to. No one forced her to go through with the accusation, or to continue it. But she did and all for revenge, out of a hatred born from your father's death and your mother's inattention. Poor excuse, isn't it? But then rotten seeds make diseased trees. She was the angriest little girl I ever met, outside of myself. She could rip the world to bits in her hands and play with the tatters as if they were ribbons. And let me tell you something, don't judge her. We all have our part to play and hers was the lynchpin. She secured the farm for your cousin."

I stared at her, incredulous, and then I said something I hadn't even known I was feeling but I realized was no less true.

"Who cares?"

She blinked.

"What?"

"Who cares? You think any of us would choose the farm over undoing...all of that? You think Mom or God even Dad, or Grand-dad—any of us would choose that?! You had no right, none, you had no right to choose for us."

"Are you simple?" she sneered. "Do you know what I am talk-ing about? He was trying to get your grandfather to sell it, to give it to some goddamn food manufacturer. Wooing him and Piper, who frankly I expected more from, with his tales of money. How the last farm they'd bought, which had been nearly five hundred acres less than ours, had sold for a million dollars. As if that was all that counted. As if that meant anything. We were more than just the success of the farm by then. We were a name, we were our land. We built this home from nothing. Nothing—" She gave a furious chok-ing noise. Instinctively I reached for the water but my hand stopped before the jug. It didn't matter; she didn't stop speaking for long.

"But he didn't know. Jude never did understand. He didn't love it, he didn't feel it. It was just a thing, a large toy to be played with and handed over at will. But your grandfather—God, I was so disappointed in him. But he would keep turning to the outside *for influence instead of looking in. And I knew then, I knew that I had to teach him a lesson, one that would mean he would never look outside this home again. Home is all there is."*

I dropped my gaze to the floor. *"This was Claudia's home,"* I half whispered.

"And it will be again," she said, frowning. *"Patience, Meredith."*

"Do you know what Mom would do if she knew this?"

"Are you deaf? She already knew. And she dealt with it as best she could. I don't blame her."

"I don't know why I listen to you," I said, my voice breaking.

"You listen because you're interested, my girl," she said, smiling, her hooded eyes blinking heavily. *"And I talk so that someone will remember, after I cannot."*

Claudia was sent away by our mother less than a month after she accused Jude of trying to rape her that night by the barn. Our mother still had some relatives on our maternal grandmother's side in Boston. She was to finish her senior years of high school there. It was explained to all of us as a fresh start for her, away from a place with too raw a memory. We did not question our mother's decision. We were too afraid of the answer she might give. The night before she was due to leave, Ava and I hovered outside her bedroom after Mom had gone to sleep, gently scratching the door so she would know we were there and let us in. But even though we could see the shadow of her night-light underneath her door, it remained firmly closed.

The next morning our uncle drove her to the airport with Ava and I in the back of his truck. We had insisted on coming with her to say goodbye. Our mother did not try to stop us nor she did she accompany us. Instead, she handed Claudia her suitcase at the door.

"Phone me when you arrive," she said. She did not embrace my sister, who stood there, rigid with hate, but she did not drop her gaze from hers, either. For a moment there was silence and then Claudia turned her back and left.

Ava and I were silent in the back of the truck on the way to the airport. Claudia sat staring straight ahead and no one tried to make conversation. When we arrived, Ethan stepped out of the truck and went to get her bags and suitcase. I put my hand on the door handle but Claudia stayed where she was. She dropped her head and for the first time in my life I thought I might see my eldest sister cry.

Ava, who was behind her, unbuckled her seat belt and stretched out a hand through the gap between Claudia's seat and the car door to stroke her shoulder. Claudia let it stay there and I saw her shoulders tremble.

"Will you write?" I asked, my voice sounding small in the air.

Claudia hesitated and then shook herself. Ava removed her hand. Our uncle stayed outside, the bags piled up on the sidewalk, smoking a cigarette.

Claudia opened the car door. "I'd better go or I'll miss my flight," she said and shut the door firmly behind her. Ava and I remained in the truck. Even though we never said the words we knew that we would not see her much again. I had fought Claudia my whole life, but until that point I had no memory of a life without her. She had been there since the day I was born. That was all I knew. And so, I began to cry.

Jude, to my then incorrect and partial knowledge, never came back to Aurelia, and I never saw him again. He had been living in the main house, and we were half a mile down from it, so we never got to see the shouting match between him and my grandparents, or him packing his bags, or the kick of dust from his truck that shot both gravel and a curse into the face of the white home with its beautiful promises.

I wish I knew more about what really happened that winter between those three people, but I don't. I may have gotten the bare facts from the bedside of my mentally deteriorating grandmother, but still the whole episode is shrouded in mystery, as if I am viewing it through a semitransparent sheath. I'll never know the full extent of what that episode did to him, nor really what happened in those evenings between Claudia and Lavinia at the house after my father's death, that would make my sister revere my grandmother to such a degree that she would throw away her mother and sisters at the asking.

After the incident with Claudia, my grandfather started to drink again, my uncle beat his wife and my mother locked the bedroom of my eldest sister and forbade us to ever go in there, while my cousin Cal Jr. progressed from haunting spirit to flesh and bone once again. And with a pace that, when I look back on it was almost frightening, this soon became normal.

In our house my eldest sister and I sorted through the possessions of our youth. We did not bother about the furniture. We were not sure if we could even take it, so instead we sorted through the boxes of photo albums, of trinkets and jewelry, china plates and dolls, tea sets and toys. Methodically we opened and went through each of our parents' possessions in an unspoken rule of saving everything that recorded their lives before and after us.

I found the tea set they had bought from the honeymoon in Quebec. I held the cup to my lips, remembering all the times I had drunk air from its chipped blue rim.

Claudia's quick hands went through and sorted each possession, her eyes weighing both their monetary value and their sentiment. She did most of the work, really. I sat there

on my knees, picking at the objects she placed on the floorboards for bubble wrap.

We did not speak. We did not stare at photographs and
reminisce; we did not remark on the mutual memories that
taunted us as we smelled our blankets and ran our fingers
with care over that which we had once handled with so little
thought.

It was after seven in the evening before we unloaded the
last box in Claudia's car.

"There's one more thing," I said and ran back up the stairs
into the house. I found the loose floorboard by the window
and lifted it up. The letters were still there in a plastic bag.
I picked them up and went down to Claudia. She raised her
eyebrows when I stuffed them into her hand.

"What is this?" she said.

I held them out to her. "Open them."

But she didn't need to. Her face said it all when she turned
them over and saw her writing and the postmark on the envelopes. And I dared not look at her face and she dared not
look at mine, and suddenly it seemed to me that ours was not
a home, it was a grave and we were the ghosts that haunted
it because those before us at least had death and all its release,
whereas we were still anchored down by memory.

No matter how white they look, scars are still marks as
raw as they were when first made. And for the first time
ever I knew that running away had been my only salvation,
because to stay and confront what I knew…

She turned from me and looked at the skyline.

I did not touch her, but I did not leave.

And then eventually, she put a hand over her mouth
and clambered heavily into the car. But I waited outside. I
couldn't go just yet. There was still one more thing I had
to know.

So I turned to walk away and she did not look at me. I made my way down the dust path, winding my way through the once familiar places to the rose garden—the garden my grandmother had tended, had loved and nursed over as if it were one of her own children. It was the only thing she ever gave life to that was a success. To do it, I had to walk through the trellis walkway, which was half torn down and what was there was covered in brown and mottle. The garden was now a mass of weeds and overgrown grass. It would have made my grandmother reel to see it, but the wildness of it somehow was a comfort.

I kept my eyes ahead and when I passed the spot on which it happened, I could feel him walking with me, but this time I could not look at him. I would not. He could haunt me anywhere he liked, but not here.

And then I stopped.

I was at the clearing with the stone god fountain. Though marbled with white rust all over, it was still intact, but that was not what arrested me. I had known it in my heart before I came, but even to see it was somehow still so painful.

Where three graves should have been were thick brown disruptions of earth, left open—he hadn't even bothered to have them covered again. He had ripped them out of the earth and scattered them, God knows where, my grandparents and Piper. I wondered then when this had happened. Maybe it had been just after my mother had died and my last sister had left or maybe it was some time later. I don't know. And then I wondered if they had ever haunted him, the way he haunted me. If rousing their bodies out of the earth they had so loved hadn't wreaked havoc upon him ever since. If they had not sat in his car with him the night he crashed it and died, bringing him with them to their place of unrest.

This used to be a gravesite, a place of everlasting respite.

My great-grandparents' plot was still there, as was my uncle's, thankfully untouched. We had lowered my grandfather and my aunt in turn next to them and cried. When it came to the funeral of my grandmother I hadn't returned home. She died a few weeks before my midterms during my first semester and I had taken the timing as the excuse I needed to stop my mother from trying to guilt me into coming back for her funeral. I did not know that by then she had already been diagnosed with stage-four breast cancer, nor that she had known about it for some time. She would be dead by the following summer.

The wind stirred the gravel from the earth there and a few crumbs fell into the open mouths of the three graves.

When I returned to the car, my door was still open and Claudia was still sitting there holding the letters. I climbed in beside her. We sat for a minute in silence. I wanted to tell her about the graves, but just as I opened my mouth to speak she cleared her throat and said, "I would have done anything for her." The shock of her voice made me meet her eyes. She looked right into me and shrugged.

"She was the only one who ever knew me."

I waited for her to go on, but she didn't. Finally she turned on the lights and the engine, put the letters in their plastic wrapping to lie nestled in her lap and we drove away from the farm for the last time.

14

THE WORLD TURNED AND WITH EACH SPIN I grew older. I whispered my secrets to my last remaining sister and she fed her hopes back into me. We made a cat's cradle of our confidences. In so many ways it felt like we were all we had. My mother was never the same after Claudia left—each birthday, each holiday, the difference in her became more compounded and more obvious. Her love was not unconditional and this devoured her. She was still our Mom, still loved us, but she realized she did not love us the way she thought, because she did not forgive my sister and my sister did not ask her to.

My uncle held a knife to his wife in front of his son in 1986—six months after Jude had gone—and Georgia-May packed her bags and left for her surviving family in Florida by the end of that week. My uncle did not seem to care and he was slowly but surely relieved of his duties on the farm. The only thing that saved him from utter ruin was the fact that he was Lavinia's son. She shopped for him, cleaned his house, cooked for him, all under a mildly disguised veil of contempt. And when he was drunk and we stumbled across his path, he only spoke of Alison—not his wife and child, but a girl whom we had never met and he had not seen in twenty years. Ava called that love.

He probably died calling her name.

For the five years after his wife and son left, my uncle drank himself into a useless stupor day after day. He was a tragic joke to us, someone to avoid, someone to pity and worst of all he knew it but he had no wish to change this, he only wanted to be alone, to have some peace. And then on the 3rd of September 1991 he finally got his wish. His body was found by a dog walker in the woods midmorning. He was forty-four. His car had run through a road boundary not three miles from home and had driven off the side of the road, flipped over twice and was found upside down. He hadn't been wearing a seat belt.

Georgia-May did not come for the funeral.

And my grandmother lost her last surviving child.

She would tell me that a week after the funeral, she rose very early one morning, so early the sky was a wash of pale pink and the air was muggy with impending heat. The ground stretched before her and every place that she could see that the light touched she knew was hers, was a Hathaway's, and it gave her comfort, it gave her purpose. She placed a hand on her belly that had nurtured two lives within it and in one of her weaker moments she longed for the quiet confidence of that beginning. She had not cried at the death of her firstborn. No one had, now that she had come to think of it. And for the first time ever, she felt something that shook her, something she had not expected: a treacherous sense of regret.

And then she looked up as a wind roused the dust of

the land into a dance at her feet and she remembered who she was.

For some that day the sun simply rose in the morning, but for Lavinia Hathaway it burst.

Claudia dropped me off outside Jane's house. She helped me carry in some boxes, which we piled up in the living room with Jane's permission. Jane did not ask her how things had been, and my sister and I remained silent, only speaking when necessary. And then finally there was nothing left for us to do and we stood up and dusted down our hands and realized the time for goodbye had come.

Jane made her excuses and left us.

"How long did you know?" Claudia asked finally.

"Since Grandma got sick."

"Did you ever…" She cleared her throat but did not finish. I shifted from one foot to the other. And then she stopped and, looking me straight in the eye, she shrugged. Because what was there to say now that could possibly make any difference?

"Do you know what happens next? With the farm, I mean," I asked her.

"I don't care, Meredith," she said and she shook her head at me. "This is a good thing. You may not realize it, or want to believe it, but it is. We only ever kept it by doing the worst things for it. And I'm tired—I'm so tired of being one of us. Of being the one to live and remember. No matter where we go or what we do, it's always there and now finally, maybe with it going, we can forget. We can sleep through the night."

She pulled her car keys out of her pocket and swung them onto the loop of her finger.

"Goodbye then," she said.

"Yeah…" And I'm ashamed to say my voice broke and I looked down at the floor and saw the heels of her boots move away and, as I looked up willing something, anything, to come forward, the door closed and she was gone.

I stood there in the doorway, listening to the machinations of the car start up, and the roar, and then the dying breath of the engine as she drove away. And just like that, I was all that was left.

But still I was not alone.

So how did it come to this?

They all died, of course.

Death came to visit Aurelia in 1991 and his stay there was incredibly productive. He pitched up his scythe and put up his feet and settled into the white house for what would be an energetic sabbatical. The first person he took was my uncle and then two months after that he turned his gaze onto Piper. His gift to her was cancer, ovarian and rapid. By a twist of irony, the person who nursed her through her death was my grandmother. She gave to that woman who had been her lifelong adversary, every last piece of comfort and respite that she could; every waking hour was devoted to her care, until one night she sent for each of us to come into the room where Piper lay and say our goodbyes and the rattling sack of bones there breathed for the last time. My grandmother cried when Piper died, actually burst into tears when she placed a hand on her chest and a mirror under her mouth, and there was no shadow of air on the glass.

It was the strangest sight I had ever seen, watching Lavinia cry. Her body was wracked with sobs, her eyes bleary and red, her howls erupting with a force that even her wringing hands could not stifle. She did not cry when her sons died, she did not cry when her own husband would die, but for

Piper, whom she had treated as an enemy for over forty-five years, she cried. I don't know why. That was one of the few things she would never tell me.

So Piper went first, four months after Ethan's death, the day before Valentine's Day, and then in May of the following year, my grandfather died peacefully in his sleep of a stroke. He just did not wake. Even though the blood vessels in his brain had burst, causing a sharp slice of agonizing, white-lightning pain, it was a mere moment before whatever void there was opened up and swallowed his soul whole. He died next to my grandmother and she only realized what was wrong when she turned over in the morning and saw how peaceful he looked. She lay with him for half an hour before she told anyone. She called us all to the house and broke the news in the living room while the coroner came to take the body. I remember how they wheeled him past us in the black mortuary bag. Ava whimpered. Cal Jr. got up from where he sat beside her and shut the living room door.

It was warm the day we buried my grandfather. Uncomfortably, unseasonably warm so that my black dress stuck to my back with sweat. There was no breeze, just unremitting sunlight beating down on the assembled mourners as the same priest who had conducted Piper and Ethan's funeral droned on above our heads. I sat between my mother and Ava, my eyes unable to tear themselves away from the lacquered oak coffin. He was in there. Open it up and you would see him, see the dark blue suit that he only ever wore on formal occasions because he hated wearing suits. He was always tugging at the shirt collars, stretching his neck, or slipping his finger into the knot of his tie. My grandmother had chosen it. She had pressed and ironed it herself before she dressed him.

Get up, I thought. Get up and take it off. Get into your pants or jeans. In this heat the earth will cook you.

When he was lowered into the ground, my family and I stood up and one after another threw a handful of earth down onto the coffin. As I did so I felt like my life seemed to be the thing that filled in the gap between funerals. How many times had I done this now? My grandmother scooped the dirt in her hand, releasing it in a slow pour; my mother threw hers with a gentle toss while Ava repeated her delicate gesture and then it was my cousin's turn. Only the five of us now, when once…when once…

His actions were slow but controlled. He turned to the bowl of earth on the stand, he lifted a chunk of it into his palm, shaking his wrist to get the measure of it. Then he stood on the lip of the grave and, tightening his fist, crouched down and flung the earth onto the coffin so that it fell in a rain of dirt landing with a splatter onto the gold-embossed plaque.

The priest faltered in his speech but only for a moment, while his eyes found those of my grandmother's and the hands holding his bible clasped the spine. None of us looked at each other. We stood back as the diggers gently covered my grandfather in the dust of Aurelia. Our faces were masks that betrayed nothing to the other mourners.

My grandfather's will was read at the wake. We retired to his study after he was buried and it was there that we discovered Cal Jr. was to be the main beneficiary of Aurelia and all its assets, after the death of my grandmother. When we learned the news my grandmother smiled at him. He turned his head and looked out the window.

And then all that was left was Lavinia, but Death had a different plan in mind for her. She would die, but not quickly. Hers would be piece by piece, starting with her mind.

It started with a small thing. Her utter lack of emotion in the weeks after the death of her husband. She had lost her son, husband and sister in-law in the space of a year and a half and yet she was surprisingly cavalier. People attributed this to either coldness or stoicism, but this can-do attitude was less a conscious decision than an inability to do anything else.

And then gradually, so slowly it was almost a tease, she began to forget things. Small things: appointments she had made, that she had run out of a particular food or ingredient at home, names at the tip of her tongue but never quite able to spill over. She attributed it to getting old. She was old. And then she started to write things down whenever she could, but then she would forget where she had kept them, these bits of paper, so she kept a book. But she would forget at the end of phone calls or conversations what it was she needed to write down in the first place and she knew then that something had permanently unraveled within her like caught thread.

So she made an appointment and she saw a doctor and she came home and realized that her time had finally come. She had been diagnosed with a particularly aggressive strain of Alzheimer's and she had a year before she would come undone. She tasted the bitterness of her impending death and the manner in which it would come and it was then and there as she sat in her living room and gazed at the polished crystal and woods that she made up her mind.

No, there was no violent death for my grandmother. She would not have feared it if there had been. Hers was more torturous: she would waltz with death through dementia, as her brain slowly degenerated, taking her body with it. She would lose her memory and then her language and her speech until she was a living shell with everything she was and everything she knew gone.

And this was what stayed with her for a whole year.

When the disease began to take hold of her, my mother, my sister and I began to take turns to nurse my grandmother. My cousin was too busy on the farm to be able to help and in any case Cal Jr. didn't have it in him. We were all that remained then, and I remember how lonely that feeling was. From having a home with grandparents, cousins and aunts, we were reduced to just the five of us. Yet Aurelia remained unchanged. The farm was still as great and as prosperous as it had ever been; it had expanded while we, its inhabitants, had shrunk.

We moved into my grandparents' house. I was seventeen and filling out college applications. Ava had already graduated high school and had enrolled at Duke University, but she had deferred for a year while I was still at home and our grandmother was sick. She hadn't wanted to go at all by then. She had wanted to stay and train in the local community college as a midwife. She loved babies: with them she was utterly at home. The day we had to move into our grandmother's house, I had come out of the shower and found her in her bedroom shaking. She was sitting in the middle holding her duvet up to her mouth. I sat with her and positioned my wet head next to hers and held her. We never said a word, we didn't need to. Our mother had tried to tell us how temporary this was and how necessary, with Cal Jr. living up in the house all alone, unable to care for our grandmother, whose condition was worsening all the time.

"We're still a family," she'd said. "This is just what families do."

We moved in on a Wednesday and Ava smiled when she crossed the threshold. No one would have known there was anything wrong. Funny, but now that I think about it, that moment up in her bedroom was the last act of kinship between us in our home. We would never return to it the way we had left.

Ava got a job in town at a diner to keep her occupied, because Mom insisted it wasn't good for her to stay in the house all day. Cal Jr. had been furious. He had berated Mom for tarnishing our family name—making one of us work in a common diner as if we were desperate and needy. Mom hadn't lifted her eyes from her plate when she'd told him that despite him being the head of the family's finances, she was still head of her own household and he had no right or sway over what her daughters did. He hadn't liked that one bit. In a way, though, he had been right to be concerned, because it was only then that I began to really understand the change in my family's stature after Ava took that job. For the first time I began to read in other people's faces not the awe and respect I had known, but now a trace of discomfort. When I would first go in to see Ava where she worked, I would notice the regulars and how awkward they were about giving her orders for food and how they wouldn't meet her eye when she stretched over them to pour coffee or clear away plates. I would sit at the red-topped counter and I realized what was in their minds when she moved away. It was the same question I saw on the faces of my classmates and teachers every single day at school. *Are you okay? What's happening up there?*

But there was no one outside ourselves we could trust to tell.

So Ava worked, our mother nursed and I helped while Cal Jr. supported all of us, and honestly, this mock unit we had built worked. We became a family out of the embers of a once greater one. We took up the mantle and we succeeded, and would have even been happy but for two things.

The first began one day when my grandmother was crying out and as there was no one around but me I went into her room and she turned to me as I opened the door.

"It's you, then," she said.

"Yes, Grandma, what is it?" I stepped inside and shut the door behind me.

"Water," she said simply.

So I poured her a glass from the jug and helped her to drink it.

"You don't look a bit like your father, not a bit. You're nothing like us," she said suddenly. I had trained myself not to listen to her words as if they were truths anymore. Mom kept telling us how she wasn't herself, that her mind was unraveling and taking her body with it, but all the same I couldn't help but feel that perhaps now more than ever what she uttered was more herself than we wanted to realize, because this was her unrestrained, untempered and ungoverned. I saw her mind as a sack of fluid held together by a band that was slowly losing its shape until one day it would simply burst and pour away, but that did not mean that its contents were altered just because its frame was rotten. However, I kept these thoughts to myself. It would not have helped anyone to hear them.

"You were never like us, were you? I used to say that the tree of the Hathaways gives two kinds of fruit. Sweet and sour. Your father was sweet, your uncle and aunt sour. Your sister Claudia was sour, Ava was sweet, but you, you were never anything. You didn't fit." She stopped and looked down. "I liked that."

I wiped my hands on my jeans and then smoothed the bed covers over her.

"You never loved me, did you?" she asked. In my shock I met her eyes as I leaned over her to adjust her pillows and she smiled. "I never loved you, either. But I didn't hate you and that's more than can be said for some in our family."

Briefly I stood there and then moved away.

"Merey, do you know who I am?"

"Yes," I said. "You're my grandmother."

"Because I don't want to forget," she said, a whimper creeping into her voice. "I don't want to forget…" As her voice trailed off then her eyes sharpened into focus on me.

"Do you know who I am?" she asked again.

"Yes, Grandma," I repeated slowly. Her mouth twisted into a sneer.

"Your name is Lavinia Hathaway," I said. "You live on a farm in Iowa—you were married and had two sons. Your youngest son was my father. I know who you are."

"That wasn't my name." She leaned forward and smiled. "That's not my name." And she giggled, holding her hands up to her mouth. "That's not my name," she repeated, laughing. "It's not my name."

"It is your name."

"No, no, it wasn't." She leaned back with a huge grin and then her eyes found the curtain and something shifted and slowly the expression drained from her face.

I took my moment and left. When I shut the door, I leaned against it for a minute, utterly bemused, but I dismissed it because I mistook a moment of clarity for one of confusion.

But she did not forget, and the next time we were alone she asked me again what her name was and again I told her what I knew and it was then she grew angry and threw a glass at my head and she hissed at me, "Stupid girl, that's not my name. It's not my goddamn name." And because I was confused and shocked I asked her, I asked her what was her name.

I opened the door and let the devil in.

Sometimes I have wondered over the years if a person's ability to feed their secrets into another isn't perhaps a way of bleeding their soul into yours. You become a hollow vessel in which they slowly fill you with their lives, so that their memories seep into your thoughts and dreams. I cannot tell you the amount of dreams I have had of a girl in a gingham pinafore, or a woman walking the dusty roads to her car holding her jaw slowly swelling under her hand, or of a redhaired girl I've never met but whom I look on with hate and fear.

Since I went to the farm with Claudia, I've begun to dream again. I am walking the road that takes me to the farm. It is night. The road is silvered by the moon that dips behind clouds so that in fits and starts the road is obscured to me, but still I keep walking. I find myself back at the entrance, at the sign in curlicue black lettering, which I cannot read but whose ends look like tails swinging in the dark, and I make my way up the gravel path, winding my footsteps to a house so white it shines. The lights blaze from the windows, the open air carries voices from inside, stray breaths of conversation, raised voices, shouts of laughter. I stand before it, waiting. And then there is the sound of twigs being snapped into the earth and I hear his voice.

"Say it."

I woke up panting, not screaming. It was still late and the room was black and white, which only compounded my brief but bright fear that I was still there, still back in a world I had no wish to be in and yet, unlike this one, was one of color.

15

I RENTED A CAR, PACKED UP THE BOXES AND SAT down to the plate of scrambled eggs Jane had made me.

Over the rim of her coffee cup she asks, "Are you sure you want to leave today?"

"It's time to go back," I say softly.

"I'll let you know what happens. With the farm, I mean," she offers.

"Don't bother—I don't want to know. It's done."

"Is it?"

I look up from my plate and my fork hovers.

"Your mother's heart would break if she saw what you two had become." Jane sets down her cup and folds her hands into her lap. "It will never be done until you make peace."

"Peace," I mutter. I put down my fork. "Jane, do you know what happened the night before I left for college?"

She shifts in her seat.

"No," she says, "but I know how it broke your mother to see what had happened to you."

I shake my head. "Ava never told Mom what happened and I am glad, because I think it would have destroyed her if she had had to stop loving yet another daughter. Peace—peace is for those who can redeem what they did. And I can't. I cannot ever undo what happened and nothing good can ever come out of it."

That shook her. She blinks, her face a mask, but I could see then her mind was racing.

"Thank you for having me, I appreciate it. And I know it was Ava who called ahead before I came here and that's why you had the room ready—"

"I didn't—"

"You didn't have to, I figured it out when I got here. I had no idea I was still that predictable." I push my plate forward and stand up.

"You all used to be so happy," she says mournfully.

I can feel myself smile.

"We didn't know each other back then."

I drove for miles with the boxes carrying my family's life in the back. My cousin drove with me in the car, lighting up cigarette after cigarette but never speaking. I did not need him to, his company was enough.

And now—

And now—

I had said we were happy but for two things, hadn't I? And the second, the second was—

Ava, I did not know—I didn't.

I did not know what I was seeing.

A few hours later, I happened to pass a wedding. The people spilled out of the church, swiftly followed by the stark white and black of the bride and groom. The guests threw confetti in the air above their heads and it rippled in an array of delicate peaches and pinks. The bride bent her head and her smile shone on the roses in her hand while her new husband kissed her hair.

Their happiness was radiant.

"Do you know where my mother is buried?" asked Cal Jr. beside me.

"No, Cal, I don't."

"No..." He scratched his finger on the window pane. "Me, neither."

One night as I rested at a motel, I dreamed the dream again. I was standing at the foot of the mound but I did not go in. I heard the noise and his voice behind me and I began to shake but I did not move. The cloud slipped behind the moon, wide and bright like a silver dollar.

Like the silver dollar my father used to have when I was a child, which he would roll over the back of his fingers for my delight.

Cal Jr. stood before me, smiling.

"Say it and I'll bring the moon down for you."

We faced each other. I couldn't see her but I knew she was there somewhere listening. I wanted to be brave but I am not. I never was.

So I said it.

And he plucked down the moon and I saw that it was only ever just a silver dollar.

I am sitting in Cathy's, a little restaurant with checkered cloths on dark wooden tables and candles that throw up shadows that melt against the oaks of the restaurant's décor. I am in Ohio, specifically, Raynsville, Ohio, which is a little to the south of the state. It's been a long drive—just over two days and I am tired. I am sitting at a table to the back of the place behind a gauze of tapestry in blue. Nothing matches here, but the wait staff leave you alone and they refill your coffee without preamble or questions.

I've been here about half an hour. I scour the menu listlessly, but I don't want to eat. The table next to me has a couple who are picking at their salad. They have barely spoken to each other since they sat down and I think to myself, why do they do it? Why would they come outside among people like me, who watch their movements and lack of touch or communication and know how unhappy they are with each other? Why don't they hide it? Or do they just not care anymore? Do they want someone to see, someone to notice and tell them, yes, we know it, too, you're not making it up? Is that what they seek—acknowledgment because they cannot even get a hello from each other?

The woman stops eating and looks me in the eye. She's caught me staring. I shift my gaze.

Camel-colored coat, dark jeans, the tail of a white shirt.

"Do you mind that I'm going to NYU?" I said as we packed.

"No, I don't mind," she lied as she folded my sweaters.

"Ava, it's summer, it's like a hundred degrees out there," I said, snatching the blue sweater out of her hands.

"Yeah, and it'll be minus a hundred in the winter."

I shot her a look.

"I'll be home before then, Ava, to get some more clothes."

"I don't think you will," she said and her ponytail flopped over her shoulder as she leaned down over the suitcase.

"Of course I will," I said, hurt.

She opened her mouth to reply and then stopped.

"Nothing will change." I put my hand on her shoulder. "This is still my home."

"Then why do you want to go so far away?"

I couldn't answer. She shook her head and resumed folding.

"Don't you want to go away?" I ventured.

"All the time."

"Then why don't you?"

She stopped and stared ahead and for a second there I remembered that she was the elder one.

"Meredith, you can't always get what you want."

I shook my head, I was pissed.

"Then maybe you just don't want it enough."

I stand up when I see her, but she sits down without even looking at me and takes her bag off and slings it on the back of her chair. Her hair is in a loose bun and she hasn't taken off her hospital ID badge. She gives me a quick glance and then motions to the waitress and asks for some coffee with cream.

A cup and small jug are set down before her quickly.

"Would you like a menu?" the waitress asks.

She catches my eye and I drag mine away from her face.

"Not right now," I answer for her.

She cradles the cup in her hands. I look around the room before clearing my throat. She brings the cup to her lips and I see the flash of her wedding band. I swallow. I hadn't been at her wedding.

"So," she says, finally looking at me.

It had been Ava who had insisted on organizing a goodbye party even though there was only the five of us there. She had cooked and baked all evening, filling the kitchen with the smells of freshly baked cakes and meat. It had been Ava who had hung up the streamers around the house and decorated the table with candles and set out the fine china.

"Ava, I don't want all of this," I'd said, gazing at the ribbons of yellow and pink around the porch.

"Shut up and help, would you?"

I knew she was overcompensating; it was her way of burying her pain, but it only made it more acute for me. I could see her impending loneliness and I wanted to tell her that I didn't need to go, that I was happy to stay with her. But I wasn't. I felt like if I didn't go now, I never would.

"How was it?" she asks, staring at her cup.

"It was, um…" I clear my throat again. "It was hard."

"Different?"

"Yeah…" My voice comes out in a strangled gasp. I cough. "Um, Uncle Ethan's house is gone. He demolished it."

"But Mom's was okay?" she says, suddenly urgent. I'm surprised that she cares. It must show because her face hardens.

"Yeah, it was fine. We, uh, we found everything that you boxed away. Thanks."

There is a silence.

"Yeah, it was pretty impressive how I put everything we owned away, alone, after our mother's funeral while you and Claudia were busy…busy doing what exactly?" She shrugs, holding my eye. "Important things I'm sure."

"Yeah, well where were you this time around?" I hiss at her. "Where were you?" And then I glance around. I see the woman with her salad look at us quickly before turning back to her husband and breaking into conversation at the hostility of my gaze. I turn back to the table. Her face is impassive.

"It's gone," I say softly. "It's finally gone. We'll never see it again."

She arches an eyebrow and looks at her cup.

"I see it all the time."

I feel my eyes widen.

"I used to, feel—feel like I was still there," she says softly. "For years I would dream about it. I would turn corners on the street and see Dad or Charles. Once I even thought I—"

She breaks and I think, I'll tell her that the same thing happens to me, about my dreams, my visions. I'm not mad, I'm not alone.

Mom had raised her glass as a toast to me, the five of us sitting around the table. Everyone had lifted their glass except Grandma, who was staring at the lick of flame on the candle.

"To my beautiful, talented, youngest child who is leaving us to go back to the place where I met your father and married him. I hope that you get everything you seek and are fulfilled and happy and that you go there knowing that you are coveted and loved." She paused. "And missed. To Meredith."

"To Meredith," Cal Jr. and Ava echoed.

Mom gave me a knowing look. "Time to grow up, Merey."

"I don't really get why you called me," she says suddenly. "I mean why drive all the way up here to give me a bunch of stuff you know I don't want or need? Force my hand like this by threatening to come to my home if I don't see you? Is that how this is going to work from now on for you?"

"I wasn't threaten—"

"Because that isn't how it's going to work with me, Meredith. If you think you can just...turn up whenev—"

"I don't— I—I wasn't trying to—"

"I will not have you demanding anything from me, or making demands on my time—not you, you don't have that right anymore...."

"I'm sorry—" I suddenly break down "—I'm so sorry. I didn't..."

"Well, you know what, Meredith, that isn't really—"

"I didn't know that night, I didn't know. I heard you and I thought, I thought..." Her mouth drops and a wave of comprehension floods her features but I cannot stop.

"I thought that you wanted to. That you meant it because how you were around each other and I mean, I think, the

two of you were always…and I know, I know, I know now
that that wasn't but I didn't know it then. I mean you never
told any of us, you never said…"

She straightens in her chair and sets her cup down. "I don't
want to talk about this here."

"Well, I have to. I have to talk about it."

"This isn't appropriate."

I look at her incredulous, desperate. "I don't care."

She meets my eyes and her mouth thins.

"Going back there, seeing what he had done to the place,
I always thought the best thing for us would be to get away
from there, but we'll never get away. It's in our blood.
There's no escape. I've tried to pretend, I've tried to forget,
but I can't."

"Forget what?" she asks coldly. "Forget who? You seem
to be confused about what it is you're talking about."

"The night in the rose garden…"

She raises a hand. "I told you I don't want to talk about
it."

"Please…?"

"You need me to help you through it? You want me to
hold your hand and tell you it's all okay? I don't think so.
You went back there—you chose to go back—and whatever
issues that raised for you is on you. You're not my problem.
I've had more than my fair share of the place."

"I'm sorry I wasn't there when Mom died."

She rolls her eyes. "Yeah, you said before."

"I just couldn't stand to see you. I couldn't stand being
there, back there with you after…" My teeth chatter against
my lip. "I didn't want to believe you and it was easier because
the alternative meant that what I did, what I didn't do was…
that it made me—and I couldn't face that, I just couldn't, I
couldn't."

She stands up. "I'm leaving."

I grab for her hand but she is already going.

"No," she says and shrugs my hand away. "I told you to stop."

"Hey," I hear a waitress shout as we both stalk out of the restaurant. "Hey, where do you think you're going?"

"This looks like shit."

Mom put down her glass and stared at my grandmother.

"Shit," she said in a croak. "You're all eating shit."

"Lavinia, you're tired, you should go to bed."

My grandmother arched her neck and called out to the hall, "Cal, get in here and take this shit away."

I looked at my cousin but he leaned back in his chair and snapped his napkin onto his plate.

"Here she goes again."

"Cal, where the hell are you?" my grandmother shouted, looking at the door. Mom rose up and went to stand next to her.

"God, he's always with that slut of a daughter of his. I'm so sick of it. If only he knew what a whore she was. Simpering after her like some dumb mule. I wish to God she'd died in that stupid car wreck."

We sat there for a minute in horrified silence and then suddenly she burst into tears.

"No one ever pays any attention to me. No one!" she screamed. "Lou, are you deaf? I said to clear this mess up." She swiped a plate with her hand so that it went crashing to the floor. Mom was next to her in an instant, helping and cajoling her from her seat while Ava and I circled her.

"No, no," Mom said, batting us away. "She's had too much excitement and you'll only crowd her. Merey, help me—Ava, you clean up here, okay?"

There was the harsh scrape of the chair. Cal Jr. got up, left the room and slammed the front door as he went out into the night.

"Here, here," I say, taking out a handful of money and shoving it at the waitress as I hurry out after my sister. She is walking in long purposeful steps, but I catch up.

"I know you hate me, I know I deserve to be hated, but I swear if I could undo it, if I could go back and make it different I would." She swings around and for a second I think she'll hit me but then she just carries on walking.

"I would because I didn't know and ever since I found out, ever since I realized I've been—it's been...listen to me!" I scream suddenly, grabbing her arm which she shrugs off before squaring up to me.

"What? What's it been doing, Meredith? Hurting, have you been hurting, pining, regretting?" Her voice comes out in a contemptuous parody of a whine. "Does it keep you awake at night? Does it? Are you racked with guilt? Because even if you are, so what? So what? You think this is about that night? It's not. It's about after." I shrink back and she wipes her hand over her mouth before dropping it to her side.

"You want me to take you in my arms and tell you it's all okay? You want me to sit there and grieve with you about Mom and the farm. Let me tell you something, Meredith. Everything you are going through, you're supposed to go through because that's a consequence of what you did."

"I didn't know," I splutter. "How was I supposed to know?"

"Because I told you," she screams. She takes me by the arm and drags me into a side street and shoves me against the wall. "I told you, I wrote to you and I explained and you never returned my calls. You wouldn't help when Mom was dying—you left me there and you didn't give a damn what happened or what would happen. You left me in hell and didn't give it a second thought!"

"That's not true, that's not true."

She holds my face up by her hand and forces me to meet her eyes.

"You ran as far and as fast as you could and you did not care who or what you left behind. You left me there knowing what he did to me."

I shake my head, tears of rage coursing down my cheeks.

"No…" I hold on to her wrist. "I'd just heard that kind of story before."

"From who?"

"From Claudia, and that turned out to be a pack of lies."

I throw her hand away and release myself, standing up to her.

"You said it to him, you said it." I am panting now.

She shakes her head in disbelief. "Then you never knew me."

I'd helped Ava with the cleaning up while Mom dealt with our grandmother upstairs. It was much later when she finally came back down.

"I'm so sorry, Merey," she said, holding out her arms for me.

"No, Mom, it's fine. Don't worry."

"God, and those things she said in front of Cal, about his mother…" Her eyes skimmed the top of my head. "Is he very upset?" She looked from me to Ava.

"Cal Jr. hasn't come back," Ava said.

"Oh, God. Ava, will you go find him? You've always been good with him."

★ ★ ★

We stand there in silence, staring at anything but each other. I can barely stand so I hunch against the wall.

"I'm sorry, I'm sorry." I hold up my hands and then drop them again. I am exhausted. I grip my knees with my hands. She pauses with me.

"Why did you never come back?" she asks. "Because you were ashamed? Because you were embarrassed by what you'd seen or because coming back would mean that you'd have had to stay at home and face up to the truth? Why choose the hard thing when it's so much easier to be in New York and pretend that I was the bad guy?"

I am speechless.

"You know, I had to nurse both Grandmother and our mother until they died and I had no one but him. Do you have any idea what that did to me?"

I look at her in horror.

"You don't get to come here and say you're sorry." Her eyes are bright as she speaks. "It isn't good enough. It will never be good enough."

I open my mouth, but nothing comes out, not a sound, and then from somewhere, I begin to howl. I hold my hands up to stifle it but it bleeds through my fingers, a wounded-animal thing that seeps through the cracks and bursts like a flood, sweeping away all dams of control in a torrent of recrimination and despair unleashed.

I was calling for her. It was I who had offered to find her.

They had been gone too long, the two of them, and Mom had started to worry.

Throwing the flashlight among the darkness, it punctured the thick purple haze of the evening with circles of white. I remember how the air was full of the smell of azaleas and the sound of crickets mingled with the brush of the wind through the sycamores.

Swinging my free hand lazily, waving the flashlight around the path I knew so well, I began to think of how much I would miss my home, and for a moment I allowed myself to feel how truly scared I was of leaving the farm—of a life outside of Aurelia—and I was stricken with both the fear of the unknown and my desire for it. Though the summer winds were a welcome respite from the onslaught of heat that had been thrust on us all afternoon, I gave up a shudder.

And then I heard it.

It was the sharp snap of twigs being twisted into the earth. I swung around and moved off the path down to the rose garden. I heard them before I saw them. His voice was low, half in a whisper, but in the stillness of the night, it carried.

"Say it," he urged and then more forcefully, repeated, "Say it!"

And then another noise. At first I didn't even know it was her. It was a sound I had never heard from her before.

"Say it, say it, Ava."

There was no other noise but a slow rhythmic rustle of earth and movement. I crept around slowly and saw their legs lying on the ground, hers spread against his.

I turned off the flashlight.

"Say it!" And then I saw his legs move up and hers stretch out and she stifled a cry.

The bracken snapped further up by their heads. I could hear him grunt in exertion. Her legs were scrambling on the ground as his own grew more energetic. They looked like they were running.

And then I heard her, I heard her say it, half caught in a cry and a sob and when she said it she started to cry, soft but consistent sounds that ran from her mouth as her legs fell down and were still.

I looked through the garden then and saw the angle of her neck turned from him, her whole body utterly still as he started to gain momentum. She looked like she was playing dead, her wrists held

down by his, her dress up against her waist. But she wasn't, because
she looked up and saw me.

She opened her mouth to cry out but she didn't get the chance to.
Because I ran.

We are in her car now. I sit hunched there in my seat, all
but screaming for God knows how long, while she sits beside
me and waits it out. And then there is silence. The sounds
just die away and leave me with nothing. She shifts in the
seat and fiddles with the buckle of her seat belt.

"I'm sorry I came here," I say at last.

She sighs.

"Even now, after all these years, I still can't get away," she
says more to herself than to me. "When you'd all gone and
Mom was sick and we were the only ones left, I saw how
much he hated it. He told me how he'd always hated it,
loathed every last speck of the place."

"I don't understand," I say.

Ava sighs, staring ahead. She looks tired. "She thought he
was obsessed with it because he wanted to own it, that's why
she groomed him to take over the place, but that was never
his intention. As soon as there was no one left in his way he
was always going to rip it apart piece by piece. He blamed
it for losing his mother." She shrugs. "In the end, he always
thought it was the preciousness of the family name that made
Granddad get rid of her and he never forgave them for it. He
never forgave them for taking her. They took her away from
him, so he decided to take the one thing away from them
that they cared about."

"But they were dead," I say, confused.

She gives me a rueful look. "It must be nice, not having
to know how his mind worked."

I look down at my hands.

"When did you decide to believe me?"

There is a pause. "I don't know," I say. Lie. I knew. I remember that night, remember when I had dreamt it and the next few nights over and over. Each time I closed my eyes the memory switched onto my mind's projector until I woke up panting and I realized what I had seen. What I had run away from.

"I went away, I grew up," I continue. "I started to realize that things like that weren't just—weren't always so simple. And slowly I just... I didn't want to believe it. I wouldn't for the longest time."

She breathes deeply. "You know, for a long time I thought maybe you were the right one. That maybe I had brought it on myself, after everything that happened when I was a kid. But then I would remember that I pleaded with him and even though I said what I said, it wasn't..."

"I didn't understand what I saw."

"I know."

"Not at first."

"I know—" She stops. "But I did tell you."

I fall silent again.

"Please forgive me." It is only a whisper but it resounds in my ears.

She doesn't speak and then she leans forward and holds onto the steering wheel.

And I stay there beside her and we sit that way in her car, with those words hanging in the air, while the world keeps on running around us.

EPILOGUE

AURELIA WAS SOLD A MONTH LATER. IT WAS AN
anonymous bidder who took it. I received a letter from the
solicitors a week afterward informing me of the complete dissolution of the farm and all its assets. I put it back in an envelope and stuffed it in the back of a drawer.

My already messy apartment is now even more so. Boxes
from the clear-out with Claudia line the walls of my home in
building blocks and towers of brown and beige. I sometimes
take down a box and rummage through, lifting out things
and holding them in my hand, just staring at them, conjuring
up memories that take me through space and time to places
of comfort and warmth, before I grow tired and put them
back in their box again. I don't know what to do with them
all. I can't unpack them. I take them out like exhibits from
a museum and peer at them, using them as conduits to the
past.

I don't know what Claudia has done with the stuff she
took, or the letters. We haven't spoken since we met in Iowa.
I sense the slight chink in her armor has been hastily soldered
shut. We'll return to our routine of brief and infrequent cor-

respondence over time but in the interim we both need our space. I wonder sometimes how she does it, how she goes about her life of shopping and dinner parties so easily. But I think perhaps I am being unfair. Perhaps she, too, opens her boxes and weighs the objects in her lap, thinking of a time that was and one that could have been with the same sharp slice of regret. How would I know even if she was? It's not like she would tell me, even if I did ask.

You know, I once heard that in Greek *nostalgia* literally means the pain from an old wound. I suppose that makes me a masochist, because every night I unpick the scab and open the veins up, letting the memories pour from the scars there, until they trickle down my face in tears.

I can't stop myself.

I wish I could.

I wish I could stop thinking of that night in the rose garden, or that day in Ohio. But I replay that moment over and over again in the restaurant, in the street, in the car. I am alone with nothing but my thoughts now for company. They've stopped coming to me, my family. Ever since I saw Ava, they've gone—descended back into their graves with no warning, as quickly and with as little effort as it took for them to rise out of them.

But that doesn't mean I don't see them.

Because every night I have the dream. In a way it's a comfort. Without it I would miss them.

What do you think that means?

I am walking the road that takes me to Aurelia. It is night and the road is silvered by the moon. I find myself back at the entrance, to the sign in curlicue black lettering that I cannot read but whose ends look like tails swinging in the dark and I make my way up the gravel path, winding my footsteps to a house so white it shines. The lights blaze from the windows, the open air carries voices from inside, voices I recognize and long to hear again. I walk up the porch steps and knock on the door.

He opens it.

Behind him I can see the opening of the hallway leading to the living room and I know they are all in there, all waiting for me to join them. I want to, so much, but I have to get past him first.

"So." He leans against the door frame, a grin spreading across his lips. I look behind me but the world is black. The moon has gone.

"Can I come in?" I ask, peering over his shoulder. I can hear my father's laughter drift out into the hall.

"Sure," he says conversationally. "What's the password?"

"Password?"

"Hmm…" He pulls out a cigarette and lights a match.

"Go on," he says reasonably, "say it."

I stare at him.

"Say it."

"Say it."

"Still playing games?" I ask. "Aren't you too old for that?"

"You're never too old, girl," he says through a mouthful of smoke rings. They wobble in the air and melt near my face.

"Cal Jr., who is it?" my grandmother asks, but I can't see her because the door is pulled, blocking her from view.

"Well?" he asks.

I pause, but only for a moment.

"I love you," I whisper.

And just like that, he pulls back the door.

And I go home.

★ ★ ★ ★ ★

Acknowledgments

While writing in itself may be a solitary act, the process of getting published would not have happened without the following people: to my amazing agents Sallyanne Sweeney and Beth Davey, without whom this literally would not have happened; to my editor, Krista Stroever, who was the first person to take a chance on an unknown, and I hope this repays your efforts; to Juliet Mushens for all her amazing support throughout; to my English teacher Mrs. Wells, who was the first person to ever encourage what was before just a shameful habit; and to my husband, Jack Davy, who held me together with tape and glue and who was this book's biggest supporter, counselor and defender.

1. How much is Lavinia the architect of her family's downfall? Is she the cause of their destruction, or had they already willingly created the situations that would ultimately lead to their ostracism and exile?

2. What do you make of the role of mothers in the novel? Lavinia, Julia and even Antonia all have devastating impacts on their children. What do you make of their approaches to motherhood and their relationships with their children?

3. Meredith faces a heartrending and difficult journey back to Iowa to confront her family's past. How much do you empathize with Meredith's place in her family's history? What do you make of the final reveal of her betrayal of Ava? Do you agree with the reasons for why she fled and her need for self-preservation or do you find her ultimately as selfish and as cruel as the other members of her family?

4. What do you make of Piper's relationship with Lavinia? Why do you think Lavinia cries when Piper dies, but doesn't when she discovers Cal Sr., dead in bed next to her? How much of an adversary is Piper to Lavinia?

5. Is Julia a victim or does she deserve her exile from the farm? Is she the cruel, spoiled, capricious monster Lavinia portrays her to be, or is her character poisoned and influenced by the jealous influences of her stepmother? What effect does her abandonment have on Cal Jr.? And why do you think she never comes back for him?

6. Forgiveness is a running theme through the novel. To what extent, if any, do the characters deserve forgiveness or sympathy for their actions?

7. To what extent are the men passive participants in the novel? Are they merely puppets manipulated and controlled by the female characters in the book or do they willingly and actively participate in the family's politics?

8. To what extent can it be argued that Aurelia is the central character of the novel? What do you make of the bloodletting ritual of the Hathaways and the notion that the farm was a world in its own right? What do you make of the portrayal of the outside world compared with that of Aurelia?

9. How do you interpret the ending of the novel and the last line "And I go home"? Do you think this

means Meredith has accepted her past or is unable to escape it?

10. What do you make of the relationship between Meredith and her sisters? Do you agree with her assertion that they never really knew each other because of how much they hid from one another? Was their relationship doomed because of the effects of Lavinia's machinations or were Meredith, Ava and Claudia the cause of the break in their sisterly bond?

Set on a magnificent stretch of farmland in Iowa, The Legacy of
Eden *has a quintessentially American sensibility, so it is especially
surprising to learn that you were born and raised in the U.K.
What drew you to this time and place, and what were the
challenges of writing about it? What kind of research did you do?*

When I set out to write *The Legacy of Eden*, I wanted a
location that had great swathes of space, and I was
intrigued by Iowa's moniker as the American Heartland
and its huge agricultural presence. I knew this would
require a lot of internet and book research on farming
techniques, as I am a resolute city girl from London,
but I did not let that daunt me. Imagination has no
boundaries or maps, nor should it.

What inspired your idea for the story and characters in
The Legacy of Eden?

I fell in love with the story of family politics and the
cruel machinations of an amoral matriarch when I read

Robert Graves's *I, Claudius*. I could not stop thinking about what it would be like if this was transported from ancient Rome to modern day and to a family people could empathize with. Katherine Anne Porter once said that "In the nicest houses, in the most comfortable homes, the best people do the worst things to each other." I am paraphrasing, but that notion really intrigued me: the idea of not knowing what goes on behind closed doors. And I wanted to create a story of hubris and ambition, but one with real devastation. These are people who start off loving one another, but in the end they sacrifice each other for their own ends.

You've created such a complex and memorable cast of characters in this novel, particularly the matriarch, Lavinia. When you started the book, did you have her story and personality already mapped out, or did she reveal herself to you over the course of writing? What surprised you the most about your characters along the way?

I plotted an initial arc for all my characters, but some things revealed themselves when I was writing. For example, I didn't initially plan for Lavinia to be married to someone else with a different name... I firmly believe that you can make a character as hideous as you want to, just as long as the reader can understand why they behave the way they do. Although Lavinia does horrendous things, it is clear why she does them. In the end, she triumphs, but the reader knows that the farm fails. All the sacrifices and devastation is ultimately all for nothing, and Lavinia never knows it.

Aurelia comes to life in the novel, almost as if it's a character itself. Why did you choose to focus the story on a farmhouse in Iowa? What about the rural setting appealed to you, and how did it inform and enrich the novel as you were writing it?

I love novels in which the setting becomes a character in itself. The best example of this I can think of is Manderlay in *Rebecca*. I wanted to create a place that was vast and alluring, but that also had an unbreakable hold on the characters. When I travelled to America, I was struck by the sprawling farmlands full of crops, and I thought that it must be incredibly rewarding to start off with a blank piece of land, cultivate it and, in the end, yield enough crops to feed a family and make a living. The idea really seduced me, though obviously I romanticized it even more so for the book.

Aurelia is an unusual name for such a sprawling rural estate. What is the significance?

This is going to sound strange, but I think it was divine providence. I thought I had made up the name when I began writing. But then I discovered that there actually was an Aurelia in Iowa. After researching it further, I discovered that Aurelia means golden, and everything came together. It was so organic, yet so perfect.

The Legacy of Eden *is divided into sections for each of the four leading female characters: Meredith, Lavinia, Julia and Ava. Why did you choose to structure the novel in this way, and why these characters?*

I chose to structure the novel this way because ultimately this is a tale about the women, and each of them has a pivotal role in their family's history. Meredith's acknowledgment of the past and her resolving of her family's dissolution are crucial to the story; Lavinia marks the beginning of the family history; Julia's breaking of her father's heart leads to horrendous consequences; and what happens with Ava is the final nail in the family coffin. Though the farm is governed by men, it is the women who make this story, who guide their present and who are instrumental in shaping their history.

Can you describe your writing process? Do you outline first or dive right in? Do you write the scenes consecutively or do you jump around?

Writing is hard. It takes so much patience, and drive and constant revision. I always start with the characters, plotting out every detail from their backstory to what they look like to what they eat. Inevitably (and this is when I know the story is working) they will take on a life of their own; my initial kernel of an idea will develop into fully fleshed characters that feel like real people, and the story will grow from them. I always write chronologically. I'm a traditionalist in that way.

Aside from being a writer, you also work in publishing, so you must find yourself having to read quite a bit of other material while you are writing. Do you find this distracting or does it help to inform your own work?

It is never distracting. My writing style is my own; I have my own voice, and reading another person's work does not make me insecure. In fact, I know how personal writing is and I am always so excited to find fresh new talent. I love being able to give others the same chance I have been given. I know how much writing and publishing means to them because of how much it has meant to me.

Can you tell us about your next book?

I am loving writing my next book. It is set in Louisiana in 1963 and charts the civil rights movement and Martin Luther King's nonviolent protest as seen through the eyes of a white child from a middle-class family and the black son of her family's maid. The two form a beautiful and loving friendship, but the racial politics of the day threaten to pull them apart and destroy everything they have known. Once again, a character I did not intend to be major has completely taken over, but that is why I love writing. Even though you start off in one place, something unexpected yet so exciting comes out without you ever intending for it to happen.